Advance Praise

"An elegy for a lost father, an unforgettable fable of the power of art, *Ghost Horse* weaves a singular spell, captivating the reader and never letting go."

—Adam Johnson, author of *The Orphan Master's Son*,
winner of the Pulitzer Prize for Fiction

"An adventure of feeling and intelligence, frightening in its penetration to the depth of a child's anguish, *Ghost Horse* is a masterful novel. The reader's heart opens to McNeely's characters, and does not ever quite close again. This brave compassion is what fiction is for."

—James Carroll, author of *An American Requiem*,
winner of the National Book Award

"The rich interior life of a boy among boys whose home life has gone disastrously wrong; the origins of evil; the secrets, and the secret codes, of school bullies; the terrible things that we do to find, or avoid, sex; how adults manipulate each other, and what they try to get from children; ancient Rome; stop-motion animation; the binding of Isaac; the story of Cain; the history of race and class in Houston; the fallout of what looks like a slow-motion divorce—these are just some of the pieces that click into place within McNeely's terrifyingly sensitive novel, which finds a whole world of deceit and imagination among a couple of families and a boys' grade-school cabal. McNeely's prose—superbly attentive to what goes on in Buddy's head, and why— sets up scenes few readers will forget: it's a novel whose beautiful sentences match the wrong-way turns, the blood-red futilities, and the available insights, of its rough lives."

Stephen Burt, author of *Belmont and Close Calls*
with Nonsense: Reading New Poetry

"In *Ghost Horse*, his excellent debut novel, Thomas McNeely skillfully offers up the dark mysteries of the adult world through the eyes of a child. Wise, insightful, and exquisitely written, it lays bare the heartbreak of family life and lost friendship against the backdrop of class and racial difference. *Ghost Horse* is that rare fictional rendering that truly illuminates real life."

—Rishi Reddi, author of *Karma and Other Stories*, winner of the L. L. Winship / PEN New England Award

"Thomas McNeely is a beautiful writer. I've read drafts of this book over the last ten years and I've been waiting all that time for the finished product. This is an incredible book about love and family and growing up. But mostly it's about the mysteries of the human heart."

—Stephen Elliott, editor of *The Rumpus*; author of *Happy Baby* and *The Adderall Diaries*

"Thomas H. McNeely's moving, darkly beautiful debut novel, *Ghost Horse*, turns the emotional messiness of family life into something gripping and mysterious. One boy's coming-of-age in 1970s Texas becomes the deeply compelling story of all who have ever shouldered an unwanted secret. McNeely is an astoundingly gifted writer exploring—to great effect—the vagaries and surprises of desire."

—Daphne Kalotay, author of *Russian Winter* and *Sight Reading*

"*Ghost Horse* is a wrenching, poignant, and beautiful novel. McNeely evokes the searing landscapes of youth and South Texas with nuance and power. This is a story that stays with you like the long days of your last childhood summer, shading everything in your memory."

—Bret Anthony Johnston, author of *Remember Me Like This* and *Corpus Christi: Stories*

-"In this dark, swirling, atmospheric novel Thomas McNeely brings to life the world of Buddy Turner and his deeply troubled parents and grandparents during a few desperate months in the mid-70s. Even as Buddy struggles to keep faith with his film about the ghost horse and his collaborator, Alex, the adults around him keep changing shape, keep lying. I know of few other novels that so powerfully evoke the chaos and powerlessness of childhood, even fewer that do so with such power and brilliance. Ghost Horse is a wonderful and compulsively readable debut."

—Margot Livesey, author of *The Flight of Gemma Hardy* and *The House on Fortune Street*, winner of the L.L. Winship / PEN New England Award for Fiction

"Combining Southern Gothic surrealism, animated movies, and characters who are both larger than life and painfully real, *Ghost Horse* gallops off the page."

—Pamela Painter, author of *The Long and Short of It and What If? Writing Exercises for Fiction Writers*

"Thomas McNeely writes about the social tensions of class and race in 1970's Houston, Texas with breathtaking depth and beauty. Buddy Turner is a protagonist not to be forgotten and his pain is brilliantly rendered. *Ghost Horse* is a stunning novel."

—Annie Weatherwax, author of *All We Had*

"*Ghost Horse* pulls the reader back to the not-so-sweet Seventies, a decade when America suffered a nationwide nervous breakdown. Set adrift among a broken family, tenuous loyalties, distrusted institutions, and class conflicts, middle schooler Buddy Turner retreats to a world of imagination, focusing on the one thing in his troubled environment he has control over: making a home movie with a comic-book script that expresses his underlying angst. With *Ghost Horse*, author Thomas H. McNeely adroitly captures the dynamics of a confused and conflicted time, when those individuals who lived through it, as with his novel's characters, coped with the decade's emotional, cultural, and spiritual crack-up as best they could."

—Tim W. Brown, 2013 Gival Press Novel Award Judge and author of *Second Acts*

Ghost Horse

by Thomas H. McNeely

[signature] Houston, TX
Blue Willow
8/15/15

Winner of the Gival Press Novel Award

Gival Press

Arlington, Virginia

Published by Gival Press, an imprint of Gival Press, LLC.

For information please write:

Gival Press, LLC
P. O. Box 3812
Arlington, VA 22203
www.givalpress.com

First edition
ISBN: 978-1-928589-91-4
eISBN: 978-1-928589-92-1
Library of Congress Control Number: 2014947586

Cover art: © Tyler Olson | Dreamstime.com.
Photo of Thomas H. McNeely by Jude Griffin.
Book Design by Ken Schellenberg.

for my mother and father

That which the world really admires as shrewdness is an understanding of evil; wisdom is essentially the understanding of the good.—Søren Kierkegaard

1.

Last day of fifth grade, Houston, Texas, 1975; the time before *Star Wars*. At Queen of Peace, there are piñatas and sugar cookies frosted unnatural pastel colors and too-sweet fruit punch, mammas in sunglasses chatting with priests, white boys and brown boys making summer pacts. But this is no concern of theirs, of Alex Torres and Buddy Turner's, already hurrying home along the White Oak Bayou, to Alex's house. It is Buddy's last day at Queen of Peace. Next year, he will go to a new school across the city where everyone is white; but he and Alex won't talk about this. They won't talk about what will happen when Buddy's father comes back at the end of the summer. They have known each other too long to talk about such things. They are hurrying home, now, anxious to catch the three o'clock movie on Channel Thirteen.

In bare-dirt yards along the bayou, dogs bark, pulling at ropes and chains; and Alex seems to fade, to disappear. Both of them, Alex and Buddy, have heard the story that the dogs' owners teach them to bite Mexicans, a story that they know probably isn't true; and yet, Buddy can't help but feel glad that he himself will be safe; and as soon as he thinks this, he's ashamed. It has been like this since he found out about the new school, as if he is watching himself in a movie.

In Alex's backyard, Ysrael barks. Alex checks his watch. With a sideways glance as he opens the heavy glass storm door and jabs first the deadbolt, then the knob lock with his keys, he lets Buddy know to get the snacks, to warm up the TV. Then he yells at Ysrael in Spanish to shut up, before he barges out the back door. Buddy stands in the particular silence of Mr. Torres' empty house, breathing its smell of cooking and furniture polish, as close and tight as a shoeshine box. He doesn't go to the dark hall that leads to Alex's room, papered with drawings, almost as familiar to him as his own. He doesn't go to Mr. Torres' room, which he has glimpsed only a few times. He stands as long as he can, listening to Alex in the backyard, almost seeing him unlock Ysrael's cage. From atop the dark wooden TV console, huge and weighty as a ship, Mrs. Torres, dead in a car crash before Buddy met Alex, watches him, frozen in black and white, a wedding veil like a crown on her dark hair, inside a silver frame.

All of this lasts only a moment. Already, he is clicking on the TV, hearing it crackle and hum as the faint hair on his forearm lifts as it brushes the screen. Already, he is turning a corner of a beaverboard wall into the kitchen (all of it, the kitchen, living room, dining room, actually one single room, unimaginably small when he remembers it years later, after it's lost to him; at the time, it is capacious, teeming with mystery); already, he is recovering from various stashes in various cabinets, a system known only to Alex and himself, the tube of Pringles and bag of Cheetos that will stain their fingers orange and turn them shiny with grease. Later there may be candy peanuts, as cushiony as Styrofoam, or peanut butter cups, whose edges they will bite into starlike shapes. But for now, he tucks two cans of grape Nehi under one arm, listening to Ysrael bark as Alex lets him out into the yard, as he himself sinks into the wraparound couch, as Alex crosses the screen and drops into the corner, one cushion away, pulling the Cheetos onto his stomach. Buddy can still remember when they didn't think of where they sat, when sometimes they would end up slumped on each other's shoulders, asleep, when Mr. Torres came home. He knows what the boys at school call them — *gorditos, maricones*, fatasses, faggots. Alex and he have told each other that the secrets of the three o'clock movies, and the movies they will make, will protect them from what the boys say, though of course, they haven't exactly said this. If they had said it, it would now be even more flimsy than their silence, belied by the careful distance they keep on the couch.

Of course, they do not talk about this. They sit, tensed, waiting, for the three o'clock movie: Vincent Price, stop-motion monsters, Godzilla flicks, Hammer Horror, the original *Dracula* and *Frankenstein* and all the remakes. And there are other movies, ones that seem too strange, and sometimes too dirty, to really be on TV — silent films with hurdy-gurdy music like *Nosferatu* and *Metropolis*; or the split-second in *Vampire Circus* when they were sure they could see the vampire girl's bare chest; and even in the movies that are supposed to make sense, like *The Pit and the Pendulum*, scenes that don't, like the one when the woman is tied to an altar, screaming, as she's circled by a kind of witch-doctor, a scene that seemed to go on forever, because it made no sense, because the woman seemed to be laughing as well as crying.

What is the joke?

❧ ❦

The walls of Alex's room are covered with flattened-out grocery bags, and on them, drawings of turtles and gulls from the bayou, of the bayou itself; and mixed with these, rampaging across the city, as if they were just as real, monsters and vampires, robots and demons, leveling skyscrapers with jets of radioactive fire.

All summer, since Buddy visited his father at Fort Polk, they have worked on the Horse, in Alex's room, which smells of sweat and pencil lead and the red-hot cinnamon candies that Alex keeps hidden in his desk. Each summer, almost for as long as they can remember, they have planned movies — a mystery about a madman who dumps his victims in the bayou, a cartoon about a gull who follows the bayou back to the Gulf — but none of it has come to anything, until the Horse.

To make the Horse look real, Alex says, they will have to shoot hundreds, maybe thousands of drawings, each drawing filmed six frames, a third of a second of film. Day after day they have labored, Alex sketching four horses to a page, handing each page to Buddy to color and number and cut into four separate pieces. They live within a dream, bleary-eyed, backs aching, nerves jangling with sugar. They don't go outside or watch the three o'clock movie or even the cartoons that play on the far reaches of the UHF channels. Sometimes they forget to eat. Each day folds in on itself and vanishes, and all that is left are the drawings, messages from another world.

At the end of each day, they take stock: How many seconds they have finished, what is yet to be done. They have a tripod, borrowed from Mr. Torres, and a desk lamp to light the drawings and backgrounds. They have the Super-8 camera and five yellow boxes of film that his father took for him from Gramma Turner's house, when he visited Houston not long after Buddy went to Fort Polk.

What they don't have, aside from a tape recorder and money to process the film, is a finished script. Maybe it's halfway done, maybe a third; Buddy isn't sure.

"¿Porqué no?" Alex says.

Alex paces, clicking a cinnamon candy against his teeth, glowering at Buddy, who sits at his desk. Buddy shrugs, concentrating on cutting out the day's drawings of the Horse with an X-Acto knife.

"*No tenemos más tiempo,*" Alex says.

Buddy knows what Alex means, that next week he will start at the new school; but he doesn't want to think about it. He doesn't want to think about what will happen when his father comes back from Fort Polk.

"*Lo haré,*" he says. I'll do it.

"*Este es el Gran Momento,*" Alex says. "*Si hacemos un buen trabajo, nos mostran a los estudios. Entonces hacemos una película de verdad.*"

This is what Alex always says — that if they can make a good enough short, the studios will give them a contract. Buddy has seen him on drawing jags before, but nothing like this: The edges of his fingernails are permanently black; on his right middle finger is a callus the size of a dime. Buddy doesn't know if he can believe what Alex says about the studios, but he knows that Alex's questions about the script are fake; Alex could make the movie himself.

"I'll do it," he says.

Outside the room, the doorbell rings, then come muffled sounds of Mr. Torres opening the front door, and Buddy's mother's voice. Usually, by this time, Buddy has gone to Gramma Liddy's house, where his mother will pick him up. He looks from Alex to the drawings of the Horse, imagining the scene in the living room: Mr. Torres, stocky, crew-cut, still wearing his work shirt and slacks from his office job with the city, smiling as stiffly as a manikin, his eyes watchful, having nothing to do with his smile; his mother, her arms crossed over her white hospital uniform, her weary face beautiful, transformed, as it is not when she sees his father.

Alex eyes him, like Mr. Torres. Then he reaches past Buddy, opens a drawer, thumps a stack of paper on the desk: the drawings they have made that summer.

"*Coge la máquina,*" Alex says.

Buddy hesitates, listening to his mother and Mr. Torres in the living room; they know about the movie, of course, though he wishes they didn't. He wants the movie to astonish, to annihilate. Unfinished, under adult eyes, it is only childish.

"*Andale,*" Alex says.

From under Alex's bed, Buddy retrieves the black leather bag, and unzips it, releasing its smells of cedar and oil and the faint bitter smell of Gramma Turner's house, the smell of the tree-shaded streets near Rice. Among the five yellow boxes, seventeen and a half minutes of film, is the camera: Super 800 Electro, reads its metal plate. There are dials to record the length of film in meters and feet, dials to adjust shutter speed and widen or narrow the aperture to film indoors or out. He presses the trigger; its sleek black metal feels powerful, irrefutable, in his hands.

"*Andale*," Alex says. "*Mira.*"

Alex presses down on the top of the stack of paper with one hand, holding up the other end with his fingertips: a flip-book.

Buddy uncaps the lens. The pages are dirty and smudged, ones he has seen a thousand times. But in the camera's dark box, its square screen, what he sees is already different, somehow, part of a story. In herky-jerky motion, as the pages blur past, the Horse bursts from the ground, no more than a skeleton, his eyes edged red, like glowing coals; his coat turns smooth, his wings fan out; he tosses his mane, striking lightning from his hooves, his eyes like quicksilver mirrors. It is not how Buddy remembers the horse he saw with his father, or even how he imagined it; and how he remembers and imagines it don't matter anymore.

Alex raps the side of his head, hard.

"*Piense en las cosas buenas*," he says. "That other crap is just crap."

"Just crap," Buddy says, knowing what he means.

What he means is what Buddy told him will happen when his father comes back. What Alex means is the whole adult world. Buddy doesn't know if he can believe him.

$\approx\!\sim$

His father lived on the outskirts of Fort Polk, Louisiana, in what looked like an abandoned motel: two strips of cinderblock barracks that faced each other across a patch of yellow grass. For two years he'd been away, first to finish medical school in Detroit, then to serve out his time in the Army. In the summers, Buddy and his mother visited him, and at Christmas and Easter, his father came to Houston. But last Christmas, his father stayed with Gramma Turner.

That summer, Buddy's mother had sent him to visit his father alone; he was old enough, now, she said, almost twelve. Buddy knew this wasn't the real reason, but he didn't know what the real reason was. No one would tell him the truth. He'd gone to Fort Polk to bring his real father home.

His real father had gone to the beach with them, and worked on his car at his mother's house, and applauded at the magic shows that Alex and Buddy performed. His real father was gentle, not like the one Buddy heard when he listened to his mother and father argue on the phone, their voices vicious, unrecognizable.

Who left who? his father said. *I didn't mean to,* said his mother.

His mother said that his father loved him; she said he was very sad and very lost. Each time Buddy saw him, he seemed more stiff and strange. But this was only a mask, Buddy knew. Beneath this mask, his real father was still there.

His last night at Fort Polk, after they'd seen the horse, they sat at a folding card table in his father's barracks and ate take-out Chinese food. The day before, when they'd gone to the base hospital, his father stood behind him, hands clamped on his shoulders, and introduced him to the other doctors. The doctors told Buddy that his father was the best, hardest-working pathologist they'd ever had. Buddy understood that they were telling him these things because they couldn't say them to his father. His father was uneasy with doctors, even now, when he was one of them.

In his barracks were things Buddy remembered from his visit the summer before: his father's battered yellow bike, the chin-up bar across his closet, his medical manuals, thick as telephone books, with his name — J. Turner — marked in permanent ink across the pages. There was the bottle of Paddy's Whiskey, whose glinting yellow liquid reminded Buddy of parties in their kitchen in the time before his father left, his mother flushed and beautiful, his father telling long, elusive jokes.

But there was also the postcard. The postcard was exactly the same as one his father had sent him, a sunset silhouette of a wagon train. On it, in blocky capital print, was a single sentence: "One day we'll look back on our suffering and not remember who we were." It was unsigned, and the handwriting wasn't his mother's. Heart pounding, Buddy slid it back beneath a refrigerator magnet. The sentence played in his head like an evil spell. He knew he couldn't ask his father what it meant.

Buddy looked at the air pistol target and the bottle of Paddy's, the ropy muscles in his father's arms, his jaw working under his skin. He glanced up, curious, expectant, as if Buddy had something important to say.

"Tell me about something," his father said. "Tell me about your movies."

Of course he'd told his father about the movies that he and Alex planned to make. And though he imagined his father watching them one day, astonished, amazed, now he wished that he hadn't told his father anything.

"Nothing, sir." He shrugged. "We can't do anything until we get the camera."

"Maybe I can help you with that."

"Yes, sir," he said; he didn't believe that his father would help them.

"Are you excited about your new school?"

His father asked him this question every night. Gramma Turner had said it wasn't *right* for him, a white child, to go to Queen of Peace, and his mother was no kind of mother for sending him there. He hadn't told his father what he thought.

Now, he would. "No, sir," he said.

The muscles in his father's arm tensed. "Why not?"

"It'll be harder to make the movies, sir."

"You can still make movies. You just need to start thinking about your future."

This was something else Gramma Turner said.

"Look," his father said. "We just have to tell my mother what she wants to hear for a while, then we can do what we want. We can go on trips together and go for bike rides and make movies. Whatever you want. Okay? Look at me, Buddy. Okay? I won't let anybody keep us from being together. I promise."

His father leaned toward him, looking him in the eye. He wasn't looking anywhere else. Something like anger poured off him in waves of heat; and Buddy felt his own heart lift. He reached across the table to touch his father's arm.

"What are you going to do, sir?" he said.

His father flinched, as if Buddy's hand were a snake. Then he looked down at his own hand. "I'm sorry, Buddy," he said. "I wanted to talk to you about this. I'm going to have to live at my mother's house for a while."

Buddy watched him. Since they'd seen the horse, he'd known what would happen, but he didn't want to know. "When are you coming home?" he said.

"I'm not, Buddy."

A cold hand closed inside his chest. "Why not, sir?"

"Because I can't, Buddy," his father said. "I just can't. I've got a good job waiting for me in Houston. Pretty soon, I'll be able to buy a house. What would you think about coming to live with me?"

Buddy wondered, for a moment, if it was a joke; but he could see, in the stillness of his father's face, that it wasn't. He knew he should be thinking of his mission to bring his father home. But he was thinking of Alex and his mother and the movies.

"I don't know, sir," he said.

"Will you think about it?" his father said.

"Yes, sir. I'm sorry, sir."

"It's okay, Buddy," his father said. "But I need you to promise me you won't tell your mother I asked you this, okay? I could get in a lot of trouble."

"Yes, sir," Buddy said.

For a moment, his father sat very still. Then he crouched next to Buddy, and drew him into an embrace; and Buddy closed his eyes, feeling the warmth of his father's skin, smelling his clean smell, and beneath it, his milky odor of sweat. That summer, he'd begun to picture his father in the barracks, in his white T-shirt, in the darkness of the pines and the cicadas' patient burr. He thought of what his mother had said, that his father was very sad and very lost; and then he was ashamed of what he'd thought. He tried to see himself and his father from far away, as if it was a movie. But he couldn't; his father's stubble rasped his neck; he wept almost silently, like a slowly pounding fist.

"I'm sorry, Buddy," he said. "I'm sorry. I didn't think it would be like this."

⧽⧼

The day was very warm, the sky frosted with a high, thin haze the color of beach glass. Tall grass nicked his arms with small, stinging cuts. Across a clearing, his father waited, holding back vines that grew over skeletal trees. Buddy hurried toward him, hugging his arms against his chest, and ran stiffly. His hair was hot and stuck to his ears; his jeans swished, he thought, like skirts.

He ducked under the vines. The cool, dark air smelled sweetly of decaying leaves. Last year, when he visited Fort Polk, they'd found a cow's skull, and seen vultures wheeling high above, as if painted against the flat blue sky. His father sent him specimens — a rattlesnake in formaldehyde, a tarantula in a jar — and Buddy remembered, or imagined that he did — mysterious tree-hollows, giant spider webs. But now, in the swamp, there were only slim, crowding pines, and beneath the wet, leafy smell, another smell, like meat at the supermarket, but worse.

Over a log, past a copse of bushes, his father stopped in a kind of clearing. They stood near a pool of orange scum that disappeared into a thicket of vines and bushes and shadowy trees. In the shadows, something moved. At first, Buddy didn't see what it was. Then he saw it, past the vines and bushes, in the dappled, moving shadows: the head and neck of a horse, its teeth bared, its eyes frightened and wild.

And then, as quickly as he'd seen the horse struggling, it was still. Flies spun around its head, the only part of it visible above the scum; and in the silence, Buddy could hear their steady burr, and through the shadowy vines, two dark, hollow sockets stared out at him, where before he had thought there were eyes.

His father opened his mouth, opened his hands, but didn't talk. Buddy breathed, now, without tasting the smell. He knew what his father would say, if he turned to him. But he didn't look at his father; he looked at the horse.

"All this ain't real?" he says.

Buddy doesn't look at him.

"What are we gonna do without the Horse?" Alex says.

"*No sé,*" Buddy says.

"That's right, *loco*, you don't know, 'cause there's nothing. There's nothing, no movie, without it. *¿Qué es más real que el caballo espectral?*"

Buddy knows what he means. Alex has given him this speech before.

"Maybe," he says.

"*Por si acaso no,*" Alex says. "Finish the script, then we finish the story boards. Then we can start filming. Then we can send it to the studios."

Buddy keeps his back to Alex. He wants to ask Alex why he doesn't just make the movie himself. On the wall are pictures of horses jumping, horses grazing, horses fording a river. Next to each real picture is a drawing. Even then, it is clear to him that Alex is studying horses so he will understand what it is to be one, just as he has drawn monsters and vampires and herons until he becomes them. The horses prance, gallop, seeming to move even when they are still.

But at the moment, all of it seems fragile and foolish. Inside Alex's room, he believes what Alex says, but outside, it sounds crazy, in a way that makes Buddy afraid that he will go crazy, too. He hasn't told Alex about the sounds he's heard when his father came to Houston that summer, after Buddy visited him at Fort Polk, his mother crying out, as if she was in pain. He still hasn't turned to him; but he can picture Alex in his stained shirt, with his stained hands. *El Toro Loco*, the boys at Queen of Peace called him, because he cried sometimes, for no reason, and punched kids flat. He can picture them from above, two fat kids in a room full of stupid drawings. He knows what Simon Quine would say, what any of the boys at St. Edward's would say, and it frightens him, because it is still there under his tongue.

"Okay," he says. "I'll try."

❧ ⚜

In Sacred Studies, Mrs. Gray talked about *The Pilgrim's Progress*, an old-fashioned book about a man who walks to heaven. She discussed how Christian, guided by Evangelist, left his wife and family to seek salvation through the Wicket Gate; and then, as sometimes happened, Mrs. Gray slipped into the story of her own son's divorce. Her daughter-in-law was a feminist, she said; that meant that she didn't care what happened to her son. Now, she said, her daughter-in-law was fighting for custody of their children, who had never hurt anyone.

"Divorce," she said, "is a disease caused by the lies of feminism and secular humanism. You must pray for your parents, my children, so they will see through those lies. I will pray for you, and hope you take some comfort in my prayers."

She stood at the front of the classroom, which smelled of dirty cleaning solution and a foul-tasting orange drink the school sold at lunch, her large, square hands clasped at her waist. On the bulletin board behind her were smiling jack o' lanterns, but no witches or ghosts; Mrs. Gray claimed that witches and ghosts were Satanic.

The boys, in khaki shirts and pants, shifted uneasily. Sam Fahr, slumped low in his desk, raked his long, black bangs over his eyes. Everyone knew that Sam's father had disappeared that summer. Except for Sam, Buddy had been careful not to tell anyone at St. Edward's that his own father was gone.

Directly in front of Buddy, Simon Quine raised his hand. Simon sat at the head of the class. Each day, Buddy watched his broad, straight shoulders, the cleft at the base of his skull furzed with blond hair, the movement of the sides of his neck as he recited his homework almost silently to himself: *Carthagenian, quodnam est, integer.* Looking at Simon, Buddy remembered the buzz cut his father had made him get, the way his belly folded over his belt. Since he'd been there, Simon hadn't said anything to him; Buddy wasn't sure if he was glad of it, or not.

"I'm sorry, ma'am," Simon said, in a voice so faint it was almost a whisper. "I think I'm confused. Isn't it true that divorced people go to Hell?"

Mrs. Gray gripped her hands at her waist, her whole boxy shape stiffening. "No, Mr. Quine," she said, finally. "That is not always true. Divorced people may ask Our Heavenly Father for His Forgiveness."

God's Perfection, Mrs. Gray reminded them, was boundless, as was His Mercy; we have only to believe in Him, she said, to share in His Perfection and dwell in His Mercy. Buddy's throat ached with a feeling like laughter and crying together. His mother said they needed to pray to bring his father back home, but he didn't believe her; he didn't have any use for her prayers.

Shielding his notebook with his arm, he wrote:

SCENE ONE: NIGHT. HUGH *searches for the* HORSE *in the swamp.*

"Mr. Turner?" His name came from far away. "Mr. Turner?"

He looked up. The boys watched him with pale, avid stares. Except for Sam, who shook his head, and Simon, who sat bolt-upright, still facing Mrs. Gray, who held out her hand. "Bring me that, please, Mr. Turner."

The boys tittered. Mrs. Gray ordered them to be silent. As he walked the few short steps to her, holding the weightless sheet of paper, he felt like throwing up. She creased the page from his binder and slipped it into a fold of her dress. Up close, her plump, sleek face was terrible and adult.

"Be seated, Mr. Turner. You will see me after school."

Buddy turned back to his desk. Sam still hid behind his hands; but Simon watched him, his cool, blue-eyed gaze curious, and not unkind.

ॐ∽

After school, he strode down an empty hallway, framing a shot of himself, a shadow reflected in smooth cement. He wanted to kick something, a trashcan. But when he imagined the dull thud, the clattering of its lid, he saw Reverend Toy, with his pomaded black hair and pale bulldog's face, swoop from the shadows in his swishing cassock; or Mr. Gamph, who was said to patrol the bathrooms and hallways after school, swinging his paddle. As he passed the front office, he wanted to smash its plate glass windows, but it was useless. Smashing them would only get him in trouble.

Each day, Sam Fahr and he went to the parking lot on the roof of the mall, to smoke cigarettes that tasted like burning leaves, which Sam kept hidden at the bottom of his backpack in a rolled-up sock.

They stood in the parking lot, looking out across the freeway, at the bayou that wound past the low houses near the school, past the medical center, where Buddy's father worked, and the gray wedge of Rice Stadium, near Gramma Turner's house, and in the far distance, the gray glass buildings downtown, and the blinking lights on the Folger's plant, near his mother's house; and Sam told him about the bands whose names were tattooed on his backpack in blurred black marker — Black Sabbath, Iron Maiden, Blue Oyster Cult — how KISS stood for Knights In Satan's Service, how they kidnapped young boys at their concerts to sacrifice to the Devil. Other times, they were quiet, and Buddy thought of the silence in Sam's house: the dark, wood-paneled hallways, the spotless white couch and delicate figurines in Mrs. Fahr's parlor, the silence there which seemed thick, as if someone had always just finished crying.

That day, Mrs. Gray had told him that she understood the standards at Queen of Peace might not have been as high as they were at St. Edward's. But there were many children, she said, from circumstances even more distressed than his own, who would take his place in a minute. Did he know what she meant? she said. He did. Gramma Turner had told him what happened to children who got lost on the streets. He wanted to tell Mrs. Gray they could have his place. But he was afraid of what his father would do, if he got kicked out of St. Edward's.

Medium shot: Crossing scabby lawn, where boys in khaki shirts and pants and girls in blue smocks waited for their parents to pick them up. He hurried toward the corner of the school, toward the round, pink belly of the church's apse, where he met Sam under a shade tree each day after school. Now, under the tree, was a group of boys – Sam, Gene White, and Simon Quine.

Simon stood closest. Gene slouched against the tree, thin arms folded across his chest. Gene was a pale boy with a skeleton-face who laughed in sharp bursts, as if he was in pain. Buddy had seen him circling the soccer field with Simon at P.E.; but Simon didn't treat him like a friend.

Near the curb, backpack slung over his shoulder, Sam kicked a patch of grass. Buddy stopped at a safe distance. Both Gene and Simon stood half a head taller than he and Sam, but he knew if they were caught fighting, he and Sam would be blamed.

Simon kept his hands joined behind his back. His uniform was uncreased, as if still on cardboard in its package. Not only his height, or the metal wristwatch he wore, made him seem older; he looked to the side of Buddy, like an adult, and like an adult, there was something about him that was distant and lonely.

"*Quod facis, novus puer?*" he said. *What are you doing, new boy?*

"*Nihil,*" Buddy said. *Nothing.*

Simon grinned, nodding, as if Buddy had passed a test. "What were you drawing in Mrs. Gay's class?" he said.

Buddy shrugged. "I don't know."

"You don't know?" Simon said, almost gently. "What's wrong with you?"

"Maybe he don't want to tell you," Sam said.

"You went to Queen of Peace," Simon said, to Buddy.

No one at St. Edward's knew about Queen of Peace, Buddy thought, except for Mrs. Gray. He felt as if Simon had reached out and touched his bare skin. Sam shook his head, once. "How do you know?" Buddy said.

Simon only grinned. "That's where spics go, isn't it?"

It was the word his mother had told him never to use. When one of the white boys at Queen of Peace called him a spic, Alex had broken his nose.

"Sure," Buddy said.

"Let's go," Sam said. "Your mom's gonna be here soon."

"We don't need your lip," Simon said, half-turning to Sam. "Maybe Turner here doesn't want to hang out with someone like you."

Sam stared at Buddy, then started toward the street. Reluctantly, Buddy followed him, shielding his chest with his books and binder, keeping wide of Simon, who mirrored him, arms loose at his sides. Gene unraveled himself from the tree.

"I know where you're going," Simon said to Buddy, though he seemed to be talking to Sam. "You're going to the roof at the mall to smoke cigarettes. One day you'll get caught, and sent to a boy's home, and never see your family again. But I guess that doesn't matter, because you don't really have a family. Right?"

His heart pressed breath from his chest. No one at the school knew. Simon couldn't be talking about him. If he could make it to the street, where Sam was waiting for him, he would be safe.

"Maybe I'll tell him about your mom," Simon said, to Sam.

Sam whipped around, his fists clenched.

"It's a movie," Buddy said. "I'm gonna make a movie."

He hadn't needed to tell him. That was why Simon smiled; and Buddy turned from him, afraid, and ran across the street to Sam.

3.

On the Saturday that Buddy discovers the woman, he waits for his father in his room, a notebook open on his lap. The silence in his mother's house is like a stopped clock. Sometimes his father comes at ten, or twelve, or three. It's impossible to say when he will arrive.

His room smells of formaldehyde and a slight rottenness, the snake in a jar that his father sent him the summer before. One wall is taken up by a giant, dark closet. In the closet are built-in shelves he climbed when he was young, believing them to be as tall as a tower. On the shelves are the stuffed animals he and his father dissected, and the film editor, with its hooded screen and two arms to hold reels of film, and the movies he found in Gramma Turner's den. In the closet, the blue jeans and loud striped shirts that his father wore when he lived with them float, suspended in darkness.

He looks down at his notebook, where he is supposed to be writing the script. He has tried to write about the Horse, but can't; he wants to write the real movie — buildings and trees, gray sky and gray cement — bits and pieces that don't make any sense.

The real movie is what he heard from his mother's room when his father visited that summer, his mother crying out, as if she was in pain.

The real movie is what he saw at St. Edward's after school that week, Gene White and Simon Quine in a grove near the soccer field. Gene knelt, hands clasped in prayer. Simon stood over him, his arm raised, holding an imaginary knife.

My son, God will provide, Simon said, and Buddy recognized the words from a Memory Verse — the story of Abraham and Isaac.

Please, Gene said. *Please, I promise I'll be good.*

Simon traced a cross above him, and drove the knife in. Gene fell, waving his hands to ward off the blows; but it was no use. Simon straddled him, stabbing him, and for a moment, Buddy thought they were joined in an embrace; and something caught in his stomach, a warm, frightening emptiness.

Outside, his father's car rumbles into the driveway. Buddy slides the notebook under his bed. Panic scatters like birds in his chest. The notebook — the script — has to be hidden, even though there is nothing in it.

Outside, the gate latch clicks, his father's leather shoes scritch up the back porch steps, the back door slams shut.

Voices bleed through the closet. Buddy sits on his bed, holding his books and binder on his lap. He tells himself that he should get up, burst into the kitchen, yell at his father to leave his mother alone; but he waits, holding himself rigid, trying not to listen.

I know you didn't want this, his mother says.

Who didn't want it? his father says. You already made your choice. I'm trying to be fair. You'll get all the support I can afford.

You didn't need to go to Detroit, his mother says. Dr. Marcuse could've cared less where you went for your residency. You could've stayed at Galveston. You could've gone across the street from Rice to Baylor.

What about this summer? his mother says. Was that meaningless?

His father is silent.

Tell me the truth, his mother says. Tell me what's really going on.

But his father's footfalls shudder through the house; his shadow lengthens, filling the hallway, like the scene in *Nosferatu* when the vampire, Count Orlok, casts his shadow outside his final victim's room, before he is caught in sunlight. Then his father is there. He wears a dark two-piece suit, tie loose at his collar, slacks slung low on his hips like jeans. He is always at work, doing autopsies, reading slides.

"Let's go," his father says.

In the kitchen, his mother stands near the back door, arms folded across her chest, her eyes struck with a kind of blindness, as if his father has cast a spell on her. Buddy tries to signal to her with a look that he will stay, but she follows his father, catching the screen door before it closes.

Outside, his father stands, his back to them, facing the sand. Since he returned from Fort Polk, he has torn out the fence near the driveway, driven a truck into the yard, dumped sand there, to keep it from flooding. He has replaced the water heater and laid paving stones and installed burglar bars on all of the windows.

The sand is piled waist-high to him, stubbled with grass. The air smells of coffee from the Folger's plant and the ship channel's gasoline smell. Buddy imagines that he is a camera, hovering above the tiny yard — up, above the two-story, mottled-brick house, and the second story on Mr. Knight's house next door that looks like a mobile home has landed on it, and his mother's muddy yard, where nothing has grown for a long time – up, above the railroad tracks at the end of the street, and beyond them, the field where boys were buried, killed by two madmen, and beyond the field, the giant steel derricks that march, carrying power lines to the Gulf.

Later, he will see how young his father was; he will see his mother's graying hair and careworn face. But now, he does not see these things; theirs is the only story that he knows. "I'll get out here soon," his father says, "and spread that sand."

"It'll be fine," his mother says, "if you fix the fence."

"It's not fine," his father says. "I'll get out here soon and finish it."

His mother descends the porch steps, picks a thread from his father's jacket.

"We'll talk later?" she says.

His father pivots from her, stalks toward the driveway, opens the gate in the scrap of fence that remains. His mother's eyes are glassy, wounded, as if his father has hit her.

"Go on," she says, to Buddy. "Go."

❧ ☙

All the way to Gramma Turner's house, Buddy steals glances at his father. He doesn't dare to actually look at him. His father stares ahead, gripping the steering wheel, not looking at him, either. The horse follows them, galloping above the freeway. Each Saturday since his father has returned, they have spent at Gramma Turner's house, where she and Buddy will sit in a tiny room, correcting Buddy's schoolwork. It is why Buddy holds his books and binder on his lap, digging the edge of the binder into his hands. Along with how his father has treated his mother, it is why he hates his father, then.

His father parks on the street behind Gramma Turner's, then sits, staring ahead, as if he is still driving. Then he gets out and opens the trunk. Buddy turns to see what he's doing, but the trunk blocks his view. The houses' sharp-peaked roofs glower down at them like faces of teachers. He touches his door latch, squares the books on his lap. He is furious with his father, furious with himself for leaving with him.

His father puts a pair of slim black shoes and mustard-colored shorts on the hood. He still doesn't look at Buddy. He pulls off his tie, begins to unbutton his shirt. A huge car idles past; his father waves. Buddy turns from him, not knowing what to think. He is thinking of the sounds he heard from his mother's room when his father visited that summer, how he lay in bed, frozen, pretending not to understand.

The trunk clunks shut. His father taps his window.

"Come on," he says.

Buddy unlatches his door, holding the books and binder against his chest.

"You don't need those," his father says.

There is an edge of impatience in his father's voice, even contempt. Buddy puts the books on the floor of the car. When he looks up, his father is gone.

Across the street, his father advances on a two-story, powder blue house, his mustard-colored shorts, his pale, hairy legs, naked-looking. Buddy follows him, leaving his books in the car. He has an idea what his father is doing, though it makes no sense. But this is why his father is impatient, because he should already know.

"Sir?" he says. "What are we going to do?"

His father doesn't answer him. He stares ahead, as he has since he left the car, at a point that only he can see, and opens a gate in a chain-link fence. Inside the house, a dog barks, scrabbling against a door. In the back yard is a sagging kiddie pool, a blue rubber ball in the grass. At the end of the yard is a high wooden fence, and near it, a tall, spindly oak whose lowest crook is almost as high as the fence.

"What are we going to do, sir?" Buddy says.

"What do you think?" his father says. "Think you can make it?"

"Yes, sir," he says, though he isn't sure.

His father gives him a leg up into the crook of the tree. Buddy's sneakers slip on the smooth bark. He balances on the fence, still holding the branch. Far beneath him, farther than he's ever jumped, is a carpet of dead leaves and lichen-plated branches. It is Gramma Turner's backyard, though it is like a picture, as if he has never seen it before.

He closes his eyes, lets himself drop. The ground hits his legs, and he tumbles, leaves crackling, a branch stabbing his side. A moment later, his father lands next to him, wincing, holding his knee. "You okay?" his father says.

"Yes, sir."

"I bought you a bike," his father says.

His father looks at him, radiating heat, like he did at Fort Polk. Buddy doesn't know what to think. "Yes, sir," he says.

"It's in the garage," his father says. "We can't go up the driveway, because my mother will see us. So I'm going to get it. When you see me come out, run up, grab it, and go. If we get caught, my mother will put our asses in a sling."

"Yes, sir."

"Therefore, we cannot get caught."

"Yes, sir," Buddy says.

His father stares at him a moment longer, as if he is about to say something else, then takes off across the yard, keeping clear of the kitchen window that looks out on the driveway. Buddy waits. He hasn't been this far back in the yard since last Easter, when he was sweating in an itchy suit, pretending that he hunted bright plastic eggs in a forest. Now he is not pretending. He and his father are on a mission. The red brick house looks like a miniature house, a house from a postcard. Behind the garage, behind the sliding-glass doors that look out on the yard, a dead eye, flat black, Grampa Turner rests in his bed, and Buddy wonders if he can see them, and if he is laughing at the joke they are playing on Gramma Turner.

The garage door rolls up. A bicycle ticks out. Buddy runs across the yard, watching the kitchen window. Above it, the window of the room where his father says that he lives, that Gramma Turner has never let Buddy see, is curtained, as always. He can't think of that now. He is in a movie, the movie of him and his father. He grabs the handlebars, curled like ram's horns, wrapped in green metallic tape. He runs the bike, gripping the handlebars, and jumps up, swinging a leg over its seat, somehow landing on it, wobbling, finding the pedal, as he pumps down the driveway; as sunlight streaks through his wheels; as he shoots, weightless, into the street.

4.

They ride past the Village Theater, into a shade that is deeper, the houses grander, where oak trees spread above the streets like phantoms. Here is Dr. Red Duke's house, with its tennis courts and terraced roses; here is Dr. DeBakey's, with its wavering coach lamps and curtain of dark ivy. Through the spangling leaves, the horse gallops, almost invisible. The air smells of mothballs and roses. In the time before his father left, Buddy imagined living here, on the tree-shaded streets; he can still imagine it.

Ahead, his father stops, still straddling his bike, in front of a red brick house, three-storied, its windows beetling down at them under deep eaves.

Even before his father turns to him, his face bright and open, his real father's face, Buddy knows what he will ask. Though his father has never mentioned it to him since he returned to Houston, Buddy hasn't forgotten what his father asked him at Fort Polk.

"What do you think?" his father says.

"Think about what, sir?"

"What do you think of the house?"

The house's ivy-covered lawn and wavering coach lamp are mysterious. For a moment, in one of its upper windows, he thinks that he can see another boy, looking down at him. But it is only a shadow, a reflection on dark glass.

"I don't know, sir," he says.

"Can you think about it?"

"Yes, sir."

His father pushes off from the curb. Buddy sees him flinch, as he did at Fort Polk, as if he thinks that everything he does is wrong; and Buddy knows that he's a liar, for pretending not to understand what his father has said; the house is beautiful and terrible, the most beautiful house he's ever seen.

❧◦❧

They have ridden around the bayou until they reached River Oaks' gray stone gate, then turned and headed back downtown. His father wanted to do it twice; Buddy has ridden until his feet slipped from his toe guards, numb, trying to catch his father's fleeting shape.

At Gramma Turner's house, his father's plan is to sneak their bikes back into the garage, then tell her he's had another autopsy. In the driveway, Buddy sees a curtain in a front window rustle. He starts to call out, but too late. Gramma Turner's voice strikes down like lightning:

"Where in the hell have you been?" she says.

His father freezes, then starts slowly up the driveway again, his bike ticking next to him. He is like Jason in *Jason and the Argonauts*, Buddy thinks, going to behead Medusa. Above them, the horse stamps the sky, tosses his mane.

Gramma Turner peers down at them from a tiny porch between the back door and garage, her chin lifted, visoring her eyes with her hand. Her hair is a jet-black helmet, her eyes hidden behind thick, horn-rimmed glasses. At the collar of her purple dress is an ivory cameo, a profile of a woman that Grampa Turner bought her in Rome, long ago. Buddy can't think of Gramma Turner without thinking of the woman in the cameo; and like the woman, there is something royal about Gramma Turner that makes him ashamed that they have tried to fool her.

"What do you think you're teaching him, sneaking around like this?" she says.

His father stares ahead, as still as a statue.

"I don't know, mamma," he says.

She descends the porch steps, grips Buddy's arm, kneading it to test his solidity. Her eyes, in her glasses, are huge, all-seeing. "Hungry?" she says.

There is no fooling her, she says. Never once in all her forty years of school teaching has a student lied to her, and gotten clear with it.

Buddy's stomach growls; but he will never admit to her that he is hungry.

"No, ma'am," he says.

His father rolls up the garage door with a tremendous crash, staring ahead, as if willing himself to vanish. "Let him go," he says.

"Jimmy," she says. "I need to talk to him about his school."

"Let him go," his father says.

Gramma Turner lets go of his arm. His father has disappeared. Buddy raises his kickstand, thinking that he will walk the bike into the garage. "Get on inside," Gramma Turner says. "Your daddy and I need to talk."

He looks for his father again, then leaves his bike in the driveway, climbs the cement steps to the tiny porch. He opens the door to the tiny yellow kitchen, closes it behind him. To his left is the tiny, dark, wood-paneled room where he will spend the day with Gramma Turner. On one wall is a framed drawing of a steep mountain, from whose summit shine golden rays. Sprawled along a road that winds up the mountain are fallen travellers, wallowing in Drunkenness and Sloth and Debt; at the bottom is its title: The Road To Success.

His grandmother's and father's voices bleed from the garage. He goes to the window in the back door. Three feet away, maybe, across the porch, is a door to the garage. Slowly, he opens the back door, lifting it by its doorknob, so that it won't stick on the sill. His fingertips throb, blood beating from his heart. He is afraid of what his grandmother will do, if she catches him.

You go over there and she lies to you, just like she always has, Gramma Turner says, and then you don't know what to think.

It's not like that, mamma.

Then tell me, Jimmy. Tell me what it's like. You need to come back, so we can take care of this mess, and you can take care of your daddy. You can't keep paying, honey, for a mistake you made twelve years ago.

Buddy opens the screen door. The horse hovers over the garage. He is in the trees, part of the trees, in their bare, gray limbs. Buddy doesn't know what Gramma Turner means, when she says that his father has made a mistake; but he understands that she is calling his mother a liar.

Last Christmas, the adults gathered here, at Gramma Turner's house. You don't have a right, Gramma Turner said, to his mother. You don't have a right to be his mother. You don't have a right to be his wife. You tricked him.

He doesn't know what Gramma Turner meant when she said that his mother tricked his father, but he knows it is something dirty, like scenes in the three o'clock movies that don't make sense.

The door swings open. Gramma Turner is there. She catches his wrist, shakes it, her eyes locked on him, huge in her glasses.

"What are you doing?" she says.

"Nothing, ma'am."

"Were you listening? Did your mother tell you to listen?"

"No, ma'am," Buddy says.

"You sure about that?" She shakes him. "You sure?"

The horse will shoot down, crash through the roof, pin her with the points of his hooves; he will tear off her skull with his square yellow teeth, his face a death-mask of shrunken skin. He will dash out her brains, pinkish gray in the dust, so that her face will be only a mask. "Yes, ma'am," he says.

Behind her, in the garage, his father watches him, his face in half-shadow.

"Let him go," his father says.

"Jimmy," she says.

"She's not like that, mamma," his father says. "Let him go."

Gramma Turner lets go of him.

"Go see your granddaddy," she says. "I'll deal with you in a minute."

He goes through the dining room, its dark oval table and dark gray curtains and glimmering crystal, and stands at the bottom of the stairs. His heart still hammers with fear. He knows he will have to face Gramma Turner, in the little room, and later, his father, who will think that he has betrayed him.

He puts his foot on the first creaking stair. He doesn't know where his father really lives. But he is afraid to go up the stairs; he knows what he will find in his father's room, sitting on the edge of his father's bed — something not even the horse can defeat, a boy with a faceless face, as smooth and blank as a mirror.

కా౼౼ఉ

He has already stood in the den, looking out the sliding glass doors at the back yard, remembering the day he found the camera, how he'd stood, pointing it at two blue jays, their pinpoint nostrils, the water-diamonds shimmering in the air; how they were already part of a story, suddenly sharp and clear.

He has studied, as he always does, the pictures on the wall: his grandfather with men whose names he's made Buddy memorize: Eubie Blake; Calvin Owens; Bobby "Blue" Bland; Louis Armstrong, Prince Among Men. When he moved to Houston, his grandfather became Bink Turner, King of Nighttime Jazz, broadcasting nine to midnight, Sundays till one a.m. On the side, he directed high school jazz and marching bands. Buddy can still see him on a street corner at a Thanksgiving Day Parade, his snap-brim fedora raked on his head, talking easily and seriously with other men; but his grandfather has been sick for a long time.

Now he watches his grandfather's sleeping face, his wide, handsome brow and jet-black hair. He touches his grandfather's blue-veined hand.

The hand grasps his, startling him. Grampa Turner opens his eyes, smiling with the side of his face that still smiles.

"Gotcha," he says.

Some days he can't talk, and others, he is hard to understand. Today, his voice is only a whisper. "Hello, granddaddy," Buddy says. "How are you?"

Grampa Turner shrugs, as if he doesn't think much of the question.

"Mamma?" he says.

"She's fine. She told me to send you her love."

His grandfather looks away from him, frowning, his dark eyes fierce. "Movie?"

"I'm working on it."

His grandfather grips his hand. "Good."

Outside, his father's and Gramma Turner's voices rise in argument, the screen door slaps shut, something crashes in the garage. Gramma Turner bustles into the den, glancing sideways at him. Buddy isn't afraid of her, now. When she is around Grampa Turner, she is different, her eyes delicate and searching.

"How you doing, Bink?" she says. When his grandfather is silent, she says, "Jimmy's busy now. He'll come see you later."

Grampa Turner looks away, his mouth tight, as if he's tasted something bitter.

❧ ❧

For a long time, they sit on the narrow, sagging day bed in the tiny, wood-paneled room. Buddy balances a paper plate of cookies on his knees, a can of Coke. Next to the bed is a telephone table crowded with wadded tissues, a soap opera magazine, a mug of cold coffee. Since his grandfather got sick, before his father left for Detroit, Gramma Turner has slept here. On the wall above the table is a black and white photograph of his father in the yard of the house where they lived in Navesota, before they moved to Houston. In the photo, his father holds a ball, wearing a pair of striped overalls. Behind him, a chicken pecks in the yard. When they bought the house in Houston, Gramma Turner reminds him, their dining room table was a wooden spool;

but they never begged, she says, and they never forgot who they were, and he should remember, he should always remember who he is.

From the front pocket of his binder, which his father has recovered from the car, glaring at her, Gramma Turner plucks each new test and quiz. His grades that week are so low they seem white-hot or ice-cold: a fifty-four on a math quiz, a forty-two in Roman History, a thirty on a test in Sacred Studies.

After she's set aside the last sheet of paper, she takes his free hand, rubbing it between her own. He knows what will come next, the questions about his mother: how often does she clean? does she help him with his homework? does she drink two or three glasses of wine with dinner? does she ever have men friends over? He knows what her questions mean, that his life with his mother is wrong; this, and not the corrections, is why he hates Gramma Turner.

"Buddy?" she says. "Were you listening today?"

"No, ma'am."

She rubs his knuckles, worrying them like stones. "Do you know what'll happen if you tell your mother about that house you saw?"

"No, ma'am," he says.

"She'll try to take it away from him. And if she can't, she'll end up wasting all his money on lawyers and all her money on lawyers and no one will have a place to live."

He turns his face from her. His eyes sting. It is a lie that he only hates her. He knows that she is right about his life with his mother. He knows where his mother and he will go: into the darkness of the shotgun shacks near their house. He wants Gramma Turner to tell him what will happen next.

His father opens the back door. While they've talked, he has banged and clattered behind the thin wall, as he has each Saturday since he's returned, intent on his mysterious, never-ending work. Now he stands in the doorway of the little room, red-faced, dripping sweat, his white T-shirt transparent on his chest.

"Ready?" he says.

"No, Jimmy," Gramma Turner says. "He isn't."

"I'm going upstairs," his father says. "Will you be ready then?"

"No, Jimmy. We've still got a couple of hours, at least. This is what happens when you bring him late."

"Why don't you do this before?" his father says, to him.

"You know he can't do anything in that place he lives. Now why don't you go upstairs and take a shower? Then you can come and visit your daddy."

His father stares at him, then disappears, pounding up the stairs; his footfalls creak across the floor above, water sings through pipes.

"What's wrong?" Gramma Turner says. "Want another Coke?"

"Yes, ma'am," he says, though he doesn't.

His grandmother goes to the kitchen, returns with a Coke wrapped in a thin paper napkin. Buddy slowly sips the Coke he doesn't want, playing for time.

The pipes hum, the shower squeaks off. Above him, his father creaks across the landing to his room. Through the high, narrow window above the bed, Buddy sees a patch of yellowish sky. Sometimes, by the time he leaves, it is pitch black.

"Buddy?" she says. "Why don't you tell me what you heard?"

He doesn't want to answer any more questions. He doesn't want to betray his mother, or his father. He is listening, hoping that this will be the day his father will take him back to his mother's, that his father will return for good, though he knows that this won't happen. He closes his eyes, praying to the horse to swoop down, to crash through the wood-paneled walls.

"Buddy," she says, gripping his hand. "Look at me. Did your mother tell you to listen? Is she doing this to you, honey?"

The horse will fade through the ceiling; Buddy will grip his ghost-body, his ghost-mane, and fly away with him.

"Buddy? Look at me. What did she tell you to do?"

Like hoof-thunder, his father thunders down the stairs. Buddy opens his eyes. His father stands in the doorway of the little room in a light-colored dress shirt and slacks, smelling of Vitalis and Listerine, clutching a can of Coke.

"Ready?" he says.

"No, Jimmy," Gramma Turner says. "He's not."

His father stares at him, looking through him, at someone else. "What do you want to do?" he says, to Buddy.

"Don't, Jimmy."

"Is this what you want to do?" his father says.

"Please, Jimmy. Stop it."

"I'm trying to give him a choice."

"This isn't the way to do it. I'm not going to have all our hard work ruined by your foolishness. I'm not doing anything different with him than I did with you."

"Maybe that's my point," his father says.

Gramma Turner looks down at his schoolwork, shooing his father with a wave of her hand. "Go on," she says. "Go see your daddy and leave us alone."

"He's my son," his father says.

His grandmother takes off her glasses, pinches the bridge of her nose.

"He's my son," his father says.

"All right, Jimmy. He's your son. But I've been the one raising him while you've been away. And I know where you're going to take him."

His father blushes a deep, bloody red. "Come on," he says, to Buddy.

"You sit right there," his grandmother says.

"Come on," his father says.

"Think about what you're doing, Jimmy. You can't put him in the middle of this. Not for yourself. Not for him. You can't."

"If you don't let him go," his father says, "I'm not coming back."

It is like the time his father took the camera, how his father stormed from the house, Gramma Turner shouting at him that he was ruining Buddy with his foolishness. Now, as then, Buddy is glad to see her defeated. But even as his father opens the back door, telling him to come on, even as Buddy gathers his books and binder, he wants to touch her shoulder. But he is afraid of what will happen if he does; her face, bare of her glasses, looks too delicate, like a part of her that is too private for him to see.

All of this lasts only a moment. He turns from her and flies down the porch steps, letting the screen door slap behind him. Only when he reaches the car does he look back. Behind the screen door, she is a shadow, a ghost.

"Jimmy!" she cries. "When are you coming home?"

5.

In the car, his father stares ahead, street lights shuttering across his face. Usually they go for a burger at the Rainy Days Inn, then the freeway home. Now they pass the medical center, the giant pool at the Shamrock Hotel. Then they are crossing the bayou, whose huge cement banks yawn open beneath them. In the distance is the Astrodome, an ancient, enormous UFO, and between them and it, in the yellowish haze, endless blocks of apartment complexes, convenience stores, mini-malls. At each turn, Buddy tries to recalculate what new route they will take to his mother's house, but the way back, the whole shape of the city, is unclear to him. He doesn't know what his father will do. The horse is still there; but he is miles above, as high as an airplane.

At a pink brick apartment complex with a two-story, white-pillared façade, like a plantation house, or the White House, his father stops, punches numbers into a keypad in a metal box. He doesn't look at Buddy. Before them, a section of wrought-iron fence grinds slowly open. They drive past row after row of pink brick buildings, row after row of cars beneath a rusting tin shed that lines the fence.

His father parks under the shed, and straightens his tie.

"Buddy," he says, "I'd like you to meet a friend of mine. She's been a good friend. She's helped me through some hard times."

He knows that his father is lying. But it is like an alphabet with letters missing, a building that twists in impossible shapes. He watches his father speak as if he is watching a bad lip-synch. He is in a no-place, a place where there is no horse; he is in the real movie, he thinks.

"Okay?" his father says.

"Yes, sir."

Across the parking lot, in a three-story wall of apartments, is a dark, narrow hallway. At the end of the hallway are two doors, a swirl of dead leaves, a yellow light. A moth struggles against the light inside a clotted web. It is like the dungeons in *The Tomb of Ligeia*, Buddy thinks, though he knows it isn't like them at all.

His father lifts his hand, hesitating, then knocks.

⊱⊰

At first, she is only a shadow. She stands in the doorway, hesitating, clutching her hand against her chest. Then she moves, floating toward them, her small mouth slightly opened in surprise, her smooth skin like alabaster, her small sharp eyes flickering from him to his father; then she is embracing him, pressing against his belly the slight curve where her legs and belly meet, clasping him with her nervous hands. Her smell is like his mother's, a sweetish perfume, but beneath it is another odor — vampire venom — a sharp smell of flesh. In the moment it takes her to move toward him, he recognizes her, though from where and when he doesn't know; all of this is swept away in her scent, her touch.

"Oh," she says, "you don't know how long I've waited." Then, to his father, "You didn't tell me you were bringing him."

"Sorry," his father says.

"I wish you'd let me know. I could have done something special."

"I'm sorry," his father says, though not like he means it, in a voice he uses with Gramma Turner. "I'm deeply sorry from the bottom of my heart."

The woman steers Buddy into a bare hallway, gripping his arm; and he is happy to be lead, dizzied by her touch. "Here," she says. "Let me get you something."

She has led him into a small apartment: a dining area, a tiny galley kitchen. A small TV plays almost soundlessly, like his mother's, in the way of TV's left on all the time. Beyond it, a living room with hanging plants and a couch buried under velvet throw pillows. Everywhere there are glass baubles, dioramas, miniature worlds.

But he doesn't notice all of this right now. Now, he touches the rough plastic surface of the card table where he and his father sat at Fort Polk. The folding chairs are the same, and the TV stand, and the TV. He keeps his back turned to his father and the woman; he knows that he can't let them see that he has noticed.

In the galley kitchen, the woman opens a refrigerator. Behind her, his father reaches into a high shelf and takes down a bottle of whiskey. The woman cracks ice from a tray. Pieces scatter on the floor. "What's wrong?" his father says.

"I just dropped some ice," the woman says.

His father glances at him; and Buddy knows that he can see what he has noticed. "Ice," his father says, grinning at him behind his mask. "That's nice."

The woman turns to his father; and for a moment, a kind of tenderness steals across his father's face. "I wish you'd told me he was coming," the woman says.

"Ah ha-ha," his father says, in a monster voice.

The woman puts a glass of Coke on the table. She asks Buddy if he's eaten, and if he is hungry, and when he says he hasn't, and he is, she and his father discuss what they should eat. His father says it will be more efficient to have something delivered. As she and his father speak, they often use that word – efficient – and the air becomes thick in the way it did when his father and mother talked about the hospital, long ago.

His father decides that they should order a pizza, then goes to the end of the bare hallway, glancing back sharply at the woman before he shuts the door.

The woman sits across the table from him. Her red hair, against her pale skin, is like spun copper. She has just woken from her crypt. She takes his hand; her hand is almost as small as his, and something in her strong, nervous touch reminds him again of the time before his father left.

"My name is Mary," she says. "Did your father tell you that?"

"Yes, ma'am," Buddy says.

"I'm your father's friend," the woman says.

"Yes, ma'am."

"You don't need to call me that." She presses his hand. "Call me Mary."

On the refrigerator are pictures of children. He knows that she has written the postcard he found at Fort Polk, that she is the reason his father will not come home. He wants to tell her about the sounds that he heard, his mother crying out, but he won't betray his father. And it is not only this that makes him hold his tongue; he wonders, with sharp, sudden jealousy, if his picture is there.

"Yes, Mary," he says.

The woman smiles at him. "I have so many questions. It will take us a while to get to know each other, but we'll have time. Soon, we'll have plenty of time."

❧ ❧

Outside, they file through the maze of apartment buildings. His father has ordered a pizza to pick up at the front gate. He strides ahead, whistling; he is an excellent whistler, the tune subtle and complex; he is different in this secret place, his jokes, his funny voices, more like his real father's, though not the same, not exactly.

In a courtyard is a swimming pool, whose still, blue surface is lit from within. Above it is the sound of the freeway, the city's glare, and the horse, hidden in the depthless night. "It's nice," the woman says, to him. "I wish you could've come here this summer. You could've gone swimming."

His father cuts his eyes at her, as he did before he shut the door. The woman purses her lips, to trap what she's said.

"Did you have a nice day?" she asks his father.

"We had an excellent day," his father says. "Buddy did an excellent job with his school work. My mother helped him."

"How is your father?"

"Fine," his father says. "Just fine."

"You're very lucky," the woman says, to Buddy. "Most people don't have a grandmother like yours."

He was excellent, his father said. This glows in him, and almost as good is their tricking of the woman. "Yes," he says. "She's very nice."

"I didn't know my grandmother when I was your age," the woman says. "Most of the children I teach don't, either. Here. Let me show you something."

The woman takes his hand and leads him off the path.

"Look," she says.

In a pond, glimmers of orange, of off-white, brush the dark surface. Goldfish. Through his own reflection, Buddy watches their flat, untroubled eyes. Behind him, where his father stands with the woman, a thick silence gathers. Buddy stares at the goldfish, daring himself to turn. He turns, and his father takes his hand from the woman's. But he's seen it, and the dark bitter glow inside him flickers out.

❧

They eat dinner at the card table, watching *The Love Boat* and *Fantasy Island*. His father watches him hopefully; the woman asks about his friends; Buddy invents boys — Oscar and Scotty and Greg — who all make good grades, and who are all very nice. Before they leave, he asks to use the bathroom. His father tells him to hurry up; he has already gone once. *A piss-o-tron*, his father says.

In the bathroom, which smells like his father and the woman, an embalmed smell of Vitalis and hairspray and perfume, is another door, which he is sure will open into the room at the end of the hallway, which he was afraid to open before.

Outside are his father's and the woman's voices. I thought it meant, she says. No, his father says, not yet. You need to be more careful. There are some things he doesn't need to see. Then why did you bring him? the woman says. What am I supposed to do? Am I supposed to just disappear?

Slowly, he opens the door, pressing his cheek against its cool wood. Outside, in the hallway, his father is telling the woman sorry, sorry, and soon, soon, as if these words are the same. He prays for the horse to break through the ceiling, to tear through the cheap walls; but he is deep inside the honeycombed building, far from the horse; and he knows that the horse is only a childish thought.

A sliver of bare, ill-lit walls, an opened closet, his father's dresser from Fort Polk, open to him. Reflected in the dresser's two tall mirrors is a welter of dingy sheets, coiled as on a sick bed. For a moment, in the mirror, he sees his father, a single, clean bullet hole in his head; and the woman's crying is like the sounds he heard from his mother's room, his mother crying out, as if she was in pain; and he knows that he has seen the real movie, the movie where his father really lives.

"Buddy!" his father shouts, outside. "Let's go!"

6.

All the way back to his mother's house, past El Destino Club #2, where purple lights revolve, and Telepsen Tool, where sparks shower night and day, and Andrew Jackson Grammar School's cement playground, enclosed in a barbed-wire fence; past the orange duplexes at the end of his mother's street, whose porch roofs sag like heavy-lidded eyes, where Mexican children stare at his father's car, then vanish into the houses, or around corners, or under gutted cars, Buddy can never tell — Buddy presses himself against his passenger door, his forehead against his window's cool glass; and all he sees is not the same, like a film running backward; and he doesn't know which way he's seen it is real, the way he's seen it before, thinking of the streets near the new school, or the way he sees it now, strange and fragile, his home.

His father parks in the driveway. The engine ticks in the silence. Above them, in the darkness, the horse is invisible, a satellite.

"Buddy?" his father says. "Look at me. Were you listening at my mother's?"

"Yes, sir."

"You need to promise me you won't say anything — not about the house, not about Mary. Nothing. Okay?"

In the streetlight, his father's face is only a shadow; and Buddy can hear, in his voice, that he is afraid. "Yes, sir," he says.

"I'm sorry, Buddy."

"It's okay, sir."

"No, Buddy, it's not. Right now it's not okay. But I'm going to make it okay. I'm going to buy that house we saw. You and Mary and I can live there. Mary can help you with your schoolwork. We won't have to deal with my mother anymore. You can visit your mother every weekend. Your mother's a real special woman, and she should be happy. We can all start over and be happy."

He watches his father's face, waiting for something else. His mother's house looks fake, an abandoned set. He wants to ask his father if what he's said is just a joke; but he knows that it isn't. "Yes, sir," he says.

"I need you to think about it, Buddy. Okay?"

"Yes, sir."

"I love you, Buddy. I'm sorry. I need to go."

He embraces his father, breathing his clean, sweaty smell. Then he is standing in the driveway, watching the taillights of his father's car disappear. He opens the gate in the scrap of fence, latches it behind him. All of it is fake — the burglar bars, the broken sidewalk, the unspread sand.

At the top of the porch steps, the kitchen door swings open. His mother's gaze glances off him, then past him, squinting into the darkness.

"Where's daddy?" she says.

"He left. He said he'll call you later."

"What's wrong?"

He slips around her, dropping his books and binder on the steel-topped table, where they skid across its slick surface. Near his mother's chair are a glass of wine and a box of orange snack crackers. British voices twitter on the TV. As he heads for the bathroom, his arms and legs feel wobbly, and his eyes can't focus right; at each step, he is afraid that he will sink through the floor.

"You look strange," his mother says. "Are you okay?"

He shuts the bathroom door. "I'm fine."

"Are you sick?" she says, outside.

He sits on the toilet, covers his face with his hands. When his father doesn't come in, he and his mother always end up fighting about Gramma Turner. But tonight, he can't let that happen; he doesn't trust himself to face her. "I'm fine," he says.

"What else did daddy say?"

"I told you," he says. "Nothing."

Her slippers scratch outside on the wooden floor. "Did you see granddaddy?"

"Yes. He's fine."

"What about Gramma Turner?"

"She's fine, too."

"Buddy?" she says. "Are you sure you're all right?"

"I'm fine," he says. "Leave me alone."

After a moment, she goes to the kitchen. In the darkness behind his hands, he hears the television cease, water hiss through pipes, the deadbolt in the back door click. She is shutting down the house, getting ready for bed. He knows that he should get up, go to his room; but he sits, frozen, unable to move.

He uncovers his eyes. In the medicine chest mirror, his face looks different — thinner, older — as if it is not his own, as if one of the boys buried in the field is watching him through the mirror. He sniffs his shirt, detects the woman's fleshy scent: vampire venom. Evidence. He has been infected; he cannot let his mother know. Silently, he slides open the medicine chest, where his father's Bay Rum still lives, and shakes it into his hand, rubs it onto his face and neck and clothes.

He flushes the toilet, opens the door. Light from his mother's reading lamp bleeds into the hallway. He knows he should go to his room, shut the door, to pretend that he is sick, to protect his mother from the venom; but he stands in the hallway, waiting.

"Buddy?" she says.

He goes to the doorway to her room, but doesn't look at her.

"Come here," she says, patting a place on the quilt.

She sits on pillows against the headboard. The neck and sleeves of her nightgown, so thin it seems made not of fabric, but of her warm, fleshy scent, peeks out above the hem of the covers. In her lap, a brown-faced child stares up at him from the cover of a Maryknoll magazine. His mother's eyes, on him, seem to strain against their blindness. He sits on the bed, facing away from her, knowing he should leave.

"What's wrong, honey?" When he doesn't answer, she says, in a sly voice, "You smell like a cat house. Are you wearing daddy's aftershave?"

"We rode our bikes," he says. "I wanted to smell good."

"For your information," she says, tweaking his ribs, "women appreciate soap."

He jerks away from her.

"What is it, sugar?"

He stares at the quilt, knowing that he should leave.

She noodles his armpit. Snickering, hugging his sides to guard against her swift hands, he slumps onto her lap. Her hands race over him, needling him; he squirms away, trying to escape. He cannot let her tickle him; he cannot let her make him cry. That spring, when he complained about St. Edward's, or visiting Gramma Turner, he'd end up pinned, begging for mercy, crying tears more bitter than ordinary ones. But at the same time, because moments earlier, he was complaining, then laughing, all of it seemed like a crazy joke.

Now, his throat aches with the same feeling of laughter and crying together. She strokes his hair. He will tell her, he thinks, if she will let him stay; he can't, he thinks, afraid of himself, and of what he might do.

"What did you and daddy do today?" she says.

"We rode our bikes. Then I had to sit in the crappy room with crappy Gramma Turner. Then we ate a crappy hamburger."

"Please, honey," she says.

"It was crappy," he says. "I hate her."

"Please, honey," she says, shielding her eyes with her hand. "Don't start."

"It's true."

"No, it isn't. She is your grandmother and she loves you very much, and she has been very, very generous to pay for your school."

"Who cares?" he says.

"You should," she says, looking at him. "You'd be over there at Andrew Jackson if she hadn't paid for St. Edward's. You don't know what it's like, moving from school to school, Grampa Liddy chasing jobs, and Gramma Liddy no help, like she is. You don't know what it's like not to have enough."

Each time they talk about Gramma Turner, his mother blames Gramma Liddy. He doesn't believe her, but he doesn't know what to believe; he doesn't even know how to ask what the real truth is. "Why didn't we go to Detroit?" he says.

"Please, honey. We've been through this."

"Tell me."

"There was the house, and my job, and Gramma Liddy — please, honey, I don't want to get into it again."

"Tell me."

"That's it, Buddy. That's all there is to it. I made a mistake, and now I have to do the best I can to make it right. We have to keep hoping and praying that we can bring daddy back, so we can be a family again."

He doesn't believe her. He knows that she is lying. He wants to ask her what Gramma Turner meant when she said that she, his mother, would take everything, and when she said that his father had made a mistake. But he knows that he won't. If she will keep secrets from him, he will do the same. He won't tell her about the woman, or the house that his father has shown him, not only because he doesn't want to lose his father, but also because he doesn't want to lose the woman, the house, the apartment; they are secrets as powerful as magic.

He sits up, turns from her, shivering. Whatever he says, it will not be enough; and the only thing he can say to stop what is happening, he is too cowardly to say.

He rises and goes to the hallway. "Buddy," his mother says, "you've got to tell me the truth, honey. That's the only way we can help daddy."

He continues into the darkness and formaldehyde smell of his room. His mother calls out for him, but he doesn't reply. By the porch light through his windows, he finds the box of movies in his closet, and carries it to the editor.

The editor is a square plastic box with a viewing screen, an aperture, and two arms, one to hold the film, the other to wind it. From the box of movies, he takes a blue plastic canister marked with Grampa Turner's precise script: *Buddy's pool, June 1967.* There are other movies — vacation scenery, frantic parties at the hospital full of vaguely familiar faces — but this is the one he watches again and again.

In her room, his mother is crying. He clicks on the light beneath the aperture, clips the reel to the feeder arm, tucks the end of the leader into the take-up reel, aligns the film in the aperture, pulls it taut. Cranking the take-up reel, moving the feeder more slowly to keep the film true in its cogs. He knows that it is not the real movie where his father lives; but he leans closer, his face almost touching the editor's hooded portal, its lighted screen, his heart pounding slowly with expectation.

A naked infant splashes in an aquamarine pool. Water diamonds hover in the sunlit air, in the backyard outside the window where he now sits. The camera pans to Gramma Turner, perched in an aluminum lawn chair, wearing a canary-yellow dress, white gloves, and matching pillbox hat. The chair next to hers — Grampa Turner's, who is filming — is empty. She claps her gloved hands, and her red lips move, and Buddy remembers her high, clear voice.

The camera pans to the left. Grampa Liddy, in his light blue shirt and pants pulled high over his stomach, beats out time to the song with his wooden cane, wisps of white hair and craggy chin nodding along. Next to him, Gramma Liddy sits bolt upright, her silvery hair pulled back in a paisley scarf, watching Gramma Turner. But even she is singing; and he remembers their voices, and the slight chill of water on his skin.

Then his mother holds him, wrapped in a powder-blue blanket, her arms sleek in her orange and yellow sundress, in front of the back yard fence, which is blanketed in honeysuckle. She rocks him lightly, talking lightly to the camera, and beneath her quick glances is something bold and calm; and Buddy can almost smell the honeysuckle, feel her rocking, see the bees' bright patterns in the air.

The movie cuts to his father. Buddy slows the film, though it is already brittle and yellowed from when he has watched it before. His father wears a white T-shirt and jeans, and holds him, now dressed in a blue jumpsuit, so that they both face the camera. He studies his father's shy, stunned smile. He thinks that he can see, now, the darkness gathering in his face, at the corners of his eyes, a different father, just beneath the one he knows. But he cannot be sure. No matter how many times he watches the film, there is always a moment he misses, the moment when his father disappears, and Buddy cannot stop him. His father turns from the camera, turning Buddy to face him, refusing to give up his secrets. In the film, his father swings him down in a long arc, and he rises from his father's hands. And though he and his father are a blue- and white- and flesh-colored blur in streaks of sunlight and trees, he remembers the plunge, the upward heft, the moment when his father's impossibly large, impossibly strong hands release him, then close on him again.

7.

Each day he goes to the edge of the church at the new school, to spy on Gene and Simon, to watch them play the story of Abraham and Isaac, Christian and Apollyon, Reverend Toy's sermon about homosexuals and drug addicts snatching children right across the street at the mall, Mrs. Urqhart's speech that they aren't *at some second-class, public-school dump,* even things he's read in the newspaper: Simon is on border patrol and Gene is an illegal alien; Simon is a police officer, Gene is the Mexican man the police drowned in the bayou. And always, before Simon straddles Gene, before he raises the knife or aims the gun, come the trembling, secret words: *I don't need your lip, I'll give you what-for, I'll tear your ass apart.* Buddy watches them, jealous that Gene is with Simon, afraid of his own jealousy, and the hollow ache in his chest, the empty ache that has only grown since he was infected by the woman's venom. He watches with a kind of amazement: the plays make the teachers, the school, the whole adult world, seem like what it really is: a crazy, terrible joke. And more amazing is the moment when Simon rises, checking his watch, and heads to the street between the school and the mall, where a golden car sweeps up to the curb, a woman at its wheel, veiled by glare on the windshield – pale skin, a wave of blond hair; too beautiful, Buddy thinks, to be a mother – and Simon vanishes into the car, as if nothing has happened.

He hasn't told Alex about the plays. After school, he's hidden at Gramma Liddy's, or stood outside Alex's house, waiting for Ysrael to bark. He hasn't worked on *Ghost Horse,* which he knows is only childish. He can't tell Alex about the woman, or how his father's movements have stiffened, how he is surrounded by a shield of heat, so that what Gramma Turner says to him doesn't matter; and yet his father jokes and whistles, trying to play a father, and nowhere is this more true than at the woman's apartment. He can't tell Alex about the comfort he feels, hidden in her apartment, the comfort of silence, the silence that hides the change in his father that is too strange, too shameful to tell, the silence that connects his father and him, an invisible thread.

∂◦ᚥ

On the soccer field, a flock of boys wheels across mangy patches of green and brown, playing Smear the Queer; the football wobbles through the air to one boy, and the other boys chase him until, at the last possible moment honor will allow, he throws the ball to someone else, and the tide turns. They do what they want. Coach Bland never leaves his shack; it is rumored that he spends all day reading dirty magazines.

Where is the horse? Buddy, walking next to Sam Fahr around the soccer field, searches the flat gray sky above the pink brick school, above the boxy brown mall, above the houses, low and flat and eerily alike; but the horse has disappeared.

If you play "Stairway to Heaven" backward, Sam tells him, you can hear a black mass. The symbols on *Zoso* are Satanic, too. Jimmy Page made a deal with the Devil: his soul to play kick-ass guitar.

Across the field, Gene and Simon watch them. Simon cracks jokes Buddy can't hear; Gene laughs, hugging himself, as if he's in pain.

"What're you looking at?" Sam says.

"Nothing," Buddy says.

"You been hanging out with Simon?"

"No," Buddy says.

"You been watching him and Gene."

Buddy feels himself blush. "How do you know?"

"I seen you." Sam cants his chin at the grove. "Simon's not cool. He takes stuff you tell him and fucks it up. That's what he does. He fucks stuff up."

Buddy knows what he means; he's seen what Gene and Simon did to Sandy Mc-Ginty. Everyone knew that Sandy's father didn't live with him; that was why he was a mamma's boy, who never washed, who shrank and stammered and cowered. One day when Sandy's mother, a huge, red-haired woman with a flushed face, picked him up from school to practice his viola, she yelled at the boys to stop tormenting her son. Sandy was put on trial; Gene and Simon asked him if his giant mother was a drunk, if the viola wasn't even a real musical instrument. When the boys piled on Sandy on the soccer field, when they made him confess, Buddy didn't help. He knew that it was wrong; but he also knew that with each blow against Sandy, he dodged one himself.

"It's not cool," Sam says, watching him.

Buddy knows what he means, but he can't think about it, right then. "How does he know I used to go to Queen of Peace?" he says.

"I don't know."

"How does he know we smoke?"

"What're you saying, man? Everybody at school knows we smoke. What's a-matter? You scared of getting caught?"

"No," Buddy says.

"Yeah, you are. They scare you with all that Hell talk. But they can't scare me. I already know I'm goin' to Hell."

Sam stares at him, daring him to say he's wrong. Usually it made Buddy feel frightened, and a little brave; but now, Buddy doesn't quite believe him.

Across the field, Gene and Simon turn, as if at a hidden signal, and head toward them. "Come on," Buddy says. "They're coming."

Sam catches his arm. "Fuck that. I ain't scared."

He bats at Sam, twisting from him, a crazy feeling in his throat like he might cry, or throw up. It's not only what Simon has done to Sandy, or the hollow feeling in his chest when he watches Gene and Simon in the grove; it's how Simon moves through the hallways in disguise, one person in class and another in the plays, like an angel in the Bible who walks among men.

Sam lets go of him. Buddy wipes his face on his sleeve; Sam screws up his eyes, squinting at him. "I ain't scared," Sam says.

In a moment, the boys circle them, their expressions curious, mocking, eager. Behind them, on the field, Gene waves more of them on, shouting that there will be a trial. Simon pushes through the circle, grinning at Buddy, offering him a secret sign, as he did the day he spoke to him in Latin.

"What's the problem?" he says.

"There's no problem," says Sam.

"It looked like there was a problem," Simon says, to the boys. "Didn't it? Didn't anybody else see a fight?"

The boys agree, catching on. Buddy knows it doesn't matter if they saw it or not. In the circle, the air smells of their sweat, their breath. Buddy watches their hands, flinching when they move.

"Maybe it's none of your fuckin' business," Sam says. "Maybe you should go back to playing your stupid games."

The boys make a low sound, serious, and at the same time, mock-serious. A blush spreads down Simon's neck. "I think you're hiding something," Simon says.

"Fuck you," says Sam.

Another low sound spreads through the boys; some jostle, trying to get a better look. It isn't too late, Buddy thinks; they can leave. But Sam stands his ground.

"Maybe I'll tell them about your mother," Simon says.

The boys turn quiet, watching them. Sam cocks his head to one side; then he lurches at Simon, swinging his fists.

"Get him!" Gene cries.

But the boys are already swarming, grabbing Sam's arms. Hands pin Buddy, twisting his arms behind his back. A pain like a knife drives into his shoulder; he makes himself go limp, his heart thundering in his chest. Simon glances at him, a question, then looks at Sam. "Why don't you tell them?" Simon says.

"Let me go, asshole," Sam says. "I'll kick your fuckin' ass."

Simon grins. "Don't you want to know?" he says, to the boys.

"Tell!" Gene shouts. "Tell!"

The boys take up the chant, pumping their fists. Sam tugs from side to side, trying to break their grip; the circle sways with him, a mouth of arms and fists, pushing the pain deeper into Buddy's shoulder. He wishes that he could vanish; he hears his own voice chanting, too.

"Why don't you tell us," Simon says, to Sam, "why your mother doesn't pick you up after school?"

"You're a liar," Sam says. "You're a liar. You're gonna go to Hell."

"I am not a liar," Simon says. "You're a liar. If you don't have anything to hide, why don't you just tell the truth?"

Sam spits on him. The boys' chant falters. Then Simon slaps Sam, so quickly Buddy isn't sure he's seen it; and a bright line of fear opens in his chest.

The boys are silent. Sam bows his head, his arms held up on either side of him, a silvery string of snot hanging from his nose. Simon leans close to him, his expression calm and still. "Isn't it true," he says, to Sam, "that your mother thinks your house is haunted? Isn't it true they're going to take her away?"

Buddy doesn't know if what Simon says is true. But part of it is; all the boys feel it, he thinks, as if Simon has opened a secret door.

"Turner," Simon says, to him. "You've been to his house. You know."

"No," Buddy says.

"He's lying!" Gene cries.

Simon lifts his hand, to silence Gene. "Yes, you do, Turner. You know."

Sam raises his eyes to him, asking silently what he will do. Buddy looks at the sky, searching for the horse. When he first came to St. Edward's, Sam was the only boy who talked to him; he was always kind. Now he looks at Sam's torn shirt pocket, his shaggy hair, remembering the silence in Sam's house, and in his mother's house; and he turns from Sam, knowing there is still time to tell the truth.

"It's true," he says.

A shout of anger, of a kind of triumph, erupts from the boys. They press in, shoving, closing around him. Simon yells for them to let Buddy go. The hands release him; and Buddy turns, not looking at Sam, and runs across the field, toward the school.

8.

Where is the horse? That Sunday, at Queen of Peace, Gramma Liddy grips Buddy's hand, picking her way carefully across the gravel parking lot. Her shoulders are hunched, but she peers out beneath her furrowed brow, her blue eyes quick and alert. Shifts in pressure in her hand telegraph shifts in her balance, a current running between them. Ahead is the church, smooth, bone-colored limestone — *a citadel*, Buddy thinks, like the Temple in Jerusalem; but he is not sure the horse is here, either.

His mother glances back at them, impatient. As usual, Gramma Liddy wasn't ready when they came to pick her up for mass, and as usual, his mother paced outside her bedroom door, fretting that they would be late.

"Before we're locked up, " Gramma Liddy says, "tell me about your weekend."

"It was fine," he says.

"Of course," Gramma Liddy says. "Everyone's fine. Everyone's lying."

That morning, she asked his mother why she was so quiet, and his mother said that they would talk about it later. The night before, Buddy and his father went to the woman's apartment, wearing Halloween masks. When the woman answered her door, she screamed, clutching at her chest, and Buddy, behind his mask, imagined what would happen if he showed up alone, in the middle of the night: the flash of a knife, blood fanning out from the woman's neck. That afternoon, Gramma Turner and his father had talked in the garage, their voices stretched tight, like a rope about to snap: *It can't go on like this, Jimmy*, Gramma Turner said. When his father came down from his room after he showered, carrying the masks, the shield of heat that surrounded him seemed broken, and he shifted his weight uncomfortably, swallowed up in his dark, ill-fitting suit. At dinner, while the woman asked her usual questions — how were his friends? how was he doing in school? had he worked any more on his movies? — his father watched him across the table, his gaze steady and demanding. When they got home, his father went in to talk to his mother, and Buddy sat in front of his editor, trying not to listen. That morning, silence spread out between his mother and him, and now it was there, between Gramma Liddy and him, a thin sheet of glass.

His mother opens the church's heavy wooden side door; Father Peron glares down at them, his dark eyes so close Buddy can see their pupils. His mother dips her fingers in holy water, hurries down the side aisle. Gramma Liddy nods at Father Peron and follows at her own pace. Rows of brown faces watch them, dotted pink here and there – the few white parishioners, his mother says, who didn't leave when the neighborhood started to change. Buddy stares down at the yellow and aquamarine flecks in the floor, hoping that Alex and Mr. Torres are at the church down the street, where all the masses are in Spanish; they are the last people in the world he wants to see.

His mother, already kneeling in a pew, glances up sharply at Buddy, then closes her eyes, presses her forehead against clenched hands. When she prays, there is something solitary and awful about her that frightens him.

The rail bites into his knees. Beside him, Gramma Liddy sits, chin slightly lifted, catching a scent. On the wall behind the altar, Abraham glances up, surprised, dropping his knife, the Blessed Virgin spreads out her blue cloak, Christ hangs on His cross, blood flowing from a gash beneath his ribs – not like the altar at St. Edward's, with its bare, gilded cross; *Christianity without Christ*, his mother says.

Father Peron is talking about Purgatory. Buddy presses his forehead against his hands and tries to pray. But he sees his father, staring at him at the woman's apartment, and the decision that he will have to make; he sees the question in Sam's eyes – he can't forget what he's done to Sam. He glances at his mother's clenched hands, her silently moving lips. To live in sin, she's told him, is to be separated from God and the whole world; that is the meaning of the sheet of glass.

The suffering souls in Purgatory, Father Peron says, are like the unfortunates who die crossing the border, except that we might materially assist those souls in Purgatory with our prayers. Each Hail Mary, he says, eliminates five hundred years of suffering, each Rosary, a thousand; and in this way, he says, prayer for the souls in Purgatory is like the bake sales and barbecue drives for Queen of Peace itself.

❧ ❧

After mass, savory smoke drifts across the parking lot; next to oil drum cookers, men in cowboy hats hoist cans of beer. There is chicken slathered in barbecue sauce and spicy yellow potato salad and slow-cooked ribs; Buddy's mouth waters, thinking of it.

"There's your minions of Satan," Gramma Liddy says, nodding at the men. "Should we buy our lunch from them?"

"Mother," his mother says.

"Really. That was obscene, comparing Purgatory to a bake sale."

"How else is Father Peron supposed to keep the church running? He can't give homilies about the Holy Spirit every week."

"It would be nice," Gramma Liddy says, "if I could tell I was at mass."

"We could go to mass at Holy Rosary," his mother says, "and listen to Mrs. Hotze tell us that man the police drowned in the bayou deserved it."

Gramma Liddy doesn't say anything to that. "We shouldn't talk like this in front of Buddy," his mother says. "It confuses him."

"Are you confused?" Gramma Liddy says, her sharp blue eyes lighting on him.

Before he can answer — he would say no; he would never admit to Gramma Liddy that he's confused — Mr. Torres calls out to them. Gramma Liddy freezes. She looks like she does when Mrs. Orange phones, whose dim-witted son is always in trouble with the law, or Mrs. Diebold, who is dying of cancer.

Mr. Torres threads through the crowd, pausing to shake hands, short, compact, broad-shouldered, his crew cut graying above a broad, watchful face. Behind him, Alex looms, almost as tall as his father, wearing gray slacks, a clean white dress shirt; his dark gaze lifts and levels on Buddy, taking aim.

"The unfortunates!" Mr. Torres says, kissing Gramma Liddy's cheek. "Maybe he should say a prayer for Joe Campos, instead."

"It would certainly be an improvement over bake sales," says Gramma Liddy.

"The New Hope Church is having a benefit for the Campos family. We're going to send a petition to the mayor to get those policemen fired. You should come."

"We'll see," Gramma Liddy says.

"Maybe you can come, Maggie," says Mr. Torres.

"Thank you," Buddy's mother says. "We'll see."

"You haven't been around much lately. Have you been working hard?"

"Yes, but it's been fine." His mother waves away the question, blushing, glancing sideways; and to Buddy, she becomes beautiful. "It's fine," she says.

Buddy watches them, pinned by jealousy. Alex watches them, too; then both of them look away. In broken Spanish, his mother asks Mr. Torres how his campaign for city councilman is going. Mr. Torres, still smiling, says in English that he probably doesn't stand a chance. Then his smile tightens, turns cautious.

"How's Jimmy?" he says.

His mother's expression shifts, too, as if she's seen something that frightens her. "Fine," she says. "Just fine."

Mr. Torres' smile falters; he looks at Buddy. "*¿Qué te pasa?*" he says. "Is that new school keeping you busy?"

"Yes, sir," Buddy says.

"You should visit us sometime," Mr. Torres says. "Alex says he hasn't seen much of you lately. You must be very busy."

"Dad," Alex says, then cocks his head at Buddy. "Come on."

He doesn't want to go; but he follows Alex to the playground, glancing back at Mr. Torres, who can see inside him, he thinks, to Simon, and Sam.

In the low, oatmeal-brick school building, paper skeletons dance across a bulletin board; at the edge of the playground is the cement pipe that Alex and that he tried to crawl through, once, all the way to the bayou; and in the clump of trees, the aerial fort where they rained rocks and bark on boys who tried to charge it. But all of it is strange and small; it is a movie, now, too.

Alex sits on a picnic table near the playground, elbows on his knees, hunched shoulders gathering his Sunday jacket around his neck, too big for everything around him. "Quick," he says. "Who directed *Bride of Frankenstein?*"

"Easy," Buddy says. "James Whale."

"*Blood Feast?*"

"Herschell Gordon Lewis."

"*Mothra vs. Godzilla* – the American version?"

"Ishiro Honda," Buddy says. "There is no American version."

Alex grins, nodding; but he watches him steadily. "*Bueno,*" he says. "I had to see if you were real. Maybe you got infected. Invaded by aliens."

Alex watches him, his grin fading.

"Where've you been?" he says.

Buddy scuffs the toe of his dress shoe in the dirt. "Nowhere. I've been busy."

"I've seen you outside the house," Alex says. "If you don't want to make the movie, just tell me. I've got other things. Other projects. Understand?"

Buddy looks at Alex's hands. They are clean; but they are always clean on Sundays. "I'm sorry," he says. "We can work on it again."

Alex glances up at him.

"Come on," Buddy says. "I've been working on the script."

Alex looks at him.

"*¿Qué te pasa, ese?*" he says. What's wrong with you, man?

Buddy wants to tell him about the woman. He wants to tell him about Gene and Simon's plays, and the hollow ache he feels, watching them, and what he's done to Sam. But when he starts to speak, it is as if he reaches out, and touches the sheet of glass.

"*Nada,*" Buddy says. "*Las estupideces. La mierda.*"

❧ ❧

Gramma Liddy lives near the bayou in a small, gray, shingle house built, Buddy's mother said, for workers at Schlumberger Tool. Grampa Liddy bought the house when she was still at Rice; then his back gave out, and he couldn't pay the mortgage. Thank God, she says, she'd already started at the hospital, and Sister Bertille taught her how to manage the lab. When she gets fed up with Gramma Liddy's pronouncements, as she calls them, she reminds Buddy that she carries the mortgage on Gramma Liddy's house as well as their own. She never says this to Gramma Liddy, though.

Inside, the house smells of cigarettes and cooking and the faint, musty, acidic scent of paper. Newspapers and magazines, tied with old stockings for the paper drive at Queen of Peace, sit in chairs at the dining room table. Books crowd shelves behind the front door, and the low, varnished bookcases in his mother's old room, and the sewing table next to Gramma Liddy's bed. Beneath the front window, a bucket catches the drip from the air conditioner, which she uses to water the plants. In the back yard, she sets out Styrofoam plates of breadcrumbs to feed the mockingbirds and bluejays, and chicken liver on the porch for neighborhood cats.

While his mother puts the potato salad and barbecue they ended up buying, as they always did, onto plates in the kitchen, Buddy sits across from Gramma Liddy at the dining room table, reading the newspaper. The table is where Buddy has shown her his scripts, and where they've planned the miniature city, and had their conferences, as she calls them, though since that summer, he's come to the table less and less. He can't tell her about his father, or Gramma Turner, or even much about the school, because all of it makes her angry with his mother.

His mother and Gramma Liddy are talking about Poor Mr. Torres. He's a good man, his mother says. He's a *very* good man, Gramma Liddy says. God knows he suffered terribly when he lost his wife. And he worked his fingers to the bone to get that office job with the city, and to provide for Alex. But he makes her want to tear her hair out with his piety and politics; all he talks about is *La Raza Unida*, as if that can buy him a cup of coffee. Maybe it can, his mother says. Look how many businesses on Telephone are Spanish-owned. During the war, Gramma Liddy says, no one cared about the color of anyone else's skin; during the Depression, certainly no one did. Of course they did, his mother says. And think about what they did to daddy because he was in the union. If a Mexican man drowned a white man in the bayou, there'd be rioting in the streets. You're right, Gramma Liddy says, but I don't see how it helps for everyone to have their own little clique. All those cliques just mean you're easier to pick off. He's still a good man, his mother says. Yes, Gramma Liddy says. He's a very *good* man. Better than some I could name.

Gramma Liddy peers at him through the blue smoke that wreathes up from her cigarette. Buddy keeps his eyes on his Astrocast: "Make space for you. Not all understand your budget for time, energy, money."

"Did you and Alex have a good visit?" she says.

"Sure," he says.

His mother appears, carrying a bowl of potato salad. "Mr. Torres has been so good to you. It's important to keep up your friendship with Alex."

Alex and he have made plans to meet the next afternoon. Buddy still doesn't know if he believes in the Horse, but he will try. "I am," he says.

"You should visit him more often. You can't just hide out over here."

"I'm not hiding," he says.

"It's not his fault," Gramma Liddy says. "It's that absurd school, preaching Doomsday next to a shopping mall. It's a little assembly line for fascists."

"Please, mother." His mother cradles the bowl against her waist. "Don't start."

"It's true," Gramma Liddy says. "There's no difference between Queen of Peace and that place he goes now except the color of its students."

"Queen of Peace cares about color. How many black children do you see there?"

Gramma Liddy sweeps her hand through her smoke. "That's not the point. The point is why he's going one place and not the other."

"Please," his mother says. "We've had such a nice morning."

"Why not a whole nice weekend? Why not a whole nice life? It's no use — it's worse than no use — all this apologizing and pretending." Gramma Liddy fixes him with her sharp blue eyes. "You're the great white hope. Father a doctor, mother a medical professional, both graduates of Rice. Don't think Mrs. Turner forgets that for a minute."

"Please, mother," his mother says. "He doesn't need to hear this."

"Don't you want to know who guides your fate?" Gramma Liddy says, to him.

"Enough," his mother says. "It doesn't have anything to do with fate; it has to do with dollars and cents, just like it always has. I don't want to get into it in front of him."

Gramma Liddy lowers her eyes, taps out her cigarette. "Go on," she says, to Buddy. "Your mother and I need to talk."

Buddy gets up, trying not to look at Gramma Liddy, who fiddles with her lighter, and his mother, who holds the bowl, yellow-knuckled, against her waist.

In the hall outside his mother's old room, Buddy kneels and presses his ear against the heater in the living room wall, which smells of heat and dust; scraps of Gramma Liddy's and his mother's voices echo inside.

It doesn't help, his mother says, for you to talk to him like that. He's confused enough as it is. This is tearing him apart.

Whose fault is that? Gramma Liddy says.

It doesn't matter whose fault it is, his mother says. It's no one's fault. If it's anyone's fault, it's mine. Jimmy is his father, and Buddy needs him.

Jimmy, Gramma Liddy says, is mentally defective. Do you remember when he pulled that screen door off its hinges when your father wouldn't let him see you? He'd be no better off than Mrs. Orange's son if he didn't have his mother propping him up at every step. Buddy needs that man like he needs a hole in his head.

Buddy thinks of Mrs. Orange's son, who works at Mr. Gage's gas station, and stares out from a fixed, masklike face. He knows what he should think, that there is something wrong with his father. But Gramma Liddy's words run through his chest like a cold stream; he can't help but hate her, now, too.

After a moment, his mother says, Jimmy has given me until Christmas to sign the divorce. Then he's going to sue me for desertion, which will throw custody in his favor, or cost me every cent I have to fight him.

Then why don't you sign it?

Because, his mother says, there's no guarantee of custody, or even support. And if I just kick Jimmy out, I'll lose Buddy as surely as I will if they take him. If I can't get his tuition paid, he'll end up at Jackson, and I'm not willing to do that. I'm in no position to bargain, even if I could afford it, because I didn't go with Jimmy to Detroit.

It all comes back to Jimmy, Gramma Liddy says.

It comes back to Jimmy and Buddy, his mother says. He needs Jimmy, he pines for him, in ways you don't even see.

I've never made a secret of what I think of Jimmy, Gramma Liddy says. I just told you, but you won't listen. As far as I can see, he's ruining Buddy; you've let him bring nothing but shame and disgrace onto this family from the very start. It's only your pride that won't let you admit that this was all a mistake.

It wasn't a mistake, his mother says, in a small, quiet voice. It was my life.

Buddy takes his ear from the heater. He doesn't want to listen anymore. He doesn't know what his mother means, when she says it wasn't a mistake, but her life. But he knows, from his father's and Gramma Turner's voices the day before, that what she's said about Christmas is true, and from his mother's and Gramma Liddy's voices now that their world, the world of Sundays, will not survive. Christmas is less than two months away, and he doesn't know what he can do to stop it.

He goes to his mother's old room, past the gilt-edged books that Gramma Liddy won at Port Arthur High. Sometimes she still recited poems — *And I shall have some peace there, for peace comes dropping slow, dropping from the veils of morning where the cricket sings* — and her voice became beautiful with the beautiful words. She had a chance, his mother said, to go to college on scholarship, but her mother, Buddy's great-grandmother, told her that Corrigans didn't accept charity. And then she married Grampa Liddy, his mother said, and that was the end of her poetry, though his mother wouldn't tell him what that meant.

Past the bookcases, in the dim, still room, are matchboxes and miniature cars, chalk lines for seashore and roads, and on the bed, tanks and soldiers standing guard above the miniature city. But the city no longer seems real to him; it is fading, too, into the world of childish, forgotten things.

He has to do something; he doesn't know what he will do. He takes a note pad from a drawer in his mother's old desk. His arms and legs feel cold; his hand trembles, so that his own words look strange to him:

HUGH *(kneeling, praying): Ghost Horse! Ghost Horse! Please help!*

9.

Each day, when his mother drops him off at Gramma Liddy's, he hurries down the street to Alex's house. They've gone back and filled in scenes: The Horse will appear to Hugh and tell him that he'd been his horse when Hugh was a boy. But he got lost in the swamp, where he died, and then was resurrected with mysterious powers. Buddy still hasn't written the scenes, but they are forging ahead with the drawings; they work on the scene of the horse at the window, speaking silently to Hugh, before he flies away. They talk about how they will combine the live action with animation. In *Famous Monsters of Filmland*, at the grocery store, Alex has read about blue screen mattes; they will have to shoot the animation against a blue background, then rewind the film, and shoot the live action over it. When he's with Alex, it seems real. But even then, it is not the same; he can tell that Alex doesn't trust him.

Why should Alex trust him? Each day, at school, he talks to Simon.

A week after he found out about Christmas, he was standing in a shadowy walkway, watching boys in brown uniforms chase a soccer ball, when Gene and Simon appeared. One moment, they weren't there, and the next, they were.

"Tell me about your movie," Simon said.

Simon watched him, calm and patient, but Gene grimaced at him, his eyes, in his skeleton-face, spiteful, hungry-looking. "Tell him," Gene said.

Simon lifted his hand, to silence Gene, then turned to the courtyard. "Curtis," he said, pointing at Curtis Tilden, a pale boy with greasy hair who chased the ball with the others. "His dad divorced his mom. Now Curtis has to live with him. Robby Weeks," he said, pointing at another boy. "His dad makes him live with him, too. Vernon's dad," he said, glancing at Buddy, smiling, "ran off with a gay. Now Vernon has to visit him."

The boys ran across the courtyard, the same, yet different, as if they'd clicked into focus. "I told you something," Simon said. "So you tell me."

Buddy wanted to tell him everything – about his father, and Christmas, and the strange thing the woman had said. But he turned from them, and ran down the hallway, his heart beating breath from his chest.

༂ ᝪ

He's told no one, not even Alex, about his father and the strange thing the woman has said about the test. His father moved stiffly, tethered by strings, eyes hardened, going blind; Buddy knew that he was infected by the woman's venom, that she had put a curse on him. In chapel, while Buddy mouthed the dour hymns, or listened to Reverend Toy's sermons about the invasion of America by illegal aliens, another sign of the End Times, he imagined cutting the brake lines on the woman's car, slitting her throat and watching her bleed to death – he hated her, now; he knew that everything was her fault. But when he faced her, those fantasies dissolved. He hated the flattery that still coursed through him at her touch; he hated his weakness with her.

That Saturday, she reached across the ugly wood-laminate table at her apartment and took his hand. His father had gone out to pick up a pizza. "Your father is very concerned about your grades," she said. "He wants you to grow up to be a nice, healthy boy. That's all anyone wants. But we see how unhappy you are. Wouldn't you like to live somewhere you're happy? Wouldn't you like to do your best?"

She spoke haltingly, as if trying to remember her lines; she was repeating, as she often did, something Gramma Turner said. It was idiotic, her question, like all her questions; yet he couldn't help but feel a desire to please her. "Yes," he said.

"What do you think would help you do your best?"

"I don't know," he said, and then – he despised himself, remembering it, despised his bitter tears – "I'm just stupid, I guess."

"Of course you aren't." Mary – in that moment, she was Mary – squeezed his hand. "That's silly. You just need the right environment to help you do your best. But maybe that's something your mother can't give you right now."

Her face had changed; she watched him, seeking an answer. He took his hand from hers and put it in his lap, covered it with his other hand.

"I don't have anything against your mother," she said. "She's a very nice person. She wants what's best for you. We all just want what's best."

He stared past her at the TV. If he didn't look at her, he could imagine it: the knife, the blood, climbing the fence to escape.

"I know this must be hard for you," she said. "We're only trying to help. I can see how unhappy you are. When you were little, we tested you, and you made a very high score. You were so bright and happy, then, so full of joy."

Her voice stopped. She pressed her lips together, wanting to trap what she said, searching his face to see if he'd heard. A memory crystallized, as strange as the coiled sheets: colored blocks, a white room, her strong, nervous hands.

That evening, they ate with the TV on, as they always did – *The Love Boat*, then *Fantasy Island*. His father glared at him, his arms squared on the table: What was his plan for the week? he said. He needed to have a plan. When was he going to do his homework? He needed to do his homework before he got tired. If he exercised more, he wouldn't get tired, and he might lose some weight. He wasn't trying to make him feel bad, his father said; he was trying to help. Buddy glanced from his father's unwavering gaze to the woman's pious, frightened face to the TV, where Captain Steubing helped a little girl out of some sort of jam, and Mr. Roarke shook his head at his guests' folly. Look at me, his father said. I'm trying to help. Do you want to have to spend all day at my mother's again? His father's eyes were two flat metal discs. Something had shifted, something had changed: his father no longer winked or whistled; there was no tricking of the woman. Buddy knew, from how she looked at him, that what she had said to him would get her in trouble. If he told, everything might change. But he was afraid of what would happen, if it did; and for this, he despised himself, too.

On the freeway, after they left, his father stared ahead, streetlights shuttering across his face. "Your mother's a good person," his father said. "But she can't do a good job raising you right now. Understand?"

He did. The stacks of newspapers and unopened mail in the kitchen had grown, and laundry piled atop the washer; his mother worked later and later at the lab, and fell asleep while she was helping him with his homework.

"It's not her fault," his father said. "Her mother didn't do a good job raising her. Until I met your mother, she lived in kind of a dream world. I can see the same thing happening to you. You may not think it's important, right now, where you live, and how you do in school, but it matters when you grow up, and you don't know how to act with other people. Understand?"

His father's rigid face vanished and reappeared in the passing light. It was true; his mother and Gramma Liddy lived in a dream world. So did Alex. So did he. He didn't want to live in a dream world, if that was what his father hated in him.

"Yes, sir," he said.

"Have you thought anymore about living with Mary and me?"

"No, sir," he lied, pressing his forehead against his window's cool, dark glass.

"You need to think about it. You need to make a decision, okay?"

The car's tires clack-clacked on the freeway. Buddy wanted to tell his father what the woman had said; but he knew, now, that his father wouldn't believe him. He wanted to ask his father what would happen at Christmas, but he was afraid; and he was also afraid of the silence between them, which his lie was supposed to help, but didn't, which expanded – *clack-clack, clack-clack* – like the rushing darkness outside.

"Okay?" his father said.

"Yes, sir," Buddy said. "What if I can't?"

His father was silent for what seemed like a long time. "Then I'm going to have to do some things, Buddy," he said, "that I don't want to do."

∂⊷⊷

After school, Buddy and Simon circle the soccer field, near the high, chain-link fence. A flock of boys wheels across the field, playing Smear the Queer. Gene trails a few yards behind; Buddy feels his eyes on him, narrowed with envy, but he doesn't care. He doesn't care that Sam tells him he'll go to Hell, and spits when he passes him in the hallways. He isn't even thinking about Christmas, or the strange thing the woman said about the test. Simon listens, his head bowed, hands joined behind his back, lips moving silently over Buddy's words – *light meter, jump cut, fade* – as if memorizing them; and Buddy's vision sharpens on the scuffling boys, on the football wobbling through the flat gray sky; he is in a movie, the real movie of his life.

He hasn't told Simon about Alex. He knows what Simon would call him, what any of the boys at St. Edward's would call him.

He hasn't told Simon about the Horse; he's stuck to older stories, like the mad-man dumping his victims in the bayou, or made up new ones: a mystery about a woman axed to death in her apartment, a story of a mother who loses her job and has to live on the streets. Gene says the stories are gay; Simon's told him to keep his yap shut, and made him walk behind them while they talked.

The stories Simon tells are almost the same as the plays: how Mrs. Urquhart and Mr. Poole meet in the parking lot for secret dates; how Mr. McNiece, their math teacher, spends his evenings at the Bunny Club, then comes home to slap around his son, Ben; how Derek Little's sister left school to have a baby. But the stories Simon lingers over the most are of boys whose parents are divorced: Curtis, Robby, Sandy, Vernon; even the tale of Mrs. Gray's grandchildren, who he said were living with their other grandmother; and of course, Sam, who would be sent to another school, if he was lucky, when his mother was taken away. It was easy, Simon said, to find things out: sometimes, people just told him; sometimes, he listened to what teachers or parents said.

Buddy doesn't always believe him, but he knows that Simon is telling the truth, just as he was telling the truth about Sam's mother, even though what he said wasn't really true; and when Simon talks about the other boys, he wonders how Simon knew about Queen of Peace, and what else Simon knows, but doesn't say.

The football wobbles through the flat gray sky. Simon shakes his head. "I wish I could make things up, Turner. But I can't. All I can do is memorize. My dad says I'm going to be a doctor. What does your dad say you'll do?"

What Buddy has told Simon about his father — that he is a doctor, a pathologist who diagnosed cancer — was tinged with wavering candlelight, the tinkle of silver, the tree-shaded streets near Gramma Turner's house. He hasn't told Simon about the house his father has shown him, though it is there, behind everything he says. But now, he is pulled up short by the plainness of Simon's question.

"Nothing," he says.

Simon grins at him, then makes his face blank, as if to take back what he's said; it is something he often does. "When are you going to get your camera?"

Buddy kicks a tuft of grass. He's told Simon that he won't get the camera until his grades improve. He knows he can't let him meet Alex; but he also knows that the camera is why Simon is talking to him. "Christmas," he says. "Maybe."

Simon gazes across the field; he is always careful with his questions. "School's easy, Turner. We'll fix it. You can't be a loser, like Sam." He cuts his eyes at Buddy, making sure he agrees. "I was just thinking, when you get the camera, it would be fun to make movies of real people, like *Candid Camera*."

"Like who?"

"Like Mrs. Urquhart and Mr. Poole. Or Curtis and Sandy. Or Sam's mom. We could spy on them."

Why does the thought make him sick? He knows it is the real movie; but he is glad that he has lied to Simon about the camera.

"I don't know," he says. "Film's expensive."

Simon purses his lips, eying him; and Buddy wonders if Simon can see that he is lying. "You're smart, Turner. We'll figure it out."

Simon checks his watch, a cheap, digital one, Buddy has noticed, then turns, and lifts his hand; Gene shambles to a halt, takes a step forward. Simon gestures again, hitting an invisible wall, and waves goodbye. Gene stares, and then starts across the field, away from them.

Simon heads toward the grove near the soccer field. "Gene's a suck-A," he says. "His dad sends his mom dirty postcards, because he goes away for work. His mom's a big, fat slob who watches him when he takes baths and makes him sleep in her bed. That's why he's a suck-A. Isn't that funny?"

Buddy thinks of Gene, how he laughs in sharp bursts, as if someone were hitting him, how he speaks only to echo what Simon says; he is like a haunted house, Buddy thinks, haunted because it's empty.

As they near the grove, he looks at the furze in the hollow of the base of Simon's skull, wishing he could touch it, remembering Simon stabbing Gene among the shade trees where they now walked, where he has never been before; and the emptiness catches at his stomach, and at the same time fear, so that he can't tell the difference between the two things – the emptiness, and his fear.

"Isn't that funny?" Simon says, glancing back at him.

"Sure," Buddy says.

Simon makes a face, as if he can see what he thinks. "Come on," Simon says. "My mom'll be here soon. She wants to meet you."

Past the fence, across the lawn between the field and the church, the golden car sweeps up to the curb. Buddy slows his step, worried that Mrs. Quine can see inside him, too. Simon reaches the car first, waving him along; Buddy leans down through the opened passenger window, into a smell of milk and fresh paint – a hopeful smell – which he hasn't known, until then, was Simon's.

Mrs. Quine watches him, one arm cocked across the driver's-side door, one hand on the steering wheel. She is even more beautiful than he's imagined – as beautiful as a movie star, as someone on TV. Her long, sad face is tilted, asking a question, sunglasses perched like a barrette atop her blond hair. Beneath her hazel eyes are bruise-colored shadows; but they only make them more lustrous. Sadness weighs the corners of her mouth, but only makes it more full. His gaze drops down – he can't help it – past the collar of her checkered cowboy shirt, to the dark cleft inside, above which dangles a golden cross.

A wet, farting noise sputters against his ear. He jerks back, smacking his head against the doorframe, and sees a flash of white. Simon wrenches open the back door, sprawls across the seat, his fist raised. A pale boy in a white lower-school T-shirt lies in the corner, whimpering, kicking the air to ward him off.

"Boys," Mrs. Quine says, not looking at them.

"But he's embarrassing us," Simon says, in a voice Buddy has never heard before.

"We'll let your father take care of that. Right, Junior?"

Junior lets out a thin whine. Simon seems to deflate, then jabs the boy's thigh. Junior wails. "You're a stink-pot," he cries. "You're a stinky turd."

Simon raises his fist. "Junior," Mrs. Quine says, her tone darkening. "You know what we talked about; you, too, Simon. We don't want to get your father upset." A different kind of hush falls over the car. Simon and his brother look at each other; then Simon retreats. "Sorry," Mrs. Quine says, to Buddy. "You hurt your head?"

"No, ma'am," Buddy says, though his face throbs.

"Simon's told me a lot about you," Mrs. Quine says. "Says you're real smart. Also says you hang out with Sam Fahr."

"Not anymore," Simon says, in a bright, sing-song voice.

"Is that true?" Mrs. Quine says, to Buddy.

"Yes, ma'am."

"I don't mean to be ugly," she says, "but these days, you have to be careful. We're a Christian family, and we can't have any cigarettes or heavy metal or any of that mess."

"Yes, ma'am," he says.

"Simon says you used to go to Queen of Peace."

"Yes, ma'am."

Mrs. Quine looks at him as if she is asking a question; but he doesn't know what it is. "Simon tells me your father's a doctor," she says.

"Yes, ma'am," Buddy says.

Mrs. Quine's expression softens. "Simon says your mother picks you up late. Does she work, too?"

"Yes, ma'am."

"Why's that?" Mrs. Quine says.

Buddy thinks he understands, now, what the question is. "I don't know, ma'am," he says. "I guess she likes it."

Mrs. Quine looks away, seeming to consider. "I don't mean to be nosey. Simon tells me you have to wait out here for your mother, and that's how you got mixed up with that Sam Fahr. We're starting a little ride service. Maybe we can help you out. You think your mother'd be interested?"

Buddy can feel Simon's eyes on him. If they take him to Gramma Liddy's, he doesn't know how he will keep Alex, or the camera, a secret. But he isn't thinking about Alex, right then; he is thinking of the swift, golden car, and the beautiful sadness in Mrs. Quine's eyes. They live near him; it is something Simon's never mentioned. It is almost unimaginable. Looking at Mrs. Quine, he feels a giddy drop, as if he's reached out his foot, and found the next step gone.

"Yes, ma'am," he says.

"Okay," Mrs. Quine says. "Tell your mother to give me a call. We better get going. Mr. Quine likes to have his dinner ready on time."

Simon slips between them, opening the passenger door. "Tell her, " he says.

❧ ❧

He sits, knees drawn up, arms folded across his chest, stomach squeezed between his ribcage and lap, listening to the freeway whisper across the mall. The church's pink brick is clammy against his back. His books and binder lay next to him on the rubbery grass. He's watched the golden car until it shrank to a dot near the freeway. The giddy drop still spins in him; he lets out his breath, a breath he's held all day without knowing it, like he did when he was with his father. *Christmas*, the freeway says; all day, the word has beaten inside him like a pulse. He wants to go to the roof and look out at the city, to look for the horse, to connect the woman's apartment and Gramma Turner's and his mother's houses, and the house that his father will buy, to fit together Sam and Alex and Simon. And then the idea of fitting all the pieces together seems suddenly crazy, slips through his fingers like a fish. He closes his eyes, trying to think of the Quines, to catch their fleeting reflection, a glimmer on dark glass.

The stuttering sound of his mother's car pulls up to the curb. He picks up his books and binder, keeping his eyes closed, and follows the car's sound, bumping into the car, palpitating it until he finds the door handle.

The door squeals when he closes it. The heater blows dusty air in his face.

"What's wrong?" his mother says.

"Nothing," he says.

"Why've you got your eyes closed?"

"I don't know," he says.

"Well, open them. You're giving me the creeps."

He opens his eyes, and trains them on a crack on the bottom of the windshield. Yet he can't help but peek at her, too: at her hammy arm and weathered-looking hand, her chest and stomach bunched up under her white uniform, the deep circles beneath her eyes, her mouth's rigid, fragile line.

"Sorry I'm late, sport," she says.

She is always late. Sister Bertille makes her stay until blood draws are done, then she has to go back to set up evening rounds. Sometimes she takes him to McDonald's for a treat, but mostly, they go straight to Gramma Liddy's, before she returns to the lab.

"It's okay," he says.

The car shudders into motion. "I can't keep leaving you out here," she says. "We've got to do something about a carpool."

"It's fine," he says.

She turns past the mall. "How was your test?"

For a moment, he doesn't know what she means. Then he remembers the test he took that morning on the pacification of the Gauls. When he faced the blank white spaces, all they studied flew away. "It was fine," he says.

She glances at him, sharp-eyed. "You've got to start doing better, honey. We can't give them that ammunition."

That is what she always says, as if they are fighting a battle. They sink back into murky silence that has taken what he studied. It is idiotic, he thinks; it is impossible. Everything gets lost. "I used to be smart," he says.

"You're still smart, honey. You just need to work harder."

Outside, identical houses pass: a cock crows on a mailbox, a black jockey offers a brass ring. He is a prisoner, going to the big house. Until he starts speaking, he doesn't know what he will say. "I took a test one time," he says.

"You've taken lots of tests."

He presses his forehead against the cool glass. An elf waves from a porch; a ceramic frog squats under a birdbath. "It was a long time ago," he says. "It was a test with blocks. I took it at the hospital. I made a high score."

"That's right," his mother says, after a moment. "You took one with that little woman, the children's counselor. What made you remember that?"

Along the bayou, a strip of weathered gray fence hides the houses, but he can see a cream-colored eave, the crown of a mimosa tree, a weather vane shaped like a submarine. "Nothing," he says, frightened, now, of what he is doing.

"That's strange," his mother says. "Do you remember her name?"

"No," he says; he is a prisoner, looking for a house, a particular house, trying to imagine in it Mr. Quine, who likes his dinner ready on time. "No," he says. "I don't."

10.

Through the wall comes Mr. Torres' voice repeating a phrase from a speech, as he often does—*el mejor beneficio para la raza es el mejor beneficio para la ciudad*—mixing with the sound of the rain. Buddy has written the first two scenes and they are filling in theirs. On Alex's desk is a thick pile of paper – storyboards. On each sheet, he prints the dialogue and action below four cells, where Alex has sketched each shot. Each shot, mixing live action and animation, has to be carefully planned, they've agreed, so that it will look real.

Alex heaves himself up off the floor, than stands beside the desk, his white dress shirt untucked, stained orange, a sheaf of paper in his hand.

Mira, he says.

Alex lays the papers on the desk, pressing down on one end of them with his palm. It is the scene he has worked on for weeks, the Horse fading through Hugh's window. Alex has sketched the Horse in white pencil on blue paper, so that when they film the live action over it, the background will be invisible – a blue screen matte.

At first, the Horse is only the barest outline of white marks. Then, the lines coalesce until the Horse is there in every detail – his quicksilver eyes, his folded wings; still ghostly, yet more exact, somehow, because he is a ghost.

"What?" Alex says.

"Nothing," Buddy says, afraid of what will happen next. "It's great."

 ঌ৵ ৵ঌ

Light from the sliding glass doors floods the den, reflecting on pictures of Grampa Turner with famous men; but the end where his grandfather sleeps is as dim as the back of a cave. His grandfather sleeps, as he does more often when Buddy visits, though he always keeps one dark eye opened, so it is impossible to tell if he is really asleep.

On his manila-colored report card is a line of sharp C's, an A in Latin, and in Sacred Studies, a D. Sitting on the edge of his bed at his mother's house, reading his grades in the weak winter light, Buddy has pretended they were someone else's; they got switched, somehow, with Sam's. Then the truth closed over him again, a rolling wave, a giant hand. *How could you do this to us?* his mother told him; then, pressing her fingers against her eyes, she said she was sorry, it was her fault, she needed to help him more. But he knew that what she first said was true.

He's in trouble, his father said. It's not your fault; you've got too much on your hands. But we've got to get this over with. We need to think about him.

I'm thinking about him. If you think I'll sign those papers, you're crazy. Why don't you tell me the truth? What did he mean when he told me about that woman?

I don't want to go to court, Margot.

Don't threaten me. I'll go to court and spend every last cent I have, if that's what it takes to find out who's behind all this.

You made a choice, Margot, but now you can't accept it. Who do you think will look better to a judge, you or me?

After a moment, his mother said, You don't really want him, Jimmy. You wouldn't know what to do with him if you had him.

His father didn't answer her. What his mother said wasn't true, couldn't be true, Buddy thought; hate flashed through him, a thin, bright line.

Now, at Gramma Turner's house, he listens to his father and Gramma Turner in the kitchen, clutching his gym bag on his lap. When his father picked him up at his mother's house, he told Buddy to bring it, though he didn't tell him why.

What did she say? Gramma Turner says.

She said she won't sign it, his father says, until I tell her the truth.

What would she know about the truth? You see what's happened, Jimmy, now that you've dragged him into this. You know what we need to do. I just wish you'd let me do it. Have you told him about his punishment?

No, mamma. Not yet.

Why not? It was good enough for you.

Gramma Turner calls his name. Buddy looks into Grampa Turner's fierce, staring eye. *What do I do?* he says, silently.

Run, Grampa Turner says, silently. *Run away.*

He imagines running to the sliding glass doors in the den, but he can't; he can't let his father think that he has betrayed him.

In the yellow kitchen, at the tiny round breakfast table, Gramma Turner sits, resting her forehead on her fingertips. His father leans against the sink, wearing a white T-shirt and mustard-colored shorts, his arms crossed over his chest.

"I'm so worried, honey," Gramma Turner says, lifting her hand for him to sit in a chair at the table. "I know you're worried, too. You've got too much worry and confusion on your little mind. Am I right?"

"Yes, ma'am," he says.

"That's why you can't study, honey," she says. "Because you're too worried. You've got everything you need right here. But if you don't start using it, you're going to fall farther and farther and farther behind. And then no high school's going to take you, and no college will accept you, and no one will give you a job. And then you'll have fallen lower than the lowest nigger on the streets."

He flinches at the word his mother has told him never to say; Gramma Turner squeezes his hand, to reassure him.

"It's true, honey," she says. "A white man can turn more nigger than a black, if he's wasted what's given to him. I've seen it myself — good boys, from good families, end up out there under the freeway at South Main, begging for liquor money, so beat up and pitiful I can hardly recognize them. Somewhere, they took a wrong turn, and then they just kept falling. And one day, they woke up, and they were lost. One day, they woke up, and they said, 'Help me, Lord! I'm lost, and I'm all alone!' But no one's there to help them, Buddy, not their mommas, not their daddies — no one."

He knows that she is lying; it is all an act, as corny as Vincent Price in a three o'clock movie. But at the same time, he is falling into darkness, the darkness behind the porch screens, in the shotgun shacks. He glances up at his father, but his father looks past him, at something that only he can see.

"It doesn't have to be like that, honey," Gramma Turner says, gripping his hand. "There's still time to make it right. All you have to do is tell Gramma Turner you want to live in a nice, clean, safe place where you don't have to worry, where you can grow up to be the nice, sweet, smart young man we all know you can be." She presses his hand, gives it a little shake. "Just say it, honey. Just say you want to live with me."

He knows that it's fake, but he clings to her hand like a rope.

"Okay, mamma," his father says. "That's enough."

Gramma Turner cuts her eyes at him. "Jimmy," she says. "It's the only way."

"He's my son," his father says.

Gramma Turner lets go of his hand, sucks in a sharp breath. "Change your clothes," she says. "Your daddy's going to take you running."

ᔆ∼ᔆ

He follows his father across Greenbriar, dodging cars that leave wakes of mist. His father glances back, not looking at him, his breath making steam in the air. He wears his white T-shirt, mustard-colored shorts, white sneakers with dark socks. Buddy wears a pair of sour-smelling sweat pants, a thin school jacket, a white St. Edward's T-shirt. Invisible rain needles his face.

His father disappears through a fence. Buddy slips through a gap between gate-posts, following him, the metal pole cold and bitter-smelling on his hand.

His father stands, facing a moss-colored stoop and two sets of double doors. In a concrete rectangle above the doors, embossed letters bleed black: AD 1947. It is the school where his father went, and Gramma Turner taught, and Grampa Turner directed his first high school band; Buddy has never been there before. His father turns, as if a switch inside him has been thrown, and starts toward a corner of the building. At the corner, behind a clump of cypresses, is another stoop, and a single set of doors. Past a chain-link fence, in the gathering dusk, windows glimmer like windows of model railroad houses. Between the fence and the school stretches a vast, empty field.

His father stops near the corner, turned so that Buddy can see only a sliver of his face. His black hair looks slicked down on his head, his white T-shirt stuck to his shoulder blades in flesh-colored patches, already soaked through with rain.

"There's the track," his father says, pointing at the field. "We'll do ten laps. We'll need to stretch out first, so we don't pull our muscles."

His father bends over and touches his toes. Buddy leans down; the backs of his knees stretch tight, his fingertips quiver at mid-calf.

"Is that as far as you can go?" his father says, behind him. "Don't they have P.E. at that fucking school?"

His father presses down on his shoulders. "Don't bend your knees," he says.

Buddy straightens his knees; his sneakers recede. "Okay," his father says. "Now touch your toes." Buddy reaches, quivering, his stomach bunched under his ribcage, afraid that his knees will pop.

"Goddammit," his father says. He locks Buddy's shins with the edge of his sneaker, pushes down on his shoulders. Buddy's fingers hit the grass.

"There," his father says. "You did it."

His father lets go of him. Buddy stands, knowing he's done nothing. His father is already in the field. Buddy walks past him, not looking at him; he thinks that he knows, now, why it is better not to.

"Set the pace," his father says. "Stay in the middle lane."

Buddy sets off down the track. His sneakers squish, his hair is wet, his jacket slick and dark. As he nears the fence at the opposite end of the track, he sees a family in a window of one of the houses — father, mother, two children — gathered in front of a TV; he imagines the warmth of the room, the softness of the couch where they sat. Then the school's long, ugly flank, its rows of dark windows, stretch out, and the vast, empty field, a shadowy smudge of oaks at its end, and his heart clenches and sickens. He closes his eyes. But in the darkness, he hears too clearly the slap of his shoes on the track, his catching breath, his father padding lightly behind him; in the darkness, he hears too clearly someone else beside him, telling him to stop.

He opens his eyes. He is almost at the stoop at the corner. In the gap between the school and the trees, past the fence on Greenbriar, a car like his father's sweeps by, a face in its passenger window, looking out at him.

"You're doing good," his father says. "Nine more."

He runs like this, past the house, and the school, and the oaks, then back toward the house. His father calls out eight more, then seven.

"I can't," he says, as they close on the house again.

"Yes, you can," his father says.

"I can't," he says, hating his own, childish whine, not knowing if it is he or the voice beside him who is speaking.

"Yes, you can," his father says. "Don't think about it. You're doing good."

He tries not to look in the window; but he glimpses the television, the father leaning forward to stroke his child's hair, or pick up his drink. The dark windows on the side of the school stretch out, and the smudge of oaks, its shadows mysterious and deep.

"Please stop," he says.

"If we stop now," his father says, "we'll have to start over next Saturday, and the Saturday after that, until you get it right."

He turns to his father, but sees only a pale, dim shape, charging behind him. "Don't turn around," his father says. "Keep going."

He looks down at the track, so as not to look at his father. The track is made of hard, red stuff painted with white lines. Each granule passes slowly beneath him. He feels as if he'd woken and found himself running, as if he and his father will keep running forever. *Stop*, the voice beside him says. *Give up*. But he can't; he can't let his father think that he's betrayed him.

In the gap between the school and the trees, cars sweep past, their headlights lit. His legs shamble beneath him. "Come on," his father says. "We're almost there."

He shuffles, hating his own weakness, waiting to see what will happen.

"Come on," his father says, shoving him.

Buddy stumbles forward. A bright line of fear opens in his chest. He runs, past the dark oaks, turning the corner toward the house.

"Sorry," his father says.

Buddy doesn't answer him. He is running, now, his jacket hot, its smell sharp.

"I'm sorry," his father says.

He glimpses the flickering television, the dark windows, the field, a sickly feeling spreading through him, a far-away sadness like when he looked out at the city from the roof at the mall. His throat is parched, a rough, strange catch in the cold. He unzips his jacket. Something taps his shoulder – the water bottle.

"Thirsty?" his father says.

Buddy runs ahead. He is almost at the stoop again.

"Five more," his father says. "You're doing good. You need to zip up your jacket, so you don't catch cold."

He passes the shadowy oaks. Rain coats his face, trickles into his ears.

"Buddy?" his father says. "You need to zip up your jacket."

He closes his eyes. The horse will swoop down, bowing his head to let him alight, and they will fly above the city. A stitch cuts into his side, a pain like a knife beneath his ribs. "What's wrong?" his father says.

He opens his mouth, and found he can not talk.

"What's wrong?" his father says.

Buddy turns.

"Don't turn around," his father says. "What's wrong?"

"It hurts," Buddy says.

"Don't think about it. Talk to me. Tell me what you're thinking."

"I hate you," Buddy says; but it isn't what he's meant to say. What he meant to say has gotten lost; everything got lost.

"Okay," his father says, calmly. "Four more. Why do you hate me?"

He shambles past the smudge of oaks, holding his side. His legs feel as if they might snap. "You're a robot," he says, not knowing if it is him, or the voice beside him who is speaking. "You're trying to kill me."

"I'm not trying to kill you, Buddy. I'm trying to help you. Is that what your mother says, that I'm trying to hurt you?"

His T-shirt is cold on his chest. Ahead, in the house, are the Quines.

"What about Christmas?" he says.

"Did your mother tell you about that?" his father says, his voice changed.

"No, sir," he says. "I heard her."

The Quines are in the house, but he can't see them. Then the dark field spreads out before him, the shadowy oaks, the cars almost invisible except for the streaks of their headlights. "Three more," his father says. "What do you want to do, Buddy?"

The pain splits his side. But it is better, now, than stopping.

"What do you want to do?" his father says.

The Quines aren't home; it is his mother's house; it is the house where he will live with the woman and his father.

"You're not my father," the voice beside him says. "You killed him."

His father shoves him again, harder, this time. "Shut up," he says. "I'm your father, and I love you. That's why I came back."

He sprawls ahead, cartwheeling his arms to keep his balance. He runs, holding his side, past the school's dark windows. "Two more," his father says. "What do you want, Buddy? Do you want me to leave?"

He runs, following the white lines that shine in the dark, a phantom, a ragged ghost. The family in the house are ghosts, and in the school building, ghosts of children press their faces against the dark panes of glass. His father calls out the last lap. "What do you want, Buddy?" he says. "Do you want me to go away?"

His legs shamble beneath him; he is a robot, fitted together from spare parts. He shuffles off the track, and falls to his knees, trying to soothe the pain that splits his side. The cold ground sends a shock into his chest. He grips the wet grass, trying to be still, to make it stop. "Get up," his father says, behind him.

He keeps his face turned from his father, listening to the rain whisper on the track. "Get up," his father says, nudging him with his shoe. "We'll have to do it again."

He kneels on the ground, squeezing his eyes shut.

"Is this what you want?" his father says. "To lay out here in the dirt?"

He keeps still, not daring to turn, to look at his father.

"You know what's going to happen, if you don't learn to finish what you start? You're going to get your ass kicked the rest of your life."

"I don't care," he says.

"You don't care about getting your ass kicked? You want to live out there with your mother and get your ass kicked, or do you want to live here, with Mary and me?"

"I don't care," he says. "I don't want your shitty houses."

"Fine," his father says, his voice changed. "That's just fine. I'm going back to my mother's. I'll see you later. Have a nice life."

He listens to his father's footsteps recede across the track, willing himself not to move. All of it is a lie, all of it is a joke, and he's believed it; but he won't believe it anymore. He rises, trying to zip his jacket, pulling it closed with trembling hands, then turns to the oaks, and starts toward Greenbriar, toward the passing cars. His sweat pants slap his legs; his toes ache with cold. He is lost, he is a nigger, he is alone; but he will not go back, he will never go back, to Gramma Turner's.

As he passes the shadowy oaks, spirits of the boys buried in the fields, and the raggedy men on South Main, flit, beckoning him. He keeps his eyes on the fence. And then, past the cypresses, another ghost appears. He will not go back, he will never go back. Then he is running, as if not he but another boy was running, and in the darkness, he sees his father, his face convulsed, transformed by grief.

11.

That Monday, his mother drives past Queen of Peace and the Heinke's where Mr. Torres used to work, where spray-painted plywood covers the windows and weeds sprout in the parking lot. They pass the crumbling Paradise Hotel, and next to it, the Tiki Lounge, whose dark doorway is already opened to the gray morning air.

Gramma Turner has said she would pay more than thirty dollars a month for Buddy to ride with Simon. Mrs. Gray has told her all about the Quines. Mrs. Quine doesn't have to work, and Mr. Quine is an up-and-coming businessman. Simon, she says, is exactly the kind of boy Buddy needs to know.

They cross the bayou, into a neighborhood he's never seen before, where trailer homes hide on gypsum lots and stores sell vacuum cleaners and dishwashers and keys, their windows yellow with dust, nestled between buildings with ill-painted names: The Oriental Club, The Other Club, The Business Man's Lounge. In oyster-shell lots, behind hulking, battered cars, are portable signs: Veterans Here and We Won and Fight For Freedom and Unwelcome Imigrant Go Home. None of them are in Spanish. He's imagined the Quines live in an enclave of graceful brick homes near the bayou; he keeps waiting for another, hidden neighborhood to appear.

"What are you going to tell them if they ask about daddy?" he says.

His mother creeps along, craning over the steering wheel to read street signs. "I'll tell them the truth," she says.

"You can't," he says, gripping his binder. "You promised."

"I promised I'd think about it. You shouldn't have friends you have to lie to."

"He's not my friend."

"Then why are you so crazy to ride with him?" She nods at the portable signs. "I hope Mr. Torres doesn't have to see all this."

"Who cares about Mr. Torres?" he says. "You promised."

She shakes her head, not looking at him. "I promised I'd think about it."

❧❧

The day before, on Sunday, his mother and he went to the lab. She said she just needed to catch up on a few things, so she could get a jump on the week. Sister Bertille was still on her about her hours. It wasn't the afternoons, now, but the mornings; someone needed to be there to help with first blood rounds. If she had to go to part-time, he'd heard her tell Gramma Liddy, she didn't know how they would make it.

Glass doors hissed open on the hospital's rear entrance. Up a flight of stairs, and he could taste the chemical smell. All of it was there: boxes of reagents, green trays holding vials of dark blood, the gurgling, clicking hum of cryostats and autoclaves. Here, in the time before he was born, his father slept on a cot, tending the delicate machines.

At the work benches, the techs—Barbara and Yolanda and Yun-sen—faces from parties his mother threw when they graduated from the courses she taught — peeked over their microscopes. His mother asked if her students' tests were in her office. Yolanda, who'd been there the longest, who wore her hair in an amazing confection, winked at him, and said they were.

Behind them, in the hallway, a voice called his mother's name. She turned, wearing a trapped grimace. Carol, the weekend supervisor, who looked a little like Jackie Kennedy, rushed toward them, explaining that one of the night techs had to go home because her baby was vomiting, and she couldn't find anybody to fill in. His mother groaned, then answered in the commanding voice she used only at the hospital. You need to keep someone on call, she said. Someone who wants the overtime.

They turned down another hallway, past framed illustrations of men in togas and ruffled collars dissecting corpses throughout the ages, which Sister Bertille had nailed into the ceramic brick walls. Sister Bertille herself emerged around a corner, her long, pale face framed in a black wimple. His mother stiffened. Without glancing at him, without greeting, Sister Bertille began to ask if his mother had had time to review the time card reports. *Soon, sister,* his mother said. *If you can only work part-time, Margot,* Sister Bertille said, *we can only pay part-time. Please, sister,* his mother said. *Can we talk about this later?* Sister Bertille peered down at him, and her expression shifted. She gripped his arm, the cold smell of the convent breathing from the folds of her habit.

"I didn't even see you," she said. "How is your school? How is your father? Are you glad to have him back home?"

His mother's eyes were flat, entirely blind. "Yes, sister," he said.

"Tell him to come visit us," Sister Bertille said, releasing him; then, to his mother, "We'll talk about the other matter later."

All the way home, he pleaded, wheedled, threatened, begged. In the kitchen, he unearthed the school directory from the stacks of bills, opened it to the Quines' listing, put it in front of his mother on the lab table. He prodded, harangued, insinuated, cajoled: Wouldn't it be better, he said, if she didn't have to take him back and forth every day? Wouldn't they save on gas money? What would happen if she lost her job? They could end up starving on the streets.

"All right," she said. "I'll call her. Leave me alone."

He took the phone from her desk and put it on the table, then retreated, closing the kitchen door, and stood outside, listening. There was one more thing he hadn't asked; he hoped he hadn't made another mistake.

At first, his mother's voice was light and brittle, as it always was when she talked to strangers; she agreed with Mrs. Quine that they were very lucky to live so close; a ride would be a great help. Yes, she said, her voice narrowing, she had to work. No, she said, her husband couldn't help with rides. Of course, she said, her voice sharpening to a point. I understand you have to charge. I'll have to think it over.

He opened the door. She sat, facing the TV, touching her fingertips to her mouth. "I thought you were doing your homework," she said.

"What did she say?"

"What kind of people are the Quines?"

"They're nice. Did she say anything about daddy?"

"No," his mother said, watching him closely. "The nice Mrs. Quine wants thirty dollars a month to give you a ride. I don't like the sound of her."

"They're normal," he said. "Simon's at the head of the class."

"Why do you care so much what they know about daddy?"

He stalked toward her around the table, the muscles in his neck like cords. "Why do you care what Sister Bertille thinks? Why do you care what Manil thinks?"

She squinted at him, trying to bring him into focus. "What is going on, Buddy? Where did daddy take you yesterday?"

"Nowhere," he said. "Are you going to let me ride with them?"

"I've got to think about it," she said. "It's expensive."

"Gramma Turner'll pay."

"I don't want her to pay. That's not the point. The point is I've already let things go too far. I don't want you mixed up with the wrong people."

He took the phone and pulled it as far from her as the cord would reach.

"Who are you calling?" she said.

"Gramma Turner," he said. "I'm gonna call Gramma Turner."

∂∘⌐

They turn at the Hellfire Club, a blood-red shack whose edges are painted with licking orange flames. Across the street, a white wooden church spire pokes into the sky. They turn again, onto a street of low brick houses that seem to sink into spongy lawns, to a two-story, gray-stone house whose sharply-peaked roof looks slightly crooked, like a house in a fairy tale. His mother pulls into its driveway, stopping halfway up. Outside, a lawnmower drones. Buddy looks at his mother, at her hammy arms and graying hair and white uniform. "I'll just go," he says.

"Not so fast, sport," she says. "You're not getting rid of me that easily."

A tall, barrel-chested man in dark slacks and a light dress shirt strides toward them, slapping a newspaper against his thigh. Behind him, a dark shape slips out from the garage, then ducks its head and disappears.

"Leave your books," his mother says.

Buddy leaves his books and binder in the car, hoping they've made a mistake.

"Dan Quine," the man says, offering his mother his hand. "Sorry about the dog." His black eyes pass over Buddy like a searchlight, his head thrown back, as if from a great distance. Then he turns, nervously, abruptly, and starts toward the house. "I expect you want to talk to Lorraine," he says. "This'll help her on gas money, save you some driving. Hard times for everybody, now."

"I'm so glad we can help," his mother says; then, "You have a beautiful house."

Mr. Quine glances over his shoulder, lips pursed, pleased.

"It's a fixer-upper, an investment. We're planning to move, soon; move up. I hear you're over by Hughes Tool. Nice houses there, if you can get the Mexicans out."

Mr. Quine smiles, testing his mother, offering her a secret sign, as Simon did the day he spoke to him in Latin. His mother lowers her eyes; Mr. Quine slaps the newspaper on his leg. Buddy wants to shake her.

As they approach the rear of the house, the sound of the lawnmower grows louder. Mr. Quine halts, one foot on the porch's cement steps. Past the porch, on the other side of the house, is a vacant lot. In it, a blond-haired boy in blue jeans and a white St. Edward's T-shirt pushes a lawnmower across a vast, weed-grown field.

"Get those ditches cleared?" Mr. Quine says.

The boy looks up; and at first, Buddy doesn't recognize him as Simon.

"Yes, sir!" Simon says.

"Good boy," says Mr. Quine. "Time to wash up." Then, to his mother, "He's a good boy. Just a little soft."

His mother looks at Buddy, a look he cannot name; it is the same way she looks at him when he goes with his father on Saturdays.

Mr. Quine holds open the door. *Keep your mouth shut*, Buddy says to her, silently, as she disappears inside.

The sound of the lawnmower stops. Simon pushes it toward the garage, glaring at Buddy, warning him not to approach. But when he comes out again, he still seems smaller, somehow, than he does at school.

"Chores," he says. "What a pain. Does your dad make you do them?"

"Sure," Buddy says.

Simon looks down at his hands. He shakes his head, and Buddy sees that he is embarrassed. Then Simon glances up at him, his eyes sharp.

"Did you meet Toby?" he says.

"No," Buddy says.

"What's a-matter? Don't you like him?"

"I don't know," Buddy says.

"I bet you hurt his feelings. He'll like you if you let him."

Before Buddy can answer — he isn't sure what he will say, but he is sure he doesn't want to meet the dark shape that slipped behind Mr. Quine — Simon whistles. Toby runs out from behind the garage and stops, braced on his hind legs, snapping his teeth. Simon orders the dog to sit, then kneels beside him, rubbing his flank, nuzzling his neck against his face. In a childish, sing-song voice, he tells Toby what a good dog he is; and something reaches inside Buddy, something like sadness, but sharper, as if he watches Simon behind the sheet of glass.

"Come on," Simon says. "Let him smell you, so he'll know who you are."

Buddy hesitates. "Come on," Simon says. "Don't be scared."

Buddy closes his eyes, holds out his hand, steeling himself to feel the dog's teeth sink into his skin. A wet muzzle brushes his fingers, sniffing, then a silken-furred skull butts his palm. Toby peers up at him, his brow knit, whimpering.

"See?" Simon pets the dog's neck. "There's nothing to be scared of. He likes you, now that he knows you're a friend."

The back door opens. Mr. Quine stands on the porch. Toby ducks out from under Simon's arm. Simon still kneels, staring down at his hands.

"Did I tell you to play with Toby?" Mr. Quine says.

"No, sir."

"What did I say?"

"I was letting Toby smell him, sir."

Mr. Quine's gaze swivels from Simon to Buddy and back again. "That's not what I told you to do, is it?"

"No, sir," Simon says.

"Then get in here. Your mother's already late."

Simon rises, blushing from the tips of his ears. Mr. Quine's dark eyes shift to Buddy. "Sorry," he says. "But we've got rules around here. If you're going to ride with us, you'll have to learn how to follow them."

"Yes, sir," Buddy says.

"But he wasn't doing anything, sir," says Simon.

Mr. Quine looks at Simon, and Buddy remembers Simon hitting Sam, his hand so swift he wasn't sure he saw it; and he feels himself move toward Simon, to take his place.

The back door swings open. Buddy's mother appears, wearing a brittle smile, and behind her, Mrs. Quine. Next to Mrs. Quine's, his mother's face is rigid, ugly-looking. Buddy wonders what she's said.

Simon holds out his hand. "Thank you for letting Buddy ride with us, ma'am. He's one of my best friends. We promise we'll take good care of him."

Buddy wonders if it is true, what Simon says, that he is one of his best friends; he wonders what Simon sees, when he sees his mother. "Thank you, Simon," his mother says, shaking his hand. "It's nice to meet you. But I have to go."

"Go where, ma'am?"

"Simon," says Mrs. Quine.

"I have to go to work, Simon. I work at a laboratory."

Simon smiles at her, a smile for adults; but his gaze is level and curious. "I'm going to be a doctor, ma'am. Maybe you could tell me about the lab sometime."

"Simon," Mr. Quine says. "Don't get smart."

"Sorry," Mrs. Quine says, to Buddy's mother, ruffling Simon's hair. "Simon's just like that. Always into everything."

"Maybe we'll talk about it later, Simon," His mother says; then, to Mrs. Quine, "Thank you for your time. I think I need to talk to Buddy a minute."

His mother takes his arm, sweeping him with her along the driveway. The Quines stand on the porch, watching them, sealed in the same, unspoken thought: that he is a mamma's boy, and his mother is a weirdo. After his mother and he pass the corner of the house, Buddy wrenches his arm from her grip.

She grasps his arm again, brings her face close to his. "I don't like this, honey. I don't like this one bit. We can get in the car and I can take you to school and you can tell Simon that your mother made a mistake."

"Did you tell her about daddy?"

"No, Buddy. That's not the point."

"Give me the keys," he says.

"Listen to me, Buddy. I know these kind of people. I grew up around them."

"Give me the keys," he says, tugging away from her.

"They're not like us, honey."

"Give me the keys," he says, afraid that the Quines will see them.

She shakes him. "Listen to me. You're not helping anything, doing this."

He twists away from her, his throat tight and aching. "They're normal," he says. "If you don't let me go, I'll tell Gramma Turner you won't let me ride with them."

"Go ahead," she says, her voice rough and strange. "Go ahead. Do your worst."

"I'll tell her," he says. "I'll tell her I want to live with her."

His mother looks at him, an adult look of distaste. She drops his arm, digs in her pocket, throws the keys on the driveway. He picks them up, opens his door, his hands trembling, gathering his books and binder under his arm.

"Please, honey," she says. "Don't do this."

He keeps going. The porch is empty; the wet morning air smells of freshly-cut grass. Behind him, her car door clunks shut. A string stretches tight in his chest, pulling him back to her; but he keeps going until it snaps.

12.

Mornings in the golden car, a holiday spirit reigns. Mrs. Quine plays the country music station, nodding her head, sometimes singing along. She takes a different route to the school than his mother does. On the freeway, they pass a sea of clapboard houses, where Buddy imagines madmen lurking in the huge cars with tinted windows that ply the streets like sharks, searching for boys to drug and bury. They pass heaps of scrap metal and a drive-in theater overgrown with weeds and a sickly-looking building that one week is a Giant Furniture Warehouse 50% Off Everything Must Go and the next is a gun store. They pass the Astrodome and Astroworld, and in the distance, the skyscrapers downtown, all of it covered in a thin, gray mist of decay; but the world outside the car doesn't matter as much as the one inside. Each morning, in the back seat, Simon quizzes him on his homework; Mrs. Quine chimes in, telling him how smart he is when he gets the answers right, tutting when he's wrong.

Simon, she says, is a modern miracle; he only has to read something once, and he memorizes it. It's all because of her, Simon says, wrapping his arms around the seat to hug her, so that the car swerves, and she yells at him, laughing, and almost crying, too. It's all because of you, Simon says, in his sing-song voice. When I'm a doctor, I'll buy you a house. That's sweet, Simon, Mrs. Quine says. What'll we do with your father? I don't know, Simon says. I'll buy him one, too.

Some mornings, they tell jokes. At first, Buddy keeps quiet when they tell them; then Mrs. Quine asks what's wrong. My mother, he says, knowing it will get his mother in trouble. She doesn't like those kind of jokes, ma'am. After a moment, Mrs. Quine says, I don't mean to be ugly, Buddy, but your mother's wound a little tight. She ought to loosen up a little bit. A joke's a joke. Know what I mean?

Yes, ma'am, he says; he does, and the next time, he laughs along: What did the black man say, running to catch the elevator? *Hodedo, hodedo, hodedo!* Why did the black man keep getting in fights with the Mexican? *That's nat'cho cheese,* he said, *that's nat'cho cheese!* Even Junior grins, eyeing them warily. Sometimes, they sing:

High hopes! He's got hi-i-igh hopes! And Buddy can't believe his luck, that he is with them, now, in the swift, golden car.

෯෨෮

Each morning, after his mother drops him off, stiff and offended, he goes to the Quines' back door, having learned to quiet Toby, and peeks through the window in the kitchen door. The panes of glass are covered with paper. But in one corner, the paper is pulled up, just a sliver, and through it, he watches Mr. Quine read his newspaper. There are two kind of people in Houston, his mother says: those who read the *Post* and those who read the *Chronicle*. Each morning, Mr. Quine sits at the breakfast table, holding a *Chronicle* in front of himself like a screen; Buddy fills in the details of the kitchen from memory: the floors covered with newspaper; the cans of paint along the baseboards; the doorless cabinets, their cups and plates and bowls exposed; the hopeful scent of milk and paint, which he believes he can smell through the glass. Sometimes, Mr. Quine snorts, shakes his head in mock disgust, then turns the page with a smart crackle. He is always there, the same, wearing his light dress shirt and dark slacks. When Buddy knocks, and Mr. Quine tells him to come in, Buddy suspects that Mr. Quine knows he's been watching him. Then Mr. Quine rustles the paper, and turns to that day's item.

"It says here," Mr. Quine says, "that the government is giving thirty thousand dollars apiece to Vietnamese fishermen in Kemah. Thirty thousand dollars. How do you think white fishermen can compete?"

"I don't know, sir," Buddy says.

"They can't," says Mr. Quine. "The Vietnamese work like bastards and save every cent. So what do you think is going to happen?"

"I don't know, sir."

"What's going to happen is the Vietnamese are going to take over Kemah, then they and the Mexicans are going to take over Houston, and pretty soon, you won't know who you are. That's what'll happen. Your tax dollars at work."

Buddy imagines the Huns sweeping into Rome. He thinks of Alex and Mr. Torres. But he can't think of them, here.

"Yes, sir," he says.

"All right." Mr. Quine snaps the paper to the next page, his black eyes flashing out at him, suspicious. "There's your lesson for the day. Simon's upstairs."

Through the den, past baskets of laundry on the couch, down the hallway where one wall is painted dark blue, the other white, he can breathe now that he's away from Mr. Quine; but at the same time, he wishes he said something to show he agrees. His mother's answers to Mr. Quine's questions are vague and weak. The government owes the Vietnamese every cent it gave them, she says. The policemen who drowned the Mexican man should go to jail; the idea of the Ku Klux Klan patrolling the border was absurd. Not that he's told her what Mr. Quine says; he never tells her anything the Quines say, but he listens to her talk to Gramma Liddy. What she says doesn't matter at the Quines'. There is nothing she can say; his grades are up, Gramma Turner is pleased. Somehow it all rings together in a single chord: the Quines' daily bustle; Mr. Quine's questions, which paint a world, like Bible stories, of shining and embattled certainty.

Up the scuffed stairwell from the front hallway, each morning, Simon sits at his desk, a book open before him, lips moving silently, as if in prayer. Behind him is a metal bookcase, and the room's low, slanted ceiling, its single window, where a tree branch waves like a skeleton's hand. There are no pictures or posters on his walls; Mr. Quine says marks will lower the house's resale value. In the bunk bed Junior sometimes hides, already dressed, pretending to sleep.

Simon raises his hand, palm out, in their secret Latin greeting: "*Salve*."

"*Salve*," Buddy says, matching his signal.

"Did you study the Verse?"

That day, the Memory Verse is an arduous passage from *The Pilgrim's Progress*. Though Buddy has studied it with his mother the night before, he can't remember it. He shrugs, slouches, makes his voice rough and world-weary, like he always does with Simon: "I don't care," he says. "Mrs. Gray can go to Hell."

Simon laughs silently, silently clapping his hands. Buddy looks at the bed, to make sure Junior isn't there, then takes another step into the room.

"You're not gonna be anything," he says, jabbing his finger at Simon. "You're gonna live under the freeway with the bums."

Simon grins, wavering; both of them know they can't play like they will that afternoon at Gramma Liddy's — not in the silent house with Mr. Quine. All Buddy wants is a little taste; he wants to make sure it will really happen.

Simon shrinks from him, raises clasped hands. "Please, mamma," he says. "Please! Don't hurt me!"

"I'll give you what for," Buddy growls. "I'll tear your ass apart."

"Boys!" Mrs. Quine calls, downstairs.

Simon gathers his books, his face already becoming the one he wears to school. As quickly as it appears, it vanishes — the moment that tells Buddy his secrets are safe, that he and Simon will share, that afternoon, a secret deeper than any Buddy has told him. A hollow ache settles in his stomach, sharper for having been fed.

But the day, the hours between then and the afternoon, is already starting. Junior slips out from under the covers, calling them faggots; Simon lands a slap upside his head that sends him howling down the stairs.

Simon tucks in his shirt, his mouth grim. "Come on, Tuber," he says.

In the kitchen, Junior presses himself against Mrs. Quine's slim flank, glaring at Simon, his snuffling face so pale Buddy can see blue veins at his temples, squinty eyes and small teeth and bright red lips like a rat's. The shadows beneath Mrs. Quine's eyes are darker; sadness weights her face like a mask.

Mr. Quine sits at the breakfast table, his hand curled into a fist. "I can't live like this, Lorraine. You've got to get these kids under control."

"It's not her fault, sir," Simon says.

Mr. Quine looks up at him. "Whose fault is it?"

Simon shrugs, the tips of his ears red. "I don't know, sir."

"He hit me!" Junior whines. "He's a liar!"

"Junior," says Mrs. Quine, in her warning voice.

"Is that true?" Mr. Quine says, to Simon.

"Yes, sir," Simon says, lowering his eyes. "But he called us a dirty name."

Mr. Quine's gaze shifts from Simon to Buddy and back again. "Get out of here," he says, "before I tan all your hides. I'll deal with you later, Simon."

"Sorry, Buddy," Mrs. Quine says, as she hustles them out the door, in a voice that isn't really sorry, that blames him. "I'm sorry you had to hear that."

Outside, Toby trots next to Simon, leaping up to nuzzle his face. Junior already stands at the side door of the garage, leering back at Simon. Junior's taunts don't reach him; Buddy knows Simon could catch him, if he wanted. He knows what Mr. Quine means, when he says he will deal with Simon later. Some mornings, when they play too loudly, or Junior runs crying down the stairs, Simon is called to the kitchen alone, and Buddy listens to the pop of Mr. Quine's belt. His own hunger seems petty, then; he wants to tell Simon that he understands. But when he catches up with him, Simon stares ahead, his face like a statue, as if he doesn't know who he is.

෫ඁ෴

Mondays, when Simon finishes quizzing him, Mrs. Quine turns down the radio. "So, Buddy," she says. "How was your weekend?"

"Fine, ma'am," he says.

"How's that Other Grandmother of yours?" she says, using their code for Gramma Turner: Other Grandmother: O.G.

"She's fine, too, ma'am. She made me do all my homework over again, then she made me correct all my tests. Then she yelled at my dad."

Mrs. Quine tuts, pauses, about to ask the question she always asks. "It's funny your mother makes you go over there every weekend, Buddy. Why is that?"

Junior watches him, his head resting on top of the front seat like a head on a platter. Simon watches him, too, his face somewhere between the one he wears at home and the one at school. One day – Buddy can't remember when, or why he took the step that is still more like flying than falling – he started telling them about Gramma Turner.

"I don't know, ma'am," he says.

"Well," says Mrs. Quine. "I don't understand how you can have one grandmother who's so nice, and another one who acts like that. It just goes to show, you can have all the money in the world, and still not be happy."

"Poor Tuber!" Simon says. "We should kill her, so he can live with us."

"Simon," says Mrs. Quine. "That's not nice. I'm sure Buddy's fine, living where he is. You just remember, next time you get mad at your daddy, that you could have a grandmother like that. No offense, Buddy."

He feels only a little – a pinprick. It's worth it; pity courses through him, a sweetness he can almost taste. He turns to his reflection in the window, wondering what it would be like to live with the Quines. When he tells them about Gramma Turner and his father, he is different, as if he can see them clearly, in the real movie of his life.

෫ඁ෴

At school, he marches with Simon through the swarm of girls in blue smocks and boys in brown uniforms, the upper-school girls in tartan skirts and boys in white shirts and gray pants, through the pink brick buildings' cement hallways, the stink of bathrooms and echo of voices and glimpses of half-familiar faces. Looking out from the Quines' world, all of it seems like a crazy cartoon.

Simon's face has changed, as it always does at school: he stares straight ahead, searching out an enemy. Then he purses his lips, makes his voice a fruity warble, doing Mrs. Gray: "Let us now recite the Memory Verse."

"Let the Kingdom be always before you," Buddy says.

"And believe."

"And believe steadfastly concerning things that are invisible."

"Let nothing."

"Let nothing. I don't know. I can't."

Simon cuts his eyes at him, critical, disappointed. "If you don't get your grades up, Tuber, you won't get that camera. Right?"

This is the story he's told Simon; he doesn't know how he will get the camera from Alex. Buddy looks away from him. "Don't be a loser," Simon says.

While Simon stands next to him in chapel, pretending to sing the hymns, silently mouthing their words — *there is a green hill far away, without a city wall* — and while Reverend Toy preaches about the feminists and communists and homosexuals who are beating down the doors of America, he says, like barbarians at the gate, and while the usual parade of teachers — Mr. McNiece, Mrs. Urquhart, Mrs. Poole — appear in the classroom, their faces sour with suspicion, or wiped clean by a kind of fanatical rage, demanding the boys' attention, always with the paddle a hinted threat, and while Sam Fahr hovers, as he always does, at the corner of his sight and thoughts, Buddy recites the Verse silently, stopping, circling back, checking the sheet of notebook paper he's copied it on; and as the words coalesce in their proper order, he takes comfort in them, as he did in Gramma Turner's voice when his father banged and clattered in the garage, as he used to when he thought about the horse. This is the real secret that Simon has taught him: that school is real, and a joke; that only losers don't follow rules, and only losers believe in them. In the evenings, as he slogs through the Peloponnesian Wars, and Pilgrim's captivity with the Giant Despair, and his Latin translations, whose conjugations and declensions are like a secret code, he feels Simon next to him, and knows he can do for him what he can for no one else. And if his grades could stem the tide of Christmas — that is his hope, his real hope, which he tries to keep hidden, even from himself.

⧼⧽

By Sacred Studies, the last period of the day, he is ready. He stands at the front of the classroom, in its stuffy heat and smell of sweat and pencil lead. On the bulletin board are pictures of the Star of Bethlehem, the Three Wise Men, the Baby Jesus, but none of Santa Claus, the reindeer, a tree; Mrs. Gray claims that they are pagan. She looks out at the boys above her half-glasses, her thick hands folded on her desk.

"Let the Kingdom be always before you," he says, and stops, his mind not blank, but swarming; he looks at Sam, who slouches at his desk, afraid another voice will say everything about Christmas, and the woman, and how his father had changed.

"Let the Kingdom be always before you," he says, closing his eyes. "And believe steadfastly concerning things that are invisible. Let nothing that is this side the other world get within you; and above all, look well into your own hearts, and to the lusts thereof; for they are deceitful above all things, and desperately wicked; set your faces like flint, you have all power in heaven and earth on your side."

He opens his eyes. The stuffy classroom and buzzing fluorescent lights are still the same. Simon smiles his approval; with his middle finger, Sam scratches his nose. "Excellent, Mr. Turner," says Mrs. Gray. "You may be seated."

⧼⧽

They stand in the cold back room at Gramma Liddy's, hands stuffed in their thin school jackets. From outside the closed door comes the babble of cartoons that Junior watches in the living room, snatches of Mrs. Quine and Gramma Liddy's conversation at the dining room table. Through the slatted blinds, weak winter light casts streaks on the yellowed walls. A high, soft bed juts out from one corner; around it crowds a hope chest, an armoire, a heavy desk, a wooden chair.

On the way home from school, they have done the familiar routines: Mrs. Gray, arriving at Sandy's mother's house, kills Sandy with a shotgun, and in turn, is killed by Sandy's mother; Reverend Toy, discovering Mr. McNiece beating his son, Ben, kills him, and is slaughtered by Ben. As Junior looks on, they play almost silently, using code words and secret signs. Mrs. Quine asks about their days, and receives the standard replies. Sometimes, she and Simon trade gossip about teachers and other boys' families, though none of it as dirty as what Simon has told him; and Buddy presses himself into a corner in the back seat, waiting.

"O.G.?" he says, in the room.

Simon glances at him, sly, wavering, his cheeks splotched pink.

"O.G.," he says.

Buddy sits in the chair. Simon backs away from him, screwing up his face. Then Simon charges, waggling his finger.

"You're never gonna be nothin'," he says. "You're just a nigger, you hear?"

"I don't care," Buddy says.

"Are you sassin' me, boy? I'll tan your hide."

"I don't care. You can go to Hell. You can eat shit and die."

Simon laughs, hiding his mouth with his hand, then makes his face blank. "That's it," he says. "I've had enough of your lip! Jimmy! Get in here!"

Buddy springs up, slumps his shoulders, makes his face an idiot's mask. "Goddammit, mamma! I'm tryin' t' clean th' garage!"

"Forget the garage!" Simon shouts. "Your son's goin' to Hell!"

"O-kay." Buddy climbs the porch steps, head bowed. "There he is, mamma." He points at the chair. "Whuddaya want me to do?"

They look at the empty chair.

"Do?" Simon says, glancing at him.

"Do?!" Buddy says, Gramma Turner, now. "I'm tired of doin' what you want! We've done enough of what you want!"

Simon raises clasped hands. "Please, mamma! Please don't hurt me!"

"I'll do what I want!" Buddy says, jabbing his finger at Simon. "I'll make your daddy take you runnin'! I'll send you up to your room! You're never gonna be nothin' unless you do what I say!"

"I'll do it, mamma!" Simon says, laughing, afraid. "I'll do anything!"

"Damn right you will! I'm sick and tired of having to do everything myself! I'm sick and tired of cleaning up this mess!"

"Oh, please, mamma!" Simon says, wringing his hands. "Please, mamma! I'm sorry I made a mess!"

Buddy claps his hands in front of Simon's face, stage-slapping him. Simon sprawls across the bed, then rises, whimpering, giggling. Buddy slaps him – again, again. He hates him – hates his bright blue eyes, his blond hair; he hates him because Simon doesn't really know what he means.

"What'd you think, Jimmy?" he says. "You think this is just a joke?"

"No, mamma, please, mamma."

"You think you can do what you want? You think everything's for you?"

"No, mamma," Simon says, laughing, crying – Buddy can't tell. "No, mamma, please, mamma; I won't do it again."

Simon sways, fluttering his eyes. Buddy grabs his collar, touching his damp skin, drawing an imaginary pistol, pressing it against Simon's head.

"Please, mamma, please, mamma," Simon says.

It's too late. Buddy pulls the trigger. Simon's head wrenches, twisting sideways; brains spatter the wall. He shudders, making the death-croak. Buddy lets him drop, and sits in the chair, trembling, now, with emptiness and fear and expectation of what will happen next.

Simon stands over the chair, gazing down at him, his head thrown back, eyes glassy, unseeing; he sways from side to side, flexing his hands into fists.

"What'd you think? Think you'd get away?"

Buddy shrinks into the chair. "No, sir."

"Think you can outsmart me? Think you're smarter than that dog?"

"No, sir," Buddy says.

Simon snatches at him, his fingers like claws, face twisted with rage. "You better start runnin'. 'Cause when I catch you, you'll wish you'd never been born."

Buddy springs from the chair, scrambles across the bed. Simon comes after him, barking threats – he'll do for him, he'll do for all of them, and the farther he runs, the worse it will be. Buddy careens onto the hope chest, crashes into the armoire, scrambles to the other side of the bed, leaps onto it again. How're you gonna take it? Simon says. You gonna take it like a man? The bedcover slips through Buddy's fingers, catches on his shoes; he plunges off, striking his head on the chest, and howls. Tears sting his eyes, his fear real, and not-real. He is not himself, and Simon isn't Simon; they have turned into something else.

Simon grasps his ankle. Buddy falls, panting, face-down on the bed. Simon straddles him, pinning his arms with his hands, pressing his leg between his legs. His heart pounds against Buddy's back, his breath flutters against his neck. Buddy lies beneath him, thinking of his mother's warmth and smell. For a moment, they are still, as if balanced in another world; and Buddy watches himself outside himself, matching his breath with Simon's, knowing that Simon understands. Here is blessed peace and the end of the hollow ache. Here is the secret, deeper than any he can tell.

Then Simon rises, and moves across the bed. Buddy squeezes his eyes shut, hides his face in its dusty-smelling cover. His back is cold, colder now from the ghost of Simon's warmth. He tries to keep still, to catch which face of Simon's is real – the one at home, or at school, or in the car. Already, it's beginning – the ache, the doubt.

"Come on, Tuber," Simon says.

Simon stands beside the bed, his cheeks sticky pink, tucking in his shirt with quick jabs. "Mrs. Gay said you got your grades up?" he says, not looking at him.

"Yeah," Buddy says.

"So you're going to get the camera?"

Buddy doesn't answer him.

"Don't you want to make our movie?"

Simon stares at him, his face like flint. Maybe nothing has happened, Buddy thinks. Maybe it is all a lie, a different kind of joke.

"Sure," he says.

☙ ❧

After the Quines leave, he stands in the doorway to the living room, across from the couch where Junior watched cartoons, a breakfront and china cabinet. On the TV, the coyote plunges silently off a cliff. Gramma Liddy sits at the dining room table, staring at the front door. When he and Simon come out of the room, Mrs. Quine is always there, talking in a quick, low voice. Sometimes, she turns from them, shielding her face with her hand, and Simon glares at her, his eyes murderous.

Come on, mamma, he says. It's time to go home.

"What do you know?" Gramma Liddy says.

"Nothing." Buddy shrugs. He sits across from her, his hands in his pockets, in a creaky, straight-backed chair. Behind her, the blinds on the French doors are opened; smoke from her cigarette twists through bars of shadow and light. She pushes a pack toward him, then catches herself, and frowns.

"What are you working on in there? Anything good?"

"Nothing." He looks down at the tablecloth, pocked with cigarette burns. "Just making fun of people, I guess."

"That doesn't get you anywhere," Gramma Liddy says. "Though I daresay there's enough in your life to make fun of."

He glances up at her, afraid she's told Mrs. Quine about his father.

"Don't worry," she says. "Your secrets are safe with me."

She leans closer, so that he can smell the cigarettes on her skin. "You must be very careful with them, Buddy. Mrs. Quine does the best with what she has. So does Simon. So does Junior, that poor imp. They are perfectly innocent; they see only themselves wherever they look. But that doesn't mean you should trust them. It doesn't mean you should hide from them, either."

He hunches lower in the chair, fingering a hole in the tablecloth. She doesn't know the truth about the Quines, he thinks; she doesn't know about the moment of peace, or the pop of Mr. Quine's belt – it is happening, right then.

"Buddy? Your mother has told me what your father wants to do. She's told me that he has asked you to decide where you want to live."

He keeps his eyes on the tablecloth, fire spreading over his skin.

"Do you know what I'm talking about, Buddy?"

"Yes," he says.

"Has your mother spoken to you about it?"

"No."

"Have you decided what you want to do?"

He can't go back to the room where he's been with Simon; he can't go to his mother's room, to the miniature city. The house – the bookshelves and couch, the newspapers and smoke drifting through bars of light – seems infected; she is betraying him, in a way he can't even name.

"Can I go to Alex's?" he says.

She sits back in her chair, her chin lifted, studying him. "You haven't been over there in quite some time."

"I know," he says. "Can I go?"

She lowers her eyes. "Very well. Make it good."

He leaves without looking at her. Outside, the shingle houses seem bare and deserted and strange. He zips up his jacket, shoves his fists in its pockets against the cold. He doesn't know where he will go; but he runs to the street, as if pursued.

13.

If he turns right, he will reach the bayou, and the bridge where Telephone Road crosses it, not far from the Quines'. Left, toward Alex's house, is the freeway, and vacant lots where houses were cleared to widen it. The freeway, like the bayou, runs north to south, to the Gulf. Before the freeway is the low, roofless cinderblock building dedicated to oranges. Inside are theaters with tractor seats and old-fashioned iron fences and colored tiles, a steam engine that turns a miniature boat around a pool like a clock, a museum which claims that Adam and Eve ate oranges before the Fall. Oranges, a sign in the museum says. The Secret To A Happy Life.

Since he started riding with the Quines, he hasn't been to Alex's. Sometimes, Buddy has seen him from the golden car, walking down the street after school, and he knows that Alex has seen him, too. He has stopped working on the movie again; the movie seems childish, though he still dreams of the horse.

He turns left, telling himself he won't really go to Alex's; he will only take a look. Mr. Torres' white truck, with its bumper sticker — Torres Councilman 5 — is in the driveway. His mother has told him that Mr. Torres lost the election. Empty planters decorated with mirrored glass flank the storm door. He waits for Ysrael to bark in his cage, for the curtain in Alex's window to move, the damp air biting his face. Like the traffic whispering on the freeway, two currents run inside him — one to go to the house, one to leave; the one to go is daunting, the one to leave, petty and mean, like his disbelief in the horse. And then he is moving, as if not he but someone else is moving him, not out of courage, but out of fear of his disbelief.

Before he reaches the porch, the front door sucks open; through the storm door's tinted glass, he can see Mr. Torres' unsmiling gaze.

"*El Amigo*," Mr. Torres says, opening the storm door, using his nickname for him when they are alone. "*¿Cómo estás?*"

"*Bien, senor.*"

Mr. Torres sweeps his arm out like a doorman. "*Entre, por favor. ¿Tienes frío afuera, no? No deberías estar en la calle. La policía pensará que vas a robar la casa. Pero con ese uniforme no van a pensar que eres ladrón.*"

Mr. Torres smiles. *You shouldn't stand in the street,* he's said. *The police will think you want to rob my house. With that uniform, though, they won't think you're a thief.*

Buddy is sure that Mr. Torres is making fun of him, sure that he can see the jokes he's laughed at with the Quines. He hates Mr. Torres' secret smile; and he is sure that Mr. Torres can see this, too.

"*Lo siento, señor,*" he says. "*¿Está Alejandro en casa?*"

Mr. Torres' smile wavers. "*¿Porqué?*" he says. "*¿Deseas visitarle?*"

Buddy looks at the picture of Mrs. Torres atop the silent TV; he knows that coming there has been a mistake. "*Sí, señor,*" he says.

Alex fills the doorway to the living room. "*Está bien, papá,*" he says.

Mr. Torres looks at Alex, and they are silent. "*Está bien,*" Alex says, signaling with a tilt of his head for Buddy to follow him.

Past the couch, past the pictures of Mrs. Torres, Buddy feels Mr. Torres watching him. In the hallway, Alex opens his door, and Buddy glimpses drawings: of the ghost horse, of herons and monsters, of a white gull, circling the room.

Alex glances back at him, then pulls the door shut. "Let's walk," he says.

☙❧

They walk down the street toward the bayou. When Alex took Ysrael out of his cage, Mr. Torres asked where they were going; Alex told him The Orange Show.

Buddy digs his hands into the pockets of his jacket, his head bowed against the wind. Ysrael circles them, bounding off to sniff and mark trees, returning, glancing up at them under his shaggy brow. Alex wears a trench coat over his white dress shirt and gray slacks, so that he seems more than ever like a spy. He doesn't look at Buddy.

"What do you want?" he says. "You have a fight with your friend?"

"No," Buddy says.

"Then why do you want to talk to me?"

"I want to work on the movie." Buddy doesn't know if it was true, but he wants it to be true. He wants to believe in the horse again.

"Don't lie," Alex says.

"I'm not. I'm going to get the camera."

"Good for you."

"It's 'cause I got my grades up."

"I'll give you a gold star."

"It's hard there," Buddy says. "You wouldn't understand."

Alex makes a fist in his pocket. Buddy wishes he would hit him. At the end of the block is the bayou, though from where they were, it looks like nothing, an empty field. Beyond it are sulfur-colored buildings, and above them, a livid orange sunset, a rip in the flat, gray sky. "Have you made any more drawings?" Buddy says.

"That's none of your business," Alex says. "When are we going to work on it? After you're done hanging out with that white boy?"

"I don't know."

"I don't know, either, man. I don't know why I'm even talking to you."

They cross a wide, curving road that follows the curve of the bayou, where teen-agers race cars. On the side of the road opposite the bayou is a shadowy park, where no one goes, even in daytime, and past it, the row of shacks where the poor whites lived. When they walked home from Queen of Peace, they stayed on the side of the road where they were now, away from the park and the whites' barking dogs.

Past the shacks is the Telephone Road bridge, and the wide, green ditch of the bayou, hidden past a bend of its bank. White specks cross the sky above it, swooping and gliding – gulls on their way back to the Gulf.

"I had to get a ride," Buddy says. "My mom was going to lose her job."

Alex takes a tennis ball from his pocket and shies it up the path. Ysrael bounds after it. "That's tough," Alex says, watching Ysrael.

"I don't even like him," Buddy says.

"Then why do you hang out with him?" Alex studies him. "You could bring him over. I could meet him. We could all hang out."

"I can't," Buddy says.

"Why not?"

"I don't know."

"Yeah, you do," Alex says; then he glances down the path. "*¡Ysrael!*" he calls. "*¡Ysrael! ¡ Perro estúpido! ¡Bajo de aquí!*"

Alex lumbers toward a storm drain, where Ysrael snuffles, rooting in the tall grass. Buddy follows him, watching him as he wades in. Mr. Torres has told them to never go near the drains, squat cement houses with metal girders like teeth around bottomless mouths, because of the snakes that lived there. Once, they ventured into the grass and woke cottonmouths, curled on the cement; the snakes lifted their heads, as if lifted by strings, their mouths as white as blankets.

Alex tugs at Ysrael's collar; the dog whimpers, barks, scrabbling at the grass. "He wants his ball," Alex says. "Can you hold him?"

"I'll get it," Buddy says.

"I don't want you to get it."

But Buddy is already moving into the grass, parting the tall, sharp-leafed reeds.

"¡Estúpido!," Alex shouts, struggling to hold the dog. "¡Estúpido!"

Buddy follows a line where Ysrael pointed, lifting his feet high in the thicket. The ground slips out from under him; he grasps a fistful of reeds, afraid he will slip into the drain, or be bitten, his heart pounding, the leaves cutting into his hand.

Alex is silent, watching him, his face changed.

The tall grass swims with shadows, the drain's dark mouth close enough to touch. He reaches, leaves whispering against his skin, closing his eyes, tamping the wet ground, waiting to hear the slither, to feel the needle-sharp fangs. He wishes it would happen.

"Got it," he says.

 ❦

Alex pockets the ball, snaps a leash on Ysrael's collar. He looks at Buddy differently, now, and Buddy feels different, too — sharp and clear, as if the cold air whips through him. "What's wrong with you?" Alex says.

"Nothing," Buddy says.

"What if I had to get my dad out here 'cause you got bit?"

"Sorry." He shrugs.

He starts across a bridge of land between the drains, toward a bluff that looks down on the bayou. Alex follows him, Ysrael next to him, sniffing the grass. Behind the sulfur-colored buildings, the sun's dull orange disc is almost gone.

"We need to get back," Alex says.

"Just a minute," Buddy says.

Beneath the lip of the bluff is a broken line of branches and old tires and gas cans. Bleach bottles and Styrofoam and clothes glow white in the dark — junk borne out to the bayou in storms. Sometimes, they found good things, useful things — molded Styrofoam, a steering wheel, a bicycle, once. Beneath the line of junk, the bayou moves, though its motion is visible only from the nodding of reeds along its banks, tugged by the current like dead men's hair. Nowhere — nowhere, at least, that he can see - are the ripples around turtles' heads, the rustle of beaver and nutria, the rare splash of fish they've seen when it was light. The water moves, invisible, a river of shadow, and above it, the white gulls ride its current, tilting their wings.

"Nothing good down there for a while," Alex says, next to him; then, "My dad says I shouldn't hang out with you until you show me some respect."

Headlights and taillights stream like cells across the Telephone Road bridge, where the bayou vanishes around another bend. "What if you had to choose," Buddy says, "between your mom and your dad?"

Alex is silent. "I don't want to talk about that crap."

"What if your dad turned into a robot?" Buddy says, waiting for Alex to hit him. "What if he told your mom he wanted to take you away from her at Christmas?"

Alex flexes his fist in his pocket.

"What if your dad had a girlfriend?" Buddy says. "What if he wanted to take you to live with her? What if you couldn't tell your mom about her, 'cause your mom would sue him and never let you see him again?"

"Is that true?" Alex says, not looking at him.

In the dark, Buddy can't see Alex's face. Now that he's said it, it's different, like himself and his father and mother and Gramma Turner when he told the Quines. But he feels no different; the hunger, the doubt, still beat in him.

"I'm just saying what if," he says.

"What's your mom going to do?" Alex says.

They look at each other, like when Mr. Torres and his mother talked at Queen of Peace; but now, Alex doesn't turn away. "I don't know," Buddy says.

"What are you going to do?"

"I don't know. Don't tell anyone."

Headlights sweep the grass. Behind them come a rumble of motors, crunch of tires on gravel, tinny oompah of the Spanish station. The huge cars with tinted windows are gathering along the edge of the park for the night. Ysrael turns, letting out a fretful bark; Alex yanks his leash taut. "Who'm I going to tell?" he says. "Come on."

They set out along the edge of the bayou, keeping wide of the cars, toward the bend where it disappears. Buddy wonders if the bayou is the same one where he and his father rode their bikes, and if it isn't, where the other one is, and how they fit; he wonders where his father is, right then, in the vast, unmappable city.

Alex strides ahead, hidden in darkness. "The next time that white kid comes over, I want you to bring him to my dad's house. *¿Entiendes?*"

"Sure," Buddy says, watching the place where the bayou disappears; and for a moment, he feels as if he's slipped and let something break. But it is only a tiny crack; all around it, the other thing, the terrible thing, rolls out of the darkness in waves, as if his words have released it: *I don't know, I don't know, I don't know.*

14.

His mother sits across the living room, unraveling a piece of string in her lap. Between them is the tree his father bought the weekend before, reflected in the large, oval mirror above the small, round table that holds the Advent candles. All day, it seems, they have waited, though his mother was up before him, cooking a roast, as she always does on Christmas Eve; and he has tried to write the scenes that he and Alex imagined: the Horse's return to the cell where Hugh was held; the Horse's capture by the mysterious stranger, who has a root that sapped his strength; the Horse's release of Hugh, using his waning powers, so that Hugh can bring back an antidote to the root from the swamp. But all of it seems fake, compared to the movie he's in, the real movie of his life.

His mother glances up, narrow, disappointed — suspicious, he thinks. Since he started riding with the Quines, she hasn't asked him where he's been when he comes home from the woman's, though she eyes him, just like this. He frames a shot of them — her, in her white blouse, green velvet skirt, and fancy shoes; himself, wearing his itchy Easter suit and Christmas tie. *What are you going to do?* he says.

I told you, honey. We'll either go to five-fifteen mass, or have dinner with the Torreses, and go to midnight mass. I'll leave a key under the water heater in case you get home before I do. Don't worry. Just try to enjoy yourself.

He leans forward in his chair, the tie biting into his neck. *I won't enjoy myself.*

Please, honey.

I won't. I'll vomit on the table. I'll kill her.

Please, honey. This isn't helping. Gramma Turner has the right to invite whoever she wants to dinner. She's not the one you should be angry with.

He sis back, afraid of whom she means. *What are you going to do?* he says.

Her eyes slide past him. *What do you mean?*

What are you going to do?

She fidgets with the string. *I don't know, Buddy. It's up to daddy. We've got to keep hoping and praying that he'll do what he knows is right.*

And him, he thinks; it's also up to him. He's seen her, standing at the window above the kitchen sink, covering her mouth with her hand; he's seen the brown envelopes, their address labels decorated with scales of justice, appear and vanish from her desk; and the penciled columns of numbers on her legal pads, which he's known, with a cold catch in his stomach, is money. All of it means she's lying to him now, though how she is, he can't say. He leans forward, the tie cutting into his neck, trying to imagine what will happen if he tells her about the woman: a judge in black robes glowering down at them, picking his father clean, making her spend every last cent she had in court.

What else? he says.

That's it, Buddy, she says. *That's all there is to it.*

Outside, his father's car rumbles into the driveway. His mother quits the couch, wobbling a little in her fancy shoes, as she makes her way to the kitchen. He sits, frozen, not daring to turn to the window behind him that looks out on the driveway, listening to the clunk of his father's car door, the rattle of his keys, the luff of aluminum in the storm door as his mother opens it. In weeks past, he's heard their voices in the kitchen, low and taut — *no fault, mutual incompatibility, desertion.* Now they speak in measured tones, as if nothing has happened, though his father's voice is jerky and halting, as it has been since they ran laps.

Slowly, Buddy rises and goes through the dining room, past a shopping bag of gifts for Grampa Turner, and stands out of sight of the kitchen, to listen.

Are you sure you want to go through with this? his mother says.

His father says nothing.

There's still time, Jimmy. You can save us all a lot of grief if you just tell the truth. But if you don't, I'll have to ask him. Think about that, Jimmy. Think about what kind of man, and what kind of father, that will make you.

His father is silent. Buddy feels him hesitate, and steps into the kitchen. His mother, near the sink, cuts her eyes at him, telling him that she and his father need to talk. His father leans against the dryer, arms propped up on either side of him, his dark suit bunched around his shoulders. Since they've gone running, Buddy can never be sure, when he sees his father, which father he will meet. Now, his father looks out at him, trapped behind his mask, and crosses the room, and embraces him.

Merry Christmas, Buddy, he says.

Merry Christmas, sir.

His mother watches them, touching her fingertips to her mouth. *There are some presents here, Jimmy, for your father.*

Thank you, his father says. *He'll appreciate that.*

There's something for you, too.

Thanks. I'll get it later. My mother's expecting us.

It will only take a minute.

We need to go.

His mother faces the window above the sink. His father looks down at him; Buddy doesn't move. *Okay. Just for a minute. Then we need to go.*

They're in the dining room, his mother says.

In the dining room, his father stands across the table from him, checking his watch. Outside, oak leaves tumble along the buckled sidewalk. Buddy tries to imagine what will happen that night, but he can't; he can't even look at his father.

You did a good job on that tree, his father says.

Yes, sir.

My mother says you got your grades up. You worked hard on that, Buddy. We're all real proud.

Yes, sir.

His father checks his watch, lets out an impatient breath. *Margot?*

I'm getting a glass of wine.

We need to go.

His mother enters, carrying two glasses, her quick, hopeful glance averted from his father and him, and fishes a red-wrapped gift from the shopping bag. His father sets his glass on the table and stares at the gift, as if he doesn't want it. Slowly, he unwraps a thin, black, leather book. *I'm sorry, Margot,* he says.

His mother grips his sleeve, the hope in her eyes now fierce. *Let Buddy see it.*

His father's brow is gathered. Buddy takes the book from him, unsure he wants to see it. Inside, two photos, black and white, face each other: one, a picture of himself, a bald baby in a christening gown; in the other, two people, a man and woman, stand in front of a church with an old-fashioned belltower, palm trees, a mountain. At first, he doesn't see who they are. Then he sees his father's stunned smile, his hair already thinning above his thin face, his face not older than an upper school boy's; his mother holds his arm, facing the camera, her gaze bold and calm.

Do you know who those people are? his mother says.

Buddy looks at the picture, afraid of the fierceness in her voice. *Yes,* he says.

Tell me.

It's me and you and daddy.

That's right. It's you and me and daddy. The picture of daddy and I was taken the summer of 1964, the year before you were born. Daddy was still at Rice, interning at the lab in the summers, and we went to help our sister hospital in Guatemala in an exchange program. People did those kind of things, back then; they went to Selma or Birmingham or Guatemala and helped people and fell in love.

Goddammit, Margot, his father says. *I'm sorry.*

His mother keeps hold of his sleeve. *You don't need to be sorry. You don't need to be sorry ever again.*

We're late, his father says.

Just one more thing, and then you can go, and do whatever it is you need to do. Just light the Advent candle for us.

His father starts for the small, round table in the living room. His mother lets go of his sleeve. Buddy puts the album on the dining room table; then, checking to see if they are watching, he slips it into his coat pocket, and follows them.

His father lights the candles, three pink, one purple, to signal the coming of Christ. From a stained booklet that comes in the box with the wreath, he begins to read, as he does each year — *that the coming of your son may bring us healing in this life and salvation in the life to come.* In the mirror above the table, his mother's bowed head and closed eyes look terrible, like a house shut tight; next to her, his father's face seems heavy and foolish, as if he is impersonating his father. And he, in his itchy suit, watches them — pale, bloated, a spy. He wonders how the Quines, looking at them from the other side of the mirror, will see them. Then he lowers his eyes, as if to stop them from looking — not at their ugliness, but at the candles' pale tongues of flame, the tree lights' pinkish glow, how, for a moment, the room is fragile and holy.

❧ ❦

His father drives fast, cutting off other cars, and exits the freeway near Gramma Turner's. Buddy watches the big houses slide past in the dusk, their colored lights and plastic reindeer like patches of a dream. The album is still in his jacket; they didn't notice it was gone. His father stalked from the house, his mother trailing behind him, pressing the shopping bag into his hands, saying *come back later? we'll talk?*

In his grandmother's driveway, his father ratchets the brake. Buddy presses his forehead against his window; the air outside is cold and fragrant with wood smoke.

We better get inside, his father says.

His father opens the door. Buddy reaches into the back seat for the shopping bag. His father ducks into the car; and for a moment, in his face, Buddy glimpses his real father's face.

Leave those, his father says. *We'll get them later.*

When his father opens the back door, the woman stands in the kitchen, holding a casserole dish, her hands in huge oven mitts, cartoon hands. He's known she would be there, and has imagined ways to kill her: tampering with appliances she might get, slipping poison into her food. But it is different, seeing her there; he doesn't know if killing her will do any good.

You're late, Gramma Turner says, to his father.

Gramma Turner watches them, her chin tilted, arms crossed over her chest, wearing a dress that matches the woman's; but her eyes, behind her glasses, look trapped and uncertain. His father glares at her; the woman vanishes into the dining room.

Look at you! Gramma Turner says, to Buddy. *Don't you look handsome! I just need to talk to your daddy a minute, then we'll have a big Christmas! Why don't you go and help his little friend!*

In the dining room, the woman places silverware on the table, her back to him. He will show her the album, he thinks; she will shrink from it, like a vampire from a cross. But both of them stand still, listening.

What did she say? Gramma Turner says.

Nothing, mamma.

She must've said something, Jimmy. You can't just keep waiting, and hope this will all go away.

His father doesn't answer her.

I'm scared, Jimmy. I'm scared for you and Buddy. I asked Mary what you're going to do, and she says she doesn't know. Just tell me what you're thinking, honey, and I can help.

I don't want to talk about it, mamma, his father says. *I don't want your help. I told you — I'll take care of it.*

༚ ᕗᣦ

Candlelight glimmers in crystal, in red and green cut glass; behind his father, shadows waver in the curtains on the dining room windows, and on the curtains on the bay window behind the empty place set for Grampa Turner. Everything is there, the same: the turkey and stuffing, the mushroom soup and green bean casserole, the spicy spinach and cheese, the eggnog cup shaped like Santa's smiling face, placed in front of Buddy's plate by Gramma Turner's invisible hand. But it is not the same; not only because of the woman, who keeps touching his sleeve, reminding him to sit up straight, to thank Gramma Turner as she passes the dishes; not only because of the empty place at the head of the table, where he imagines Grampa Turner in his checkered coat and loud striped tie, asking if they can listen to Louis Armstrong; not only because his mother should be there, but isn't, and the woman shouldn't be there, but is.

Something else shadows Gramma Turner, who sits stiffly, bolt-upright, her eyes delicate and searching as only at Christmas; and the woman, who compliments Gramma Turner, her voice like an animal testing a branch. Both of them look at his father, who keeps his head bowed over the table, the muscles in his jaw churning as he eats.

It sure is nice, having everyone here, Gramma Turner says.

Everything is perfect, grandmother.

It's especially nice, Gramma Turner says, *having my two nice strong young men here. What about you, Jimmy? Are you having a nice Christmas?*

His father stares down at his plate.

What about you? Gramma Turner says, to Buddy, touching her napkin to her lips. *What do you think Santa Claus'll bring you?*

His father doesn't look up. The woman prods Buddy's arm.

I don't know, ma'am, he says.

Well, what do you want him to bring you? Do you think you've been a good boy?

His father stares at his plate, heat pouring off him in waves.

I don't know, ma'am, Buddy says.

I think you have. I think you've done real well. You just needed some help. I hope pretty soon you'll get all the help you need. But don't you feel good, now, honey – now that you got your grades up, like a nice, little man?

His father's forearms flank his plate, his fists clenched.

Yes, ma'am, Buddy says.

So why don't you tell us, honey? Gramma Turner says, tugging at his sleeve. *Why don't you tell us what you want Santa Claus to bring you?*

Leave him alone, his father says.

I'm just trying to cheer him up, Jimmy, Gramma Turner says. *I'm just trying to give him a nice Christmas.*

Your mother has worked very hard, Jimmy, to make this a nice dinner.

Gramma Turner touches her napkin to her lips. *I don't understand why you have to be like this, Jimmy.*

Like what? his father says, leaning across the table, his jaw rigid. *What am I like?*

∾⊷

After dinner, the woman asks his father to take pictures. His father says they don't need any more pictures, but Gramma Turner and the woman insist. His father sets a timer on his camera, scuttles back to his chair. The timer whirrs, a red light blinks. His father grimaces; Gramma Turner wears a fake, brittle smile. Buddy, next to the woman, rolls up his eyes, a zombie, a corpse. It is part of the fake story that covers the real one — the story of the pictures in the album, and the coiled sheets in the mirror, and Grampa Turner's empty chair — and now he is part of that fakery, too.

∾⊷

In the den, the Christmas tree's colored lights float in the darkness beyond the sliding glass doors, and on the pictures of his grandfather with famous men. In the living room, on the piano, as he does each year, his father picks out "Silent Night." From the kitchen come Gramma Turner and the woman's voices, as his mother's and Gramma Turner's have in the past. Grampa Turner watches Buddy from his bed, propped up on pillows in a royal blue robe.

The last few weeks, his grandfather hasn't talked. But since his father took him running, Buddy has believed that he can hear, sometimes, what his grandfather has thought. *Merry Christmas, Grampa*, he says.

Grampa Turner grips his hand, leveling on him his dark, commanding gaze. *Merry Christmas*, he says, silently.

My mother sent you some presents, Buddy says. *They're in the car. Daddy'll bring them to you later.*

His grandfather turns his head from him. *No, he won't*, he says, silently.

Buddy leans closer, unsure he's heard him. In the living room, the piano has stopped; Gramma Turner and the woman coax his father toward the den. Buddy touches the album in his pocket, to show it to his grandfather; but there isn't enough time.

Grampa? he says. *What's going to happen?*

Grampa Turner turns to him again, his dark, fierce eyes full. *I don't know*, he says, silently. *No one knows. It's up to you.*

His father stands in the doorway. Behind him crowd Gramma Turner and the woman, who holds a tray of food. His father's eyes shift from Buddy to Grampa Turner, trapped-looking, as if he's heard what they said.

Merry Christmas, daddy, his father says, holding out his hand. *How're you feeling? You do those exercises I showed you?*

Gramma Turner takes the tray from the woman and brings it to the bed. *He can't do those things, Jimmy. He just needs you to sit with him and visit.*

Grampa Turner grips his father's hand; his father tips sideways, grimacing, as if they are wrestling. *Goddamn, daddy*, he says. *You're gonna break my fingers. Nothing wrong with you. Strong as a fucking horse.*

Language, Jimmy, Gramma Turner says.

Grampa Turner stares at his father; and Buddy feels the old joke coming, an ache in the back of his throat. *I'm sorry I haven't visited, daddy*, his father says. *I really am. I feel for you; I really can. But I can't quite touch you.*

Grampa Turner laughs, a faint, bitter, rasping laugh, turning from his father, still gripping his hand. His laughter turns into deep, hollow coughs. Gramma Turner and the woman circle the bed. Gramma Turner pushes past his father, lifting Grampa Turner from his pillows; the woman plumps the pillows behind him; Gramma Turner lowers his grandfather back down. His father stands next to the bed, his hands at his sides; and Grampa Turner keeps his face averted from him, drawing deep, hungry breaths.

The woman stands next to the bed, holding his grandfather's hand. His father watches them, the darkness in his eyes like the darkness outside the window; and Buddy wishes that she would disappear. *I'll listen to his chest before we leave*, his father says.

Gramma Turner leans over the bed. *How're you feeling, Bink? You want some supper? We made everything you like.*

Maybe he doesn't want supper, his father says. *Maybe he wants to open presents.*

He needs to eat, Jimmy. It'll get cold if he doesn't.

What do you want to do, daddy? Do you want to open presents?

Please, Jimmy, Gramma Turner says. *Don't do like this.*

He wants to open presents, his father says. *So let's open the goddamned presents.*

༚ ༚

Across the table from him, his father sits, sipping whiskey from a shot glass, only his head visible, facing Gramma Turner and the woman across the den. Buddy sits near the tree, sunk in a low-slung chair, his stomach squeezed between his rib-cage and belt. From the candy that spills out of his stocking on a TV tray, he picks Hershey's kisses, rolling the tinfoil into pellets he secrets in his pockets, letting the sugary goo coat his mouth, imagining it mixing in his stomach with the turkey and green beans and two servings of stuffing he's eaten. Grampa Turner watches them from his bed. Near the door, the woman sits in the chair where his mother sat, folding used wrapping paper, stacking boxes. Gramma Turner weighs gifts from under the tree, checks their labels; then, as they are opened, she looks on expectantly, pinching the hem of her dress.

Outside, in the darkness, the birdbath floats like a plume of smoke; and Buddy remembers the sharpness of the bird the day that he found the camera; and he tries see it all clearly — what has happened, and what is happening — so that he will know what he should do.

Two gifts remain, one for his father, one for him. Gramma Turner has told them they are the last ones; but from the wrapping paper, which on these gifts is always the same, and from her anxious glance, Buddy already knows. Already, she's given the woman a frilly blouse, a silk scarf, a Waterford traveling clock; and Grampa Turner, a tartan blanket, a plush blue bathrobe, a pair of sheepskin slippers; and his father, an electric tire gauge, a tie and button-down shirts, a certificate for a tailored suit, a box of monogrammed handkerchiefs, a book called *People Sense: Learning to Communicate at Work*; and for him, a shirt and sweater set, a box of socks and underwear, a scientific calculator, a certificate for that year's Easter suit, a book called

The Young Person's Steps to Success, a book called *The Shark: Deadly Hunter of the Deep*, which two years before, he would have liked.

Inside his father's card, a boy in footed pajamas kneels before a tree surrounded by presents. Next to the boy is a column of years that Gramma Turner has written, one for each year his father has gotten the gift, which was always the same.

For a long time, his father stares at the card. Then he shakes the box next to his ear. *I wonder what it is?* he says.

Gramma Turner dabs at her mouth with a tissue. *You know what it is, Jimmy. I've had about enough of your foolishness.*

Slowly, his father cuts the tape with the edge of his thumbnail, then lays the wrapping paper on the floor next to him, so as not to wrinkle it. From the box, he lifts a pair of black leather shoes identical to the ones he wears.

Shoes! he says. *What a surprise!*

Go on, now, Jimmy, Gramma Turner says, dabbing at her eyes. *You never know when you'll need them.*

His father drops the shoes in the box, and stares at Gramma Turner, seeming to look through her; but at the same time, it is as if there is no one in the room but them.

The woman glances between them, perched on the edge of her chair.

Why don't you thank your mother, Jimmy, for your presents?

Neither Gramma Turner nor his father look at her. But something in his father shifts. He rises, grunting, hunched over, arms dangling at his sides, and dances toward Gramma Turner, hopping from foot to foot.

Thank you, mamma, thank you, mamma, thank you, mamma, he says, flapping his arms around her in a kind of embrace.

Gramma Turner shrinks, batting at him. *Stop it, Jimmy! Stop it!*

Stop, Jimmy, the woman says. *Please. You're frightening her.*

His father looks at Buddy, smiling, his face shiny with sweat. It is something he and Grampa Turner often do at Christmas — joking with her.

I'm sorry, mamma, he says. *I guess I got carried away. I appreciate the shoes; I truly do. I appreciate everything.*

His father stands over her, his expression changed; he reaches down to touch her shoulder. Gramma Turner shoos his hand away, covering her face with her hand.

Maybe you should sit down, Jimmy, the woman says.

His father sits, and pours another glass of whiskey. Gramma Turner gives Buddy his gift, her shoulders bowed beneath the terrible weight. Buddy opens the card, for him a jolly Santa, and looks at the column of years. Slowly, he unwraps the gift.

Inside the box are tissue paper, and a bicycle helmet.

That's just part of it, Buddy, Gramma Turner says. *Your daddy's still working on the other part. Why don't you tell him about it, Jimmy?*

His father doesn't answer her.

Your daddy ordered you a special bicycle, Buddy, all the way from England. He's almost finished putting it together. Your daddy loves you, Buddy. Remember that.

Thank you, sir, Buddy says.

His father stares across the room at Gramma Turner. Buddy looks away, afraid of what he will do, not wanting to humiliate him. Outside, the room where the other family lives floats in the dark trees. He imagines they are really switched, that the other family is inside, and they are trapped outside. Gramma Turner watches him, her eyes delicate behind her glasses. The album is a gun, a bomb, that can blast through all the fakery. He rises, touching his pocket. He will show her the pictures; he will show her who his father really is.

Ooga-booga! his father says.

His father springs from his chair, and dances toward Gramma Turner.

Ooga-booga! he says.

The woman reaches for him, but his father slips past her, circling Gramma Turner, who struggles out of her seat.

Ooga-booga! his father says, hovering around her, feinting, pinching her arms.

Gramma Turner swats at him, screaming, stumbling past the woman, her arms outstretched, like a sleepwalker. *Everything's ruined!* she says. *Ruined!*

In the living room, a door slams shut; from behind it comes the sound of his grandmother weeping. His father smiles at Grampa Turner, who stares at him, his eyes blazing, his hand raised, as if he is about to speak. The woman looks from Buddy to his father, her small, frightened, chiseled face, and flees to the living room. His father turns to him, still smiling, though there is no pleasure in his smile.

Come on, he says. *Let's go.*

❧ ❧

His father drives past the colored lights on Tellepsen Tool, past the field where the boys are buried, past the men outside El Destino Club #2. Since they left Gramma

Turner's, he hasn't spoken. Buddy remembers Grampa Turner's dark, accusing stare. He still doesn't know what he will do. But what his father has done has given him hope; it is almost something his real father would do.

They turn down his mother's street, where the night air smells of firecrackers and brisket from oil drum cookers, and tinny music swells and fades from backyards, like the streetlights on his father's face. Buddy thinks of how the freeway snakes from Gramma Turner's through the vast, dark city. He still can't picture it; and he wonders if he will ever go back to Gramma Turner's again.

Downstairs, the front windows in his mother's house shine with the tree lights' pinkish glow, and in the window above the kitchen sink, blue light flickers from the TV. The driveway is empty; his father's grip on the steering wheel relaxes, and Buddy feels a weight lift from his own chest. His father parks the car, then sits, facing the windshield, while the engine ticks in the silence.

Where's your mother? he says.

At the Torreses', sir.

His father nods, still facing the windshield. *Joe Torres is a good man.*

He's okay, sir.

His father glances at him. *You should keep those pictures, Buddy. Okay?*

But they're yours, sir, Buddy says.

I know, Buddy. But you should keep them. You know I can't do anything with them. You should keep them, and always remember that I love you.

His father turns to his window; and a cold hand reaches into Buddy's chest.

What do you think you'd want to do, Buddy, if we didn't have to deal with all this crap? What if we could just ride our bikes, and I could go to work, and you could go to school and make your movies? What do you think you'd want to do, then, Buddy? Do you think you'd want to live with me?

Yes, sir, he says. *I think so, sir.*

But we don't live in that kind of world, do we, Buddy?

No, sir, Buddy says, not knowing what he means.

His father takes a white envelope from his coat pocket, and holds it out to him, not looking at him. *I need you to give this to your mother. But I need you to promise me something. I need you to promise me you won't read it. Okay?*

What about my decision, sir?

You shouldn't have to do that, Buddy. It's not fair. It's not right.

But what if I want to, sir?

His father lifts his hand from the steering wheel, then lays it down again. *It wasn't right, Buddy, what I did over at my mother's tonight — how I acted. It wasn't normal. It wasn't right for me to take you out to that track. It wasn't right for me to go to Detroit, and not try harder to be with you and your mother. Understand?*

No, sir, he says.

His father shifts in his seat, rubs the steering wheel with his free hand. Beads of sweat glisten on his face like beads of glass. *There are a lot of things in this world, Buddy, that just don't make sense. Some people, they're just different, you know? Maybe they can do most things all right, maybe they can get along in the world, but they don't really know how to be with other people. Understand?*

No, sir, he says, though he does.

His father holds the envelope out to him, not looking at him. *Just give this to your mother, Buddy. Okay? Then everything will be all right.*

The house looks hollow, a fake house. Buddy grips his door handle, angry with his father, angrier than he's ever been. *What if I can't, sir?*

Please, Buddy, his father says.

Why don't you give it to her, sir?

Because I can't, Buddy.

Why not, sir? Buddy says.

His father strikes the steering wheel, rocking forward, his movement swift and awkward and adult. *Because I can't, Buddy. I just can't.*

Buddy takes the envelope from him, opens his door, pulling the shopping bag across his legs. His father touches his coat sleeve, but Buddy struggles away from him; he knows that if he turns to his father, he will see his father's face, in the weak yellowish light. *I'm sorry, Buddy,* his father says.

Yes, sir, Buddy says, not looking at him.

I love you, Buddy. I'm sorry.

Yes, sir, he says, shutting his door. *I love you, too, sir.*

☙ ❧

Inside, the kitchen is dark, except for the bluish, shifting light. Buddy locks the back door and goes to the TV, bringing his face close to its screen. The Pope leads a procession of priests inside a huge church. Outside, his father's car still hums in the driveway. Everything he's said is crap, Buddy thinks. *Leave*, he thinks, staring at the screen until his eyes burn, until the sound of his father's car has vanished.

He carries the shopping bag through the dining room, past the living room's pink bubble of light, into the darkness and formaldehyde smell of his room. He takes the album from his coat pocket, then feels for a rip in the box springs of the bed where he's hidden things before, and shoves the album in.

From outside comes hollow thunder, railroad cars coupling on the tracks, the crackle of fireworks, like feet on dry twigs. Then, silence, and out of the silence, a whispering sound like the freeway's breath — the boys, buried in the field, moving toward him through the tall grass.

He goes to the living room, carrying the shopping bag. Inside the tree lights' pink glow, he is safe. On the sealed white envelope, in his father's writing, as lumpy and awkward as his own, are his mother's name, and the name of the hospital where his father works. He turns on the desk lamp, careful not to look in the oval mirror, where he knows a boy from the field is watching him, his dark eyes and shaggy hair like Sam's. He holds the letter against the bulb, and can see only a thicket of curving lines. He pries a corner of the flap, but it tears.

If he opens it, he can't show it to his mother. If he opens it, his father will know he's betrayed him. He rips it open, before he can think anymore.

December 23, 1975

Dear Margot,

I am writing to you from my new office. The techs here aren't as good as the ones at the old lab, but they try hard, and I think if I can train them half as well as you did me, they will do a good job.

There are tears in my eyes now as I think of all the help you have given me at Rice and medical school and the lab. You are a good person, Margot, and I know that all you wanted was to make a family. But I think that whatever is inside people that keeps people together with a family is not there inside me.

I think you know there is someone else now, and it is simpler. I won't try to take Buddy, because I know that the same thing that happened when I tried to make a family with you will happen again. I will give you all the support I can afford, Margot, but I can't be with you and Buddy. I am sorry, Margot. Please forgive me.

He reads the letter, then reads it again, warmth ebbing from his hands and face. Someone else, not his real father, has written it. Maybe the woman. Maybe it is all a joke. Because it cannot be true that his father has betrayed him; if he tells his mother about the woman, it will mean that he will never see his father again. He folds the letter tightly, digs its point into his hand, to remember this. Outside, the boys press their faces against the windows, jeering at him, beckoning him.

Headlights sweep the windows. For a moment, he thinks it's his father, coming to take the letter back. Then he hears his mother's car rattle and sigh. There is still time to leave the letter on the table, find the boys who scattered from the headlights, and go with them. But he stands, trapped, as the gate latch clicks, and the back door rattles open, and a dark shape fills the doorway to the kitchen.

You're home. The figure comes toward him, her movements stiff, her voice flat, like a robot's. *Is daddy here?*

He left, Buddy says.

Did you have a good time?

He sidles toward the hallway, lifting the shopping bag. *It was fine.*

What did daddy say?

Nothing.

His mother catches his arm; on her breath is the faint, sour smell of wine. *Please, honey. I'm tired of all this.*

Buddy ducks away from her; she catches the bag, ripping it, but he makes it into the hallway, shutting the bathroom door, locking it behind him.

Please, honey, she says. *You need to tell me.*

He covers his face with his hands, with the smell of alcohol and reagents on the letter, the smell of the lab. *Leave me alone,* he says.

Please, honey. Don't do this. You're hurting yourself. I'm not talking about daddy anymore. I'm talking about us. Lying is a mortal sin.

He crouches on the tile floor, closing his eyes.

I don't know what you're talking about, he says.

You're not helping anyone, Buddy. Not even daddy. Especially not daddy. This will eat him up. It will take all that's left of him.

She doesn't know what she's talking about, he thinks; she doesn't know what's really going on. *You're a liar,* he says.

Please, honey, she says, trying to stifle the sound of her crying. *Please don't do this. Just tell me who she is.*

He holds himself very still.

I'm sorry, honey, she says. *I'm sorry I'm asking you this.*

You're crazy, he says. *Leave me alone.*

Please, Buddy, she says.

Leave me alone, he says, squeezing his eyes shut. *You tricked us. You're not really my mother. You're not really his wife.*

What do you mean? she says, her voice changed.

Her voice frightens him. He doesn't know what he means. *What do you mean, Buddy?* she says. *What did they tell you?*

He keeps still, listening; outside the door, his mother weeps, deep, wracking cries, as if something is being torn from inside her.

He knows that he has said something dirty, like what he has glimpsed in the three o'clock movie, but he doesn't know what it is.

The door to her room slams shut. He opens his eyes, and unlocks the bathroom door. In her room, his mother is silent; he tries her door, but it is locked. He rattles the knob, pushes against it. He beats on the door with the side of his fist, steps back, slipping on the sweater his grandmother gave him, throws himself against it. He didn't mean what he said; he didn't know what he meant. Even he isn't there, not really.

He is in a movie, the movie of his life. He is remembering, as if it was happening right then, the morning Grampa Liddy died. When he'd woke, gray light filtered through his windows, a time of morning he'd never seen. A lamp still burned over the chair where his mother read him to sleep the night before. In her room, her bed was a smooth, white slab. He didn't see the note she left that said she went to Gramma Liddy's. But he knew, then, that she and his father had died, and he beat the walls, trying to follow them. Now, he knows why she won't open her door; he knows why she won't answer him. It isn't he who cries out; it isn't he who beats her door. Someone else has taken his place – a monster, a madman.

Mamma! he cries. *Mamma! Please let me in!*

15.

SCENE ONE: NIGHT. HUGH searches for the HORSE in the swamp. Lightning flashes. HUGH sees the HORSE and goes to him. The HORSE is dead. HUGH kneels and prays. Lightning strikes the HORSE. The HORSE rises up from the ground, glows in the sky, and spreads his wings. HUGH reaches up to him. The HORSE nods and lets HUGH know that he will be all right. The HORSE flies away.

SCENE TWO: HUGH sits next to his window. He hears a noise and looks out. In the window across from his, GILDA beats WOODY to death with a metal bat. HUGH sits down, nervous, then kneels at the window.
    HUGH: Ghost Horse! Ghost Horse! Please help!

SCENE THREE: NIGHT: GILDA and MYSTERIOUS STRANGER carry WOODY in garbage bag to bayou. HUGH watches from trees. STRANGER dumps WOODY in water. GILDA turns to STRANGER.
    GILDA: Did you hear something?
    STRANGER looks at trees. HUGH moves back. STRANGER points gun at him.
    HUGH puts his hands up.
    GILDA: What did you see?
    HUGH: Nothing.
    MYSTERIOUS STRANGER: You are lying.
    HUGH: No. I saw nothing.

SCENE SIX: HUGH waits in cell. He sees a shape fly across the moonlight. It is the GHOST HORSE. HORSE fades through the roof.
    HUGH: Thank you. It's dangerous here. We need to escape.
    HORSE (silently): You killed me.
    HUGH: What do you mean?

HORSE *(silently)*: *When you left me in the swamp, I died.*

A door opens. GILDA *and* MYSTERIOUS STRANGER *are there.* HUGH *tries to step in front of* HORSE, *but* HORSE *spreads his wings.* STRANGER *takes a root from his pocket. He shoves it in* HORSE's *mouth.* HORSE *tosses his head and falls down. He turns into the* SWAMP HORSE. STRANGER *laughs.*

STRANGER: *He can't help you now. He's going to die.*

GILDA *(to* HUGH): *We'll be back soon. You're going to help us.*

GILDA *and* STRANGER *leave.*

HUGH *(kneeling next to* HORSE): *What can I do? What can I do to help?*

SWAMP HORSE *(silently)*: *You have to go to the swamp. You need to find an anti-dote? I'm sorry I can't go with you. You need to hurry.*

HUGH: *I'll help you. I'm sorry. I'm sorry.*

SWAMP HORSE *(silently)*: *I'm sorry, too.*

Eyes of HORSE *glow red.* HUGH *fades through roof.*

SCENE SEVEN: HUGH *walks through swamp. Moonlight comes through dark trees. Camera watches him through trees. He hears a sound and stops.*

STRANGER *steps out. He holds a knife.*

STRANGER: *You can't escape.*

HUGH *runs through trees.* BATS *and* GOBLINS *screech at him. A* GIANT SPIDER *sits on a hollow stump.*

SPIDER: *Come here. You'll be safe.*

HUGH *looks at her nervously.*

SPIDER: *I can help you. I know the Horse.*

HUGH *goes into stump. The* SPIDER *turns on a light. They are in a cave.*

SPIDER: *I can give you the antidote. But you have to bring the Horse back here after you give it to him. The Horse has a mission you do not know.*

HUGH: *What is the Horse's mission?*

SPIDER: *I can't tell you because it's secret. You have to go now to save him.*

ॐ∾৶

"This is pretty good," Alex says. He paces, holding the script, clicking a cinnamon candy against his teeth. Outside his room, it is raining.

"When are you going to bring that kid over?"

"When school starts. You can't tell him about the camera."

"Why not?"

"You just can't."

Alex eyes him, clicking the candy. "Your mom looked sad when she was here."

"That's just crap," Buddy says. "Let's talk about the movie."

16.

Rain veils the houses near the Quines, and the empty-looking buildings and portable signs. His mother drives cautiously, hunched close to the steering wheel, as if she can see better that way. On Christmas, she and Buddy opened gifts and went to Gramma Liddy's, as always. His mother no longer looks at him suspiciously. Since Christmas, she seems not to look at him at all, but at some point above or beyond him that he can't see. At mass, which she goes to, now, almost every day, she presses her forehead against clenched hands, then stares at that point, leaving him far behind. She hasn't tried to call his father; but sometimes, Buddy has heard her alone in the kitchen, talking to him: *If you want to wait, I'll wait. I'll give you enough rope to hang yourself.* When the weather is good, she pulls up the honeysuckle that turned gray when his father dumped the sand, and puts it in a compost pile in the corner of the yard. Buddy watches her from his room. She wipes her flushed face, studying the un-spread sand, then glances up at him, her eyes fierce. And he retreats into the darkness of his room, from the fierceness of her love, from the question she askes.

Water laps across the gray hump of the Quines' street from its ditches. They are early. Over the holidays, his mother went in to set up morning blood rounds, and left him at Gramma Liddy's when he was still half-asleep. That morning, they already got in the car before she remembered that they were going to the Quines.

"Tell Mrs. Quine I'm sorry I didn't call," she says, pulling into the driveway. "Tell her I can pay a little extra if I can drop you off early."

She hands him a folded check, which he slides into the pocket of his binder; then she touches his hair, and her expression softens.

"Have a good day, sport."

He ducks from her, opening his door; he still doesn't trust her soft looks.

Sheets of rain sweep the driveway. He straddles puddles in long strides, anxious to get to the house, afraid that Toby will dart out, and bite him. Since school ended, he hasn't talked to Simon. Once, he called, but Mr. Quine told him Simon was busy, and he knew not to call again. He doesn't know what he will say to keep Simon away from Alex; he can't tell him about the camera. He can't tell him anything.

He stops outside the back door, rain wetting his face, listening.

Where's the money going to come from, Lorraine? Mr. Quine says. *What am I supposed to do if I can't trust you?*

Over the holidays, Gramma Liddy and his mother talked about Poor Mrs. Quine. Gramma Liddy said the best thing Mrs. Quine could do would be to get as far away from Mr. Quine as she could. Buddy shouldn't have to go over there, his mother said. He shouldn't have to see those kind of things. But he knows they are wrong; they didn't really know about the Quines.

He draws closer to the porch, holding his breath, still imagining that Toby will dart out.

I'm sorry, Mrs. Quine says. *I'll do better, I promise.*

He climbs the steps, peeks through the sliver in the paper on the window. Mrs. Quine sits at the breakfast table, wearing a dressing gown, shielding her face with her hand. *Please,* she says. *They'll hear us.*

Mr. Quine moves into the frame, his back to the window – a white dress shirt, a clenched fist. Then his arm swings down, so swiftly Buddy isn't sure he sees it, and knocks Mrs. Quine against the table

For a moment, he waits for Mrs. Quine to move, to look at him. Then he runs, splashing through puddles, into the street, not slowing until a stitch cuts into his side, half a block away; he is shivering, his jacket clammy, his hair wet. He searches the sky, but the horse is not there. The boys buried in the field snicker at him, fleeting shapes in the silty rain. He can't go to Gramma Liddy's; he will have to lie, or tell what he's seen. He wonders if he's imagined it. Then he sees Mr. Quine's arm swing down, Mrs. Quine's head hit the table like a doll. It is the real movie, like the coiled sheets, and Grampa Turner's empty chair, and his mother weeping alone in her room.

He is a coward. He turns back, imagining himself breaking down the door, sweeping Mrs. Quine into the car, all of them escaping.

When he reaches the house again, it is quiet. Toby is still hidden somewhere, maybe behind the garage.

Mr. Quine sits at the breakfast table, reading his newspaper. Everything is the same – the doorless cupboards, the newspaper-covered floor, the scent of milk and paint.

Mr. Quine turns a page with a smart crackle, then glances up at the window.

"Come in," he says.

Buddy stands on the porch, shivering.

"Come in," Mr. Quine says.

Buddy opens the door; Mr. Quine holds the newspaper in front of himself like a screen. "You're early," Mr. Quine says. "It says here the D.A. won't file charges against those policemen who drowned that Mexican. What do you think of that?"

The chair where Mrs. Quine cowered, and the table where her head struck, are the same, though not exactly. Buddy looks at Mr. Quine, and hates him. In that moment, he hates him more than he hates anyone else. "I don't know, sir," he says.

Mr. Quine lowers his paper, and his black eyes sharpen.

"How long have you been out there?" he says.

He will tell him; he will tell him what he's seen. "Not long, sir."

"Don't lie to me, boy."

"Yes, sir," he says. "I'm sorry, sir."

Mr. Quine's gaze shifts. Mrs. Quine stands behinds Buddy in the doorway to the den. The gold cross glints at her neck; she wears her Western shirt and jeans. Buddy searches her face for recognition that he's come back, but sees nothing, only fear.

"Come on, Buddy," she says. "Don't bother Mr. Quine."

Mr. Quine rises, touching his belt. "Who do you think we are?" he says. "Do you think we're funny? Do you think we're something you can laugh at?"

He will tell him that he hates him; he will tell him what he's seen.

"No, sir," he says.

Mr. Quine unbuckles his belt, cinches it into a loop. "Did your mother send you over here to laugh at us?"

"Come on, Buddy," Mrs. Quine says, touching his arm.

"You see what happens, Lorraine," Mr. Quine says. "You're going to have to find another way to get your pin money."

Buddy watches his pale, meaty hands, imagining the dry pop, the red-hot stripe on his skin; he wishes it would happen. "Please, Dan," Mrs. Quine says. "Don't make it worse." Then, to Buddy, shaking him, "Come on."

Mr. Quine moves toward them around the table, stretching the belt between his fists. Buddy stumbles, his shoes tearing newspaper from the floor, letting Mrs. Quine pull him backward through the den. She leads him into a bathroom in the hallway where one wall is blue, the other white, and shuts the door, then crouches in front of him, glaring at him, her hands trembling. "What happened?" she says.

He is shivering all over, now. "I'm sorry, ma'am. My mother has to go to work early. She said to tell you she can pay extra if I can come early, ma'am."

"Lorraine!" Mr. Quine shouts, outside.

"But what happened?" Mrs. Quine says, shaking him.

"I don't know, ma'am. I got scared, then I ran away, then I came back."

She watches him steadily. "Your mother should have more sense. And you should know not to mess in other people's business."

"Lorraine!" Mr. Quine shouts.

"I'm sorry, ma'am," he says.

Mrs. Quine lowers her eyes. "Never mind," she says. "Dry yourself off. Let me see what I can do about your clothes."

When she opens the door, he sees a flash of Mr. Quine's pale face, his staring eye. Outside, their voices come, low and quick, then silence. He peels off his clothes, still listening, and dries himself with a rough towel. It is quiet, and his skin feels cool and damp; he is naked, inside the Quines' dark house.

Someone knocks. The door pushes open a crack; Mrs. Quine holds out a white bathrobe. "Buddy?" she says. "You better get upstairs."

He climbs the scuffed stairwell, holding the robe closed. Silence ripples out through the house from the kitchen. He thinks of what Mr. Quine said about pin money; it will mean that he won't ride with them again.

Buddy stops at the top of the stairs. Simon sits at his desk beneath a reading lamp, framed in the doorway to his room, a book opened in front of him, his lips moving almost silently, as small as when Buddy saw him mowing the field. *Augustus, Tiberius, Gaius,* Simon says, *Claudius, Nero, Galba* — the names of Roman Emperors, which they won't have to learn until next year; and Buddy waits, knowing Simon has heard him, the hollow ache catching at him, a warm, frightening emptiness in his chest.

Simon rises, glancing at him, his face almost the one he wears at school; then turns his back on Buddy, and goes to the room's single window.

"*Salve,*" he says, lifting his palm.

"*Salve,*" Buddy says, matching his signal.

Buddy enters the room; he knows Junior is there, under the comforter, though he can't see him. The room's bare walls look strange, as if Buddy has never seen them before. "Did you get the camera?" Simon says.

"Yes," Buddy says, before he can stop himself; he ache has said it, not him.

"Good," Simon says. "We can make a movie. When can you bring it?"

"I don't know," Buddy says. "It's a secret."

Simon faces the window, where the tree branch waves.

"If my mom finds out about it," Buddy says, "she'll take it." He is thinking of Alex, and the Horse. "Where's Toby?" he says.

Simon's jaw tightens. "He bit a nigger. He bit a nigger who was trying to break into the house, and my dad had to shoot him."

Buddy takes a step closer; he doesn't believe him.

"That's a lie," Simon says. "He took him to the pound 'cause he was eating too much. He took him to the pound and left him."

Buddy wants to tell him he hasn't seen anything; he feels himself move toward Simon, like he did the first day at the house, when he imagined Mr. Quine hitting him. Simon turns to him, his eyes full, his face like a clenched fist; and Buddy stops, afraid, Simon's face, his true face, will disappear.

"I hate him," Simon says. "Do you know what I mean?"

"Yes," Buddy says, keeping very still.

"If you tell anybody, I'll kill you."

"Yes," Buddy says.

"I hate him." Simon swings at the window frame, beats it with the edge of his hand. "I hate him, I hate him, I hate him."

Buddy reaches, trembling, like water at the edge of a glass. He doesn't care if Junior sees him. When he touches his shoulder, Simon pivots, striking at him, and Buddy lets the robe fell open. Cold air flashes over him; and for a moment, before he pulls it closed, Simon stares at him, his eyes frightened and wild.

"Buddy?" Mrs. Quine says.

She stands in the doorway, holding his folded uniform, her gaze shifting between Simon and him. Buddy doesn't know how long she's been there.

"Come on, Buddy," she says. "We're late. You better get downstairs."

∽∾

In the golden car, Mrs. Quine nods along with the country music station, turned so low it's a murmur, her eyes hidden behind her sunglasses, though the rain has made a false dusk. When they went through the kitchen, Mr. Quine glanced at them over his newspaper, and said nothing. Now, they pass the abandoned drive-in, the sickly-looking warehouse, the ocean of trees and houses sinking into the earth. His shoes are still wet, his uniform damp, itchy, too-tight. Junior is sunk in the front seat, vanished. Simon, next to him in the back, stares at a rubber-band cat's cradle he weaves between his fingers. Since they left his room, he hasn't looked at Buddy.

"Stop gawking at me," Simon says.

Buddy turns to his window, where silver beads of water creep across the glass. He doesn't know if he will ride with them again. But this is not why he will tell them what he will tell them; he wants to tell them, so he will be like them.

"I've got a secret, ma'am," he says, to Mrs. Quine.

Mrs. Quine doesn't answer him.

"My dad and I stole a movie camera from O.G.'s. My mom doesn't know about it. She wouldn't let me keep it if she did."

Mrs. Quine is silent. Simon weaves the rubber band between his fingers; but he keeps his head very still. Buddy's heart thunders, taking his breath; he watches himself outside himself, as if he is someone else.

"My mom doesn't know," he says. "'Cause she wasn't there."

Simon eyes him. Junior tilts his head sideways between the seats.

"Why's that, Buddy?" Mrs. Quine says.

"It's 'cause he doesn't live with us, ma'am."

Except for the murmur of music and the clop of windshield wipers, the silence in the car is complete. But he keeps his face turned from them, watching silver beads of water travel across the window outside, pulling focus between them and his own reflection.

"He's got a girlfriend, ma'am," he says. "My mom doesn't know about her. He'd get in trouble if she did."

"I'm sorry about that, Buddy," Mrs. Quine says.

"Thank you, ma'am. Please don't tell anyone. It's a secret."

"What's her name?" Simon says.

"Simon," Mrs. Quine says. "Maybe Buddy doesn't need to tell you that."

He hasn't thought of a name for her; now, looking at Simon, he does.

"Tightface," he says.

Simon eyes him; then he grins, and silently claps his hands.

"Tightface!" he says.

"Buddy?" says Mrs. Quine. "Are you sure you're telling the truth?"

"Yes, ma'am."

"Well, what's this Tightface character like?"

He doesn't know how to say what she's like. He doesn't know anything about her. He can't tell them about the test or colored blocks or her strong, nervous touch; he can't tell them about the pictures of children on her refrigerator, how sometimes he imagines that he is one of them. "She's fake," he says. "She never leaves her apartment. I have to go see her every weekend. All she does is lie."

"That's terrible, Buddy," Mrs. Quine says.

"Poor Tuber!" Simon says. "We should kill her, too."

"Simon," Mrs. Quine says; then, "What do you mean, Buddy, all she does is lie?"

He hunches his shoulders, makes his face sharp, his voice a high-pitched, fruity warble. "Oh, grandmother. Everything is perfect! The flowers are perfect and the presents are perfect and the roast is perfect! And you are perfect, too!"

"Tightface," Simon growls, "don't you ever tell the truth?"

"Oh, I guess you could say I do. You can say one thing, and I can say another thing, and the thing you say can be just as true as what I say. Who can say if what you say or who can say if what I say or who can say if what anyone says...."

"Shut up!" Simon shouts, mock-throttling him. "Shut up!"

Buddy lets his head loll, making the death-croak, Simon's fingers warm around his neck. "Boys," Mrs. Quine says. "Be careful back there."

Simon lets go of him. Buddy slumps against his door. He knows they are watching him; but for a moment, he wants to be still. The hatred in him ebbs, like adrenaline. He can't think of what he's done; he hopes it will be enough. He opens one eye and looks out at the wall of clouds, framing a shot. He hasn't told them anything, he thinks; he hasn't told them what he's done to his mother, and what has happened to his father, and how his father — the real one, or the false one — has betrayed him. He hasn't told them what he really is — a monster, a madman.

∂∞∞

By the time they get to Gramma Liddy's, he's told Simon almost everything. All except the coiled sheets. All except the real truth; the real truth is still too shameful to tell. That morning, Mrs. Gray asks if he's had a blessed Christmas, peering at him over her glasses; then she asks why his shoes squish and his uniform is in such disarray. He sees Simon's jaw tighten, something no one else would have seen, or known what it meant, before he told her he stepped in a puddle. All day, Simon never left his side. It kept Sam away, and Simon told Gene to leave them alone. And when he saw Simon's taut, anxious face, he knew Simon's fear that he might tell what he'd seen at his house would keep his own secrets safe; and he watched Simon, his broad, straight shoulders, his bright blue eyes, the cleft at the base of his skull, the hunger like a fever in his limbs.

That afternoon, in the back seat of the golden car, they rehearse a new play: Tightface pours scalding soup down Buddy's throat, killing him. Then O.G. bursts through the door, and executes Tightface and his father. But it is not the same. In Simon's face, he sees real hate. Simon chops the air with his hands, signaling a guillotine; Buddy, as his father, slumps against the passenger door. As the car slows, then stops at Gramma Liddy's, Buddy closes his eyes, savoring and fearful of the moment when all doubt will be quelled, the coming moment of peace.

He opens his eyes. The back seat is empty. He lurches up, gathering his books and binder. Simon stands next to the car, his mouth opened in a half-smile.

At the far end of the block, a dark figure lumbers toward them. Alex raises his hand, and waves.

"Do you know him?" Simon says.

"Not really," Buddy says.

Simon squints at Alex, pulling him into focus.

"Let's talk to him," he says. "I've never talked to a Mexican."

Before Buddy can say anything — he doesn't know what to say; he doesn't know how he will explain Alex to Simon — Simon calls out to Mrs. Quine, already halfway across the lawn, telling Junior to wait until she gets there to ring the doorbell.

"Is he a good friend of yours, Buddy?" she says, peeking over her dark glasses.

He doesn't know which answer is right.

"Yes, ma'am," he says.

"I guess it's okay," she says. "Just don't be gone too long."

"Yes, ma'am," Simon says. "Go on," he says, to Buddy. "He's your friend."

As they come closer, Simon trails a little behind him. Alex smiles; but even from far away, Buddy can see his smile is stiff and uncertain.

Leave, Buddy says to him, silently. *Go home.*

Alex raises his hand. *"¿Cómo te va?"*

"Bien," Buddy says, before he can stop himself, and speak English.

"¿Está el Simón?" Alex says, nodding at Simon.

"Sí. No le digas nada de la película. No le digas nada de la máquina." Yes. Don't *tell him about the movie. Don't tell him about the camera.*

Alex's grin wavers. Simon jogs up next to Buddy, studying him.

"What did you say?" he says.

"Nihil," Buddy says. *Nothing.* Then, quickly, *"Non ei dici de movie. Non ei dici de camera."* Don't *tell him about the movie. Don't tell him about the camera.*

Simon screws up his eyes. Buddy can't tell if he's understood; but they are too close for him to say anymore.

Alex stops in the street, keeping very still, and holds out his hand.

"I'm Alex," he says.

Simon shakes his hand, holding himself still, too. He seems as small as he did when Buddy saw him reading alone in his room. But this is only a trick, Buddy knows. And Alex isn't really there, either; he's gone away, fading like he did when they walked past the whites' barking dogs. Only his dark eyes are still angry and vivid.

"Buddy's told me a lot about you," Alex says. "He says you're his friend."

A blush spreads up Simon's neck; Buddy tries to catch his eye, but Simon won't look at him. "Yes," he says. "I'm his friend."

"He says you go to school with him."

"St. Edward's is one of the best schools in the city. Where do you go?"

"Queen of Peace."

"That's a good school, too," Simon says.

"We should go," Buddy says.

Neither Alex nor Simon look at him. Buddy knows Alex wants to tell Simon about the movie, and he feels himself move toward Alex, to stop him. *Shut up,* a voice beside him says, silently. *Shut up, you stupid spic.*

Alex stares at him, as if he's heard what he thinks.

"We should go," Buddy says.

He turns and starts back to Gramma Liddy's; he knows that Simon is too afraid of Alex to stay behind. "Nice to meet you," Simon says, to Alex. "I'll see you soon."

Buddy looks back. Alex's stare is leveled on him. He tells himself that he is keeping Simon away from Alex to protect the movie, but he knows this is a lie. The hunger is an ache in his throat, a pain in his chest. He knows that Simon hates him, because of what he'd seen at his house that morning. If he can be alone with Simon, and see the face he's seen that morning, the face when Simon said he hated Mr. Quine, he will know what to do about everything, even Alex, and the Horse.

Simon stalks beside him. When he opens the front door, Mrs. Quine, sitting at the dining room table, turns from them, shielding her face with her hand. Gramma Liddy glowers at them, silently telling them to leave. Buddy starts to speak, but Simon looks through him, as he has on mornings Mr. Quine whips him, as if he doesn't know who he is. "Come on, mamma," he says. "Let's go."

17.

"That poor woman," Gramma Liddy says, after the Quines leave. Buddy stands near the front door, next to a tattered reading chair and a shelf of magazines. On the TV, a cartoon plays, the one where Elmer Fudd pretends to be a rabbit.

"I can't make heads or tails of what she's saying. It's all mixed up with her brand of religion. All I can tell is that her husband is the Devil."

She peers at him through the smoke that hangs over the dining room table, her blue eyes sharp behind her glasses.

"Do you see anything over there, Buddy? Anything that scares you?"

"No," he says. "It's fine."

"We haven't had a chance to catch up," she says. "Why don't I fix some tea?"

She pushes herself up out of her chair, and her arms tremble with the effort. He moves toward her, to help her, but stops himself.

"Can I go to Alex's?" he says.

She slowly lowers herself into her chair again. "How's your horse coming along? Is Simon going to be in it?"

"Maybe," he says.

"Buddy. We've worked very hard on our friendship with the Torreses. It's important for your mother. Do you understand?"

"Yes, ma'am," he says. "I better go."

He hurries down the street, his uniform pants still itchy and too-tight. Clouds roil above him like paint in water. He doesn't know what he will say to Alex; he doesn't even know if Simon is coming back.

He rings the doorbell, then stands in the yard, watching the curtains in Alex's window. The driveway is empty; Mr. Torres, at least, isn't there.

Alex opens the front door. "*Que pasa?*" he says.

"We can't tell him about the movie," Buddy says.

"*¿Porqué no?*"

Because we can't trust him, Buddy says, in Spanish.

Alex folds his arms over his chest. *When are we going to make the movie?* *Sundays,* Buddy says. *After he leaves.*

Alex studies him. Fat raindrops plat the grass, spattering Buddy's head. *Come inside,* Alex says, opening the door. *We can work on the new scenes.*

"I better get back," Buddy says, but doesn't move.

"¿Qué te pasa, hombre?" Alex says. *What's wrong with you, man?*

Behind the rain, Alex is a ghost. Or maybe he is a ghost, Buddy thinks, looking out at his friend. "Nothing," he says, turning from him.

∂>∽

On Saturday, he waits for his father in his room. The letter is secreted in a front pocket of his jeans. Since his father called Thursday, he's thought of what he will say: He will tell his father he's read the letter, and it's a bunch of crap. He will tell him he should just disappear.

He listens to his mother in the kitchen. Since Thursday, she's bustled around, cleaning the house, gathering force, it seems, like a hurricane. At mass, she's prayed through Father Peron's homily, and when Buddy was supposed to be doing his home-work, she stood at the window above the sink, whispering, her voice hissing and sharp. Her eyes, too, focused on the far-away place, have turned fierce, as if she is always expecting to see his father. But it is clear that his father hasn't told her about the letter; Buddy is afraid of what will happen when he does.

He goes to the hallway, where the smell of ammonia reaches from the kitchen, and touches the letter in his pocket, making sure it's there. His mother stands at the stainless-steel table, her back to him. She wears an old white blouse, denim skirt, and tennis shoes, like she had when she pulled up the honeysuckle. On dishcloths, the silver, and all the china from the china cabinet, is laid out in neat rows. Her shoulders shake, working at something in her hands.

He creeps into the kitchen and stands next to her. She squints at a fork in a bitter-smelling rag. "What are you doing?" he says.

"What does it look like?"

"Cleaning stuff."

"Very observant."

On top of the refrigerator, the moldering bread has vanished, and on her desk, the legal pads and unopened mail are gone. A kind of shock runs through him; he liked it better before. "What're you going to do?" he says.

She buffets the fork with the rag. "Daddy and I are going to talk."

"What're you going to say?"

"I won't know that until we talk. Don't worry about it, honey. I've already worried you too much."

She still doesn't look at him. He doesn't know, from how she's said it, if she's really sorry. She isn't blind, not exactly; she stares into that other place, the one where she's gone since Christmas. He touches the letter in his pocket, trying to remember what the horse has told him, the key to make things right. Each night, the horse stares down at him, trying to send a message, a clue to what he should do. But he can't think like that; he can't let himself believe in childish things.

"What's going to happen?" he says.

She lays down the fork; her face seems tired and fragile, and in it, he thinks, is the question, and an accusation he hasn't seen before.

"Nothing's going to happen, Buddy. No matter what happens between daddy and me, nothing will happen to us. I promise."

Outside, his father's car rumbles into the driveway.

"Go on," she says. "Daddy and I need to talk."

The gate latch clicks. His father passes outside the window, pale, haunted-looking, like was at Christmas.

"Go on," she says, her eyes fierce.

He retreats to the hallway, listening to the back door rattle, his heart pounding breath out of his chest.

What did you want to talk to me about? his mother says.

His father is silent.

I'm giving you one last chance, Jimmy. We can talk about this here, or we can talk about it in court. Nothing is worth what this is doing to us.

I'm sorry, his father says. It's my dad. He's sick. I think he's dying.

Oh, God, Jimmy, she says, after a moment. What happened?

Stroke. My mother found him the day after Christmas. They took him to Hermann. His pulse was sixty, seventy. Sunday, they finally did a CT scan. Massive stroke in the right hemisphere. Pulse was steady, about seventy. Still no response.

Monday, he woke up, but we couldn't move him. Tuesday, we took him home. Pulse is still weak. Mid-seventies. I don't know what's keeping him alive.

Buddy's skin tingles, imagining Grampa Turner motionless in his bed. For a moment, he forgets about everything else. But even in the hallway, he can feel the thickness of his mother's and father's voices in the kitchen.

I wish you'd told me, his mother says. I could've done something. Your mother must be run ragged.

She's fine.

Can I do anything? Bring groceries? Something?

She's fine, his father says, his voice tightening. We got someone in to help. Then, in a different voice, I'm sorry, Margot.

Don't worry about that now. You need to help your mother.

I want us to be happy, Margot. I want to make it right.

Hush, his mother says. We'll talk about that later. Go and see your son.

☞ ☜

On the freeway, his father keeps glancing at him. Buddy presses his forehead against the passenger window, watching railroad tracks and power lines, warehouses and vacant fields, flash past him in the gray winter day. He touches the letter, unsure he can trust what he sees in his father's face. His father — his real father, the one he's seen at Fort Polk, and when they ride bikes, almost the one he's seen in the movies — peeks out from behind his mask. He touches the letter in his pocket; he doesn't know, anymore, what he should do.

"Getting enough air?" his father says.

"Yes, sir," Buddy says. "I'm fine."

"I'm sorry about what happened at Christmas, Buddy. I shouldn't have said any of that. That was all just a bunch of excuses."

"It's okay, sir."

"No, it it's not. It's not okay. But I'm going to try and make it okay." His father glances at him, rubbing the steering wheel. "Did you give your mother that letter?"

"No, sir."

"Good." His father's grip relaxes. "You're a lot smarter than I am. What did you do with it?"

He hesitates, but only for a moment. "I tore it up, sir. Then I threw it away. In a trash can at school."

His father nods, staring ahead. Buddy looks at him: the stubble darkening his neck though it was not yet noon, the slight pad of baby fat under his chin, his baggy suit bunched around his shoulders, his pale, hairy, blue-veined hands; but he can't fit the pieces together, he can't tell which father he really is, and he knows it is because he is looking at his father through his own lie.

"My mother's pretty upset," his father says. "But don't worry about it. She's got other things on her mind."

"Yes, sir."

"I was thinking maybe we could ride our bikes. It's a nice, cool day to ride. What do you think? Think you'd like that?"

"Yes, sir," he says, not looking at him. "What are you going to do, sir?"

His father doesn't answer. "What are you going to do, sir?" he says.

His father stares ahead, his face rigid, trembling, almost his face at the track. "I don't know, Buddy," he says. "I don't know."

❧ ❦

When they reach the overpass to Gramma Turner's, his father exits downtown, and parks near his mother's hospital. Buddy follows him past the meaty-smelling cooling plant and the convent where the nuns who own the hospital live, thinking he should stop him, wanting to see what he will do. They slip up a back stairwell, into the laboratory, into the click and hum of cryostats and autoclaves, the smells of alcohol and reagents, the smells from the time before his father left.

Yolanda, at her microscope, looks up at them, and waves. "Jimmy Turner," she says. "I haven't seen you in a blue moon."

His father shakes her hand, takes a handkerchief from his pocket, touches his face; and behind it, his face seems to convulse. "Everything looks real good here, Mrs. Evans. Everything looks real clean. That Coulter looks brand new."

"The night shift does a pretty good job straightening things up. And you know between Sister Bert and your wife, no one can get away with sloppiness. We don't have anybody who knows these machines like you did, though, that's for sure."

His father nods, blushing, and puts his hand on Buddy's shoulder. "Thank you, Mrs. Evans," he says. "This is Buddy, my son."

Yolanda's smile wavers. "Of course I know Buddy. I've been knowing him since he was a little baby. How you doing, Buddy?"

"Fine, ma'am," he says.

"We're real proud of him," his father says. "He wants to make movies."

"Is that right?" Yolanda says, glancing from him to his father. "Are you sure I can't help you with anything, Jimmy?"

"I'm fine, Mrs. Evans." His father turns from her, and starts down the hallway. "I just wanted to check on a couple of things."

Buddy follows him past the window for Specimens and Requests, near the door they'd come in. Yolanda stands, watching them; Buddy looks away. His father heads toward the hallway to his mother's office. The door to Sister Bertille's office is open; she glances up at them; his father turns, hiding his face from her, as she rises to greet him.

"Jimmy," she says. "What a blessing. What brings you here?"

"Nothing, sister. I just dropped by to see the lab. Everything looks real clean. Everything looks real good."

Sister Bertille studies him. "You must come to lunch sometime, Jimmy. It's been far too long. Sister Paulinus and Sister Gregory ask after you. We all have so many questions about your new job."

His father touches his face with his handkerchief. "Yes, sister," he says. "That would be fine."

Sister Bertille's calm dark gaze moves over his father's face like a searchlight. "Very well, Jimmy. We all pray for you."

He follows his father down the hallway, past pictures of men in togas and ruffled collars dissecting corpses throughout the ages. He knows that Sister Bertille watches them, but he doesn't look back. They turn down another hallway where one wall is covered with sliding cabinet doors. His father opens one of the doors, his face suffused with grief, and takes out a cardboard box, and puts it in his coat pocket. He opens another door, takes out a larger box, and puts it under his arm. Buddy glances down the hallway, worried that Yolanda or Sister Bertille will appear. His father hands him an armload of boxes — sterile syringes, test tubes, surgical gloves, Buddy sees from their labels — then tips his head for him to follow. At the end of the hallway they push through a pair of swinging doors. Techs look up from their microscopes; his father waves at them, then opens a walk-in refrigerator and from a cardboard pallet begins to gather an armful of clear plastic pouches. Then he lifts the whole pallet in his arms, his face trembling, already the one at the track; and Buddy follows him out, past his mother's office, through the sliding-glass doors.

At Gramma Turner's house, his father ratchets the brake, then gets out, and loads boxes onto the pallet, which he balances on the lip of the trunk. Buddy stands next to him, waiting to help. The red brick house seems strange and small, as it did the day they snuck out the bikes; Buddy thought that he would never see it again.

Gramma Turner opens the kitchen door, peering out at them from the little porch, her hand on the doorknob, her helmet-hair gray and ragged at its edges. His father hefts the pallet, slides past her up the steps. Buddy tries to follow him, but Gramma Turner catches his wrist, steering him into the little room. Through the doorway to the den, he glimpses the woman, next to his grandfather's bed, turn to his father, small and frightened, as she was at Christmas. His grandfather stares at him, motionless; and Buddy looks away, ashamed of his own fear.

Gramma Turner sits him down on the day bed, his side touching hers, holding his books and binder on his lap. On the telephone table are a water glass, a can of Coke, packets of orange peanut butter crackers. She takes his hand, rubs his knuckles, worrying them like stones. Her eyes, behind her glasses, are rheumy and tired, and he pities her; but he can't let himself pity her, he thinks.

"It wasn't right, Buddy," she says, "what you and your daddy did at Christmas. It wasn't right, before, taking that camera. You know that, don't you?"

"Yes, ma'am."

From the den come his father's and the woman's voices, scissoring at each other in argument. Gramma Turner grips his hand. "We've got to help your daddy, Buddy. Right now, your daddy needs all the help he can get. And the best way to help him is to come live here where you belong, where you won't have to worry, and none of us will have to worry about any of this mess again."

He looks at her, trying to pretend she isn't real. He wants to tell her he has the letter; he wishes that she already knew, so he could say he lost it. "I'm sorry, ma'am," he says. "I don't know what you mean."

She studies him. "I'm worried about your daddy, Buddy. I'm worried about what he's going to do. I think you're worried about him, too."

"Yes, ma'am," he says, lowering his eyes.

"So I want you to think, Buddy," she says, giving his hand a little shake. "I want you to think very carefully. Gramma Turner's not going to be around forever, to help and protect your daddy and you. That's a hard thing for my little Buddy to think about, that his daddy might need so much help. But I want you to think about it, Buddy. I want you to think about what's really best for your daddy."

She doesn't know what she's talking about, he thinks; his father doesn't need any help. But his face burns with anger and shame.

"Yes, ma'am," he says.

She leads him through the living room, and he glimpses his grandfather's face again. Even from a distance, he can tell it has changed. He tries to feel sympathy for him, but can't; all he can feel is dread at its stillness.

Why do you have to be like this, Jimmy? the woman says. Why are you making it so difficult? All of this could be over, if you wanted it.

Maybe I like it this way, his father says. Maybe I like things to be difficult.

When they enter the den, the woman turns, covering her face with her hand. His father, next to her near the sliding glass doors, grimaces at Buddy, as if what is happening is a joke. The room smells of urine and dead skin. A plastic bag like one they took from the hospital hangs from a metal pole next to his grandfather's bed; a tube snakes into his arm, and another from under the covers on his bed. A machine blips in time to the jagged progress of a dot across a TV screen, and in the corner is another machine with metal cylinders, like a diver's oxygen tanks.

"Look who I brought to visit!" Gramma Turner says, gripping Buddy's hand, her voice false and bright.

The woman crosses the room and embraces him. Buddy lets his arms hang loose at his sides, makes himself as stiff as a corpse. Then she lets go of him, and holds his arms in her strong, nervous grip; and he sees a hard glint in her eyes, as if she can see the pleasure he felt, listening to her and his father fight.

Gramma Turner smoothes the covers on his grandfather's chest, touches his hand. "How're you doing, Bink? You about ready for your lunch?"

Grampa Turner looks up at her; Buddy thinks he means yes. His grandfather's gaze shifts to him. What Buddy saw in his face before was real; both sides of it are slack. The flesh on his forehead has shrunk, and on his neck, it hangs in folds as delicate as tissue. But his grandfather's eyes are still like dark fire.

"Why don't we go to the living room?" Gramma Turner says, to his father and the woman; then, to Buddy, "You and granddaddy can have a nice visit."

"Don't worry, daddy," his father says, as he leaves.

When they are alone, Buddy puts his hand on his grandfather's, then draws back; it is cold and rubbery, a fake hand at a joke shop. Grampa Turner watches him. And though Buddy can't yet hear him, he knows that his grandfather wants him to touch his hand. He puts his hand on his grandfather's again. Its coldness is like the coldness he felt outside the Quines'; and he tries to think of the coldness, and how alone he would feel if he were trapped inside it.

We can take care of him, his father says. I can get him everything he needs right here. I know what those places are like. He'll be septic in twenty-four hours.

I know this is hard, Jimmy, the woman says. It's hard on everyone. But a rest home would be safer, more efficient.

She's right, Jimmy, Gramma Turner says. We're trying to do too much.

"I'm sorry about the camera," Buddy says.

Be careful with it, Grampa Turner says, silently.

I know what you're trying to do, his father says. I'm sick of being efficient.

His grandfather's eyes shift to the living room, then back to him. *Tell the truth*, he says, silently. *It's the only way to help.*

A cold hand closes over Buddy's chest. "Yes, grampa," he says.

I haven't got much time, Grampa Turner says. *I want you to promise something.*

The cold hand tightens. "Yes, grampa," he says.

Don't let him hurt your mother. Don't let him hurt the Horse.

18.

On Monday, when he sees his father outside the school, haunted-looking in the swarm of children, of yellow and tartan, blue and white and brown, his first thought is that his father has come for the letter, that he's found out about it, somehow; then, he thinks that Grampa Turner has died, and he is afraid, remembering the coldness of his grandfather's hand, and ashamed he hasn't thought of that first.

After his father left that weekend, telling his mother he needed to get back to Gramma Turner's, his mother stood at the window above the kitchen sink, whispering, her voice sharp, chiding, cautioning herself against the hope that lit her face. Buddy didn't know what would happen to the woman; the question still beat in him, like his promise to Grampa Turner; but he carries what he saw in his father's face, his real father, inside his chest, a delicate, glass-spun globe.

He turns from the portico of the walkway above the yard where his father stood. Behind him, Gene snickers at a story Simon is telling, hugging himself, as if he's in pain. Since Simon met Alex, Gene has started hanging out with them again. Each day, Simon asks about Alex — how long has Buddy known him? did Alex teach him to speak Mexican? was he making a movie with him? — his voice light and bantering, letting Buddy know it's just a joke, though Buddy knows it isn't.

That week, they haven't done the play, the real play, because Mrs. Quine hasn't visited Gramma Liddy; but even if she had, Buddy doubts they would. He knows Simon hates him, because of what he saw at his house, and because he didn't tell him about Alex; and he watches Simon, his bright blue eyes, the cleft at the base of his skull, hating him, too, the hunger like a fever in his limbs.

He can't let his father see Simon; if he sees them, he would see what he'd told Simon about the woman. He can't let Simon see his father; he will see that what he has told him about the woman is true, and everything will be ruined.

"Let's go to the church," he says.

Gene glares at him. Simon eyes him, curious, scenting his fear.

"Why'd you want to do that, Turner?"

Buddy shrugs. In the yard below, his father has disappeared; soon, he will be coming up the stairs. "I don't know," he says. "It's faster."

Behind him, Sam slips out of the classroom, thumbs hitched in his belt, staring at them; it was something he did, Buddy thought, to show he wasn't afraid of them. "What are you going to do?" Simon says. "Are you and your friend going to ambush us?"

Simon's voice is false, more false than the one he uses in the car, than the one he uses when they were alone.

"What do you want to do, Turner?" he says. "Do you want to do the play?"

Buddy turns from Sam, blushing, and reaches for Simon's sleeve. "No," he says. "Come on. Let's go."

Simon recoils, cradling his arm against his chest. "Don't touch me. What's a-matter with you, Tuber? Are you gay?"

Gene leers at him. Brown-uniformed boys swarm into the hall. He can't let his father see Gene and Simon. He lurches from them, pushing through the boys, glancing back at Sam; and he believes that Sam knows what he thinks – that if his father calls out to him, he will pretend he doesn't know who he is.

Ahead, his father rises up the stairwell, tie loose at his collar, searching the boys in the hallway. Buddy pivots, turning back to Gene and Simon, who are still watching him. "Buddy?" his father says.

Around him, boys fall silent, masked and cautious at the approach of an adult. He keeps going, shoving through them, holding his books and binder against his chest.

"Buddy?" his father says.

He wedges himself through the boys, who stare at him, scandalized, amazed. His father touches his shoulder, and Buddy smells his clean smell, and sees the sadness in his face, which he knows, now, that he has caused. But he steels himself against this, too. "Buddy?" his father says. "Are you okay?"

"Yes, sir. I'm fine."

"Did you hear me?"

"No, sir. Is everything okay, sir?"

His father's eyes slide past him, avoiding his lie. "Everything's fine, Buddy. I came to see if I could give you a ride."

Gene and Simon watch him, bland and ghostly, nothing like who they really are; and Buddy is afraid that his father will see the moment of peace, and what he's done to Sam. "Are these your friends?" his father says. "Can you introduce me to them?"

They come forward — Gene, Simon, and Sam. Simon studies him furtively, blushing, tight-lipped. Gene grimaces at him. Sam stares at him, wide-eyed, no swagger in his step. "It's nice to meet you," his father says. "I haven't done a very good job of meeting Buddy's friends, but I'm going to do better, now."

The boys bow their heads, like they do when Mrs. Gray talks about her grandchildren; but there is no sign of mockery in their faces. Only Simon studies him evenly, a kind of tightness around his eyes.

"Sir?" he says. "Can I ask you a question?"

Buddy feels himself move toward Simon, to stop him; but Simon doesn't look at him. "Is it hard, sir," Simon says, "to be a doctor?"

Simon looks down at his hands, a blush rising on his neck; then he faces his father again. "I'm going to be a doctor, sir," he says.

His father smiles at Simon, not seeing the hardness in his stare. "It's not difficult, Simon. You've just got to work at it. The important thing is to want to help people." His father checks his watch, and his expression shifts. "Maybe we can talk about this later, Simon. Right now, I need to get Buddy home."

His father says goodbye to Gene and Sam. Simon watches him as he did before. Buddy can't tell what he is thinking. As he starts down the hallway, he tries to think of what his look meant. Boys still lurk, eyeing him, but the hallway is almost empty. Only a few more steps, and he will be safe.

"Sir?" Simon says. "What should I tell my mother?"

Buddy feels pulled up short, a rope inside his chest. His father glances at him, confused. "Is Buddy going to keep riding with us, sir?" Simon says.

"I don't know, Simon." His father looks at him, and his expression becomes tender, almost as when he'd looked at the woman. "Tell her we'll call her later."

Simon watches him evenly. Buddy can't tell what he is thinking. But beneath the face that Simon wore for his father is another face, almost like the one when he said he hated Mr. Quine; and he sees that Simon hates him, now, with a new hate, the bitter hate of betrayal. "Yes, sir," Simon says. "I'll tell her, sir."

᠀

On the freeway, his father leans over the steering wheel, staring ahead at a distant point, trying to get there faster, afraid it might disappear. He talks about what they need to do at his mother's house — spread the sand and tear down the fence; clean the heater and rewire off the main breaker and paint inside and out. When he asks about Buddy's friends — Oscar and Scotty and Greg — Buddy remembers the boys he made up at the woman's apartment, long ago; and he presses his forehead against his window, trying to escape his father's sadness, the question beating inside him like a pulse.

"None of that matters, Buddy," his father says. "Nothing matters, as long as we can be together. I couldn't see that before, but now I can."

His father watches him, rigid, ready to flinch, like he did at Fort Polk. Buddy turns back to his window. "Yes, sir," he says. "What are you going to do, sir?"

"I'm coming back, Buddy," his father says, as if he should already know. "What do you think, Buddy? Would you like that?"

Outside, the glass buildings downtown pivot, delicate and unreal, a miniature city, a movie set. He knows his father is trying to trick him. But he also knows that isn't true. "Yes, sir," he says. "That's fine."

"I'm sorry, Buddy."

Buddy keeps his face turned to his window. "Yes, sir," he says. "It's fine."

᠀

At his mother's house, the rotted fence, the oyster shells lining the walk, the statue of St. Francis — all of it looks delicate and strange. From his pocket, his father takes a square key, different from his mother's, and unlocks the kitchen door, then vanishes into the back of the house, telling Buddy that he needs to change his clothes. Buddy lays his books and binder on the steel-topped table in the kitchen, listening to coat hangers scritch in the closet in his room, imagining his father there, in his closet, in the formaldehyde smell, riffling through the clothes that he wore when he lived with them. His father is only a few feet from the letter. Buddy hopes he will find it. But if his father finds the letter, he doesn't know if he will come back. He picks up the phone on his mother's desk, listening to its dial tone. He doesn't know whom he should call; and hate flashes through him, so sharp and sudden it takes his breath.

He dials Gramma Liddy's number. The line buzzes; he squeezes his eyes shut, trying to send her a message to pick up. "Where are you?" she says.

"At home, ma'am. My dad took me home."

"God help us. Are you okay?"

"Yes, ma'am," he says. "I'm fine."

His father strides through the kitchen, wearing a white T-shirt, blue jeans, black leather shoes, as he did in the movies; he glances at Buddy, then slams the door open.

"I'm sorry, ma'am," Buddy says. "I better go."

Outside, the yard is empty, the gray sky and bare chain link fence and smell of the coffee plant silent and strange. For a moment, he imagines that he's only dreamed his father has brought him home; and a bright wave of panic overtakes him, and he zips up his thin school jacket, and hurries toward the driveway.

From the garage comes the clatter of metal on concrete and his father's muffled curses. He crouches among cardboard boxes and coiled Christmas lights and cans of paint, rooting inside a squat wooden cabinet, his back to Buddy; and Buddy remembers when the cabinet had been a house, a ship, a cave.

"Do you know where that crowbar went?" his father says. "The big one I got from Mr. Gage? We'll need it to tear down the fence."

"No, sir," he says.

His father pulls something loose, a dull, compact thud, and swears under his breath. "Who was that on the phone?"

His father will know if he lies to him; and he doesn't want to lie to him anymore. "Gramma Liddy, sir. I called to tell her I'm home."

A cascade of metal rains down inside the cabinet; his father curses sharply, stands up straight, wiping his forehead. "It's okay," he says. "We'll get to the fence later. Let's spread that sand."

From a dark corner, his father pulls two shovels, one long and square-bladed, one green and short, its blade folded against its neck — the foxhole shovel he bought for Buddy the first summer he was at Fort Polk.

"Remember this?" his father says, handing it to him.

"Yes, sir."

"Remember how to open it?"

"No, sir."

His father takes the shovel from him and twists a metal ring where the blade and handle met, and unfolds it, and Buddy tells himself that he should have remembered, that he would remember, next time.

His father hands him the shovel again. "Okay?" he says.

"Yes, sir."

"Okay," his father says. "Let's go."

Buddy follows him down the cement walk, past the statue of St. Francis. His father stands on the mounds of sand between Buddy's room and the garage, gazing out at the distant point. Behind the garage is the patch of yard where his mother buried the compost, and along the side of the house, a kind of alley between his mother's house and their neighbor's, where the ground is a slimy blackish-green, bare of grass. It is because of the water that collects there, his mother says, and the pecan tree in their neighbor, Mr. Knight's, yard, and the shadow from the second story Mr. Knight put on his house, a bubblegum-pink box which looks like a mobile home has landed on its roof. It was a miracle anything ever grew there, she says. But in the movie, Buddy knows, there was grass, rights where his father stands.

"We'll start down there," his father says, pointing his shovel at the alley. "We'll need something to carry the sand." He peers past Buddy at the trashcans along the cement walk. "What do you think? Do you think your mother'll mind?"

"No, sir," he says, knowing that she would.

They dump the garbage and drag the stinking trashcans back to the sand, trampling the ivy around St. Francis; and Buddy wonders what will happen when his mother comes home, whether she will look at his father as she did when she stood at the window in the kitchen, her face lit with hope. He hopes she will, and then he is afraid that she will; and then, he doesn't know what to hope, anymore.

With the point of his shovel, his father shows him how to cut hatchwork patterns in the grass that has grown over the sand. They set to work. His father drives in his shovel, his face already flushed, beaded with sweat. Except for the moan of freight trains and tinny music from passing cars, the chuff of their shovels is the only sound in the yard. They fill both trashcans, then drag them to the far end of the alley and dump the sand in the shallow standing water. The trashcans' thin metal handles bite into Buddy's fingers, his shoes are caked with mud, the cold air and heat inside his jacket dizzies him. He tells himself after the next shovelful, after the next load of sand, he will ask his father what will happen to the woman. But each moment passes, deepening the silence, and is gone.

When they've built a mound of sand at the end of the alley as tall as Buddy's waist, his father says they can start spreading it. His T-shirt is pink with sweat. He tips the blade of his shovel, and they spread the sand like pale brown icing, painting the ground in smooth, circular waves. It is important, his father says, to angle the sand, so that water will drain into the front yard, and the sand will stay there, permanent.

And in the cold and silence and smell of the coffee plant, the yard seems like only what it is — a memory, and a movie, all at once — as if no time has passed, as if he can catch the moment in the movie when his father disappeared. He wants to tell his father what he's seen at the Quines, and that each time he looks at Alex, he thinks the word, *spic*, and that he is worried about the Horse. He wants to tell him about Grampa Turner's movies, and his mother weeping alone in her room, and to ask him why she closed her door on him at Christmas. But when he starts to speak, it is as if he reaches out, and touches the sheet of glass.

Dusk settles in the yard. His father urges him on, telling him that if they hurry, they can finish before his mother comes home. He carries the trash cans back to the mounds of sand, and begins to dig, and Buddy follows him, slipping in the muck, the question still beating inside him like a pulse.

Before they've filled the trashcans again, the headlights of his mother's car sweep through the gap in the fence. His father stands holding his shovel, his face rigid in the glaring white light. His mother's headlights dim, her door clunks shut, the gate swings open. She moves toward them, a swift, white shape in the dusk.

"What happened?" she says. "Is it your father? Is he alright?"

"He's fine," his father says, laying his shovel on the ground. "Everything's fine. Buddy and I are spreading the sand."

His mother stops near the garage; even in the darkness, Buddy can see her sharp gray eyes flicker over the garbage bags, the trampled ivy, the trashcans.

"What are you doing?" she says.

His father moves toward her, palms uplifted, hands at his sides. "I'm coming back, Margot," he says.

His mother looks down at her purse. Her mouth tightens; she shakes her head, once. "Are you out of your mind? My mother is beside herself. How did you get in here? How did you get in the garage?"

"Listen to me, Margot," his father says, moving toward her, wincing. "I'm coming back. We won't need to deal with your mother anymore. I can fix up this house and buy you a new one. You can keep this one and rent it out or sell it, whatever you want. I can give you everything I promised."

"Answer me," his mother says. "How did you get in here?"

His father stares at her, his hands at his sides, his fists clenched. "Spares," he says. "Last summer, I got spares."

"Give them to me."

His father stares at her, his mouth slightly open, his face lost in the darkness. "I've got clothes in there, Margot. All my clothes are in there."

"Give them to me," his mother says, holding out her hand.

Slowly, his father digs a set of keys from the front pocket of his jeans, and puts them in her hand. "Now leave," his mother says.

"I'm coming back, Margot."

"Not like this. Not coming in here and tearing everything up and dragging him into the middle of it. That's not how it's going to work, not this time. Go home and be with your mother, where you're needed. You can come back later and we can talk. I can't talk to you when you're like this."

"Like what?" his father says.

His mother looks down at her purse. His father draws closer to her, bowing his head, and touches her arm. "What am I like?" his father says.

Buddy turns away from them. When he looks up again, his mother holds her hand against his father's chest.

"Please, Jimmy," she says. "Please just go."

His father comes toward him, and presses him against his sweat-damp shirt; and Buddy closed his eyes, listening to his father's heart pound inside the cage of his chest.

"I'm sorry, Buddy. I'll see you soon. We'll finish spreading that sand."

After the garage door rolls shut and the padlock clicks and the sound of his father's car has faded, his mother stands near the statue of St. Francis, watching the driveway. The yard is dim and still, and streetlights flicker in the dark trees beyond. She turns to him, covering her mouth with her hand.

"Are you okay, sport?"

"I'm fine."

"Your poor father," she says, turning from him again.

He knows that she is lying; he knows that she has made his father pitiful. He wishes a sheet of fire would cut through the yard; he wishes she would disappear. But the questions still pulse, there, in the darkness: What will happen when his father comes back; what has happened to the woman.

19.

That Wednesday, as they drive down Gramma Liddy's street, Mrs. Quine peeks up at him over her glasses in the rearview mirror. Since he saw Mr. Quine hit her, she hasn't asked about his father or Gramma Turner. The next morning, his mother dropped him off, and Mr. Quine glanced up at him over his newspaper, but didn't speak to him. Mrs. Quine didn't say anything to him either, then, though she looked at him differently, now; in the sadness that weighted her mouth, and the weariness that shadowed her eyes, he thought there was also a share for him.

"Buddy?" she says. "Have you heard from your father again?"

Simon, next to him in the back seat, keeps his eyes on his history textbook, *The Roman Warriors*. Since his father picked him up, Simon has watched him with a wariness, and a kind of respect; they haven't done the play, even in the car, anymore, but each day, Buddy still hoped they would.

"I'm sorry, Buddy," Mrs. Quine says. "I'm not trying to be nosey. I just want to know how you're doing, if you're still going to be riding with us, you know?"

"Yes, ma'am," he says.

"So what do you think? You think you're going to keep riding with us?"

"Yes, ma'am. I think so."

"I guess that Tightface character's not around anymore, though?"

Simon's eyes skitter up from his book. Buddy turns to his window; he can't let them see that he doesn't know.

"No, ma'am," he says.

"I'm sorry, Buddy," Mrs. Quine says; and he heard in her voice that she really was. "I'm sorry. That wasn't very Christian."

He leans forward between the seats, not looking at Simon. Junior gapes up at him, huddled against the passenger door. All week, something has itched him. He knows he has to ask it, that asking it might send a message to his father; but he doesn't know if asking will be a mistake.

"Ma'am?" he says. "Please don't tell my mother. It's a secret."

Mrs. Quine stiffens. "Of course not, Buddy," she says, her voice tinged with adult distaste. "Of course I won't."

Simon, smiling, meets his eyes; and Buddy knows he's made a mistake.

Mrs. Quine pulls up at Gramma Liddy's, then sits, touching the keys in the ignition, biting her lip, like she did when she was thinking. Each day, she asks Buddy about Gramma Liddy. "Just for a minute," she says, as if to herself.

Junior springs up, and unlatches his door.

"Just for a minute," she says, warningly. "I just want to check on Mrs. Liddy."

Buddy gathers his books and binder, imagining the bare green walls in Grampa Liddy's room, the soft, dusty bed. At night, he lays in bed, waiting for his father's call, replaying the moment he let the robe fall open, imagining Simon's warmth and weight; and he knows it's a kind of craziness, and he has to keep it hidden.

Simon holds himself stock-still.

"Mamma?" he says. "Can we visit Buddy's friend?"

"I guess that's okay," Mrs. Quine says. "Is he a good friend of yours, Buddy? Have you known him a long time?"

He doesn't know what to say; he doesn't know which answer would make Mrs. Quine think less badly of him than she already does.

"Yes, ma'am," he says.

"He's not mixed up in one of those gangs, Buddy, is he?"

"No, ma'am."

Mrs. Quine bites her lip. "I guess it's okay. Just don't be gone too long, Simon. And play nice. Mexicans are good people, but you don't want to upset them."

"Yes, ma'am," Simon says; then, in a different voice, "Be careful, mamma."

Mrs. Quine pushes her glasses over her eyes; and Buddy knows Simon means she shouldn't talk to Gramma Liddy about Mr. Quine.

"I'll be fine, Simon," she says. "Don't worry about me."

Simon stalks down the street toward the freeway, toward Alex's house. Buddy jogs up next to him, arms and legs weighted with lead, as if he is in a dream; he is afraid of what Simon will do.

"What are you doing?" he says.

"I'm going to visit your friend, Tuber. I'm going to ask him to be in our movie."

"You can't."

Simon stares ahead, his mouth a tight line. "Why not, Tuber? I bet you're lying. I bet you're already making a movie with him."

Buddy watches him, trying to understand how he knew.

"You can't," he says.

Simon smiles at him. He didn't know about the movie, Buddy saw; but now, he does. "What if I don't show you where he lives?"

Simon shakes his head, as if sadly; and Buddy knows that he will show him where Alex lived; it is a dream where everything slips away from him.

"What are you going to do?" he says.

"Nothing, Tuber," Simon says, annoyed, somehow hurt, though Buddy knows this is only a lie. "I'm not doing anything. I just want to be in your movie."

Mr. Torres' white truck is in the driveway. In the back yard, Ysrael barks in his cage. The house's yellow vinyl siding, its skirt of rock and mortar, embarrasses him, as if it was his own house. Before they reach the front door, Alex opens it, ghostly, unsmiling. "*Hola,*" he says. "*¿Qué tal?*"

"*Nada,*" Buddy says. "*No le digas nada.*" Nothing. Don't tell him anything.

"Hi," Simon says, in his false, bantering voice. "It's nice to see you again. I'd like to know about your movie."

Buddy glances up at Alex, but Alex doesn't look at him.

Shut up, the voice beside him says, silently. *Shut up, you stupid spic.*

"Sure," Alex says, to Simon.

ھ∽

Simon sits at the picnic table, reading the script, his lips moving almost silently. Leaf-patterns, and winter sunlight through the orange tree above him, shift on his back, on the blonde furze at the base of his skull. Alex and Buddy stand next to the table, a few feet away. All of them – Alex, in his trenchcoat; Buddy and Simon, in their thin school jackets – have stuffed their hands in their pockets against the cold. Ysrael circles the table, sniffing at Simon, who reaches out, not taking his eyes from the script, and touches his head. When they came through a side gate, Alex let Ysrael out of his cage. Ysrael bounded toward them, barking at Simon; and Simon, hesitating, not looking at them, reached down and rubbed Ysrael's neck, talking to him in his sing-song voice. Alex said they had to stay outside because his father was inside, working. Buddy knew that wasn't true; he knew Alex didn't want Simon to come inside because he didn't want him to see the drawings. He's glad; he doesn't want Simon to see the drawings, either, or the couch where they'd watched the three o' clock monster movie, or the picture of Mrs. Torres. He's glad that Alex doesn't trust him.

Now, watching Simon, he remembers a birthday party there long ago, a piñata in the orange tree, the clamoring circle of girls and boys; and a bright wave of panic rolls over him. *No le digas de la máquina,* he says. *Don't tell him about the camera.*

"¿Porqué no?" Alex says.

Simon's shoulders tense.

"Just don't," Buddy says. "He can hear us."

Alex's dark eyes flicker over him, his mouth tight with distaste. *"¿Porqué te preocupas tanto por lo que el puede oír?"* Why do you care so much what he can hear?

Simon closes the notebook, and regards Buddy narrowly, as if he isn't sure, anymore, who he is. "It's cool," he says.

"Cool," Alex says. "Which part do you like?"

"The Spider."

Alex shakes his head, grinning. "That's not real, man. It's a drawing."

"You mean it's a car*toon?*" Simon says.

Alex's grin fades. "Part of it is," he says, cautiously.

"How's it going to work? With the real parts and the drawings?"

"We should go," Buddy says.

"What's wrong with you?" Alex says, turning to him again. "If I want to tell him about the movie, I'll tell him."

Alex explains to Simon how they will make the movie: the live action, the storyboards, the blue screen mattes; and though it sounds as strange as Buddy has feared, like an enormous, awkward flying machine that will never fly, Simon listens patiently; and when Alex is finished, Buddy sees no mockery in Simon's face, but something worse, what he saw when his father picked him up, the bitterness he saw before, the sharp, bitter hate of betrayal.

"Do you have a camera?" Simon says, to Alex.

"No," Buddy says.

Simon doesn't look at him. "How are you going to make a movie?"

"I don't know," Alex says.

"Where are the drawings? Can I look at them?"

"We should go," Buddy says.

Alex turns to Buddy, his head bowed, flexing his fists in his pockets. *What's wrong with you, man?* he says, in Spanish, in a low, even voice. *First you tell me he can't be in the movie and now you bring him over here and I have to lie to him and look like an asshole. What's going on?*

Simon eyes them, grinning, unsure.

We can't trust him, Buddy says.

Why not? Alex says, moving toward Buddy, drawing his fists from his pockets. *Don't lie to me. Don't feel sorry for me, man.*

The back door opens. Mr. Torres pokes his head outside, smiling stiffly. "How are you boys doing?" he says.

"*Bien, papa,*" Alex says, stuffing his hands back into his jacket.

"*Bien, senor,*" Buddy says.

Simon rises, bland, innocent, yielding, a face he wore for adults; and Buddy sees that he is afraid of Mr. Torres, and he is glad of this, too.

Mr. Torres shakes Simon's hand. "You must be Simon. Alex says you go to school with Buddy. Do you live near here?"

"Dad," Alex says.

"Yes, sir," Simon says, uncertainly. "Telephone and Six-Ten, sir."

Mr. Torres nods, smiling. "That's a long way to drive to school. Why don't you go to Queen of Peace?"

"Dad," Alex says.

Simon looks at Alex, blushing, slit-eyed. "I don't know, sir," he says.

"I'm just curious," Mr. Torres says; then, to Buddy and Alex, in Spanish, "*¿Qué pasa aquí? ¿Qué están discutiendo?*" *What's going on? What are you arguing about?*

"*Nada, papá,*" Alex says. "*Está bien.*"

Mr. Torres eyes them. *Don't speak Spanish around him,* he says. *It's rude.* Then, to Alex, *Don't fight in front of him. Don't let him see that. Okay?*

Mr. Torres looks at Buddy, and Buddy knows that he can see inside him, to his craziness, and the hollow ache that he feels for Simon.

Mr. Torres shuts the door. Simon still watches the door, his eyes narrowed with the bitterness Buddy saw before, but sharper.

"Let's do a scene," Buddy says.

Alex glances at him, surprised. Buddy's surprised, too, but it seems right; he is sick of everyone seeing inside him, thinking that everything is his fault.

"Let's do the scene when Hugh's captured," he says. "We can use the cage."

"My dad built that cage," Alex says. "If we hurt it, he'll get mad."

"We won't hurt it," Buddy says. "I promise."

"Who's going to do it?" Alex says.

"He is," Buddy says, nodding at Simon.

Simon studies him, narrow-eyed, suspicious. Then he smiles at Buddy, as if they share a secret; and Buddy smiles back, hating him.

He starts toward the cage. Ysrael follows, sniffing at him. Alex tries to catch his eye, but Buddy won't look at him.

The cage is a squat, sturdy wooden frame in a far corner of the yard, bolstered with cross-beams and corner wedges, covered in a thick, chicken wire mesh. For as long as Buddy can remember, it has been there, first to keep chickens, and then when the chickens died, to keep Ysrael when he tried to dig under the fence. He looks toward the sky, searching for the horse; he looks at the spine of chain-link fences that runs down the block, the yard next door where two beautiful Anglo girls keep rabbits and chickens, the yard behind filled with rose bushes tended by an old woman they never saw; and something catches at him, telling him to stop, but he can't, not yet; and he doesn't know what to think of it, his craziness, his hard-heartedness.

Ysrael circles the cage, whimpering and barking. Simon ducks into it, then turns, bent double, glancing up to face the door; Buddy smiles at him, and swings the door shut. "Lock it," he says.

"No," Alex says.

"Come on," Buddy says. "It'll be better. It'll be more realistic."

Alex studies him. Simon studies him, too; and Buddy smiles at him again, letting him know it's just a joke. "Come on," Buddy says. "He won't hurt it. I promise."

Alex keeps looking at him, asking the same, silent question; and finding no answer, turns from him, and takes a padlock from his coat pocket, then closes his fingers over it, as if he was about to put it back again. Then he snaps it onto the hasp of the latch on the cage. Ysrael barks, once, sniffing at the lock.

"Okay," Alex said. "Do the scene."

Simon closes his eyes, raises clasped hands. "Ghost Horse!" he cries, his face twisted in mock-fear, mock-prayer. "Ghost Horse! Please help!"

Simon is trying to make fun of the movie. But he isn't, not really, Buddy thinks. In the cage, he is as small as he was in the room, in the field; he is only making fun of himself. "Ghost Horse!" Simon cries. "Ghost Horse! Please help!"

"Never!" Buddy says. "You can go to Hell!"

Simon peeks at him, grinning, unsure; he closes his eyes, and reaches out like a sleepwalker, and threads his fingers through the mesh; he shakes the cage, his eyes squeezed tightly shut. "Who do you think you are?" Buddy says, leaning closer. "You think you're better than that dog?"

Simon shakes the cage, fingers red at their tips, bone-white where the wire cut into them, loosening staples from the wooden frame. Alex takes a key from his coat pocket, and bends down to unlock the cage. Buddy touches his arm. Alex watches him. Buddy smiles at him; but Alex watches him as if he doesn't know who he is.

We need to get him out, Alex says.

Just wait, Buddy says.

We need to get him out. He's hurting the cage.

Just wait. You'll see.

Simon yanks at the mesh, barking the words, until they are no longer words, just noise, his face twisted, a clenched fist, tearing mesh from the staples. Buddy presses his forehead against the mesh. He will punish Simon. Only a moment more, he knows, and he will see Simon's true face, the face he'd seen when Simon said he hated Mr. Quine; and he wishes that he could keep Simon there, inside the cage, forever.

"Who do you think you are?" he says. "You better find some other way to get your pin money! You better get those kids under control!"

Simon's eyes snap open; he shakes the cage, staring at him, his teeth bared, as if he would kill him.

The screen door slaps shut. Mr. Torres marches toward them across the yard. *What are you doing?* he says, in Spanish.

Alex shoves Buddy aside, fumbles with the lock.

I'm sorry, papa. I'm sorry. I didn't know.

Mr. Torres pushes past them; in one, swift motion, he unlatches the door. Simon lurches forward, staring at Buddy; and Buddy knows that he can see what he wished.

What are you doing? Mr. Torres says, pulling him from Simon. *Have you gone crazy? What are you doing to this bad little one?*

₧₨

Mrs. Quine told Mr. Torres that she was very sorry. She was sure Simon meant no disrespect; she herself, she said, had only the deepest respect for his people. Mr. Torres stood in Gramma Liddy's living room, smiling rigidly; he told Mrs. Quine and Gramma Liddy the boys locked Simon in the dog cage, and Simon got frightened, he thought, and went a little wild. Gramma Liddy glared at them from the dining room table. Junior watched from the couch, gaping at Alex and Mr. Torres. Alex stood near the front door, his head bowed, almost invisible. Simon wore the same, grim, half-sleeping expression he did on mornings he hit Junior, knowing Mr. Quine would whip him. Neither he nor Alex looked at Buddy. Buddy listened to the adults' talk from far away. He knew he should be sorry, but he wasn't, not really; he was only afraid that Simon wouldn't come to Gramma Liddy's again. It didn't make sense, when he mocked him, when he wanted to keep him in the cage forever.

After Alex and Mr. Torres left, Mrs. Quine looked — he was sure, and Simon looked at him as if he can see his craziness. Then Mrs. Quine and Gramma Liddy looked away from him, as if something else was in the room, something they knew but wouldn't name, as if Mr. Torres was still there, watching them with his dark, unsmiling gaze. "I'm sorry, Mrs. Liddy," Mrs. Quine said.

Gramma Liddy sat at the dining room table, her mouth bitterly set. "I'm sorry, Mrs. Liddy," Mrs. Quine said. "I didn't know they would do that."

Gramma Liddy didn't answer her. Mrs. Quine grabbed Simon's arm and pulled him toward her and told him to apologize. Simon did as he was told, the tips of his ears bright red, his hard eyes downcast. Then Mrs. Quine told Gramma Liddy that she would make sure Mr. Quine heard about what happened, and when Gramma Liddy still said nothing, Mrs. Quine, hesitating, turned her weary, beautiful face from Gramma Liddy, told her again that she was sorry. Then she was herding Simon and Junior out the door; and now Buddy was alone with Gramma Liddy in the dim, quiet room.

"Come here," Gramma Liddy says.

Buddy stops in the door to the hallway, half-in, half-out of the living room. The light through the slats in the blinds on the French doors is deep orange, the rest of the house dark, except for the lamp on the dining room table, and the TV, which still plays, as it has the whole time Mr. Torres was there.

"Turn that off," she says.

He turns off the TV and sits across the corner of the table from her in the creaky, straight-backed chair. Smoke from her cigarette wreathes up through bars of light from the French doors; her eyes, behind her glasses, are fierce and sharp.

"Why did you let Simon go over there?" she says.

"I don't know, ma'am. He didn't do anything."

"If you mean he didn't call Alex a wetback or a spic, he didn't have to. His behavior said more than enough. And you let it happen."

"Yes, ma'am," he says, looking down at the table. "I'm sorry, ma'am."

"Mrs. Quine's very sorry. Everyone's very sorry, but it doesn't do any good." She leans closer, pressing his hand with hers, trying to send a current between them. "I know your father says he's coming back. And I know your mother thinks he deserves another chance. Everything in your life right now is telling you to be like Simon Quine. But you are not like him, Buddy, and if you trick yourself into believing you are, you'll have lost everything – you'll have lost who you really are."

She grips his hand, her gaunt face close to his. He ducks away from her, looking at a cigarette burn in the tablecloth. She doesn't know what he's done to Simon, he thinks; she doesn't know who he really is. And thinking this, he watches her, and himself, from far away, as if he is in a movie.

"Can he come back?" he says.

"Who?" she says.

"Simon."

She keeps hold of his hand, watching him differently, now, as he knew she would. The front door opens. His mother stands in the dark living room in her white uniform, glancing from him to Gramma Liddy. "What?" she says.

"Simon Quine had a tantrum. At Mr. Torres' house. In the dog cage."

His mother slumps into the reading chair by the door, covering her face with her hand. "Oh, no," she says, peeking out at Buddy through her fingers. "That poor boy is crazy. We've got to find you another ride."

"He wouldn't need a ride," Gramma Liddy says, "if he went to Queen of Peace."

"Mother," his mother says, shielding her face again; then, to Buddy, "How could you do this? What were you thinking?"

He can't tell them what he was thinking; he can't tell them that he knows that he is crazy. "I don't know," he says.

"You better figure it out," his mother says.

The doorbell buzzes. His mother heaves herself up, but Buddy lurches from his chair, knowing who it will be.

Behind the screen door, Alex floats like a phantom. Ysrael pants next to him, pale in the dark blue light.

"Alex?" his mother says. "How are you, honey?"

"Won't you come in for a minute?" Gramma Liddy says. "I've got some of that pound cake you like. I can fix some tea."

"Thank you, ma'am," Alex says, looking at Buddy. "We ate."

When Buddy closes the door behind him, Alex's expression shifts. He takes his fist from his coat pocket, looks down at the grass, as if deciding what he should do. Then he hits Buddy's shoulder, hard, pivoting him sideways.

Buddy holds his arm, which feels loose in its socket, glad of the pain.

Spic, the voice beside him says.

Alex punches his other shoulder, turning him again.

Wetback, the voice says. *Nigger.*

Alex studies him, his brow knit, as if he can hear what he is thinking; and Buddy thinks of how he cried for no reason and punched kids flat.

"What's wrong with you, man?" Alex says.

"I told you. We can't trust him."

"No, man. With you. What's wrong with you?"

Buddy doesn't know how to answer him. He can tell him that his father is coming back, about his craziness and hard-heartedness. He can tell him that he doesn't know if the woman is really gone; but he knows that all of this is a lie. The truth is what he feels for Simon, the hatred, and the hollow ache in his chest. Alex watches him, waiting for him to speak, then turns from him, and starts down the street; and Buddy stands, watching them go, until even Ysrael has faded.

20.

He finds the first drawing in his Latin textbook, *The Approach to Latin*, in study hall the next day. At first, he thinks the extra thickness wedged between the pages might be a love note; he's heard Sam and some of the other boys talk about them, even seen the pieces of paper folded in clever shapes. But at the same time, he knows that isn't what it is. In the desk in front of his, Simon holds himself very still. Only the movement of muscles on the sides of his neck, and a faint, skittering whisper, tell Buddy he is reciting his homework, and Buddy knows that he is listening.

He takes the square of paper from his binder and unfolds it, keeping an eye on Mrs. Gray, who sits at the front of the room, grading tests. Simon keeps perfectly still, a book opened in front of him, the tips of his ears dark red. At first, Buddy sees nothing, only vague shapes. Then the shapes become figures with gaping mouths and blunted limbs and huge, goggling eyes, pressing into each other from behind, as if to devour one another; he has seen them before, he knows who they are, he is not surprised – Tightface, O.G., Buddy, Buddy's Mother, Buddy's Father.

Simon is silent. All around them, boys are reading, finishing their homework, their heads cradled on folded arms. The paper is worn and dirty, passed through many hands. Buddy wants to reach out and snap Simon's neck; then the hollow ache catches inside his chest. He knows he's let something loose. He can't let Mrs. Gray find it; he can't let his mother see it. He looks at the drawing again: The figures are nothing like who they are supposed to be; but their ugliness seems truer, somehow, as if Simon has seen the craziness inside of him, and made it real.

Slowly, quietly, his face burning with anger and shame, he tears up the paper, then goes to the trashcan at the front of the room, clutching the pieces in his fist. Simon stares at his book. Gene grimaces at him; and here and there, boys watch him, waiting to see what he will do. "Mr. Turner?" Mrs. Gray says, peering at him over her glasses. "Do you wish to make an announcement?"

The boys stir, curious, tittering. Buddy stares at Simon; but Simon keeps his eyes on his book. "No, ma'am," he says, and lets the paper drop into the trashcan.

જ્જ

That afternoon, while they wait outside the church, Simon talks about the history test that week on the Gracchan Reforms, and the chapter they have to read in *The Pilgrim's Progress*. He jokes about their teachers, smiling, inching closer, daring him, Buddy thinks, to say something about the drawing.

"When are you going to bring your camera?" Simon says.

"I don't know," Buddy says.

"Don't you want to make our movie?"

"I don't know."

Simon edges closer, but when he speaks, it is in the same light, bantering voice as before. "I bet you don't even have a camera. I bet it's all a lie."

"No, it isn't," Buddy says.

"Then why don't you bring it?"

A car approaches, but it wasn't Mrs. Quine's. "Why don't you bring it?" Simon says, clutching his arm.

Buddy shrugs him off. "Maybe I don't want to."

Simon studies him, his brow knit, as if Buddy has hurt him. Then he reaches up, so swiftly Buddy doesn't see him, and presses his thumb into the hollow of his neck. Buddy twists from him, but Simon holds him, digging his thumb deeper. Then Simon shoves him away, and Buddy covers his neck with his hands; but he can still feel Simon reaching down inside him.

"When are you going to bring it, Tuber?"

"Soon," Buddy says. "I promise."

When the golden car pulls up, Mrs. Quine glances at him in the rearview mirror, as she did that morning, as if she isn't sure, anymore, if she wants him there.

"Are you okay, Buddy?" she says. "You look strange."

Simon stares straight ahead. "Yes, ma'am," Buddy says. "I'm fine."

જ્જ

Someone bangs outside on the kitchen door. It's the Ghost Horse, thundering his hooves; it's a madman, swinging his axe. It is his father's empty suit; but his father, in his white T-shirt and blue jeans, is inside, getting his gun, to protect them. Then his mother's slippered footsteps pad toward the kitchen, and Buddy wakes, remembering that his father isn't there. He rolls over inside his blankets' warm cocoon and looks out his window. His father stands on the porch, holding a white paper bag. Then he raises his fist and bangs again in a steady beat that says he isn't leaving.

The wooden floor is icy under Buddy's feet. He pulls on a pair of uniform pants and snatches a white T-shirt off the reading chair and hurries to the hallway, shivering, worried that his father has somehow seen the drawing, hoping, even if he is only his other father, that he can save him.

No, his mother says. Not like this. Not at six thirty in the morning when I have to go to work and he has to go to school. You could have called me. You can come back later and we can talk and you're not going to set foot in this house again until we do.

I thought you wanted me to come back, his father says, his voice hard and strange, like it was at Fort Polk. What am I supposed to think you want?

I want you to treat me with respect.

Buddy rounds the corner into the dining room. In the kitchen, in her housecoat, his mother wheels on him, squinting, stricken.

"Go back to bed," she says. "Daddy and I need to talk."

In the darkness, his father smiles at him, raising the white paper bag. "I brought us some hamburgers," he says.

"Don't, Jimmy," his mother says. "Don't do this."

"They're good hamburgers," his father says. "I got them at that place we used to go down by the hospital. I thought I could give you a ride."

In the darkness, his father's smile is sickly and fearful, a ghost's. The smell of mustard and pickles is like the smell of alcohol and formalin at the lab; and Buddy knows he has to go with him, that now is his chance.

ॐ∽

When they hit the freeway, it's almost empty. Smokestacks of refineries blink like candles against the sunrise. After school, his mother said, his father is to take Buddy to Gramma Liddy's and drop him off. Do not speak to her, she said. Do not collect two hundred dollars. Do not pass Go. She's upset enough as it is. His father said he wouldn't bother her; he told her he would wait with Buddy until the school opened, and pick him up that afternoon.

Before they left, his mother crouched down, and peered at Buddy, blinded by worry and love. Are you sure you want to do this, sport?

Yes, he said. I'm sure.

"How's your hamburger?" his father says.

The hamburger is delicious, tart and vinegary, just like he remembers it.

"It's good, sir."

"Good." His father stares ahead, rubbing the steering wheel. "Your mother's pretty mad at me, isn't she, Buddy?"

"Yes, sir."

"You haven't told her anything else, Buddy, have you?"

The hamburger sticks in his mouth. He turns to his window, gripping his door handle, and a cold wave of anger rushes through him. "No, sir," he says.

His father is quiet. "I'm sorry, Buddy. I'm sorry I asked you that. But do you know where your mother put those keys?"

The keys are in a milky white glass bowl in the cabinet above his mother's desk in the kitchen. Buddy saw her put them there after his father left.

"No, sir," he says.

His father nods, staring ahead. "We won't need them to fix the fence and spread the sand. But we're going to have to get inside to re-do the wiring and clean the wall heater. Do you think you could find them?"

Buddy presses his forehead against his window. Outside, the glass buildings downtown move past like cardboard cutouts. "I'll try, sir."

His father is quiet again. "I'm sorry, Buddy. I'm sorry I'm asking you to do all this. But we've got to show your mother we're serious. We've just got to keep going, then we can forget that any of this ever happened."

⁓∾

When they pull up at the school, the lights in the front office are lit. His father says he will wait with him until school starts, but Buddy tells him he needs to study for a Latin test. His father embraces him, telling him that he loves him. Buddy pulls away, mumbling that he loves him, too, and gets out, glad to breathe the cold morning air, and climbs the sweaty-smelling stairs to Mrs. Gray's room.

It is empty. He stows his books and binder inside his desk, checking it first for drawings. He sits in his desk, waiting; but the stillness and buzzing fluorescent lights seem to watch him; he wants to go to the roof, to think of what he should do about his father, but he is worried that Sam will be there. He goes out, down the stairs, past the front office. From the courtyard come the shouts of boys and the *thwup* of a soccer ball. Sam might be there; it won't be so bad to talk to him if they're alone.

When he turns the corner, a blond boy sits on a low wall that borders the walkway along the courtyard, a book opened in his lap. Buddy ducks into the lower-school boys' bathroom, but too late; Simon raises his hand.

"*Salve*," Simon says.

"*Salve*," Buddy says, matching his signal.

Simon smiles, distant and wary. In the courtyard, a pack of boys chases a soccer ball, calling out to each other; Junior runs with them. "Your mom called," Simon says. "So my mother took us early."

Buddy stops a safe distance from him, his hands stuffed in his jacket.

"What do you think you'll get on the history test?" Simon says.

"I don't know."

"It'll be easy. All Bevel-head does is read from the book. Did you study it?"

Buddy doesn't answer him.

"What's wrong, Tuber?" Simon says, in his false, sing-song voice.

"Nothing."

"I bet there is. Are you sad you didn't ride with us?"

"No," Buddy says.

Simon's smile turns brittle; he lowers his eyes. "Of course not, Tuber. I bet you're glad your dad's taking you now."

He doesn't know what Simon means; he doesn't know if Simon is somehow mocking him. He isn't angry about the drawings anymore; he is angry like he was when his father asked him if he told his mother about the woman. He feels himself move toward Simon, his fists clenched, trying to steel himself against the hollow ache that still beats in him. "Leave my dad alone," he says.

Simon looks up at him, smiling. "What do you mean, Tuber?"

Buddy comes close to him, so close that he can feel Simon's breath on his face. "Leave him alone," he says. "Or I'll tell what I saw at your house."

Simon lowers his eyes again, blushing, and stiffens. For a moment, Buddy thinks he will reach up, and grab his neck. But Simon rises, gathering his books under his arm, tucking in his shirt one-handed. Buddy wants to tell him he hasn't meant what he said, that it is just a joke; but Simon slips past him, not looking at him, and Buddy sees that his eyes are hard and glassy and filled with tears.

❧ ❧

That afternoon, he makes up a Latin test, and leaves out the history test he was sure he failed. He can't think of what he's done to Simon. All day, Simon avoided him. Buddy wanted to apologize, but he knew this would only be another mistake; he is glad he hurt Simon; he is glad that Simon is afraid of him.

Thick silence fills the car, like the silence when his father first came back; his father hunches over the steering wheel, staring ahead at the distant point.

"You only get one chance at a good life, Buddy," his father says. "A normal life. And if you throw it away, you end up on the streets, like some kind of bum. That's what I did, Buddy. I had a good life with you and your mother, and I threw it away, and now all I can do is to keep trying to get it back."

Ahead, the green highway sign for Telephone Road rises up above the freeway's gray hump. Beneath them, railroad tracks and steel derricks march, carrying power lines, into the bright afternoon haze. On Gramma Liddy's street, the low shingle houses and wood-frame houses, the tidy pick-up trucks and battered cars, Alex's house with its skirt of rock and mortar — all of it looks delicate and strange.

"What are you going to do today?" his father says.

"I don't know, sir," he says.

"Do you think you could help me over at your mother's?"

Buddy presses his forehead against his window, knowing he should ask his father about the woman; but he can't, not then.

"I bought us a couple of new shovels," his father says. "We've got a lot of work to do. I could really use your help."

Buddy keeps his face turned to his window. His father parks the car, then sits, staring through the windshield. Then he gets out. Buddy follows him, holding his books and binder against his chest. The small gray house looks made of cardboard, as if his father might sweep it away with his hand.

"Sir?" Buddy says. "It's okay, sir. You can go."

His father presses the buzzer, and stands, staring at the door, his gaze hard and sad. "Sir?" Buddy says. "You can leave."

His father doesn't look at him. Gramma Liddy opens the door. She wears a navy blue woolen suit dress, a pearl-colored blouse. Her silvery hair is pinned back. She studies his father, her chin slightly lifted, as if she were at mass.

"Jimmy," she says. "Won't you come in?"

Past the reading chair, past the hallway to his mother's old room, Buddy glimpses the high, soft bed, and flushes, breathless, worried that his father can see, somehow, the moment of peace he shared with Simon. Gramma Liddy peers at him, her sharp blue eyes cold and kind, as though she can see this, as though she can see even what he did to Simon that morning. "How are you?" she says.

"Fine, ma'am."

"Of course," she says. "How else could you be?"

She offers his father the chair where Buddy usually sat, which creaked under his father's weight. His father joins his hands in front of him, hunched over the table, too big for the room. Gramma Liddy sits across the table from him. Buddy stands next to them, wanting to stop them, unable to move. For a moment, the room is quiet, dappled by sunlight shifting through the French doors, and he tells himself that nothing will happen; but he knows that this is only another lie.

"Buddy?" his father says. "Why don't you go outside?"

"No," Gramma Liddy says, peering at his father. "He should stay. I think he should hear what we have to say to each other."

His father looks down at his hands. "Okay, Mrs. Liddy. I'd like to take Buddy to Margot's house to do some work. I think Buddy would like that, too."

Buddy tries to meet her eyes, to give her a secret sign that he will stay; but she doesn't look at him. "Has Margot given you her permission?" she says.

"No, ma'am," his father says.

"Then I don't see what the question is, Jimmy. I can't let you to do that."

His father looks down at his hands. "I know I've made a lot of mistakes, Mrs. Liddy. But I'm going to make up for all that. All I want to do is give Margot and Buddy the kind of life they deserve."

Gramma Liddy leans across the table, her gaze sharpening on his father. "Why do you think you have any idea, Jimmy, of the kind of life they deserve?"

His father stares down at his hands.

"Why do you think Margot should trust you, Jimmy? Why do you think I should trust you, after what you've done to her?"

His father glances back at him again, the tips of his ears a deep, bloody red. "I don't, Mrs. Liddy. I'm coming back because I want to help them."

Gramma Liddy leans closer to him. "Your idea of helping people, Jimmy, is very strange. All roads lead back to you. I think the best way to help Margot and Buddy would be for you to simply disappear."

Gramma Liddy glowers at his father, as if she can make him vanish with her stare. His father looks down at his hands. Buddy stands, frozen, wanting to stop them, wishing that both of them would vanish.

"How much did you pay for this house, Mrs. Liddy?" his father says.

Gramma Liddy stiffens, lifting her chin, sitting back in her chair, away from his father. "You know how much I paid."

"Margot's had to work hard all her life because of you, Mrs. Liddy," his father says. "I don't see how you've ever helped her. When I first met her, she was afraid to even talk to me, because she thought you'd find out. I can see you're doing the same thing to Buddy, wrapping him up in a kind of dream world."

"That's enough," Gramma Liddy says.

His father rises, towering over her, and for a moment, Buddy thinks he will reach out, and tear down the flimsy walls.

"I don't care what you think of me, Mrs. Liddy," his father says. "I can give Buddy and Margot what they want, and you can't. I just think you're afraid, Mrs. Liddy, of being left out here alone."

"That's enough." Gramma Liddy strikes the table; but when she turns to him, Buddy sees that she is afraid. "Get out," she says, to his father.

"Let's go," his father says, to him.

Gramma Liddy watches him, gaunt and severe. Buddy wants her to tell him not to go, but he knows she won't; and he doesn't want her to. He doesn't want to think of what he's done there with Simon. He doesn't want to think of what he is doing, right now. "I'm sorry," he says.

She turns from him, her mouth a bitter line.

"I'm sorry, gramma," he says.

She doesn't look at him; she knows that he is lying.

His father takes his arm. In a moment, they are at the door. Gramma Liddy sits, facing away from him, as still as if she were a painting. Then they are outside, and his father lets go of him, and the cold white air stings his eyes.

❧

At his mother's house, he watches his father as he pulls two shovels, one large, one small, from the trunk of his car, as he shrugs off his suit coat, his dress shirt and tie, and changes into blue jeans in the driveway, as he opens the gate and empties the garbage cans and carries them to the mounds of sand, swinging them easily upright, one in each hand, and begins to dig, his face already flushed, beaded with sweat, not looking at him, as he hasn't since they left Gramma Liddy's; he watches his father, gripping the shovel his father has given him, searching his face for signs of triumph, daring his father to look at him, knowing that if his father meets his eyes, he will turn away from him, afraid, but he sees nothing, only the same hardness and sadness he saw before; and without a sign from his father, without even a glance, he begins to ladle gouts of sand into the stinking trashcan, still watching his father, trying to see which father he really is.

"I'm sorry, Buddy," his father says. "I shouldn't've done that. You shouldn't've had to see that. That was between me and your grandmother. We've just got to keep going, and then we won't have to think about any of that anymore."

His father's shovel chuffs the sand. Behind and before them, the yard vanishes into darkness, the sand they've spread a distant shore; and in the cold and silence and smell of the coffee plant, Buddy hopes that everything will be as it was again, that he won't have to ask the question. But he knows that this is only another lie. He is in the real movie. In the darkness, the boys from the field laugh at him, jeer at him, telling him he will never ask his father if the woman is there. But he knows he will ask him; and if his father lies, he will show his mother the letter, he will kill him.

"Sir?" he says.

His father's shovel chuffs, a dry sound, a held breath.

"Sir?" he says. "What about Mary, sir?"

His father keeps digging; and for a moment, Buddy thinks he hasn't heard him. Then his father's jaw tightens, and Buddy imagines his father will swing his shovel at him, bury it in his chest. But his father turns from him, and drives his shovel into the sand, and wipes his face with his handkerchief.

"That's over, Buddy," he says. "You don't need to worry about that anymore. You shouldn't've had to worry about it to begin with."

He pictures the woman dead in her apartment, in the room with the coiled sheets, her throat slit, her name written in her blood on the walls. It is almost as he's imagined, and he thrills with a kind of pity and satisfaction; but he has to be sure.

"She's gone, sir?" he says.

"Yes, Buddy. She's gone."

His father turns to him. In the darkness, his face is a swarm of faces, flickering like spirits: the spirit of his face at the track, and at the woman's, and in the swamp, and Buddy doesn't know if he can believe him. Then the headlights of his mother's car sweeps through the gap in the fence, and he sees his father's face, haunted with grief. But behind that face, another face, another father, watches him, trying to see if he believes him; and Buddy feels himself step back, away from him.

His mother's headlights dim, her car door slams shut; she moves toward them, a swift white shape in the dusk. "You can't do this," she says.

His father turns to his mother, then to him; and the face he's seen before is gone. "Margot," he says.

"You can't," his mother says. "I know what you're trying to do, and you're not going to get away with it. Either you come inside right now and talk to me, or you can forget about seeing him again until this is settled."

"Margot," his father says, moving toward her, his palms uplifted.

"Right now," his mother says.

"What do you want to do?" his father says, to him.

"Don't," his mother says, coming toward them. "Don't answer him."

"What do you want to do, Buddy? Do you want to keep riding with me?"

His father stares at him out of the darkness. It is almost as he's imagined; he knows he should run to his room, show his mother the letter. But when he answers, it is as if not he, but another boy who speaks.

"Yes, sir," he says.

His father nods, silently thanking him, not meeting his eyes, and gently takes the shovel from his hands. "You can't do this," his mother says.

His father slips past her toward the gate. She follows him, but his father's car door clunks shut, its engine whinnies out of the driveway; she stands, facing the fence.

For a moment, the yard is quiet, the telephone lines and ragged trees black against the sunset. A train comes closer, playing a single, rising note like a trumpet. Then she turns to Buddy, and grasps his arm, and shakes it.

"Why did you do that?" she says.

He tries to wrench his arm from her, but she holds him. "We can't let daddy do this," she says. "We can't just let him come in here and ruin everything."

He looks at the muddy yard, the bare fence, the mobile home on top of Mr. Knight's house, and imagines it swept away; he wishes it would happen.

"Why not?" he says.

"Because it's ours, Buddy. It's what we have. I'm going to call grandmother and tell her daddy can't come tomorrow."

"No," he says, catching her arm. "Please."

"Why not?" she says.

"Why not?" she says, her eyes beautiful and fierce.

He knows that she is asking him about the woman. He hides his face from her, burying it against her skirt, breathing the smell of the laboratory, and squeezes his eyes shut, making his breath catch, his back shake, until he starts to cry. It is nothing like he's imagined. He knows he is not what he seems, a child weeping against his mother; he knows there is still time to tell her what he's seen in his father's face; but a wave breaks over him, stronger than the hollow ache, stronger than anything, and he feels himself carried away from her. In the darkness, the boys from the field laugh at him, jeer at him. But he cannot go back to the gray morning, the place he'd seen at Christmas; he cannot go back to the darkness where he has lived since his father left.

∂◦◦

That night, he lies in bed, listening, as his mother paces in the kitchen. Then her voice stops, and he hears a different voice, like the voice she used at the hospital, and he knows that she is calling his father. He waits, knowing he should get up; but he waits as her voice raps out words, too low for him to understand.

He waits, listening to the scritch of coat hangers in her room, knowing that he should go to her; but when her footfalls creak outside his door, and a wedge of light opens into his room, he closes his eyes and breathes deep, soughing breaths, until she pulls his door shut. He waits, watching the porch, the house's rough brick etched in the flat light, remembering his father passing there that summer, and in his white lab coat when he came home, long ago. He knows he should get up, run to the kitchen; but he waits, pinned to his bed, his arms and legs and breath, as he hears his father's car rumble, and the gate latch click, as he watches his father pass beneath the porch light.

The back door opens; his father vanishes into the kitchen. Voices seep through the wall. Slowly, he rises, and opens his door. In the hallway, the door to the dining room is closed, and to his mother's room and the bathroom, and the hallway is dark and airless. He presses his ear against a sliver of light on the edge of the dining room door, praying to his father to tell the truth.

Please, Jimmy, his mother says, her voice like the one at the hospital, like the one he's imagined in the movies. I know this isn't what you wanted — this life. You don't need to keep paying for what happened. You just need to tell me the truth.

The silence in the kitchen is like the silence when Gramma Turner said his mother tricked his father. He squeezes his eyes shut, praying to his father to tell the truth; but he knows, now, that this is only another lie.

Is there anyone else? his mother says. Has there been anyone else?

He squeezes his eyes shut, praying to his father to keep his silence, praying to him not to betray him again. No, his father says. Never.

Are you sure, Jimmy? Are you sure that's what you want to tell me?

Yes, his father says. I'm sure.

His mother lets out her breath, as if she's held it, too. If you're lying to me, Jimmy, I'll never forgive you. Not for me. But if you lie to me, and go away again, you'll break your son's heart. Do you understand?

I'm not lying to you, Margot. I promise. I just need another chance.

His mother is quiet. You should go, Jimmy. You've given me a lot to think about, and to pray about, and now I need to do those things.

Please, Margot, his father says. I'm not lying. Just tell me what to do. I'll work hard. I can do that. Just tell me what I need to do.

You need to go, Jimmy. You need to let me think.

I'm not lying to you, Margot, his father says. I love you.

His mother doesn't answer him; and Buddy's skin prickles with shame.

I love you, Margot, his father says.

Please, Jimmy, his mother says. Please just go.

The door latch clicks; the back door opens, then shuts again. Buddy slips into his room. When he opens his door, his father stands outside his window, a shadow beneath the porch light. He raises his hand, a secret signal; and Buddy waits, raising his hand, to match him, until his father is gone.

21.

That week, the drawings appear, in his binder, in his desk, in *The Approach to Latin* and *The Pilgrim's Progress*. Tightface couples with his father, his father couples with Gramma Turner, Gramma Turner couples with Grampa Turner; Buddy couples with his mother, his mother couples with Mr. Torres, Mr. Torres couples with Alex; Alex couples with Gramma Liddy, Gramma Liddy couples with Mr. Torres, Mr. Torres couples with Ysrael: Buddy's Spic Friend, Spic Father, Spic Dog. At lunch, at recess, in the hallway between classes, boys shove him, throw punches at him. They ask if Tightface is really tight, if his father likes screwing her; they ask if he talks Mexican and grew up with Mexicans and sucks Mexican dick. But he doesn't care, not really; he knows that all of it is a lie.

In chapel, as he sings along in the sea of sleepy voices, he pictures himself in a wide shot of the rows of brown-uniformed boys, and wonders what will happen if the boys knew, not what Simon told them, but the real story, the whole story, which he hears each night in bits and pieces when his mother and father talk outside in the yard; and he feels himself lifted up, because they don't know the real truth, and an heroic, far-away sadness glimmers in him. Sometimes, he watches Simon, his hard blue eyes, the blond furze at the base of his skull, and the hollow ache grips him, and he wishes that he could apologize; he still worries that Simon would tell his mother what he knew. But he doubts it; he doubts Simon will let it. Simon seems only pitiful to him, now, as unreal as the drawings he tears up and throws away; he knows that Simon can't touch his real life, the vivid life that he lives each day with his father.

❧ ❧

At Mr. Torres' house, the driveway was empty; Buddy let out his breath. His father parked the car, and sat, silent, staring ahead. Buddy opened his door. He had already told his father that they couldn't tell Mr. Torres what they were doing there. Behind the fence, Ysrael barked, and in Alex's window, the curtain parted, and as he walked toward the small, yellow house in the gray winter day, he hoped that he could redeem what he had done to Alex and Gramma Liddy.

Each day, on the way to school, they ate hamburgers, and his father talked about what they needed to do at his mother's house. They'd almost finished spreading the sand; his father told him he was getting stronger, and that he noticed he'd lost some weight. And each day, without saying it, his father told him that he would tell his mother about the woman. "I talked to your mother last night," his father said, a week after they had gone to Gramma Liddy's. "There's still some things I need to talk to her about. I'll talk to her soon, Buddy, but I can't right now. Understand?"

Something had shifted, something had changed. Buddy knew that his father was lying to him. But his father's lying made him feel adult, almost like their tricking of the woman; he knew that his father would never tell his mother about the woman.

"Yes, sir," he said, touching the keys. All week, his father hadn't asked about them. Buddy had a plan, but he didn't know if it would work. He closed his eyes, and pressed his forehead against his window, and felt the giddy drop.

"I've got the keys, sir," he said. "But I need you to help me do something. I need you to help me with the movie."

Behind the storm door's dark glass, Alex watched him, ghostly, unsmiling. His father caught up with him, and reached out to touch his shoulder. Buddy didn't look at him. Buddy knew what Alex saw, when he saw his father: the woman, and his father making him lie to his mother, and suing his mother, so that they would have to live on the streets. None of it was true, anymore, not in any way that Alex could understand.

Spic, the voice beside him said.

Alex opened the storm door, not looking at him, and shook his father's hand. "It's nice to see you again," his father said. "Is your father home?"

"No, sir," Alex said.

"Let's go," Buddy said.

His father glanced at him, a kind of sadness and distaste. Alex opened the door, stood aside to let them pass, eyeing Buddy. Inside, the wood-paneled living room smelled of furniture polish and heat. Mrs. Torres peeked out at them behind her veil atop the silent TV. His father nodded, looking around the room; and Buddy wondered if bringing him there had been a mistake.

"It's nice," his father said. "Your dad's kept it up in here real nice."

"Yes, sir," Alex said, lowering his eyes.

"Let's go," Buddy said. "Let's show him the drawings."

His father started to speak. Alex shrugged, and started toward his room. Buddy followed him, feeling his father watching him. In the hallway, Alex hesitated, glancing back at them, before he opened his door.

His father filled the room, awkward in his suit. The room seemed smaller, its smell of cinnamon candy and pencil lead childish, as if he hadn't seen it for a long time; but the drawings, which his father examined, did not seem childish. Buddy remembered what Grampa Turner had told him; and he felt himself move toward his father, knowing he'd made a mistake.

"Are these yours?" his father said, to Alex. "Did you do all these?"

"Yes, sir," Alex said.

"They're really good. You're a real artist. You should be proud."

"Thank you, sir," Alex said.

"Is this what you're working on?" his father said. "Is this part of your movie?"

"No, sir," Buddy said.

"Can I see what you're working on?" his father said.

Buddy glanced at Alex, warning him not to show his father the drawings; but Alex shrugged, opened a drawer in his desk, took out a thick stack of paper. Buddy thought he would only let his father leaf through them, but Alex put the drawings on his desk, and pressed down on the paper with one hand, and with his other hand, let the pages slowly fall. It was the scene of the Horse's flight from the cell, which Buddy hadn't written, yet. In the flickering pages, the Horse reared up, spreading his wings, and flew through the walls, an effect Alex had worked on for days, sketching the Horse more lightly, frame by frame.

His father watched, his mouth slightly opened, as if he were seeing something else. Then he turned to them, his face bright and open, his real father's face.

"That's beautiful," he said, to Alex.

Buddy kept his eyes on the Horse; and he knew that bringing his father there had been a mistake. "I haven't been around much for Buddy," his father said. "I'm going to do better, now. I'd like to help you with your movie."

Alex didn't look at his father; Buddy wanted to shake him, and felt a sharp stab of jealousy. "Yes, sir," Alex said. "Thank you, sir."

Outside, Mr. Torres' truck chugged into the driveway.

"*No podemos dejar a tu papá saber.*" Buddy said. *We can't let your dad know.*

"*¿Porqué no?*" Alex said.

"Porque mi mamá no le gustará." Because my mother won't like it.

"Alejandro?" Mr. Torres said, in the hallway. *"El amigo 'sta 'quí?"*

His father reached for the door, and opened it; and when Mr. Torres saw him, his grin tightened, turned ghastly.

"Jimmy," he said. "Good to see you again."

His father shook Mr. Torres' hand, not looking at him. "Good to see you, Joe. Sorry to barge in like this. Alex is an excellent artist."

Mr. Torres grimaced, his dark eyes flickering over Alex and Buddy. "That's fine, Jimmy," he said. "Margot said you were around."

His father nodded, looking down at the floor. "Buddy and I've been over there doing some work. Spreading sand. I want to take out that old fence."

"That sounds good, Jimmy," Mr. Torres said. "That sounds like a lot of work. Is Margot thinking of selling the house?"

"I don't know, Joe," his father said. "We'll see."

"It can't hurt, Jimmy. That's a lot of work, though. What brings you over here?"

His father glanced at him; and Buddy felt himself move toward him, ready to stop him from telling Mr. Torres about the movie.

"Nothing, Joe," his father said. "We just came for a visit."

Mr. Torres nodded, smiling, not believing him. "Let me get you a beer, Jimmy. You can tell me what the Army's been up to at Fort Polk."

"I appreciate that, Joe. We should go. I don't want to be in your way."

"Not at all, Jimmy," Mr. Torres said. "You're not in my way."

His father glanced back at him. Then Mr. Torres and his father were gone, and he was alone with Alex in the small, quiet room. Alex watched him, his gaze leveled, still somehow adult. Then he pulled the camera bag out from under his bed. Buddy's father's and Mr. Torres' voices bled through the thin walls, and Buddy wondered what they were saying, what his father was telling him. Alex unzipped the bag, lifted the camera out by its stock, and aimed it at Buddy.

"Why can't we tell my dad?" he said.

"I told you," Buddy said.

"Your dad's going to help us with the movie, but my dad can't?"

"I guess so," Buddy said. "What else are we going to do? He picks me up from school every day. How else are we going to make the movie?"

Alex moved closer; the camera whirred, its lens revolved, zooming out, zooming in. From the living room, his father and Mr. Torres approached, his father telling him they needed to get back. "Is your mom going to sell her house?" Alex said.

"I don't know," Buddy said, reaching for the camera; but Alex swung it away. In the living room, his father was thanking Mr. Torres, saying that maybe next time they could have a beer, but right now, they needed to get back.

"How're we going to make the movie if you don't even live here?" Alex said.

"I don't know," Buddy said.

Alex watched him, hard and ghostly; he stuck the camera in the bag, shoved it under his bed. "I don't care, man," he said. "I don't care about any of that crap."

∂◦⌐

In the afternoons, they go to Alex's to work on the movie, and then to his mother's house to work in the yard. His father has asked him what kind of film they needed and what kind of batteries they would use; he asked where they would shoot the movie and where they would take the film to be developed and how they would light the drawings for the animation. He's bought a tripod and batteries, yellow boxes of movie film like bricks of gold, a light meter, spotlights, the kind they used for autopsy photos, swaths of seafoam-blue material from an operating room for the blue-screen shots. He's built an editor for the negatives, an old microscope with hand-cranked reels and arms he's soldered to its base and a red light bulb beneath the slide tray, so they can match the numbers on the sides of the negatives to the footage chart they will make, so they will know exactly where to start the animation. He's built a stand for the camera, a metal frame attached by four metal legs to a smaller frame above it, where the camera will be held in place with clamps. He's bought a shutter wire, a thin metal cable that fits in a hole at the bottom of the camera's stock; Alex has explained to him how they would do the blue-screen shots. When they film the animation, his father says, they will clamp the camera to the metal stand, and use the shutter wire to click off frames, one at a time, just like counting red cells and white cells. The shutter wire and the stand will keep the camera steady; it's important, he says, to keep the camera steady, just like when you shoot slides, so that the animation won't look fake, it will look crisp and real.

In the afternoons, his father colors the backgrounds of drawings so they will blend into the live action shots, bent over Alex's desk, his hands swift and patient.

Alex, on the floor, makes new drawings, chewing the eraser on his pencil. Buddy, sitting on his bed, tries to write the new scenes; his father says he needs to hurry up. But somehow, with his father there, he can't write the script. And so he watches his father, the back of his balding head, his dark, baggy suit, and Alex, sketching rapidly, frowning at his work, watching them from far away. Soon, his father will check his watch, and say they should get to his mother's; or Mr. Torres will knock on the door, his grin tightening each day, and his father will go with him to drink a beer, and offer to help him work on his truck. Then Alex will look at him, when he looks at him at all, with the same adult look Buddy saw the first day that he and his father had come. Buddy lowers his eyes to the script, to the blank page barred with faint blue lines. But even when Alex stares at him, even when his father talks to Mr. Torres, Buddy feels a kind of peace, like the peace at the woman's apartment, like the peace he felt, knowing that Simon won't tell his mother about the woman; and he wonders if what he is watching is his real life, or the movie of his life, or something else that he can't even imagine.

By the end of the week, they are ready to start filming, his father says. All that's left is for Buddy to finish the script. What did they think? he says. Did that sound alright? Buddy says that sounded fine; Alex nods, not meeting his father's eyes, as he does each time his father leaves, as he did when his father brought the tripod and editor and camera stand, the batteries and spotlight and swaths of blue material that his father kept in the trunk of his car. On the way out, Mr. Torres pulls up, and his father tells him he was sorry, that he'll get a beer later, and asks when they can work on his truck; and Mr. Torres thanks him, his gaze hardening with adult distaste.

On the way to his mother's house, his father is silent. He unlocks the back door with the keys Buddy still kept, and changes into his T-shirt and jeans in Buddy's room. He takes the crowbar he found in the hall closet, gives Buddy a smaller crowbar he's bought for him; and Buddy knows that something is waiting in his silence.

Outside, the telephone lines and ragged trees are black against the sunset. They've finished spreading the sand; now they need to start on the fence. His father points his crowbar at the ground, at jagged stumps in the gap where the fence was. "Pilings. Sunk in concrete. It's going to be hard as hell to dig them up."

"Yes, sir," Buddy says, waiting to hear what he will say.

"It's not right, Buddy," his father says. "Keeping your movie a secret. It's not fair to Joe Torres. It's not fair to Alex. Understand?"

Buddy turns from him, weighing the crowbar in his hand.

"Listen to me, Buddy," his father says, crouching down, so that he looks him in the eye. "It's not fair. It hurts them. We need to tell Joe about the movie. Understand?"

The crowbar is cold and heavy. He doesn't know what his father is saying; he only knows that he is betraying him.

"Listen to me, Buddy," his father says. "I know what I've done, what I've asked you to do, it isn't right. But that doesn't mean it's right for you to do it. It's not good for me, either, to keep more things from your mother than I already do. Understand?"

He will show his mother the letter, and tell her what he'd seen in his father's face. But he knows that this is only another lie. His mother's car stutters into the driveway, her headlights sweeps the gap in the fence; he turns to the yard, hiding his face from her. "No, sir," he says. "Please, sir. Not yet."

His father, his real father, watches him; and in his face is a terrible sadness, like the weight he carries in his voice. His mother's headlights dim, her car door swings shut. His father stands and turns to the gate. His mother opens it, regarding them warily.

"Sister Bertille wants you to call her," she says to his father. "She wants us to come to lunch at the convent this weekend."

"Let's go," his father says.

His mother makes a dubious noise, then ruffles Buddy's hair. "Okay, sport. It's time to start your homework. Let's get inside."

"I want to help daddy," he says, ducking away from her.

"You've helped daddy enough for one day. Come on. I'm too tired to fight."

"Go on," his father says. "Do what your mother says."

He starts away from them, clinking the tip of the crowbar against the cement path. Shadows swam in the yard, and when he turns at the statue of St. Francis, his mother and father are shadows against the orange sunset and ragged trees. He can hear the thickness in their voices, though it was different, now, as if his father already told his mother about the woman; and he wonders if that was what his father really wanted to do.

How long do you plan to be out here? his mother says.

Don't know, his father says. Until I get tired.

It'll be dark soon, Jimmy. You won't be able to see what you're doing.

It's fine, his father says. I'll be fine.

His mother clasps her hands at her waist, watching his father, who cups one hand on a wooden plank in the fence. I'm going to make supper, she says.

His father tugs at the plank, testing it. That's fine.

Please, Jimmy, she says. You need to go home.

The plank snaps. I'm fine, his father says. I'll be fine.

☙ ❧

Later, he lies in bed, watching his father pass back and forth through the porch light in the yard, stacking wooden planks against the chain-link fence. In the hallway, amber light from his mother's lamp frames her door, and he knows that she is watching his father, too. He looks through the blinds on his window, watching his father move back and forth through the porch light, trying to think of his words, his heroic words, the real truth that he hears in bits and pieces between his mother and father every night: that he doesn't give a shit about upsetting Gramma Turner, and she's fucked up his entire life, that she was why he ran away from them. He knows, from his father's voice, that it's the real truth; and as he watches his father trudge back and forth, as if battling a fierce wind, more ghostly, more real than he was, he remembers him climbing the back porch steps in his white lab coat each night when he came back from Galveston, and welding the beams that held up the second story on Mr. Knight's house, sparks shooting from their blue-flamed torches, their faces hidden behind iron masks. He watches his father, his breath making steam on his window; and it seems his father has always been there, laboring, protecting them. He knows the woman isn't there, can't be there, that what he saw in his father's face was a mistake. He presses his face against his window, wanting to reach out, to tap a secret signal on the impenetrable glass; but he waits in his covers' warm cocoon, watching his father in the darkness, just outside.

22.

The big houses move, stately, mysterious, outside his father's car, flickering in the sunlight like frames in a movie. Buddy sits in the back seat, itchy in his Easter suit, his jacket and Christmas tie. His mother, in the front seat, wears an ugly yellow dress Gramma Turner gave her long ago; his father hunches over the steering wheel in a dark suit, his gaze set on the distant point. That morning, when his mother told Buddy that they were going to Gramma Turner's, she eyed him narrowly, and he thought that she was afraid; and now, in his mother's and father's clipped voices, too low for him to understand, he hears that both of them are afraid, and their fear grates on him. There is nothing to be afraid of, he thinks.

He turns to his window, away from the smell of hamburgers and French fries, trying to glimpse through the houses' dark windows secret signs of the lives inside. There is Dr. Red Duke's house, with its tennis courts and terraced flowerbeds; there is Dr. DeBakey's, with its wavering coach lamps and ivied walls. He closes his eyes, trying to remember trips to Gramma Turner's house when he sat in the back seat in his itchy suit, listening to his mother's and father's voices, his father's sly and joking, his mother's quick and halting, even then.

We're late, his mother says, now.

It'll just take a second, his father says.

I don't want to upset her, Jimmy. This is going to be hard enough as it is.

Please, Margot. This is important. It'll just take a second.

The car turns. Tree-shadows shift across his face. For a moment, he imagines that they are going to see the woman, that all of them will sit on the couch with velvet pillows, and his father will whistle and joke, and everything will be alright.

He's asleep, his mother says.

No, he isn't, his father says. Just playing possum.

His father pokes his chest. Buddy squirms away from him. When he opens his eyes, his father looms above him, studying him, a kind of tightness around his eyes.

"Come on, Buddy," he says. "I need your help."

His mother stands on the sidewalk, clutching her purse, watching the house, the same house that he and his father stopped at the day they snuck out the bikes: the same red brick and blankets of ivy, the same oak trees hovering outside. It is strange, coming here with his mother. Buddy looks for the figure he saw in the window, but there is nothing, not even a trick of light.

"What do you think?" his father says.

"It's nice, Jimmy," his mother says, quick and delicate and alert. "It's very nice."

"That's not what I meant. Do you like it? Do you think you could live here?"

His mother's eyes light on the house, then dart away. "Of course I like it. That's not the point. We shouldn't even be talking about this."

"What do you think?" his father says to him.

"I like it, sir."

"I got a key from the realtor," his father says. "We can take a look."

His mother glances at his father, like she did at the house. "Later, Jimmy," she says. "We need to get to your mother's."

His father grimaces. "Just for a minute, Margot. It won't take a minute."

His mother watches the house as if it might pounce; his father strides past her up the red-brick walk. Buddy follows him, glancing back at his mother, her face sharp with irritation, like it was when they met the Quines. He remembers what his father said about living there with the woman. None of that is real anymore. He wants to ask his mother why she can't take a joke.

Near the front door, bay windows lower down at them beneath the roof's sharp prow. When his father opens the front door, the smells of sawdust and shellac and paint expand in the air like a breath. His father leads them past a dark wooden staircase, through large, empty rooms, into an arsenic-green kitchen whose shelves and cabinets seem impossibly high; he leads them through a pantry, a bathroom, a low, wood-paneled den where trees seem to reach through a wall of windows, a room whose fireplace and mantle and glassed-in bookcases look slightly sinister, like a room from a fairy tale. His father talks about plumbing and wiring, motion detectors and magnetic alarms; but Buddy can't listen to what he is saying.

Each time he thinks that he has grasped the house's shape, they turn another corner, into another room; the house seems to go on and on, like a house in a dream. At any moment, he thinks, the woman will appear. And as they climb creaking stairs to a second story, and a third, his mother telling him they can do this later, they need to leave, his father saying it will take just another minute, the clean, hopeful smell of the first story recedes, and a warm, spicy must takes its place, the smell of the family who lived there before. "We need to go," his mother says.

His father stops outside a closed door, wincing when his mother speaks. "This will be your room," he says.

The room is large and bright, twice as large, at least, as his room at home; he wonders what Alex would think, if he could see it. He steps cautiously across its wooden floor, as if it is ice, imagining it might dissolve, glancing back at his mother, who watches him, worried, like she did at the Quines. One wall is three windows, the other, two windows, and opposite them, a closet, and on the closet, what looks like writing.

Pen marks hatch the doorsill, and next to them, in a precise, slanting script: *Sarah 6; Michael 4; Sarah 5; Michael 3; Katharine 2 ½*. Behind him, above him, in the house's third story playroom, they watch him, their skin as pale as milk: the children he has seen in the houses near Rice, and in Gramma Turner's Easter egg hunts.

Outside, through the windows, is another house like the one where he stands. Around the corner, above the tree-shaded streets, he glimpses the bone-white tip of Rice's campanile; and he feels as if he is floating, borne up into that other world. He remembers the boys at St. John's, their even stares, their button-down shirts; and he imagines looking out from their world, his limbs turning tanned and lean and taut. "What do you think?" his father says.

"I like it, sir," he says.

His mother touches his shoulder, her face pinched and fearful. "Let's go, Jimmy," she says. "We need to go."

⌒⌒

On the way to Gramma Turner's, his father keeps glancing at his mother, asking her if she's alright. His mother stares ahead, tree-shadows flickering over her face, saying that she is fine. Buddy tries to think of her expression at the house; he knows it was only fear. But they have nothing to be afraid of, he thinks. He is glad of his itchy Easter suit, his Christmas tie; he knows that to face Gramma Turner, he has only to look out at her with the boys' distant stares.

His father pulls up at Gramma Turner's, ratcheting the brake, asking his mother again if she's alright. His mother opens her door, still silent; his father follows her, cursing faintly under his breath.

Gramma Turner stands on the small back porch, her hand trembling on the porch railing. She wears a purple dress, the cameo of the Roman woman pinned at her collar, her eyes invisible behind her glasses; but her helmet hair is even more ragged than when Buddy saw her last time he was there, when the woman was still there.

His mother stands in the driveway, clutching her purse; his father, next to her, stares at Gramma Turner, caught behind his rigid mask.

Without greeting them, Gramma Turner reaches for the screen door. His father takes his mother's arm, pulling her toward the porch, but his mother wrenches her arm from him; and Buddy sees that she is not afraid.

Above the driveway, the windows of his father's room watch him like two blind eyes; his father turns to him, his glance sharp with irritation.

"Come on, Buddy," he says. "Let's go."

Inside, Gramma Turner moves ahead of his mother and father, toward the living room, where the door to the den is shut, reaching out to steady herself on a door-sill, a television set, the little room's wood-paneled walls. His mother and father and Gramma Turner move ahead of him into the living room. In the little room, on the night table next to the green corduroy covered day bed, is a bright yellow envelope decorated with a picture of a smiling family – an envelope of photographs.

Buddy stands near the table, hesitating, watching them; then he reaches out, and slips the envelope into his coat pocket.

"I'm sorry, Mrs. Turner," his mother says. "I'm sorry we're late."

Gramma Turner creeps crabwise from them, her back to them, touching the wing-backed chair; his father stands near the couch.

"I'm sorry, Mrs. Turner," his mother says. "I know this is hard. I don't want to make things harder than they already are."

"Jimmy?" Gramma Turner says. "Did you get those pads? He needs those pads, Jimmy. He's getting sores."

"No, mamma," his father says. "I'll get them today."

Gramma Turner makes a skeptical noise. "He's asleep, Jimmy. He was awake when you said you'd be here, but now he's asleep."

"I'm sorry, Mrs. Turner," his mother says. "We can come back later, if you'd like. I know it must be a great deal of work, taking care of him."

Gramma Turner grips the wing-backed chair, keeping her back to them.

"Do you have anyone in to help?" his mother says.

Gramma Turner doesn't look at her.

"If there is anything I can do, Mrs. Turner," his mother says. "Anything at all."

"What you can do" — his grandmother turns to his mother, steadying herself on the chair — "is to leave my son alone."

"Mamma," his father says.

His mother stands very still. "I hope we can talk about that, Mrs. Turner."

"I've got nothing to talk to you about," Gramma Turner says. "Who do you think you are, coming around at a time like this?"

"Mamma," his father says.

"I am still Jimmy's wife, Mrs. Turner."

"If you were really his wife," Gramma Turner says, "you wouldn't need my help. But you aren't really his wife, are you?"

"Mamma," his father says. "That's enough."

"Please, Mrs. Turner," his mother says. "I've told him that he needs help. But we need to help him. You know this is hard on him. You know he gets confused."

"He's confused because you won't leave him alone."

"Please, Mrs. Turner. You know that's not true. We've talked about this before."

Gramma Turner touches the wing-backed chair, then lowers herself into it, her arms trembling, like Gramma Liddy's.

"There's nothing wrong with my son," she says.

"Please, Mrs. Turner," his mother says.

"There was nothing wrong," Gramma Turner says, "until you tricked him, because you were too old to get a child any other way."

"Goddammit, mamma," his father says.

"Please, Mrs. Turner," his mother says. "I'm trying to help."

"That's what you tell yourself," Gramma Turner says. "But I see what you really want. You may pull him in for a little while, because he feels bad about his father. But when his daddy dies, he'll be right back over here again."

"Goddammit, mamma," his father says, stalking toward her, his hands clenched at his sides, his face a mask of rage. "That's enough."

Buddy's mother puts her hand on his arm, to stop him. For a moment, none of them move. Then his father looks out at Buddy from the living room, his face like his face at the track. "Buddy?" he says. "Why don't you go outside?"

Through the doorway, Gramma Turner's gaze lights on him; he holds very still, thinking that she knows he has the envelope.

"Look at you!" she says, in her false, brittle voice. "Don't you look handsome! Don't you look nice! Why don't you go and get yourself a Coke!"

He stands his ground, knowing he has to help his father, to stop, somehow, what they are doing to him. But his mother turns to him, covering her mouth with her hand, her eyes shattered, terrible, fierce.

"Go on," she says. "Go."

He goes out, down the porch steps, past the side of the house, not listening to the voices that seep through the front window of the living room – his father's voice, telling Gramma Turner that he is going back to his mother, and there is nothing she can do to stop him; his mother's voice, telling him nothing has been decided, telling him not to speak like that to Gramma Turner. He runs across the front yard, clenching his fists, because there is nothing he can do, not looking at the windows of his father's room, which he knows are watching him, like blank, blind eyes.

He stops on the corner at Greenbriar above a broken storm drain, his hand on the envelope slick inside his itchy coat pocket. He knows he should let it drop down the storm drain, where it will be carried out to the bayou, and the Gulf. But he closes his eyes, and takes the envelope from his pocket; and when he opens it, what he sees takes breath from his chest, and his skin creeps, as if the drawings crept under it: the woman and his father and Gramma Turner and himself, frozen in the camera-flash, the woman's face, frightened, glinting with hardness, his own face, grimacing, the whites of his eyes exposed – pale, bloated, a death's-head mask.

None of it is true, anymore.

Across the street, past the rushing cars, is the sand-colored school; and he remembers kneeling in the dirt, telling his father he didn't want his shitty houses. But he pictures it from far away, as if it happened to someone else, in someone else's life; and he sees himself and his father escaping, striking out across the vast, unmappable city, into the other world, the world he's seen from the new house.

"Buddy?" his father says.

His father strides toward him, his face bright with hope, trapped behind his mask; Buddy holds the envelope, knowing he should let it drop; but he slips it back into his pocket. "Buddy?" his father says. "It's okay. Granddaddy's awake."

The den smells of bleach and urine. In the dim light that seeps through the sliding glass doors, the ghost of the woman watches them, as the machine blips out his grandfather's pulse. His mother stands next to his bed, holding his hand, her gaze quick and delicate, murmuring words as intent and meaningless as prayer:

"It's so very good, Mr. Turner. It's so very, very good to see you again."

His grandfather stares out from his masklike face. His skin is almost translucent; but his eyes are still furious, still burning with dark fire. Buddy looks away from him, not listening, trying not to listen to the message he sends:

Don't let him hurt the Horse, his grandfather says.

"I think that's enough," Gramma Turner says.

"Goddammit, mamma," his father says. "She just got here."

"No," his mother says, cutting her eyes at Buddy, fierce with accusation, at him or his father, he can't tell. "Your mother's right. We should let him rest."

On the way home, his mother says, "It's inhuman, keeping him there like that; it's inhuman for him and your mother. He needs to go where he can get proper care."

His father stares ahead, gripping the steering wheel. When they pull into the driveway, his father toggles the gearshift, ready to park; but his mother opens her door, and gets out.

"Go home, Jimmy," she says. "Go home and be where you're needed."

⇘⇘

But his father does not go home. In the afternoons, they go to Alex's to work on the movie, and in the evenings, he and his father build the fence. At first, when he comes to pick him up in the morning, his mother tells his father that he needs to go back home, to help Gramma Turner; but Buddy pleads with her, and his mother, defeated, regards him with a kind of weariness; and when she goes to the back yard at night to talk to his father about Grampa Turner, he sees the same glinting hardness he saw at the new house. But when she stands alone at the sink, arguing with herself, her face lightens with hope, and a kind of fear; Buddy thinks her changefulness is another sort of trick, and it angers him. But each day, as he watches her change, he knows that he is helping his father kindle the hope that he sees each night in the kitchen.

Sometimes in the afternoons, before they go to Alex's, his father and he stop at the new house and wander its empty rooms, his father talking about the work that needs to be done, Buddy half-listening, trying to grasp the house's shape, which still eludes him. At school, the drawings keep coming, in his books and binder and *The Pilgrim's Progress*; and on the soccer field, the boys taunt him, asking if his father is really Mr. Torres, if he even knows who his father really is. But already he sees them, and the school, for what they are: shabby, hardbitten, a rip off. Even Simon he sees differently, now — his cheap striving, which he hides behind his indifferent mask — and he knows that all of it, the pink brick buildings, the white, empty church, the rows of brown-uniformed boys, will be swept away, like sinners in the End Times, and he will defeat them, he will bury them all.

That Friday, Alex and his father and he stand in Alex's room, in the smell of cinnamon candy and pencil lead, tense and quiet. Alex's bed is pushed against his door, the walls in one corner bare of drawings. They are ready to start filming — only a test scene, to try out the blue screen system — but Buddy's hands still shake as he tears open the yellow wrapper, clicks the sleek black cartridge of film into the camera.

A spotlight is trained on the corner; the camera is anchored to a tripod. His father holds a light meter and the chart he's made, a mimeographed sheet with columns for scene number, footage, and take. Alex mans the camera, adjusting its focus, checking the frame against the storyboard drawing, to make sure the live action and animation will match. His father points the light meter at the corner, takes a reading, nods.

"Looks good," he says.

Alex cups one hand on the camera, to steady it, a finger on its trigger. Buddy takes his place in the corner; his entrance and the beginning of the scene will be added later, in a separate take, by rewinding the film, and using a blue screen matte.

"Ready?" his father says.

Alex nods, frowning, his eye to the camera, not looking at his father; all of them have agreed on what they will say next:

"*Ghost Horse*," Alex says. "Scene eight. Part two. Take one."

"Camera!" Buddy says. "Action!"

Alex presses the trigger; the camera flitters, a sound like flipping paper, the sound of Alex letting his drawings fall. His father watches him, a bright, hopeful look. Alex is hidden behind the camera's staring eye. The scene is the last one Buddy wrote, after they visited Gramma Turner's; he still hasn't finished the script, but Alex and his father have agreed that they need to start somewhere.

When the camera starts, when the movie starts, Buddy has imagined, he will suddenly be inside it; but his father still stares out at him, and the camera still whirs, and he cannot forget Alex's stubborn silence, or how his father flinches when Alex doesn't answer him, or that the silence in the room was there because they were waiting for Mr. Torres. He turns from the camera, closing his eyes, reciting silently what he's written:

SCENE EIGHT: *HUGH sneaks up to the cell. He looks through the window. The SWAMP HORSE is lying on the floor. He is almost a skeleton.*
 HUGH: I'm back. I've got the antidote.
 The SWAMP HORSE looks at the window. His eyes softly glow. HUGH fades through the wall.

He opens his eyes and steps away from the wall, stepping through the wall; and for a moment, he is inside something, like he was when he did the plays with Simon, like he is when he watches his mother's delicate, beautiful face. He kneels behind the line of masking tape on the floor, his mark to keep him on the right side of the frame, so he won't overlap the animated Horse, and speaks his line; it is important, he and Alex have agreed, that he say them, even though the movie will be silent:

"I'm sorry I took so long," he says.

SWAMP HORSE (silently): That's okay. Promise me you won't leave again.

"That's okay," his father says, reading from the script, his voice as flat as when he'd lit the Advent candles. "Promise me you won't leave again."

"Yes," Buddy says. "I promise."

He reaches out, careful to keep on his side of the mark, holding the flask his father got from the lab, and pours it into the Horse's mouth:

Hugh pours the antidote into the Horse's mouth. The Swamp Horse changes into the White Horse.

"We better go," he says. "It's dangerous."

He squints, holding his mark, listening to the camera flitter, waiting to give the animation time to play out, not thinking of how he hasn't told Alex about the house, or the envelope of pictures beneath his bed that he cannot throw away, or his fear when he sees his mother's face as she stands in the kitchen; he is inside something, almost inside something, and he reaches out, past the mark, to touch the Horse's silvery coat, to smell his clean scent of sweat and hay, not thinking of what will happen when the camera stops, reciting his own words silently to himself, his own words almost real: *WHITE HORSE tosses his head. His eyes glow. HUGH and WHITE HORSE fade through roof.*

23.

That week, they shoot the movie, almost all of it, all of the scenes that Buddy has written. While Buddy films outside through Alex's window, Alex, as Gilda, bashes in his father's brains with a baseball bat. In the park near the bayou, Buddy comes out from behind a tree while Alex points a plastic gun at him, and his father, as the Stranger, drags a black garbage bag full of dirt, meant to be Woody, to the bayou. Buddy kneels in Alex's room, and speaks to the Horse, and prays at the window for his return. They work carefully, checking shots against storyboards to make sure they will look real. When they leave, Alex always thanks his father, but never looks him in the eye. Mr. Torres glares at them. But all of that happens far away, as if it is a movie itself. When he kneels and prays to the Horse, when he speaks to him, Buddy knows he's inside something, like he does when he wanders the new house; and he thinks that he understands how the Horse has always been so real to Alex, and he knows that the movie will be beautiful, and that there will be nothing anyone can say when it is finished.

In the evenings, his father and he sink new fence posts, bolt crossbeams, lay on facing. That Friday, they stand with his mother in the back yard. The fence towers above the kitchen window, above the carport, its greenish, hulking flank blocking the sunset. His mother squints at it, as she has all week; and there is still something quick and fearful about her, as if at any moment she might take flight.

"That's triple-treated wood," his father says. "It'll outlast the garage."

"It's very nice, Jimmy," she says. "It looks very solid."

His father wipes his face with his handkerchief, radiating heat; and at the same time, his movements are awkward and stiff, as if he thinks that everything he does is wrong. "We can take a couple feet off the top," he says. "It might look funny with those crossbeams so high up, though."

"No, Jimmy. I'm being ungrateful. It's fine. It's very nice."

His father wipes his hands on his jeans, grimacing at the fence. "Hey. It's Friday. Why don't I take you out to dinner? Why don't we go to Gaido's?"

"No, Jimmy," his mother says, turning from them, waving the notion away. "You've already done too much."

"What do you think?" his father says, to him.

Buddy remembers racing down the Gulf Freeway to Galveston, going to Gaido's in Grampa Turner's enormous car, in the time before his father left. And now, his father looks out at him from behind his rigid mask, trusting him.

"Yes, sir," he says. "That sounds good."

His mother cuts her eyes at him, sharp with accusation, and the fear he's seen before. "It's too much, Jimmy," she says. "It's too much."

"Please, Margot," his father says. "Let me do this. I want to do this for you."

His mother turns from them, fluttering her hand; but she doesn't say no. His father says he will clean up, and check on Grampa Turner, winking at him, a secret sign. While Buddy changes into his itchy suit, his mother stretches clothes hangers in her closet, muttering to herself. Then she stalks into the hallway, wearing a cream-colored slip. "It's not right," she says. "We can't let daddy do this."

He looks down at his socks; he can't look at her, at the scent of her lotion, the warm smell of her flesh. "Why not?" he says.

"Because this is what daddy does. He gives and gives and it's never what you want, but somehow you always end up owing him."

He imagines showing her the letter, and the pictures, hidden like a gun between the mattress and box springs where he sits. But he knows that he won't; and her trickiness, her fear and glinting hardness, infuriate him.

"Then why are we going?" he says.

"I don't know," she says; and he sees that she doesn't. "Because it's been a long time since I've been to Gaido's. Because your mother's just a fool, I guess."

❧ ❧

Above the Gulf Freeway, the sunset tints clouds pink against the still-blue sky. Buddy anchors his chin against the front seat on his itchy coat sleeve, remembering Grampa Turner's enormous car, Grampa Turner cool at the wheel, grinning as he raised and lowered the automatic windows to devil Gramma Turner, who clutched at her hair, yelling at him to stop; and he remembers, smelling the sharp scent of his father's aftershave and his mother's perfume, nights when they left him at Gramma Liddy's or Gramma Turner's, his mother's sweet, dusty scent enveloping him as she kissed him goodnight, before they disappeared; and he knows, now, that he is following them into their mysterious nighttime world, the world of Grampa Turner's movie. But he also knows that it is not the same; his father hunches over the steering wheel, staring ahead; his mother keeps her face turned to her window, her expression shifting, as if shadows played over it. But when they ascend the giant bridge above Galveston Bay, she touches his father's sleeve. Look, she says. You can see the Gulf. And it's true; above the abandoned railroad bridge whose draws were always raised, dark sails against the horizon, past the orange ghost of a ferry that plies the channel between Galveston and Bolivar, whitecaps lap a silvery sheen of open water, and Buddy doesn't know if he should be glad, seeing it, if he should be glad his mother has touched his father's sleeve.

At Gaido's, his father slips a folded bill to a boy who looks to Buddy not much older than he; the boy drives off in their car. His mother takes his arm and wobbles next to him up a frayed red carpet. Above them glows a fish-shaped sign: GAIDO'S.

Inside, it is the same as he remembers, or almost: a stooped man in a short red jacket leads them through hallways encrusted with seashells, a brass diver's helmet and a giant aquarium and a smooth black statue of a mermaid holding a spear. Hallways branch off to bathrooms, a gift shop, a bar, like an underwater grotto; and he can picture Gramma Turner in her canary-yellow dress and white gloves, and Grampa Turner, his face calm and handsome, and the owner himself, Mr. Gaido, showing them to their table, waiters in red jackets trailing them like gulls.

But the dining room is smaller than he remembers it, and almost empty. Old couples stare past each other, their meals already done. Candles glimmer on white linen tablecloths, ghostly in the gloom. In a far corner, a well-dressed family sits, one of the children a girl his own age, a dark blue dress, dark eyes and pale skin; and for a moment, he thinks it is the family from the new house, and the girl is Sarah, and he looks away from them, blushing with shame.

The waiter in the short red jacket leads them to a table that looks out on the Gulf. His mother touches her silverware, her water glass, looking down at the table. His father stares at her, his mouth slightly opened, as if he wants to speak; and Buddy looks away from them, at the oil rigs that blink against the deepening blue sky, at the waves that roll toward them over the brown water, the smell of tar and sand and the ocean's clean, rank scent reaching in through the plate-glass windows.

"Is this okay?" his father says.

"Yes, Jimmy," his mother says. "It's fine. It's very nice."

"We can go somewhere else."

"No, Jimmy." His mother touches his sleeve. "It's fine."

A waiter with bushy hair and a thick mustache and a sad, long face, who reminds him of Alex, arrives to take their order. His father asks for a Bushmill's neat; his mother, hesitating, orders a glass of wine. The waiter raises his eyebrows at him, not unkindly, and all of them look at him.

"A Coke, please, sir," he says.

"How is your father?" his mother says, after the waiter leaves.

"He's fine," his father says.

"Have you looked into any of the places we talked about?"

"Not yet. I'll look into it."

His mother touches her water glass, her knife, her eyes fixed, cross with herself, Buddy can tell, since she ordered the wine. "He needs to go where he can get help, Jimmy. It's not fair to him or your mother."

"I'll look into it," his father says.

His father bows his head, studying his menu; and after a moment, his mother does the same. Outside, waves lap toward them over the darkening, cement-colored water. The waiter swoops a tray of drinks onto the table like a magician, and the smell of alcohol and shoe polish expands in the air; his mother touches her wine glass, beaded with sweat, hesitating before she drinks.

"Whatever you want," his father says. "You can get whatever you want."

When the waiter returns, his mother orders the broiled flounder with rice and broccoli. His father orders the Fisherman's Platter: fried fish, fried shrimp, stuffed fried crabs and French fries and coleslaw. Buddy says he'll have the same. The waiter asks if they would like a wine to accompany their meal. His mother touches his father's sleeve, starting to speak; his father says they will take a bottle of the house white.

"That's too much, Jimmy," his mother says, after the waiter disappears.

"I'd rather have a bottle in front of me," his father says, grinning at Buddy, raising his glass of whiskey, "than a frontal lobotomy."

"Really, Jimmy. I'm serious."

His father's smile fades. "I'll tell him we don't want it."

His father cranes sideways in his chair, searching for the waiter. His mother touches her knife, vexed, then touches his father's sleeve.

"It's all right, Jimmy. You can take it home."

"You sure?" his father says.

"It's fine, Jimmy," his mother says. "It's very nice."

His father stares at his mother. Across the room, the dark-eyed girl watches them. Buddy lowers his eyes.

The waiter, hovering a few tables behind his father, steps quickly forward, holding a green bottle swathed in a white napkin, and presents it to his father, who says it looks fine. The waiter uncorks the bottle and pours a splash for his father, who says it tastes fine. The waiter pours wine into his mother's and father's glasses, then winks at Buddy, before he vanishes again.

"We should have a toast," his father says.

His mother lifts her new wine glass, and Buddy sees that the first one is empty, though he didn't see her drink it. His father opens his mouth, closes it, staring at him. "Maybe we should let Buddy do it," he says.

Buddy raises his Coke, not knowing what he will say, not looking at the dark-eyed girl; but he hopes, now, that she is watching them.

"To Grampa Turner," he says.

His mother and father clink glasses, and his, their eyes averted from him; and he doesn't know if what he's said is right.

"That's very sweet, honey," his mother says.

"That's right," his father says. "This place was it for him. Anytime anything important happened, we always came here."

His mother touches her wine glass. His father looks down at his plate. The waiter reappears, sweeping a huge tray of food onto the table, along with breadbaskets and pats of butter and side-dishes of coleslaw, refilling his mother's and father's wine glasses, announcing each dish. His mother's is the size of their dinner plates at home, but his father's and his own are as large as serving platters. Buddy digs into the crab's brown crust, into its tender belly, then into the shrimp, pinching the last sweet meat from their shells, into the flaky and always disappointing fish, and the French fries, and the coleslaw, no longer hungry, working doggedly around his plate.

His father bows his head, glancing at his mother, who pecks at her food, pushing at it with a piece of bread. "Is it okay?"

"Yes, Jimmy. It's fine."

"We can get you something else," his father says, turning to find the waiter.

His mother touches her wine glass, touches her fork, not looking at him. "No, Jimmy. It's fine. It's very nice."

His father stares at his mother, his jaw rigid. "I talked to the guy about the house. He says he's going to put it on the market when he finishes the repairs."

"I thought it was already on the market," his mother says.

"He took it back off. Wants to get a better price. Can't blame him. Buddy and I have been over there to see what he's doing. He and I could finish it in a week, tops."

"I've been wondering where you went," his mother says.

His father winces. "The point is," he says, "every day those workmen are there, the price goes up, and I haven't made a bid."

His mother touches her wine glass, which is empty again. "You should do what you need to do, Jimmy. I don't want you to get priced out of it."

"I'm not going to get priced out of it, Margot. That's not the point. He's told me what he's going to list it for. I could write him a check for the down payment right now. I could write a check for your mortgage and a check for his down payment, and still have money in the bank. If you sell your house, that's just extra."

"That's a big if," his mother says.

"I'm just saying, Margot," his father says.

His mother touches her wine glass, smiling a secret, tricky smile. "What would we do with my mother?" she says.

"There's a garage apartment behind it," his father says. "There are lots of apartments near Rice."

His mother shakes her head, still smiling. "Don't be ridiculous, Jimmy. She'd sooner check herself into a nursing home, or an insane asylum, than live out there. She hardly speaks to me, as it is."

His father stares at her. "I don't see what your mother has to do with it."

"I'm sorry, Jimmy. We shouldn't be talking about this."

"We don't need to sell your house, Margot. You can keep it and rent it out, whatever you want. Maybe your mother can live there. It doesn't matter to me about the down payment or the repairs. The goddamned house doesn't matter. I just want to give you what I promised. I just want to give us a better life."

His mother looks down at the table, her smile gone. "I'm sorry, Jimmy. I didn't mean to upset you. We can talk about this later."

"When?" his father says.

His mother touches her wine glass.

"When?" his father says.

"Later, Jimmy," she says, touching his father's sleeve. "We'll talk about it later."

Across the room, the dark-eyed girl and her family are gone. Outside, white waves roll toward them, the water as smooth and black as stone, the same darkness in the bayou that flows down to the Gulf; and Buddy imagines them vanishing — his mother, father, and he — in the candlelight and sound of the surf.

"What was it like?" he says.

"What was what like, honey?"

"When you were here before?"

His mother flutters her hand, shooing the question away. "Which time?"

He knows that she is lying. "I don't know," he says. "It was light outside. We had to go to a speech. Gramma Turner and Grampa Turner were here."

"Do you know what he's talking about?"

His father nods, staring through him. "My med school graduation, I bet."

"Oh, yes," his mother says, touching her glass. "The day that never ended."

His father looks at her, his head bowed, uncertain. "Why's that?"

"Don't you remember?" his mother says. "I guess not. You were already here for the rehearsal, so you missed all the fun. Your mother and father and Buddy and I came down in your father's old car. He was driving your mother crazy with those windows. She'd had her hair done the day before, and was on pins and needles that everything had to be perfect. He'd gotten a suite at the Galvez so she could change her clothes before the ceremony. We sat in there for hours. Buddy was bored out of his skull and driving me crazy, and she was driving me and your father crazy with her worry."

Buddy doesn't remember the hotel, or waiting with Gramma Turner; all he sees are bright flashes from Grampa Turner's movie — his mother and father, Gramma Turner and Grampa Turner; his father, flanked by his mother and Gramma Turner, wearing a dark blue robe. "Sounds like I missed the best part," his father says.

"She drove us crazy because she was so proud," his mother says, touching her glass. "All of us were so proud of you, that day."

His mother keeps her face turned from them, watching the Gulf; and Buddy feels them waver, in the candlelight and sound of the surf.

"What about before?" he says.

"Before what, honey?"

"Before that."

"Before that," his father says, "your mother and Sister Bertille taught me all I know about histology and chemistry, and most of what I know about pathology."

"That's not true, Jimmy," his mother says. "You worked so hard. Sister Bertille always said she'd never seen anyone who worked as hard as you. Every morning, even when you were at Rice, I'd come in and see your little cot made up behind the blood bank and know you were there. You drove her and everyone else crazy. But she knew you loved that place. She knew it was your refuge."

"When I was in med school," his father says, "I used to slap myself awake, driving back from Galveston. I had classes in the morning and a shift at the lab in the afternoon, and did stats and frozen sections until I came home."

His father ascended the porch steps in his white lab coat, ghostly, heroic, beneath the yellow porch light; and it is almost real, almost as it was, again.

"You drove everyone absolutely crazy," his mother says. "But we were all so proud. There's a tech there now who reminds me of you, then, Manil Ghose. He kind of haunts the place. I keep telling him to go home to his wife and children, but he won't hear it. I want to shake him and send him home and feed him dinner and give him a swift kick in the rear, all at the same time. I know he's not going to change, but I can't stop hoping. That lab is his real home. He doesn't fit anywhere else."

His father stares at his mother; and Buddy imagines them dissolving in the darkness, in the Gulf's clean, rank smell and the sound of the surf.

"What else?" he says.

"That's it," his mother says, turning to him, touching her face with the edge of her hand. "That's all there is to it, honey. Let's talk about something else."

☙ ❧

But all the way home, on the freeway, its pocked gray ribbon unreeling before them over the giant bridge, into the wooded darkness, the no-place between Houston and Galveston threaded with miles of pipeline, forgotten, uncharted, his father has told him, which would one day blow the city to bits, in the *clop-clop, clop-clop* of the rushing car wheels, in the sharp scent of his father's aftershave and his mother's sweet perfume, now mixed with the sour smells of whiskey and wine, his mother's and father's voices weave the past before his father was gone, their faces reflected in the dashboard's green glow on the windows' dark glass: how he believed that his father, coming home at night in his white lab coat, was an angel returning from the dead, how he believed the nuns were angels, too, and their convent was Heaven, and the basement morgue was Hell; and with names that are familiar, names he's never heard, they conjure the yellow kitchen table crowded with bottles, the men with long sideburns and women in short, splashy dresses; and in the darkness, in their thick silence, their voices — his father's sly and joking, his mother's quick and hesitant — weave another story, like the story when they talked in the yard, that he knew he would never understand.

When he pulls into the driveway, his father sits, staring at the greenish fence. Since they turned off the freeway, he and his mother were quiet. Buddy leans over the front seat, his chin anchored on his coat sleeve. His mother keeps her face turned to her window, as closed and mysterious as it is to him in prayer.

"Can I come in?" his father says.

"Just for a minute," his mother says, glancing at him. "Just for a minute, Jimmy. Then you need to go home."

Inside, his father excuses himself, and disappears into the back of the house. Buddy stands in the bright yellow kitchen, watching his mother fill a glass with tap water, slide a box of orange snack crackers off the top of the refrigerator, put it back, open the refrigerator, close it again, her face still inward-looking, mysterious to him, as if she is braced for a storm from which she can't find shelter, from which she doesn't want to find shelter; and he feels something slip, as he did, listening to their voices in the car; and he knows he should run to his room, show her the pictures, and the letter. But he stands, watching her, his fists clenched over the sleeves of his itchy jacket, rooted in place, like she is, by the same, mysterious force, as his father advances through the dining room, watching him as if he knows what he thinks.

"Have you still got that bottle of Paddy's?" his father says.

"It's over the pantry." His mother squints at him, trying to bring him into focus. "I'm not having any. You shouldn't either, if you're going to drive home."

His father smiles at him, slips past him, reaching above the pantry near the front door, sets on the dissecting table a bottle of Paddy's, which glints in the bright yellow light. "Really, Jimmy," his mother says. "I'm serious."

His father takes a bullet-shaped glass from a high shelf in a cabinet next to the sink and pours the golden liquid into it, cutting off the stream with a flick of his wrist.

"Maybe I won't have to drive home," he says.

His mother squints at him. "You should get to bed, sport," she says, to Buddy. "It's time to get to bed and tell daddy good night."

"I don't want to tell daddy good night."

"He doesn't want to tell me good night." His father raises the golden glass, tips it back, winking at him. "What do you want to do?" he says.

His mother starts to speak. His father watches him; and he knows he should run to his room. "A fort, sir," he says. "I'd like to build a fort."

"Jimmy. It's late. He needs to get to bed. You need to go home. I don't want to have to clean up the living room after you two have torn it apart."

His father drains his glass, places it on the lab table with a precise click. "It's okay, Margot. Everything's okay. A fort sounds like fun."

In the living room, his father switches on the lamp near the chair that looks out on the driveway, the lamp in a corner next to the couch, the lamp on the heavy wooden desk, so that the room becomes a furnace of light, a bubble against the flat darkness that presses against the windows. His father strips cushions from the butterscotch-colored chair, from the chair near the window that looks out on the driveway, from the couch. The cushions will be the walls of the fort, levered against one another. Buddy watches him, not knowing why he said they should build a fort; he remembers crouching inside the cushions' soft darkness, and the sweet anticipation, the giddy fear that tickled his throat, as he waited for his father, a giant who raged outside, to crash through the walls. Now, in the kitchen, the refrigerator sucks open, wine hiccoughs into a glass, his mother whispers to herself, a sharp, skittering reproach, and it is not the same; it is monstrous and strange, a movie he's made, that he knows he has to stop.

He reaches out, grabbing a cushion; but his father swings it away from him, laughing easily, his face flushed, beaded with sweat, as the slick fabric slips through Buddy's hands. Buddy grasps a throw pillow, but his father plucks it, laughing, dancing away from him, watching him as if he knows what he thinks.

"What are you doing?" his mother says, her voice tricky, like her voice in the car; and Buddy doesn't know if she means what she says.

"What are you doing?" she says. "You're tearing the place apart!"

He knows that she is lying; he knows they are betraying him. He swings a couch cushion at his father, the cushion huge, cartoonish in his hands; his father dances away, vanishing behind him, everywhere and nowhere at once. Buddy closes his eyes, swinging at his father; and in the darkness, in his blindness, the drawings creep out, skittering over his skin. In the darkness, he swings at his father, lost inside a giant house, trying to batter its shifting walls, reaching out to grasp at nothing; but he swings at his father, bare-fisted, crying, now, his tears bitter and childish, landing blows on his arms and legs and chest, knowing he can't stop them.

"That's enough, Jimmy," his mother says. "That's enough."

He swings at his father, but his father catches him, and presses him against his ribcage, murmuring in a voice like his voice at the track when Buddy said he hated him, and Buddy feels himself dissolve in his warmth; but he lurches away, striking out at him, and falls, feeling himself fall, letting himself fall, and the sharp wooden desk sends pain like light through his face, and he lies on the dusty carpet, covering his face with his hands, hoping that this would stop them.

"Are you all right, sugar?" his mother says. "Is he all right? I told you, Jimmy. I told you that was enough. Are you okay, honey? Are you all right?"

His father crouches next to him, and touches his face, his hand clean-smelling, rough and strong. "Are you okay, Buddy?" he says. "Can you open your eyes?"

He keeps his eyes shut tight, smelling his own hands, grease and coleslaw and fish; he can already hear, in the thickness of their voices, that he has made a mistake.

"Buddy?" his father says. "Can you open your eyes?"

He keeps his eyes shut tight, not wanting to look at them; he knows what he will see: they will be monstrous, not themselves but their secret selves, like their reflections in the mirror at Christmas. "Buddy?" his father says. "I'm sorry."

His father pries his hand gently from his face, looks out from behind his mask, his face the one he sought in the movies, his real father's face.

"I'm sorry," his father says. "I'm sorry, Buddy. It's time to say goodnight."

᠅

Later, he lies in bed, still dressed in his itchy suit, listening to the silvery sound of a trumpet thread from a record player in the living room, and to their voices, thick with the silence he heard in the car. Then they are quiet, and his mother pads barefoot through the dining room, his father following her with his creaking tread, and the filament of light that traces the edge of his door widens, and he shuts his eyes, feeling them watch him, until the door closes again.

This is hard on him, his mother says. It confuses him.

I can go, his father says.

No, Jimmy. Then, Are you sure, Jimmy? Are you sure this is alright?

His mother is only pretending, he thinks. Her voice is nothing like her real voice, the one she uses at the lab, the one she used with his father a few weeks before. The letter and envelope are only inches beneath him; he can get up, burst through the door. But he lies, frozen by what he imagines he would find. In the darkness, the drawings swarm, opening their gaping, hungry mouths, reaching out for him with blunted, slippery limbs; and he knows what he will hear, if he doesn't get up: the sounds he heard that summer, not knowing what they meant; but he knew what they meant, even then. It isn't the sounds that stop him, or what he imagines he will find; they are only evidence of what is happening, not what is happening itself. He lies, frozen by the terrible, mysterious force, and shuts his eyes, knowing he's a coward, and drives himself down into the darkness of sleep, through the floor beneath his bed, into the cool dirt beneath the house, into another house whose walls and windows multiply, unfolding in impossible shapes, until he unfolds with them, until he vanishes in them like sand.

❧⬥❧

When he wakes, gray light filters through his windows. In his mother's room, his father snores. For a moment, he wonders if he's slipped back to the morning Grampa Liddy died, into the time before his father had left. But he knows that isn't true; he knows because of what has woken him.

He gets up, takes the movies from their shelf, digs down to the bottom of the box, past the movies he knows, to the movies he's rushed through before. He clicks on the editor, snaps a reel on one of its arms, threads a leader through its aperture, pulls the film taut, his hands trembling, knowing what he would find. There is Sister Bertille, and his father, round-faced, scrubbed-looking, not older than an upper-school boy, at a luncheon at the convent. There is his mother, her arms sleek in a sleeveless dress, trying to herd a gaggle of students out of the kitchen. There is the woman — a face in a crowd at the hospital, a face behind his father at a party in their house — though she wasn't the woman, then, but someone else; and he slows the film until she becomes only patterns of light, trying to remember who she was.

She was the hippie woman who gave him weird sugarless candy, who wore Indian-print blouses and short, splashy dresses. As he scrolls through the movies, she is a glimpse, a profile, sometimes only a shadow, in lab parties and luncheons and awkward group poses; but he remembers, his skin scalded with shame, that he thought she was beautiful, and that he wanted her to love him. He remembers her chiseled smile and strong, nervous touch, and the colored blocks in a white room deep inside the hospital where his father took him, and his father smiled too much, and the woman kept touching his hand. And then they left for what seemed like a long time, and he was terrified that he would vanish in its whiteness. On the way home, his father told him it might be better if they didn't mention the test to his mother. But his father didn't have to ask; he was glad to keep his father's secret, because it made the terror somehow less.

None of it is true, anymore. He looks up from the editor's hooded screen. Outside, it is almost daylight. On the floor is a pile of movies where he's found the woman; the ones without her are stacked in the box. He doesn't know how his mother discovered the test. He doesn't think he told her; he is sure he didn't.

In her room, his father snores. For a moment, he imagines bursting through her door, stabbing the sheets, killing them. But he knows it will make no difference. He knows what he has to do, and quickly. Soon, they will both awake.

He gathers the canisters of film into his coat pockets, replaces the box on its shelf, takes the letter and envelope of pictures from between his mattress and box springs. He moves through the hallway where his mother's door is shut, a blank face, mute and white, past the living room, exactly as it has always been, no sign of what happened there the night before. In the kitchen, shades are drawn, and in the grainy darkness, the boys from the field flit, watching him; but he isn't afraid of them.

Outside, the sky is tinted pink, the air fresh with the smell of the sea and coffee from the coffee plant, so quiet that even the freeway's whisper is hushed. He unlocks the garage, takes out the foxhole shovel, locks the sliding door again. In the ship channel, a barge moans; he worries it might rouse them. He goes to the back corner of the yard, to his mother's compost, and unscrews the metal ring on the foxhole shovel, unfolds its blade, tightens the ring again, as his father showed him; he puts the letter and envelope and canisters of film into a plastic bag from the kitchen, his hands trembling, the shovel and letter and film electric to his touch.

He plunges the shovel into the compost. Worms runnel up like water, like figures from the drawings; he cuts through them, past eggshells and onion skins and stalks of liquefying broccoli, digging under the dark, rich loam, into the clean earth below. A freight train rumbles and crashes; another plays a high, silvery note. From the branches of trees and the roofs of houses and the corners of houses still in shadow, the boys watch him, but he isn't afraid; he works silently, as swift and supple as a knife, as if he is invisible, as if he is already one of them.

24.

Some nights, when his father stays, the sounds creep out of his mother's room. Sometimes his mother tells his father to go home to Gramma Turner's after they talk, as they do each night, about Grampa Turner. Some nights, after his father leaves, he will listen to his mother roam the empty house, chiding herself; and he knows what he would see, if he could see her, the face she turns to him when his father leaves, delicate with uncertainty, though each day it grew more bold, like her face in the movies.

Some mornings, his father is there, whistling in the shower. Even when he isn't, the bathroom smells of him, of Vitalis and Bay Rum and Listerine, like the bathroom in the woman's apartment. In the mornings, they pick up hamburgers, and his father talks about what they need to do at the new house, or his mother's house, or with the movie, and Buddy presses his forehead against his window, listening not to what he says, but to the sound of his voice, for clues to whether the woman is still there.

But in the afternoons, when he sits on Alex's bed, trying to finish the script, and Alex lies on the floor, drawing, Buddy watches his father, who stands over the camera, clamped in its metal stock on Alex's desk, pushing the shutter wire, clicking off frames with a hand-held cell counter, six for each drawing, to put the animation on the film they've rewound in Mr. Torres' bathroom, that his father has taken carefully from its black plastic cartridge and replaced. His father's face, then, is as calm and patient as when he's spread the sand, as when he showed him the beautiful purple cells in his microscope, long ago; and Buddy doesn't know if he should love or hate him.

At school, the drawings have stopped. Almost overnight, something has changed. The boys still jostle him, eyeing him with a kind of wariness and distaste; but now the talk is of notes passed between them and the girls, in ceremonies profound and grave, and even boys who have no hope of receiving a note, like Sandy, knew the stories of those who did, like Sam; and suddenly, no one cared about Gene and Simon, or the rumors they spread, that Sam was already living with his grandmother, that his mother had already been taken away.

Simon himself seemed strange, a character from a book. One day at P.E., a few weeks after his father came back, Buddy found him walking alone to the soccer field. Boys ran ahead of them, dressed in shorts and white T-shirts in the warm, muggy day, shouting out teams for football, which replaced Smear the Queer. Simon followed them, reciting something, Buddy saw, from the movement of muscles in his neck; and Buddy watched his broad, straight shoulders, wishing that he could tell him about the pictures and the letter and the movies. But he knew that this was only a childish thought; he knew that Simon was nothing, and he had to show him exactly what he was.

Buddy jogged up next to him; Simon kept his eyes trained straight ahead, his face the one he wore to school.

"We're going to move," Buddy said. "My dad's going to buy a house near Rice." Simon didn't look at him.

"We're going to move there soon," Buddy said. "I'm going to St. John's." Simon quickened his pace.

"When's your dad going to sell your house?" Buddy said, wishing that Simon would look at him, wishing Simon would hit him. "What are you going to do?"

∂◦◦

That Friday, when he picks him up from school, his father tells him they aren't going to Alex's house, but to his mother's. All the way home, he keeps glancing at Buddy, savoring a secret. Buddy knows what it is. That week his mother's china cabinet has emptied, and pictures disappeared from the walls; he knows that they are leaving. But he presses his forehead against his window, answering his father lightly when he asks about his friends, and how he's done in school.

His mother's house smells of shrimp and crab boil. Her battered car parked beneath the greenish, hulking fence, the sand almost covered by a thin furze of grass – all of it looks strange, as it has since his father has returned; and Buddy steels himself, framing a shot, trying to see it as it really is.

In the kitchen, his mother glances up at them, chopping onions at the dissecting table. Beneath her apron, she wears a frilly, long-sleeved dress, a dress that the woman would wear. Since his father came back, she doesn't wear her white uniform at home. She turns to his father, to kiss him. They don't talk, as they usually do, of his mother's lab or Sister Bertille, or the techs at his father's lab; she watches Buddy evenly, trying to see if his father has told him what he already knows.

"Smells great," his father says. "I'll wash up."

His father winks at him, and vanishes into the back of the house. Buddy keeps his face turned from his mother, as he has since his father kissed her. One night that week, he found her wrapping pictures in newspaper in her room. She said nothing to him, then, and he didn't ask her what she was doing.

Now, he turns from her, heading toward the living room.

"Buddy?" she says.

He keeps going, not looking at her; the drawings creep over him, runneling through his skin. But she catches his arm, her eyes blinded with worry and love, and when she speaks, her voice is hopeful, like her voice when she talked to herself in the kitchen, and he can't tell if she believes what she says.

"It's okay, honey," she says. "It's okay. Everything's going to be alright."

☙❧

The dining room smells of shrimp and crab boil and coffee from the coffee plant, borne in on a soft Gulf breeze. Sunlight spangles through the oak leaves outside. All of it looks delicate and unreal, even his mother, fiddling with yellow potato salad on her plate, and his father, shucking shrimp from their pink shells; but there is nothing strange about it. This is how they've eaten since his father came back, in the dining room, as they did only on special occasions since his father left; and Buddy watches them carefully, from far away, trying to see who they really are.

"The shrimp are excellent, Margot," his father says. "First rate."

His mother flutters her hand over the table, over the bowls and glasses and plates. "Thank you, Jimmy. They were on sale."

"Still," his father says. "They're excellent. Perfect for a celebration."

His mother touches her wine glass, not looking at his father, and there is nothing unusual about this, either; she often speaks to his father with her eyes downcast.

"Did you get a chance to call Sunnyside?" she says.

His father shucks a shrimp. "I'll call them. We had stats all day."

His mother touches her wine glass, touches her plate. "You need to call them, Jimmy. It'll be weeks before they can get him in there, as it is."

"I'll call them," his father says.

"Have you looked into getting any more help for your mother?"

His father stills his hands, and glances at him, staring at his mother across the table. "I'm working on it, Margot. I check his vitals and listen to his chest every day. He's doing fine. I think he's even getting a little movement back."

"I know you're doing your best, Jimmy. But if you don't get some help now, it's going to be a lot harder, later, when you have to let go."

"Do you think," his father says, "that maybe we could talk about this later? Maybe when we're not trying to have a goddamned celebration?"

His mother looks down at her plate.

"I'm sorry, Margot," his father says. "I shouldn't've said that."

"No, Jimmy. I'm sorry. I didn't mean to ruin anything."

His father turns to him, trapped behind his rigid mask; and Buddy thinks of how they talk outside at night, how his mother told his father he needed to help Grampa Turner, how his father told her he didn't know how to help him.

"I'm sorry, Buddy," his father says. "I shouldn't've said that. Your mother says you're doing real well in school. We're all real proud."

At night, while his father worked outside in the yard, he sat at the heavy wooden desk, wishing his father would quiz him; and now, he can't help but flush with pleasure at his words. "Yes, sir," he says.

"We're all real proud," his father says, glancing at his mother, seeking her help. "Isn't that right, Margot?"

"Yes, honey," she says. "We are."

"I know it's been hard, Buddy. It's been hard for you and your mother. But it's going to be better. Everything's going to be better. That's why we need to talk to you."

His father pauses, glancing at his mother; but his mother keeps her eyes on the table. "Everything's going to be better, Buddy," he says. "Everything's going to change. I talked to the guy who owns the house. I wrote him a check. We're going to move, Buddy. We're going to move to the new house, and we can all be happy."

The house and living room and light through the windows seem made of glass; and his mouth is as dry as glass, and he finds that he cannot speak.

"I know you're worried about your friend," his father says; he's almost said the movie, Buddy can see it, a tightening in his face. "You can still visit him. But you'll be able to live in a better neighborhood and go to a better school. Maybe you can go to St. John's. Everything'll be different. Everything'll be better, Buddy."

His father watches him, ready to flinch, like he did at Fort Polk. "If you don't want to do that," he says, "if you want to stay here, we can do that, too. I can call the guy and cancel the check. We can all stay here and be happy. We just want what's best for you, Buddy. Understand? That's why we're doing this. All of it's for you."

He thinks of their voices outside at night — *for him*, they said, *for him*. Listening to them, his skin glowed with pride and exultation; and he knows, now, that his father believes what he's said. The light through the windows and the smell of coffee from the coffee plant and his mother's empty china cabinet — all of it will be swept away. For a moment, he imagines running to the yard, digging up the pictures and letter and movies; but he knows that he won't. He doesn't know if he loves or hates his father, but he knows he has to follow his father into the other world, the real movie, more vivid than the one they live in now; he only knows that he has to live in the world with him.

"No, sir," he says. "Let's go."

The telephone rings. His father rises, winking at him, and goes to the kitchen. His mother watches him across the table, her face hard and veiled, like it was after Christmas. "What are you going to do?" he says.

She lifts her hand, turning to the kitchen, to silence him. Buddy has heard it, too, the change in his father's voice; but he can't think of it, right then.

"What are you going to do?" he says.

His mother rises, covering her mouth with her hand, and hurries from the table. Sunlight spangles through the trees outside. Buddy turns to the window, trying not to think of what Gramma Turner has said will happen when Grampa Turner dies. In the kitchen, his father is crying, his mother shushing him, as if he was a child.

25.

Gramma Turner stares straight ahead, past vacant fields and strip malls and apartment complexes. All week, his father has asked his mother to come to the funeral, but his mother refused, saying she doesn't want to upset Gramma Turner, that it isn't her place; his father said he doesn't give a shit about upsetting Gramma Turner, that Grampa Turner would've wanted his mother to be there; then he said that everything he's done, he's done too late, that everything has been a mistake, that he was afraid of what Gramma Turner would do, now that Grampa Turner was gone.

Now he hunches over the steering wheel in a dark suit; and Buddy watches him, waiting to see what he will do.

"We're late, Jimmy," Gramma Turner says.

His father stares ahead, gripping the steering wheel, silent.

"Late," she says, making a sound like her skeptical noise, a dry, humorless laugh. "You're sure she's not coming, Jimmy? I don't need that kind of grief. Not today."

His father wrenches the car into a parking lot, under the awning of a long, low brick building that looks like a bank. On its plate-glass doors, past a strip of red carpet, gold lettering glimmers: Earthman's Funeral Home. All week, Buddy has imagined how he will answer Grampa Turner if he speaks to him; but he can't think of that, right now. His father stalks around the car and opens its door for Gramma Turner, who bats away his hand.

"Goddammit, mamma," he says. "I'm trying to help."

Buddy gets out. Gramma Turner struggles up from her seat, gripping his arm, her fingers digging through the sleeve of his itchy jacket.

"I'll see you later, mamma," his father says, waving at her, as they start up the carpet. "I'll pick you up after the service."

Gramma Turner keeps going. Buddy turns to smile at his father, to show him that he hates her; but his laughter clenches inside his chest.

"Goddammit, mamma," his father says, grimacing, no pleasure in his smile. "I'll be back in a minute. I'm going to park the car."

Gramma Turner keeps going, her shoulders bowed beneath the terrible weight. Ahead, a man in a shiny black suit and a tie printed with piano keys opens one of the plate-glass doors, and Buddy sees in his quick glance that he's heard what his father has said; and Buddy looks away from him, blushing with shame.

"Mrs. Turner?" the man says. "You probably don't remember me. I'm Rudy Vargas. I was in Mr. Turner's jazz band at Jeff Davis. I just wanted to say I'm sorry."

Behind her thick glasses, Gramma Turner blinks, and Buddy sees that she doesn't remember the man at all; but she reaches out, and grasps his hand, and shakes it.

"Rudy Vargas!" she says. "Of course I remember you! Mr. Turner sure was proud of you! Are you still playing your little music?"

The man smiles, glancing at him, not believing her.

"Yes, ma'am," he says. "On weekends."

"You're just going to have to tell me all about it, Rudy!" Gramma Turner says. "You're just going to have to tell me every little thing!"

When they enter the brightly-lit lobby, the faces of men — black men and brown men and white, who stand among overstuffed couches and coffee tables sprouting boxes of Kleenex — turn to them in a wave. They come toward Gramma Turner, extending their hands, murmuring their sympathies, reminding her that they are his grandfather's students and concert promoters, band leaders and workers at the radio station, long-time listeners to his radio show, restaurant owners and owners of clubs: The Bronze Peacock, The Silver Slipper, The El Dorado Ballroom, The Zydeco Ballroom, The Continental Lounge. Among them are faces Buddy recognizes from the pictures in Grampa Turner's den: Calvin Owens, the band leader at the El Dorado, whose neat goatee and wire-rimmed glasses make him look like a teacher; and next to him, Don Robey, the most powerful man in Houston music, black or white, his grandfather said. They loom over him like revenants, dull-eyed, alert, harbitten, suave, enclosing him in their suits' whispering fabric and man-smells of tobacco and cologne; and Gramma Turner clasps their hands, exclaiming in her high, false voice that she remembers them all; and though he hates her, though he knows that her recognition of them is fake, as fake as all of the adult world, he cannot help but feel proud when they gaze down at him, when she introduces him as her grandson.

Mr. Robey and Mr. Owens move through the crowd, past a reef of women with white helmet-hair and men with worn famers' faces. Mr. Robey extends his hands, enclosing Gramma Turner's hands in his huge grasp; he smells more beautiful than any man Buddy has ever met, and his voice rolls out as if he was speaking inside a church, and Buddy knows, from the watchfulness in Gramma Turner's face, that she sees exactly who he is.

"Your grandfather was a great man," Mr. Robey says. "He did great things. He was the first radio announcer in Houston to play my records, when no one else would play them, when even Mr. Owens here couldn't attend a concert at the Rice Hotel."

Mr. Owens nods, frowning, fingering his beret, as if he's heard an unpleasant joke. "And do you know why your grandfather did that?" Mr. Robey says. "Not out of charity — no. He did it because it made good sense to bring those same people who'd heard Duke Ellington at the Rice Hotel to hear him again at the El Dorado. Good sense, to place Bronze Peacock records at Sakowitz's as well as at Krell's."

Mr. Robey stares down at him from above his pin-striped chest, to see if his point has sunk in. "Isn't that right, Mrs. Turner?"

"Yes, sir, Mr. Robey," Gramma Turner says. "That's exactly right."

"None of this marching in the streets and burning down your own businesses. None of that foolishness."

"No, sir," Gramma Turner says.

A helmet-haired woman from the edge of the crowd comes forward and grasps his grandmother's arm. Mr. Robey glares at her. "Katie," the woman says, to his grandmother. "Where've you been?"

"Not now, Troylynn," Gramma Turner says.

"We've been waiting for you," the woman says. "The service is about to start."

"Not now, Troylynn," Gramma Turner says. "This is business."

The woman looks at Mr. Robey, then his grandmother, then clutches Buddy's arm. Her silvery hair seems to float above her head; her eyes are two hard chips of glass. "Don't you remember me?" she says. "I haven't seen you since you were just a little thing! Why don't we have a nice little visit and let your gramma talk?"

Then the woman is dragging him away, pinching muscle from bone, past the men's curious faces. She's Mrs. Treat, she says, his grandmother's oldest and dearest friend; she's come all the way from Navesota just for his grandfather's funeral. Buddy remembers her from lunches at Gramma Turner's house in the time before his father left; and he remembers that he disliked her, even then.

Mrs. Treat pokes her sharp face close to his. "Is your daddy here?" she says.

Beyond the flowered walls of the hallway where they stand, men's voices murmur, and he wishes that he was with them; and something brushes him, telling him to answer her carefully. "Yes, ma'am," he says.

"Where is he?"

"Outside, ma'am. Parking the car."

Mrs. Treat sucks breath through her teeth, shakes her head. "Your poor gramma. She sure is carrying a heavy load."

He doesn't know what she means; he knows what she means, and he despises her.

"Is anyone with him?" she says.

He thinks of his mother alone in their house, wrapping glasses in newspaper, and he wants to tell Mrs. Treat that she should be there, that Grampa Turner would have wanted her to be there. "No, ma'am," he says.

"Are you sure about that?"

"Yes, ma'am."

"You're sure? You're sure there's no one else?"

"Yes, ma'am," he says, wishing he could yell something obscene in her face. "My mother had to stay home."

Mrs. Treat flinches. Her face recedes, and he sees that she knows she's made a mistake; and the ghost hand that brushed him before closed over his chest.

Gramma Turner rounds a corner, guided by Mr. Robey, and snatches Buddy's arm. "Excuse us, Mr. Robey," she says. "I'd like to visit Mr. Turner before the service."

"Katie," Mrs. Treat says. "I'm sorry."

Gramma Turner keeps going, pulling her with him.

"What did Troylynn ask you?" she says.

"Nothing, ma'am," he says. "She asked where daddy is."

Gramma Turner squeezes his arm, and he can tell she wants to ask him something else. At the end of the hallway, she pushes through a pair of padded doors. They are in a chapel, where organ music whirrs, and stained-glass windows, jagged strips of blue and red and gold, taper to a vaulted ceiling; and in the darkness, in the chapel's deeper silence, he knows that Gramma Turner hasn't asked him the question because she is afraid, and the hand closes over him again, tightening in his chest.

"You don't have to go with me, Buddy," she says, squeezing his arm.

"No, ma'am," he says, ashamed of his own fear. "I'll go."

They start down the center aisle, between rows of pews dotted here and there with people who have already taken their seats. Ahead, on the altar, is what looks like a tiny boat with one square sail raised. Around it, men in dark suits arrange flowers, so that the boat seems borne up on a sea of white; but he knows that isn't really what it is.

As they pass the rows of pews, Gramma Turner lifts her hand, nodding at the people who wave to her, pale faces, pale shapes in the darkness.

"I know you've got those pictures, Buddy," she says.

The hand tightens, but he tells himself that there is nothing she can do, that there is nothing, now, he has to fear from her; they will escape, to the new house, and the tree-shaded streets, the real movie where they will live with his father.

"Yes, ma'am," he says.

"What do you think you're going to do with them, Buddy?"

"I don't know, ma'am."

"Come on, honey," she says, giving his arm a little shake. "Don't fool with me."

Ahead, in the little boat – *in the coffin*, he says, silently, *in my grandfather's coffin*, trying to make real what he sees with his words – he glimpses his grandfather's profile, the tip of his nose in its white, gaping mouth, and looks away.

"I don't know, ma'am," he says. "I guess I'll throw them out."

Gramma Turner is silent, and when she speaks, her voice is different from the one she's used with him, different from how she's ever spoken to him before.

"What do you think is going to happen, Buddy," she says, "when you and your mother and your daddy move to that new house? What do you think it's going to be like, carrying everything you do in your little mind? Let's say one day you don't want to keep carrying all that. Let's say one day your mother finds something out. Let's say your daddy does something, because he just can't help it. All those things come to the same thing, honey. Your mother can try to take that big, new house, and if she does, your daddy'll be left with nothing. And if she can't, and if she's sold her house, you and she won't have anything to go back to, and your daddy won't have anything left from fighting her, and then all we've worked for, your mamma and daddy and granddaddy and everyone, all of it will be gone."

Ahead, as they ascend the steps to the altar, the men arranging the flowers recede, bowing and whispering their respects. He can't look at the coffin, at its white, gaping mouth; and the flowers' thick smell presses breath from his chest.

"It's a beautiful dream, honey," Gramma Turner says, "what your daddy's told you, about living in that big, new house. But I want you to think, Buddy, about what's really going to happen. I want you to think what it's going to do to my little Buddy, carrying all that on your little mind. It might be hard, now, to show your mother those pictures, but it's going to be a lot harder if you wait. So I want you to think, Buddy. I want you to think about what you should really do with those pictures."

In the coffin, he glimpses his grandfather's face — his wide, handsome brow, his jet-black hair, his nose somehow sharper than it was before — and looks away, shrinking from the coldness that reaches out like a hand. Gramma Turner lets go of his arm, then stands, holding the edge of the coffin, her back to him, and bows her head, covering her mouth with a tissue. Her shoulders shake, and he knows that she is crying; he knows he should go to her, to comfort her, but something stops him, something holds him, like the wild, angry pride, a bitter ache in his throat.

Gramma Turner weeps; he knows there is something wrong with him, that he will not go to her. He moves toward the coffin, not looking at his grandfather; then he looks, before he can think, before he can stop himself from looking, as if touching his hand to flame. But even before he looks — after he looks, but before he can really see him — he knows his grandfather isn't there. Someone else who seems like him, but isn't him, has taken his place. The man's eyes are hidden like two marbles beneath their lids, his flesh shrunk against the bones of his face; and on his hands, folded over his chest, the blue veins which marked his grandfather's hands have vanished, as if they have been erased. He reaches out, and touches the man's hand; and the coldness and stillness shoot through him, a message from another world. He waits, listening, though he knows that he will never betray his father; but he waits, listening for his grandfather's voice.

∻

Outside, blackbirds flutter in the birdbath, fanning water-diamonds into the bright air. In the garage, Gramma Turner and his father argue, as they have since his father slipped next to them in their pew at the funeral; and Buddy presses his forehead against the cool glass doors, wishing he had the camera, so he could see the birds as they really are; but he knows, even as he thinks it, that this is only a childish wish.

He goes through the living room, past the china and sofa and wing-backed chairs, through the little room with the day bed, knowing where it is, the thing that watches him, in the darkness above him, in the thick darkness and mothball smell. He opens the back door, presses his face against the screen door's mesh, smelling its sweet, coppery scent, and the smells of wood and cut grass on the cool spring air, not caring if his father and Gramma Turner catch him, not caring what he hears; soon, they will move, and nothing they can say will matter, and he won't have to listen anymore.

I just need more time, mamma, his father says.

You haven't got more time, Jimmy. If you don't get out of this now, you're going to hurt yourself, and everyone around you, worse than you've ever known. You can't keep paying, honey, for a mistake you made twelve years ago.

Slowly, he opens the screen door, closes it behind him. Though their words are the same, something in their voices is different from when they've argued before; and he wants to know what his father's mistake was.

It's not like that, mamma, his father says.

Then tell me, Jimmy. Tell me what it's like. For the last twelve years, you've been telling me it was a mistake. We barely got you out of medical school because of all you were carrying. Now you're telling me that's what you wanted? That wasn't what you wanted, Jimmy, to live like that, with someone you can't even trust. We've worked too hard to let you live like that. That's why I'm trying to help you, honey.

I'm sorry, mamma. I don't want your help.

That's what you think now. She's already gotten what she wants. She already got herself a child. But that was just one stupid mistake, Jimmy, and now she's going to make you keep paying and paying and paying.

It's not like that, mamma, his father says. He isn't a mistake. He's my son.

The light and air and smells of wood and cut grass are different. In the distance, a lawnmower burrs, birds flitter and chirp in the bright air; but all of it is fake, as fake as a blue-screen matte. He thinks of their voices outside at night – *for him*, they said, *for him* – and he knows that they were lying; he is the mistake; and everything is different, sharp and clear, as if it is made of glass.

What are you going to do, mamma? his father says.

Gramma Turner doesn't answer him.

What are you going to do? his father says. I swear to God, mamma, if you mess this up, I'll kill you. I'll come in here and slit your throat.

Made of glass, he floats, borne up on his father's words, not knowing if they are true. In the garage, Gramma Turner weeps. Behind him, in the kitchen, someone watches him. He keeps his back turned, one hand to the iron porch rail, trying to hold fast to each moment before she is real again.

He turns; and no one is there.

He opens the screen door, closes the back door quietly behind him, goes to the bottom of the stairs. Voices still seep from the garage, distant and tinny, the patter of an abandoned TV. He puts one foot on the bottom step, then climbs the creaking stairs, gripping the wooden bannister, his heart beating breath out of his chest. On a narrow landing, the gilded spines of children's books, books his father read – *The Jungle Book, A Child's Book of Wonders* – glimmer beneath a high window. The door to his grandparents' room and the bathroom next to his father's room and his father's room are shut. Below, the place he stood at the bottom of the stairs looks strange, as distant as the bottom of a canyon, as if it is only a place he remembers.

He creeps through the darkness to his father's room, covering his mouth with his hand, against the smell of mothballs and dust. The door to his father's room recedes, like a door in a dream; and then he is there, his hand on its worn metal knob, and before he can stop, he opens the door.

For an instant, he sees a boy, sitting on the edge of his father's bed, without eyes or nose or mouth, looking down at his slick, blunted limbs, looking up at him, his no-face as smooth and blank as a mirror.

But it is only the woman who sits, watching him with her frightened, skittering eyes. She wears a light blue shift that leaves her knees and calves bare, her hair tied in a red kerchief. She does not look like anything except herself. Light from outside presses against the blinds. There is a narrow bed, a shelf of miniature boys holding tennis rackets and baseball bats, school pennants above a wooden desk, its varnish worn bare where his father studied when he was a child.

"I'm sorry, Buddy," she says.

He moves toward her, to touch her, to see if she is real; but when she lifts her hand, he draws back, as if scalded, cradling his arm against his chest.

"I'll kill you," he says.

The woman shakes her head, looking down at her hands. "No, Buddy. Your father needs me. He's always needed me. If you want to help your mother, you can tell her that. It will be better for everyone." She pauses, lowering her eyes again, searching for the right word. "More merciful," she says.

He stands, watching her, not knowing what she means. Outside, his father's and Gramma Turner's voices have ceased. He turns from her, and descends the creaking stairs, hands clenched in his coat sleeves, and sits at the small, round table in the dim, still kitchen, listening to the faucet drip in the sink. Everything is clear and strange, everything as it has always been, and he wonders if he's really seen her. But he knows what he's seen; he's always known that she is there, just as he's known what he is; and it has only been his own fear, his own weakness, that stopped him from telling the truth.

Outside, his father's footfalls scrape the porch steps, his face looms in the window, haunted, enraged; and Buddy makes his own face blank, to meet him.

26.

Everything is a lie, everything is a joke; he can see it in the boys' cowed faces as they march to chapel, as they stammer and blush when they're called on in class; and in Mrs. Gray's face, heavy with fake adult sorrow, when she says she is sorry to hear of his grandfather's passing; he can see it in his father's smooth, bland, lying face when he talks about the new house, and selling his mother's house, and how everything will change when they move; he can see it in his mother's face as she wraps china in newspaper, trusting his father, trusting him. But when they go to Alex's house, and his father stands over the camera, as calm and patient as when he showed him the purple cells, long ago, Buddy still doesn't know if he should love or hate him; and he knows that he is nothing, that he is the biggest joke of all.

At school, at night, in the afternoons, when he and his father visit the new house, he plots how he will kill the woman: steal his mother's car, or his father's, sneak over at night to Gramma Turner's, smother the woman in her sleep; he could beg his father into visiting Gramma Turner, get up to the woman's room, garrote her with a coat hanger; and he curses himself for not killing her more quietly when he had the chance — cutting the brake lines on her car, switching her aspirin with cyanide, leaving a gas burner unlit in her apartment when his father took him home. But he did nothing; and at school and the new house and his mother's house, he stares down at his own hands, clenched, useless.

At school, he picks fights with the boys, swings punches at them in the hallways and on the soccer field and in the bathrooms. He watches Simon, his broad, straight shoulders, the cleft at the base of his skull; and though Simon seems unreal to him, like a character from a book, the hollow ache still beats in him, different from before, sharp and thin; and Simon watches him, too, and he thinks that Simon knows that he has changed.

The week after he discovers the woman, he finds Simon alone in the hallway, and follows him down the sweaty-smelling stairs. He knows what he has to do; and as he reaches out to touch Simon's arm, the giddy drop spins in him, as if he is falling; and he's glad he is falling, that he's found the next step gone.

Simon flinches, wheeling on him, his blue eyes narrowed, suspicious. Boys stream down the stairwell, lingering, glancing at them, expecting a fight.

"My grandfather died," he says. "It was funny. We went to the funeral. Everyone there was black and Mexican."

Simon studies him, calm, distant, assessing; and Buddy knows what he's said isn't enough; he knows what he has to do, and he wants to do it.

"My grandfather died," he says, to the boys. "We went to the funeral. My mother wasn't there. I found my dad's girlfriend at my grandmother's house. I screwed her."

The boys watch him, avid, unsure they can believe what he's said. His hands tremble, his heart presses breath from his chest. He didn't know what he would say; but now it is different, and he is different, too.

"You lie," Gene says. "You're a liar."

"How do you know?" he says. "How do you know what me and my father do? Maybe I'm Mexican. Maybe I'm a crazy Mexican bastard. My dad's got his girlfriend locked up at my grandmother's house. He's going to keep screwing her and my mother. That's why his girlfriend let me screw her, so I wouldn't tell my mother."

The boys watch him differently; it doesn't matter what he's said. All of it is a lie, and he knows that Simon can see this. He knows Simon can see the truth, the real truth; he knows that Simon can see what he really is.

"You're a liar," Gene says, uncertainly.

Buddy starts to answer; but Simon lifts his hand, to silence him, smiling, still eyeing him warily, and silently claps his hands.

⌒⦾⌒

He lays in the grove near the soccer field, smelling the pine needles' sharp scent, the cool, rubbery grass. Simon stands over him, his face flushed and taut. That week, Buddy has told the boys how his father took him to the woman's apartment, and he glimpsed the coiled sheets; how his father lied to his mother, and his mother believed him, and the sounds that came from her room. In the stories, his father was a monster, brutal and obscene, but he knew they were only lies.

The boys listened, eager, skeptical, trying to glimpse the secret world; some chucked his shoulder, told him it must suck, having a father like that, and he feels their sympathy, a sweetness in his chest, and he feels himself recoil from it. Only Simon watches him as he knows he should be watched, as hard and pitiless as the world itself; he knows that Simon hates him, he knows that Simon isn't his friend. But it is only Simon's sympathy he wants, because Simon can see that all he says is a lie.

"Please," he says.

Simon stands over him. Buddy hides his face in his arm; and though he can't see him, he knows how Simon looks at him. He knows they have to be quick; Mrs. Quine will be there any minute, his father may already be there, searching the hallways.

"Please," he says.

Simon stands over him; and Buddy knows what he must do, and it sickens him; but he also knows that it doesn't matter, anymore, what he does.

"Please," he says. "We can make the movie."

Simon hesitates. "When?"

"Tomorrow." Buddy hides his face from him, trying not to think of what he's done. "We can go there tomorrow."

Simon hesitates; Buddy tenses his shoulders, expecting that Simon will hit him; he wonders if Simon can see what he does at night, to drive himself down into the darkness of sleep, before the sounds come from his mother's room; he wonders if Simon can see what he imagines about the woman, how she will enfold him in her strong, nervous embrace, and about him, replaying the moment he let the bathrobe fall open; he wonders if he can see how his thing stiffens, and he pulls at it, knowing he shouldn't, holding his breath so they won't hear him, how the bright flashes shutter past – the curve of the woman's belly, Simon turning to him, pressing his warmth and weight against him, his own body pressing against another warmth, a smell that expanded as he drifted to sleep; and he knows it is not what he should think; he knows he should stop, but he can't stop until the black bloom bursts behind his eyes, and he opens his eyes, and feels the shameful mess on his hands.

"Please," he says.

Simon hesitates; then he kneels behind him, straddling his legs, pine needles whispering under him, and lays on him, his legs between his legs, covering him with his warmth and weight, his thing pressing against him. Buddy keeps still, listening to the freeway, trying to think only of Simon's breath brushing his neck and his heart pounding against him, knowing that soon, he will leave, knowing he isn't his friend; but he closes his eyes, imagining himself rising into him, and Simon's sweet sympathy flows through him; for a moment, he floats, made of glass, and he is not himself, but Simon, his limbs turning lean and taut. He opens his eyes, turning his face to Simon's, knowing it's a mistake; but he needs to see what's in Simon's face, to see if what he's imagined is true; and Simon recoils, scrambles up, turning, hiding his face from him.

☙❧

They march down Gramma Liddy's street, past the Orange Show, to Alex's house. It was easy to fool Mrs. Quine, when she pulled up at the school; Simon told her the story they rehearsed, that his mother couldn't get out of work, and his father couldn't take him home.

All the way to Gramma Liddy's, in the swift, golden car, Mrs. Quine asked about his father: Where were they going to live? What was it like, having him back home? What did O.G. think of what was going on? From her questions, Buddy can't tell what Simon has told her; and he's studied her sad, beautiful face, the darker shadows beneath her eyes; and he thinks of Mr. Quine, and how he's seen her head hit the table like a doll. But he answers her in a loud, false voice, the bitter ache in his throat; he tells her how they will live on a tree-shaded street, and how he will go to St. John's, and how it doesn't matter what Gramma Turner thought, while Junior peeks at him over the front seat, and Simon glances at him sideways, unsure if he should believe him.

By the time they get to Gramma Liddy's, Mrs. Quine has fallen silent. Buddy looks at Simon, urging him silently to deliver his line; but Simon keeps his face turned from him, his eyes feverish and bright.

"Mamma?" he says. "Can we visit Buddy's friend?"

Mrs. Quine touches her car keys. "I don't know about that, Simon. I don't think that's a good idea. I think we should just check on Mrs. Liddy."

"Please, mamma. He asked us to come. He wants to be friends."

Mrs. Quine peeks up over her sunglasses in the rearview mirror, studying him. "Did he say that, Buddy?"

"Yes, ma'am," he says, not knowing what he will say, watching the small, gray house. "He said next time Simon came, I should bring him over. He said if I didn't, he and his dad would be really offended."

Mrs. Quine is silent. "Are you sure, Buddy? You're sure that's what he said?"

"Yes, ma'am."

Mrs. Quine bites her lip. "Okay," she says. "But just for a minute. And no trouble this time, you hear? I don't want to have to talk to Mr. Torres again."

છે ∾

They march down Alex's street; Simon stares ahead, his face like flint, and Buddy wonders how long it will take for Gramma Liddy to call Mr. Torres; he wonders if his father is still at the school, or if he saw him slip into the swift, golden car, and his car will come racing down the street, any minute; he wonders what will happen if his father catches them before they get to Alex's, and what will happen if he doesn't; and he worries that something will stop them, and he hopes that something, maybe God, will stop them. He searches the sky, but the horse is not there. The driveway at Mr. Torres' house is empty; Mr. Torres' white truck is gone; and as they advance on the yellow house, Ysrael barks, and the curtain in Alex's window parts, and he knows that nothing will stop them.

Behind the storm door, Alex opens the front door, grinning his tricky grin.

"*¿Dónde está tu papá?* he says. "You brought your friend."

Buddy shrugs, looking at the bits of mirrored glass in the empty planters that flank the door; he wishes Alex would slam the front door shut, lock it against them.

I thought you weren't hanging out with him anymore, Alex says, in Spanish.

Simon watches them, narrow-eyed.

"I came to show him the camera," Buddy says.

Behind the dark glass, Alex's smile fades. "*Mi papá no le gusta,*" he says. *If he comes home, he won't let you and your dad come back.*

"*Es mi máquina,*" Buddy says.

Alex raises his eyebrows, smiling stiffly, trying to make what he's said into a joke; but it isn't. Alex doesn't know him; he doesn't know what he really is.

"It's my camera," Buddy says.

Alex looks at him, his smile gone; then he reaches out, to open the storm door, and locks it. "Okay," he says. "I'll meet you out back."

છે ∾

In the back yard, Ysrael barks in his cage. An airplane shadow passes, shifting the shadow of the orange tree over the picnic table, where the piñata hung, in a movie, in another boy's life. Simon surveys the yard, his jaw clenched, his expression bright and strange; and Buddy tries to see the yard as Simon does — the patches of dirt where Ysrael tried to dig under the fence, the ripe smell of rabbits next door — and he knows that Simon hates it, that he wants to tear it apart.

In the kitchen, the telephone rings. Alex lumbers out the back door, letting the screen door slap behind him, carrying a stack of papers, thick as a telephone book, under one arm. He stalks across the yard toward the cage; and Buddy knows there is still time to turn back.

Are you going to answer it? he says, in Spanish.

Alex unlocks the cage. Ysrael bounds toward them; and Simon, hesitating, reaches down to pet him. *Are you going to answer it?* Buddy says.

"You got a dog?" Alex says, to Simon.

Simon snatches his hand from Ysrael. "No," he says, glancing at Buddy.

"You want him? Ten bucks, he's yours."

Simon eyes him, suspicious. "I want to see the camera," he says.

"In a minute," Alex says. "Now I'm going to show you something else."

Alex lays the drawings on the table, raising his eyebrows, as if he were about to show them a trick, just like he did when they had performed magic shows for his father, Buddy thinks, something he hasn't thought of for a long time. Alex places one hand on the stack of papers, and with his other hand, lets them slowly fall; and at first, Buddy doesn't look at the drawings: he looks at Alex's hands, the callous on his right forefinger where he holds his pencil, his fingernails edged in black.

In the drawings, in herky-jerky fits and starts, the Horse stands over the Spider, who lays dead at his feet; Hugh and the Horse make their way through the swamp, and in the trees above them, bats and goblins gaze down, awed and frightened; at the edge of the swamp, the Horse turns his head, speaking silently to Hugh, then spreads his wings, and disappears in a burst of light. It isn't a scene, as he thought, but a whole story; it is the end of the movie, which he hasn't yet written. In each frame is a space where the live action would be matted, carefully colored blue; and though they are rough, some only sketches, he sees that they would be beautiful, more beautiful than he imagined.

"What do you think?" Alex says.

While the drawings flip past, Simon's face is the one that Buddy has seen when he read to himself alone in his room, but now his expression has hardened, as if he pressed his face against the sheet of glass; and Buddy knows the movie is only child-ish, and he steels himself against it, knowing what he has to do.

"It's a cartoon," he says. "Show him the camera."

Alex looks at him. *We can't do that,* he says, in Spanish. *There's film in it.*

Buddy turns from him, watching sunlight sift through the orange tree.

What's wrong with you? Alex says. *My dad's coming home soon. If he catches us, he won't let you come over here again.*

Show it to him, Buddy says. *Or I'll take it home.*

Alex looks at him, and Buddy knows that he can see inside him, to what he's done with Simon. Alex looks at him, still holding the drawings against the wind; then he crouches down, and places a rock from under the picnic table on them, to anchor them; and Buddy keeps his face turned from him.

The screen door slaps shut. Simon reaches down, hesitating, and pats Ysrael's neck. Sunlight spangles through the orange tree; and Buddy wishes that Alex would lock himself in the house, that he would stay there until Mr. Torres comes home.

"What are you going to do?" he says.

"Nothing," Simon says. "I'm not doing anything."

"But what are you going to do?"

"Nothing, Tuber," Simon says, in his feverish, sing-song voice. "We're just going to make our movie."

The screen door slaps shut. Alex comes toward them, gripping the camera bag's leather strap. Simon snatches his hand from Ysrael, turning from him, pretending he hasn't touched him. Alex puts the bag on the picnic table, leveling his dark eyes on Buddy, and lifts the camera out by its stock. The camera's cool black metal shines dully in the sunlight, and Simon reaches for it; but Alex steps away, shielding it with his hand; and both of them look at him.

"Give it to him," Buddy says.

"No." Alex shakes his head. "No, man. I can't do that."

"Give it to him," Buddy says. "Or I'll take it home."

Alex hands the camera to Simon, his eyes locked on Buddy's; and Buddy knows that he can see, now, what he's done with Simon, what he really is. Simon turns the camera in his hands, examining its meters and dials, his face the one that Buddy saw when he read books at his desk in his room; then Simon's eyes narrow, and he raises the camera, and points it at Alex.

"Let's make a movie," he says.

"We can't," Alex says. "There's film in it. We're putting on the animation."

"It's okay," Simon says. "We'll pretend."

"No, man. It took a lot of work. We could mess it up."

Alex moves toward him, holding out his hand; Simon steps away, hidden behind the camera's single, staring eye, tapping his finger on its trigger.

"It's just a movie," he says. "Let's pretend."

Alex stares at Simon, flexing his hands into fists. "Okay," he says, slowly. "*Tranquillo*. What do you want to do?"

"Do the scene," Buddy says. "Like he did. In the cage."

Alex looks at him, and Buddy knows that he can see inside him, to what he really is. "No, man," he says. "My dad's coming home."

Simon taps the trigger. "It's okay," he says. "It's pretend."

Alex looks at him, silently asking a question, then turns from them, and starts across the yard. Ysrael trots after him. Simon follows him, holding the camera to his eye. In the kitchen, the telephone rings; and the long spine of fences, and the little yard, seem to shrink in the sunlight.

Alex stops near the cage. Ysrael circles it, sniffing its heavy wooden frame, its glinting wire mesh, the staples where Mr. Torres has repaired it, from when Simon had damaged it before. "Go on," Simon says. "Get in."

Alex turns to Buddy, watching him.

"It's okay," Buddy says.

Alex studies him, then crouches down, his knees tucked together, and squeezes into the cage, his hands outstretched, lurching forward, tearing his shirtsleeve on the mesh. Ysrael barks, circling the cage, sniffing at him.

"Close the door," Simon says.

Alex turns inside the cage, his white dress shirt poking out through holes in the mesh, a bloodstain spreading on his sleeve, different from the red dye and Kayro syrup they used for blood in the movie.

"Close it," Simon says.

Buddy swings the door shut, holding the metal plate over the hasp, not looking, trying not to look at Alex's shirt. "Give him the key," Simon says.

"No," Alex says.

Simon taps the trigger. "Give him the key. Or it's not real."

Alex looks at him, his dark eyes close, closer than Buddy can remember ever seeing them; and he can smell his scent of cinnamon candy and pencil lead, and the sweat that beaded his forehead, and in the dull hot smell of warm grass, the coppery smell of blood that spreads on his shirt.

"It's okay," Buddy whispers. *"Está bien."*

Alex reaches back, cracking a crossbeam, and digs the key from his pants, cuffing his arm with his other hand. He holds the key pinched between his fingers, hesitating, then threads it through the mesh. Buddy snaps the lock on the hasp, and steps back, stumbling, shoving the key in his pocket.

Alex squats inside the cage, holding his arm; and Buddy remembers him, *Loco Alejandro*, who cried for no reason, and punched kids flat; and he knows that Alex is stupid to have trusted him, and he feels himself laugh, and his own laughter sickens him, and his throat aches with the feeling of laughter and crying together.

"Dame la llave," Alex says. *Give me the key.*

Alex stares at him, gripping the doorframe, but Buddy sees him from far away, as he knows Simon does, his gaze hard and pitiless; and he knows that he is watching the real movie of his life.

"Dame la llave, hombre," Alex says.

"Shut up," Simon says; and Buddy sees that the camera shakes in his hands. "Shut up. Stop talking like that."

Alex shakes the doorframe, his dark eyes leveled on him; and Buddy knows that there is still time to turn back.

"Spic," Buddy says.

Alex stares at him as if he hasn't heard what Buddy said, as if he heard something he's known long before. "Spic," Buddy says. *Huérfano. Orphan.*

Alex shakes the cage, staring at him; Ysrael circles it, whimpering and barking; and Buddy turns from Alex, from his dark, level gaze.

"Ghost Horse!" he shouts. "Scene one! Take one! Action!"

Simon backs away, hidden behind the camera. The camera whirrs. Alex shakes the cage, cursing them, and falls forward, crossbeams and wire mesh folding over him, struggling to get out; and Buddy sees Alex as he knows that Simon does, a tiny, distant figure inside the dark box, the square frame. Under the orange tree, he reaches out, and slings the camera bag over his shoulder; he reaches out, and pushes the rock from the drawings, and heaves the drawings into the air; and the drawings rain down like falling leaves, as Ysrael bounds back and forth, snapping at them, as Alex stares at him inside the cage, a stranger, he who would have been his brother; Buddy reaches out, watching himself, and touches the rock, a pebbly chunk of cement, as Ysrael bounds toward him, as Alex cries out, knowing what he will do, as he lifts the rock, and strikes Ysrael's face, and feels the hollow crack of rock against bone.

Then he is running, out the side-gate, past the driveway, past a glimpse of Mr. Torres' white truck chugging up the street, and Simon is next to him, the camera still whirring in his hand. When he thinks of what Mr. Torres will find, his heart clenches and sickens. But he can't think of that, right now; he is running, past the Orange Show's gaily-colored tiles, past the houses with neat vinyl siding and rusting cars beached on their lawns, trying not to think, trying to hold fast to the fine, clean hate, the feeling of not-feeling, the real truth.

"That was fun," he says.

Simon doesn't answer him.

"That was fun," he says.

Simon stares ahead, blank, frightened-looking, and Buddy wrenches the camera from him, shoves it in its bag, knowing that Simon has betrayed him.

Ahead, in front of Gramma Liddy's house, his father stands next to his car, holding open the driver's-side door. Mrs. Quine is there, too, coming toward them, wearing her sunglasses, shouting at Simon, asking him what they have done. Gramma Liddy, in her housecoat, stands as still as a statue, gaunt and severe, watching them as if she knows what they have done.

Simon touches his arm, telling him to slow down, to pretend that nothing has happened; but he keeps running, past the adults on the lawn, into the darkness of Gramma Liddy's house, where Junior is lying on the couch, a Roadrunner cartoon shuttering over his face, and locks himself in Grampa Liddy's room, breathing the blankets' cool, dusty scent, trying to soothe the stitch that cuts into his side, to hold fast to the feeling of not-feeling, which slips second by second through his hands. Outside, the house fills with their voices. He takes the camera from its bag, and holds it, trembling in his hands, knowing he should smash it. But he can't do it, he cannot even do that; and he sits on the floor, cradling the camera in his lap, and weeps bitterly, knowing it is useless, thinking of all that his bitterness has destroyed.

27.

After the Quines leave, he sits across the dining room table from Gramma Liddy in the creaky, straight-backed chair. Bars of light slant through the blinds on the French doors. His father has gone to Mr. Torres', having taken the camera from him, and asked him what he's done. Gramma Liddy has called his mother and talked to her in a low, clipped voice; and now, behind the glare of the table lamp and the smoke that wreathes up from her cigarette, she watches him, and though he can't see her, he knows how she watches him, and he keeps his face turned from her, digging at a hole in the table cloth.

"How are you?" she says.

"Fine, ma'am."

"I'm afraid I find that answer unacceptable. If it's true, then you have become someone I don't know. There's no excuse for what you have done, but perhaps there is an explanation. So I ask you, Buddy: Why did you do this?"

He touches the key to the cage in his pocket, wondering when he can get rid of it. His father has taken the camera; he worries that they won't finish the movie. But there will be no movie, he thinks; and a kind of dizziness overtakes him, a rolling wave, a giant hand. "I don't know, ma'am," he says.

"Then can you tell me, Buddy, what has happened?"

He digs at the hole in the tablecloth, thinking of what he's told the boys about the woman; and he is afraid, now, that Simon will tell his mother what he's said.

"No, ma'am," he says.

"Buddy," she says. "Look at me."

She touches his hand, to still it; and her eyes, behind her glasses, are not as he imagined them. She watches him as his mother did, blinded by worry and love, though her eyes are not blinded, but somehow sharper than before.

She grips his hand, her hand cold and trembling and strong. "I'm going to tell you a story," she says.

"When your grandfather and I moved to Houston during the war, we lived in an apartment building in Riverside. We were the only family to speak English at home. Your grandfather, because he was in the union, had trouble finding a job. And coming to Houston from Port Arthur and Abilene and all the other tiny places we'd lived, I felt as though I had moved to a different country, and spoke a different language, too.

"One day, Mrs. Rosen, the same Mrs. Rosen you know, came to our back door to borrow an egg. She started to tell me in her broken English that her husband had lost his job because the new manager at his department store did not like Jews. At the time, many people blamed Jews for the war. I was not immune to that belief myself.

"As I listened to Mrs. Rosen, I felt I could not breathe. Her broken words seemed ugly to me, almost sinister. I hurried her out, telling her I was ill. Then I lay down, because I was ill, disgusted with myself, or Mrs. Rosen, I didn't know; but I knew I could not be easy until I made things right with her.

"The next day, I invited her for lunch. She brought an egg, which I suppose was why she thought I'd invited her. Our conversation was awkward. Her broken words still made me uneasy. But I forced myself to ask about her husband, and to tell her, when she asked, about your grandfather.

"I didn't know why I needed to do that. I only knew if I didn't, I could have no self-respect. That is what's most important, Buddy. That is the only real salvation — what you can make with other people, outside yourself."

She grips his hand; he thinks of the miniature city, and the Horse. But these are only childish things, lies only a child would believe. What she said has nothing to do with the real world — the new house, and his father, and St. John's.

His mother's car stutters into the driveway; the door swings open, his mother comes toward him, her face convulsed, bewildered, and shakes his arm.

"What's wrong with you?" she says. "How could you do this?"

He turns his face from her, blushing with shame, but he steels himself against this, too. "What's wrong with him?" she says, to Gramma Liddy.

Gramma Liddy sits, smoke trailing up from her cigarette, staring past his mother at the front door. "We've got to get him out of there," his mother says. "We've got to get him away from those people."

Gramma Liddy snuffs out her cigarette, and glances at a clock on the wall behind her. "It's almost five," she says. "There's a mass at five-fifteen."

"You want to go to mass?" his mother says.

"Why not?" Gramma Liddy says, pushing herself up from her chair, her arms trembling. "I thought this was what it was for."

❧ ❦

At Queen of Peace, shadows dart across the playground, past the picnic table and swing set, through the jungle gym, into the drainage ditch's dark mouth, in the crisp spring dusk. His mother and Gramma Liddy and he creep through the parking lot toward the squarish, oatmeal-colored church, whose stained-glass windows are lit from within. For a moment, he imagines that Alex and Mr. Torres might be there. But he knows they won't be there; he can't think of where they really are.

Inside, Father Peron's nasal voice echoes off the bone-colored walls, pausing when they enter the side-door. Women in scarves and woolen coats dot rows of empty pews; and the church's brightness, after the darkness outside, is like an ark, and he imagines that the women, glancing up at them, are its passengers.

His mother kneels, pressing her forehead against clenched hands, not looking at him; Gramma Liddy sits, her chin lifted, listening. The thinly-padded rail bites into his knees. Behind the altar, Abraham stares up, surprised, dropping his knife, while Isaac waits on the pyre; above the altar, the gaunt, greenish Christ stares down at him, blood dripping from his crown of thorns. He closes his eyes, trying not to think; but in the darkness, Alex watches him; and in his hand, he feels the cold weight, the hollow crack of rock against bone. He thinks of the movie still hidden inside the camera, the Horse gone, the hard-won frames ruined. He presses his forehead against his hands, listening, but he hears only silence, and he knows that his grandfather was never there, that it has only been another trick; but he waits, listening for his voice in the darkness.

❧ ❦

The next morning, the drawings come, in *The Approach to Latin* and *The Pilgrim's Progress*. When Simon walks into the classroom, stiff-legged from the whipping he's gotten from Mr. Quine, Buddy knows they will be there: Tightface squats on his father, Gramma Turner squats on Grampa Turner in his casket, Ysrael squats on him. He pretends to throw them away; but at home, he studies their empty shapes, the knotted bodies that have no beginning and no end; and he knows that he has to stop Simon, that he has to destroy him.

At P.E., he crosses the mangy soccer field, where Gene and Simon sit on the bleachers near Coach Bland's shack. He wonders if Simon and Gene shared the moment of peace, if Simon has done with Gene what he did with him. He touches the drawings in his pocket, keeping his eyes straight ahead, trying to steel himself against Simon's broad, straight shoulders, his blue eyes, calm and distant and adult.

"Dog-killer," Simon says. "What do you want?"

Gene laughs silently, hugging himself with his bony arms; and Buddy feels himself falter; he thinks of what his father told him about Ysrael, how only the automatic part of his brain was still alive; and he imagines Ysrael dreaming, twitching in half-death. "I've got the drawings," he says, delivering the line he's rehearsed. "I kept them. I'm going to show them to Mrs. Gray."

"I don't know what you mean, Turner," Simon says. "I haven't seen any drawings. Maybe you made them."

Buddy watches Simon, trying to see if Simon believes what he's said.

"You made them," he says.

"I don't know what you mean, Turner. Maybe you're making things up. Maybe you made them, and sent them to yourself, and hid them in your desk."

Simon smiles at him. Gene grimaces at him with his skeleton face; and it is not what he's imagined: Simon groveling, begging mercy, himself, forgiving him.

"But you made them," he says, moving closer.

"I don't know what you mean, Tuber," Simon says, lifting empty hands. "I wish I could help. Maybe you should ask your spic friend if he made them."

Simon smiles at him, and Buddy imagines he is caught inside a movie he's made, a movie he doesn't understand.

"Please," he says, not knowing what he means. "Please make it stop."

"I don't know what you mean, Tuber," Simon says. "Maybe you should ask your spic friend. Maybe you should ask his dead spic dog."

Buddy swings at him, to smash his smiling face. Gene catches his arm; something else knocks breath from his chest. The sky opens above him, a giant mouth, and the ground claps the back of his head. In the distance, boys run toward them, their feet thumping beneath the cool, rubbery grass, and Gene waves them on.

Simon stares down at him, his face changed, a clenched fist. "I didn't want to do it, Tuber. You made me do it. You and your stupid friend."

"I'll tell them," Buddy says.

"I don't know what you mean, Tuber," Simon says, turning from him.

"I'll tell them. I'll tell them what I saw at your house."

Simon swipes at his face with his shirtsleeve, quick, sharp, as if he is hitting himself. "No, you won't, Turner," he says. "You don't care. You don't care about anything. I'll kill you."

Simon rises to meet the boys, who stare down at him, surrounding him with their smell of sneakers and sweat. Simon orders them to carry him to the grove across the field, because they are too close to Coach Bland's shack. Hands grip his wrists, his ankles, lifting him, and he watches the faint blue sky, thinking of Simon's face before he turned from him; he didn't know, when he said it, if he would tell the boys what he saw. But now he knows he will do it; and he wants to do it, to break him.

Pine trees tilt above him. Gene shouts an order. He hits the ground, needles prickling his back, their sharp, clean scent, and the smell of grass where he laid under Simon. At night, he imagines Simon pressing against him, how he turned his face from him; he knows that he can never tell what they did.

Around him, boys gather, curious, distant, most merely glad it is he and not they who are there. He searches their faces for Sam's, but he knows it will make no difference; he knows that Sam has no reason to help him.

"Get up," Simon says.

Simon stands over him, glancing sideways at the boys; and Buddy sees that he is afraid; and he hates him for his fear.

"Get up," Simon says, nudging him with his shoe.

He rises, brushing pine needles from his legs, shivering in the heat; Simon turns from him, hands clasped behind his back. "Turner," he says. "Isn't it true your dad doesn't even have a girlfriend? Isn't it true he's always lived with you?"

Simon glances at him, then lifts his hand, to silence him. "You've seen his dad," he says, to the boys. "He's a doctor. He's normal. But isn't it true," he says, turning to Buddy again, "that you lied about him? Isn't it true you made up sick stories about him? Isn't it true you made sick drawings about him, too?"

The boys watch him, masklike, distant, like pictures of themselves. Simon eyes him; and Buddy wonders if he believes what he's said. Part of it is true; but he knows that it cannot be true, if he wants to break Simon.

"No," he says.

A murmur ripples through the boys; they jostle each other, moving closer a ragged mouth. Simon shakes his head, still smiling; but his jaw tightens, and a blush creeps up his neck. "So it's true that you screw your dad's girlfriend? It's true that he screws your mother, and his girlfriend, too?"

"No," Buddy says.

Simon shakes his head, as if sadly, and turns from him. "Isn't it true you have a spic friend? Isn't it true you talk Mexican?"

"No," he says. "He's not a spic."

"But that's what you called him," Simon says, wheeling on him, "isn't it? Right before you killed his dog. You say one thing here and another thing there, don't you? You say one thing to him about your movie and another thing to us. Don't you?"

The boys watch him, not knowing what Simon means; but they know that what he says is true. "No," Buddy says.

Simon turns from him, his cheeks splotched pink, his jaw working under his skin. "You're lying, Turner. I saw what you did. I know you lied to us about your dad. Why don't you just admit it?"

The boys watch him, and he knows they can see inside him; and he doesn't know what to say, and he doesn't know what is true.

"Why don't you just admit it, Turner?" Simon says. "Why don't you admit you made up sick stories about him? So we would tell you our secrets. So we would feel sorry for you. Why don't you admit you did sick, disgusting things with your spic friend, and that's why you locked him in a cage, and that's why you killed his dog?"

Simon stares at him, his face almost the one when he'd said he hated Mr. Quine; and Buddy sees that he believes what he says. At the edge of the crowd, Sam watches him, his face as hard and still as an upper-school boy's; and Buddy can't tell what he thinks. He looks down at the cool, rubbery grass, and a cold kind of sickness spreads through him; and he watches himself, knowing what he will say, not what he's meant to say, amazed as he sees himself say it.

"No," he says. "We did them. We did them right here."

Simon stares at him as if he hasn't heard what he's said. Around them, boys jostle, moving closer, their eyes like wooden slits. Gene cries out, *He's a liar! He's a liar!* Sam still watches him; and Buddy wonders if he can see the sickness in him, the hunger and hate, not like the sharp, clean hate before; he knows that he's betrayed Simon, but he cannot stop until he's destroyed him.

"Why don't you tell them," he says, "what your dad does to your mother? Why don't you tell them what he does to you?"

Simon hits him, so swiftly Buddy doesn't see his hand; and Buddy falls, letting himself fall, to hide from Simon.

"You're a liar!" Simon shouts. "Tell them!"

Simon hits him, battering the back of his head, his neck; then there are other hands, pulling at Simon, pulling at him — his shirt from his arms, his shorts from his legs, dragging him across the pine needles, across the cool, rubbery grass. Through the thicket of legs and hands, he glimpses the boys, some frozen, as if he has a disease they might catch, some staring at him as if they will cry. Voices shout, telling each other to get Simon, to get him, as the hands pull at him, stripping his shirt and shoes and socks; and he lays on the cool, rubbery grass, covering himself with his hands, as Simon kicks him, his face and neck and head, trying not to think of the face he saw before Simon hit him: haunted, broken, a face he's never seen before.

"Tell them," Simon shouts. "Tell them!"

❧❧

Mrs. Gray watches him above her heavy, folded hands, past the picture of her grandchildren in its silver frame, her sleek, terrible face weighted with adult sorrow. The wooden seat in Sam's desk is hard and prickly against his legs; he holds an ice pack against his head, and his ears buzz, and his eyes can't focus right.

Sam and some of the other boys brought him to the front office, still wearing only his shorts, and Mrs. Gray came to get him. Someone else got his uniform from the locker room; he dressed in the classroom, knowing what she would ask him.

"Buddy?" she says. "Can you tell me who did this?"

He looks down at Sam's desk, etched with lightning bolts and devil signs and names of bands. Shouts echo in the courtyard below, carried through open windows on the warm spring air. He touches the drawings in his pocket, wishing he could show them to her; but he thinks of Mr. Quine's arm, raised above his head, of Mrs. Quine's head, hitting the table like a doll, and he knows that he can't.

"I'm sorry, ma'am," he says. "I can't."

"You can, Mr. Turner. You must. We cannot run from the Devil. We must face him, like Christian soldiers. All power in heaven and earth is on our side."

He touches the drawings in his pocket, wishing he could show them to her; they are the truth, the real truth, just as Simon told the truth, and he only lied. He looks at her plump, terrible face, the dark circles under her eyes, the two raw marks her half-glasses left on the bridge of her nose; and he pities her childish faith in the adult world, in the world that is supposed to be true.

"I'm sorry, ma'am," he says.

"Mr. Turner. This is not a game. I cannot have whoever did this running loose in my classroom. You will tell me who did this, and they will be expelled."

He touches the drawings, wishing he could show them to her, to smash her childish faith; but he knows that he can't, not only for Simon, but for himself: for the new house, and his father, and St. John's. Shouts and footfalls echo in the courtyard, dwindling on the warm spring air, the sound of children going home; and he watches himself from far away, knowing what he will do.

"I did it, ma'am," he says.

Mrs. Gray studies him. "What did you do, Mr. Turner?"

"I took off my clothes, ma'am, and the boys beat me up. They beat me up because I was telling dirty stories, ma'am. I don't know who they were."

Mrs. Gray studies him for a long time; and he sees that she doesn't believe him. "Buddy?" she says. "Are you lying to me?"

"No, ma'am."

"Do you understand that if I accept what you have told me, I will be forced to ask you to leave St. Edward's?"

"Yes, ma'am," he says, though he didn't.

"And you stand by what you have told me, Mr. Turner?"

"Yes, ma'am," he says, shivering.

She turns from him to the windows that look onto the courtyard. "Very well, Mr. Turner. I understand that you entered St. Edward's without certain advantages. I have tried to help you, but I see that I have failed. I will take what you have said under consideration, and inform your parents of my decision later."

He gets up from Sam's desk, holding the ice pack against his head; the floor sways beneath him, as if he was on a boat. "I'm sorry, ma'am," he says.

"Very well, Mr. Turner."

She keeps her back to him, and he understands that she doesn't want him to see her face. "Very well, Mr. Turner," she says. "You are dismissed."

∂◦◦

Outside, a blond-haired boy stands in a portico in the walkway; then Simon glances up at him, his eyes hard and frightened, his other face gone.

"What did you tell her?" he says.

"Nothing," Buddy says. "I told her I did it."

Simon eyes him, not knowing what he means, then turns from him. "Come on," he says. "My mom wants to talk to you."

Buddy follows him, holding the ice-pack over his left eye. Below, his father's car is parked at the curb, his shadow waiting inside; Buddy doesn't know what he will tell him. Through the courtyard, brown-shirted boys and girls in blue jumpers and even upper-school boys in white shirts and gray slacks, watch them as they pass. Simon keeps his eyes trained straight ahead; and Buddy watches him, wishing that he could apologize. But he knows that he isn't really sorry for what he's done.

"Stop gawking, Turner," Simon says. "I meant what I said. I'll kill you."

Buddy looks away from him; the boys in brown uniforms and the upper-school boys watch him as they did Simon. None of it mattered; soon, all of it would be swept away, by the new house, and St. John's.

The swift, golden car is parked outside the church. Behind the glare on the windshield, Mrs. Quine sits as still as a statue. Simon crosses the lawn, glancing back, warning him. The front passenger window whirrs down; Mrs. Quine leans across the seat, her eyes lustrous and weary. "What happened to your face?" she says.

"I don't know, ma'am. I got hit."

"Simon says you got into a fight," she says, studying him. "He says your teacher thought it might be him."

"Yes, ma'am."

"But it wasn't him?"

"No, ma'am," he says. "It wasn't."

She turns, facing the windshield; and he doesn't think that she believes him. "I'm sorry, Buddy. I'm sorry you've got so many problems. But we're a good, Christian family. I don't think I can let you talk to Simon anymore. Understand?"

"Yes, ma'am," he says.

She lowers her sunglasses, both hands on the steering wheel, staring straight ahead. "That wasn't right, Buddy," she says. "What you and Simon did at your friend's house. Tell Mrs. Liddy I'm sorry. Tell her I didn't mean to do that. Okay?"

She doesn't look at him; and he can see that in the sadness that weights her mouth, and the weariness that shadows her eyes, there is no share anymore for him; and he feels himself move toward her, reaching for the window.

"Yes, ma'am," he says. "I'm sorry, ma'am."

The window whirrs up; Simon opens the back door, not looking at him, and gets in. Buddy watches the car until it disappears near the freeway. Then he starts out along the church's long, pink flank. He still doesn't know what he will tell his father. But he touches the drawings in his pocket — they are the truth, the real truth, and he thinks that he knows, now, why he has kept them.

28.

On Saturday, Gramma Turner calls, as he knew she would. His father closes the kitchen door, speaking to her in a voice like the one he used after Grampa Turner's funeral. Buddy slips back to his room, takes the drawings from between his mattress and box springs, where he hid them along with the key to the cage, keeping his one good eye on his mother, who works outside in the yard. Since his fight with Simon, his left eye hasn't worked right. Shadows move over it like veils. He hopes it will get better; he can still get around okay. He puts the drawings in his binder behind a history test and a quiz on *The Pilgrim's Progress*. Then he closes the binder, lays it on his bed, takes the key from under the mattress, weighing it in his hand.

The night before, Mrs. Gray called to say she still hasn't decided what she would do; his case was delicate, she said, and she did not wish to persecute him because of his disadvantages. His mother, standing in the living room crowded with dusty-smelling boxes, told him what Mrs. Gray said, then asked him what in the hell he thought he was doing with his life. His father stared at him grimly across the dining room table, trapped-looking, radiating heat. Buddy already told him some boys beat him up, but he couldn't tell Mrs. Gray who they were, because they would beat him up again. But as his father watched him, Buddy wondered if he believed what he said. Something has shifted, something has changed, like his father's voice when he talked to Gramma Turner; and Buddy knows his father is trapped by Gramma Turner's threats that she will tell his mother about the woman, and by the fact of what he is.

He weighs the key in his hand. The drawings are the truth, the real truth, and he knows that when he shows them to her, she will leave them alone; he knows that they will silence her; he knows that they will kill her.

"Buddy?" his father says.

His father looms in his doorway in a dark, ill-fitting suit.

"My mother wants to see you," he says.

Buddy turns, closing his hand over the key, gathering his books and binder from his bed, his hands trembling.

"You won't need those," his father says.

"I might, sir."

His father eyes him. "Okay," he says. "Let's go."

Outside, his mother glances at them over her shoulder, turning from the compost, wiping her forehead with the back of her arm.

"I need to take him to my mother's," his father says.

"That's fine," his mother says.

"We'll be back soon. She wants to talk to him."

"That's fine."

His father moves toward her, his hands slightly lifted at his sides, and touches her shoulder. His mother turns to him, offering her cheek, then back to the compost, and Buddy still doesn't know if he loves or hates his father; he still doesn't know if he is glad his mother has turned to him, or not.

∾∾

His father stares ahead, hunched over the steering wheel, past the field where the boys were buried, and the opened doorway of El Destino Club #2. That week, he's listened to mother's and father's voices at night in the kitchen, not wanting to listen, because they were talking about him:

This is too much, Jimmy. He needs help. He needs professional help.

He's fine, his father said. He'll be fine.

He's not fine. It's not fine, what happened to him at that school. It's not fine what he did to Alex Torres. It's not fine, what either of you did.

Even now, he grips his binder, blushing with anger and shame; and he pictures again what will happen when he shows Gramma Turner the drawings: she will clutch her chest, fall dead as a manikin; she will be struck dumb, like his grandfather, her face gone rubbery and slack; she will collapse like the apostle on the road to Damascus, knowing she can never hurt them again. Then he will clap the binder shut, and his father will never have to see the drawings; or if he does, it will be only a small price to pay for his grandmother's silence.

His father wrenches the car onto the feeder road. Ahead, the freeway's gray hump approaches, and Buddy watches his reflection, ghostly in the window, knowing that soon, what he's imagined will be real.

His father keeps going, past the freeway's entrance; and Buddy knows that his father will take him to the bayou, to slit his throat; but even as he thinks this, he knows it isn't true. And as they turn under the echoing freeway to Gramma Liddy's street, a different fear expands in him, vaster, more real than his fear before.

Mr. Torres' white truck is in the driveway. His father parks his car, then sits, staring ahead, as his engine ticks in the silence; and in his face, Buddy sees something else, like he did when his father said they should tell Mr. Torres about the movie, as if he wants to break through his rigid mask.

"We need to do this, Buddy," he says. "We should've done it before."

His father gets out. Buddy follows him, trying to think of what he can say to stop him, as Ysrael doesn't bark, and no curtain parts in Alex's window, and the small yellow house watches them, as terrible as a tomb.

"Sir?" he says, catching at his sleeve. "Please, sir. Let's go."

His father shrugs off his hand, and rings the doorbell, his jaw working under his skin. In the storm door, two shadows stare back, trapped inside the glass; and Buddy looks away, afraid of what Mr. Torres will see when he sees them.

The front door sucks open, releasing the house's smell of air freshener and furniture polish and cooking. Behind the dark glass, Mr. Torres watches them, his skin stretched tight over the bones of his face, as if his flesh has been burnt away.

"I'm sorry, Joe," his father says. "Is this a bad time?"

Mr. Torres opens the storm door, shutting the front door behind him, and Buddy sees that his face isn't as he saw it before; but his eyes are as he imagined them, more terrible than he imagined. "No, Jimmy," Mr. Torres says. "It's fine."

His father looks down at his hands. "I'm sorry, Joe. I wanted to apologize. I wanted to bring Buddy over here so he could apologize."

Buddy turns from Mr. Torres, hating him, knowing he can see inside him, to what he's done with Simon, to what he really is.

"I'm sorry, sir," he says.

Mr. Torres doesn't answer him. In the corner of Buddy's good eye, on the empty planters, in the mirrored glass, a boy watches him, moon-faced, indistinct, as though through the wrong end of a hundred telescopes; and Buddy imagines the dim, silent living room, Mrs. Torres in her bridal veil, Alex's door, shut against him.

"I'm sorry, Joe," his father says. "I know what we did, what both of us did, was wrong. I know there's nothing we can do, now, to make up for it, but I hope you'll let us know if there's anything we can do to help."

"That's fine, Jimmy," Mr. Torres says.

"I've got some two-by-fours over at Margot's. Some braces. I can rig up a frame for that cage, no problem."

"That's fine, Jimmy," Mr. Torres says. "We won't need one."

"Right, Joe. I'm sorry. How is Alex? Did you get those shots taken care of? If you need me to call Dr. Basden, get him in there sooner, that's no problem."

"No, Jimmy. He's fine."

His father stares down at his hands; and Buddy remembers the doctors at Fort Polk, how they watched his father as if they didn't know who he was; and he knows that Alex is in his room, watching him. *¿Señor?* he says. *¿Está Alex en casa?*

"No," Mr. Torres says, stiffening.

"I'm sorry, Joe," his father says, lifting his hands. "For what I did. For my part in all this. I should have told you what we were doing with that movie."

"That's fine, Jimmy. I knew what you were doing. Didn't you think I knew?"

Mr. Torres grimaces at his father, his face more terrible, more adult, than before; and Buddy knows that he is lying.

"You're right, Joe," his father says. "I'm sorry. I got carried away. That's no excuse. I was just trying to help the boys with their movie."

Mr. Torres moves toward his father, then checks himself; his fists clenched.

"Who do you think we are, Jimmy? Do you think we're here to tell you who you are? Do you think we're here to forgive you?"

His father says nothing, staring at his hands.

"You are not sorry for us," Mr. Torres says, opening the storm door behind him. "We are sorry for you. Please, leave. Please just go."

The front door sucks shut. The boy in the mirrors watches him; and Buddy imagines that he can see himself from inside Alex's room; and a different kind of craziness seizes him, a different kind of ache, a fever in his limbs.

His father starts back to his car; Buddy jogs up next to him. "Sir?" he says. "Do you still have the camera?"

"Yes, Buddy. It's in the trunk."

"Do you think we could give it to him? I think I want to give it to him, sir."

Even as he says it, he knows it's not right. His father glances at him, a flash of contempt; then he turns from him, not blaming him for what he said, and in his face, Buddy sees the same ache he feels: his father, looking back at him, trapped behind the sheet of glass. "No, Buddy," he says. "I don't think we can do that, now."

❧ ❦

They wind along the bayou, through the dark trees at the end of Hermann Park, past the medical center, into the tree-shaded streets near Rice. All the way there, they've been quiet. His father parks the car and sits, staring at the new house. Outside, leaf-shadows flicker over the windshield, gaslight wavers in the coach lamp, the new house looms over them, sharp-peaked, like the prow of a ship, and Buddy feels himself borne up into that other world, the world that Alex doesn't understand.

"Floors still wet," his father says. "Next week, we'll move in."

Buddy presses his forehead against his window, thinking he can scent, on the leaf-cooled air, the faint gasoline smell of shellac, waiting for what his father will say next. "Yes, sir," he says. "I'm sorry, sir, about the movie."

"That's okay, Buddy. That's my fault."

His father pulls his hand down his face; and Buddy turns to his window, not looking at him. "Buddy?" his father says. "What happened at your school?"

"I told you, sir. Some boys beat me up. I can't tell her who they are."

"My mother talked to Mrs. Gray. She said you told her a different story."

He presses his forehead against the cool glass, afraid that his father will see the moment of peace with Simon. "Buddy?" his father says. "Look at me."

Slowly, he turns, trying to keep his father behind the veils in his eye; his father looks out at him, his face the one when he stood over the camera, and when he showed him the beautiful purple cells, and when he lied to him about the woman.

"I know this has been hard on you, Buddy. I know it hasn't been right. But I need to know if you're still going to help me. Understand?"

He looks past his father, at the dark house; he understands what his father means, and he knows that his father is asking the question to save them from the darkness, from the coldness and stillness in his grandfather's hand, and he grips the door handle, afraid that his father will think that he's betrayed him.

"Yes, sir," he says.

"I know I need to talk to your mother. I'll talk to her soon, after we're settled in. But I can't right now, Buddy. Understand? If your mother finds out I was with Mary, I could lose a lot of money. That doesn't matter. What matters is, I'm not sure your mother would let us be together, if that happened. I don't know if I could stay with you, if that happened, Buddy. Understand?"

He keeps his eyes on the house, a dark façade, an empty set; he understands what his father means, when he says that he doesn't know if he can stay with them; and the darkness rolls over him, reaching into him, a hand inside his chest.

"Yes, sir," he says.

"I'll talk to her soon, Buddy. I tried to talk to her a long time ago. I tried to tell her about that test. Sometimes you can tell people things, but they just don't listen."

He grips the door handle, slick inside his fist, wanting to tell his father that he knows the woman is still there, that everything has been a joke, angry with his father, angrier than he'd ever been; and before he can think, he speaks, not looking at his father, not knowing what he will say to him.

"What if I tell her, sir?"

His father is quiet. Buddy keeps his face turned to his window, knowing he's made a mistake. "Look at me, Buddy," his father says.

Slowly, he turns; his father stares at him, hollow-looking, as if he is only a mask; and Buddy remembers what his mother said, that the darkness would eat him alive, that it would take all that was left of him.

"What are you going to tell her, Buddy?" he says.

"Nothing, sir. I'm sorry, sir."

"Look at me, Buddy," his father says. "What are you going to do?"

"Nothing, sir," he says. "I'm not going to tell her anything."

His father's jaw clenches; his father knows he means the woman is still there. Then his father turns, lifting one hand from the steering wheel; and Buddy watches his other hand, gripping the steering wheel, pale, hairy, blue-veined, bone-yellow at its knuckles, afraid that his father will hit him.

"All this can disappear, Buddy. All this can vanish like it was never there. All it takes is one mistake, and you're left with nothing. So I need to know what you're going to do, Buddy. I need to know if you're still going to help me."

"Yes, sir," he says. "I promise."

His father stares at the house, then shifts the car back into gear, flinching, as he did when they first saw the house, as if he thought that everything he did was wrong; they move away from the curb, leaf-shadows unreeling over the windshield, a film running backwards; and Buddy watches his father's face, the one when he stood over the camera, and when he showed him the beautiful purple cells, and when he lied to him about the woman, and he cannot tell which father he really is; but he knows the emptiness he's seen in his father's face isn't real, can't be real; and he knows that if he shows his father the drawings, if he tells his mother about the woman, he will be cast out into the darkness, he will be lost in the world without him.

⇝⇞

Gramma Turner's house looms over them, the windows of his father's room watching them, mute and white. Buddy thinks of his plans to kill the woman, and they seem only childish; he would get caught, and sent to prison, or a boys' home. Killing her would solve nothing; but killing his grandmother, or not even killing her, but silencing her, will. Even if she doesn't die, her silence will bury the woman; the woman was forgotten before, and she could be forgotten again, and forgetting her would be even worse than killing her, he thinks.

His father ratchets the break, and gets out, glancing at him, rigid, radiating heat. "Five minutes," he says. "We're going to a movie."

Buddy follows him up the back porch steps, holding his books and binder against his chest, touching the iron railing, wondering if he only imagined his father and Gramma Turner in the garage. His father unlocks the kitchen door, rattling the windowpane, glancing back at him, sharp-eyed. In the dim, still kitchen, the faucet drips, everything as it has always been; and he feels the woman above him, breathing his breaths, and he imagines that she and Gramma Turner have both already died.

"Mamma!" his father says, clunking his keys on the little table. "I'm home!"

Silence. In the little room, the corduroy cover on the day bed is unmade, Coke cans and peanut butter cracker wrappers litter the night stand. Through the living room, past the wing-backed chairs, a shadow moves over the photos in the den; and he waits for his grandfather to fill the doorway, his eyes burning with dark fire, to save him.

But it is only Gramma Turner who creeps toward them, wearing a housecoat, steadying herself on the doorframe, on the wing-backed chair, her shoulders bent beneath the terrible weight. She grasps his arm, pinching muscle from bone; her eyes drill into him, huge, all-seeing.

"Mamma," his father says, in a loud, grating voice. "Here he is, mamma. Just like you asked. We can all have a nice visit."

She grips his arm, pinching muscle from bone, to make sure that he is really there. "I need to talk to him alone, Jimmy," she says.

His father raises his eyebrows, grimacing, as if what is happening is a joke. "We can all talk here just fine. We need to go. We're going to a movie."

"I need to talk to him alone, Jimmy," she says.

His father lifts his hand, as if lifted by string, clenched at his side in a fist. "Okay, mamma. I'll just go pack some boxes. I'll be out in the den."

"No, Jimmy," she says. "You're going upstairs."

His father glares at her, and Buddy thinks of what he's said, that he will kill her; but his grandmother doesn't flinch, does not even look at him.

"Goddammit, mamma," his father says. "Five minutes. I'll be down in five minutes. We're going to a movie."

His father glances at him, warning him; then his father is gone, his footfalls thundering up the stairs, and Gramma Turner is leading him to the day bed in the little room. Above him, floorboards creak, his father rounding the landing in the darkness and mothball smell, opening his door; the woman is waiting for him, spread eagle on a welter of sheets, in the close, bitter-smelling air, fear skittering her gray eyes, as his father stands over her, shoves his thing into her, big as a baby's arm. It is happening, right then. On the little bed, Buddy sits next to Gramma Turner, his side touching hers, holding his books and binder on his lap, listening for telltale sounds, like the sounds he heard from his mother's room; but he hears only silence.

Gramma Turner takes his hand, rubs his knuckles, worrying them like stones. He listens, looking at the Coke cans and peanut butter cracker wrappers and folded tissues on the night stand, the picture of his father holding a striped ball, the framed picture of *The Road to Success*, listening to the tick of a clock on the night stand, marking the minute that has already passed; and all of it is cheap and fake and hard-bitten, all of it is a lie, hiding the truth in the darkness above him, and he tells himself to be open his binder, show his grandmother the drawings, before his father thunders down the stairs again.

"Want a Coke?" she says.

"No, ma'am," he says, though he does.

Gramma Turner squeezes his hand. "I'm not going to ask you about those pictures, Buddy. Gramma Turner's going to take care of all that. You don't need to worry about any of that mess anymore."

For a moment, he wonders what she means, when she says the pictures; and he imagines that somehow she's already seen the drawings. But it is the pictures of the woman he stole; and he wonders what she means when she says that she will take care of it; and he knows he has to stop her.

"You don't need to worry anymore about any of that mess," Gramma Turner says, rubbing his hand. "You just need to tell me, Buddy, what happened at your school."

He looks away from her, listening for sounds above him, glancing at the clock, thinking that she already knows what he is, that her asking him is a kind of mockery, a kind of trick. "I already told my dad, ma'am," he says. "Some boys beat me up. I can't tell Mrs. Gray who they are."

"Come on, now, Buddy," she says, giving his hand a little shake. "Don't fool with me. You don't need to lie to me, honey. You don't need to be ashamed anymore."

"I'm not, ma'am. I lied to Mrs. Gray."

"I know that, Buddy. We both of us know that, Mrs. Gray and I. That's why she wants to give you another chance. But we also know you need some help. Both of us have taught children too long not to see that."

He doesn't know what she means; he doesn't want another chance. He keeps his face turned from her, hating her, glancing at the clock — two minutes — imagining his father arching over the woman, engorging her with darkness.

"I don't know what you mean, ma'am," he says.

"Come on, Buddy," she says. "I haven't got much time. Mrs. Gray says you can finish out your year if you get some help. You don't have to talk to her if you don't want to, honey. You don't have to talk to me. You just need to get some help."

He doesn't know what she means. Nothing she says has anything to do with what's really going on. He keeps his face turned from her, listening for the woman. The clock ticks in the silence; and he wishes that all of it was swept away — the red brick house, the little room, himself inside it. He opens his binder, pulls a drawing from its pocket, not looking at her, not looking at it, hoping that it will kill her.

Gramma Turner holds the drawing in both hands, studying it as if it was a test. Behind her thick glasses, in the profile of her face that he can see, her eye blinked, a delicate undersea creature, drinking its breath; and he remembers, from the time before his father left, how he thought her pale pink skin was made of stuff like cotton candy. On the creased paper, across the faint blue lines, the woman squats on his father, Gramma Liddy squats on Mr. Torres, Gramma Turner squats on Grampa Turner in his casket, moaning in agony, reaching out with blunted, slippery limbs. He waits for Gramma Turner to clutch her chest, for her eyes to darken, forever blind.

But in the little room, under her delicate, searching gaze, the figures look different, their scrawling shapes only childish, meaningless. It isn't right, it isn't quite right, he thinks; and he sees that something in the drawings is dead and evil, and he knows that they will stop nothing; and he knows that he has made a terrible mistake.

"Buddy," she says. "What is this?"

"I don't know, ma'am," he says; he doesn't.

Gramma Turner takes off her glasses, rubs the bridge of her nose. Then she covers her face with her hands. Buddy stands, letting his binder drop from his lap, spilling papers across the floor, afraid of what he's done. Gramma Turner's back shakes; she's slowly pounding a fist. In the kitchen, his father's keys lie on the table like a pistol. Above him, floorboards creak, footfalls thunder down the stairs; and Buddy sweeps the keys from the table and opens the back door and runs.

29.

He runs across Greenbriar, ditching the bitter-smelling keys in the broken storm drain, the black leather bag slung over his shoulder, the camera's cold weight knocking against his hip; he runs past his father's old school, seeking cover in the winding, tree-shaded streets, imagining he sees himself through the shuttering chain link fence, still running around the track. A stitch cuts into his side, and he slows his step, trying not to think of what he's done. Behind him, his father is following him, on his bike or on foot; he is beating Gramma Turner to death with his clenched fists, asking her what the drawings mean, blood spattering the paper in the little room; he is cursing him, searching for the keys, tearing the kitchen apart with his bloody hands; he is coming for him, to thank him for what he's done, lying with his smooth, bland face, telling him that nothing will happen, that everything will be alright.

He comes to a wide gray street near the medical center where cars rush along four lanes, where the Spec's Liquor bunny winks his pink neon eye and bats his neon ear, where the green-roofed Shamrock Hotel towers above him, and next to it, wind moves over its vast swimming pool like the Holy Spirit, unsure which way he will go, afraid that his father will find him; he turns toward the medical center's jumbled buildings, looking down Main past the dark shoal of trees in Hermann Park. He can take Main downtown and find his way home; but it will be too easy for his father to catch him on the wide streets. He doesn't know where he will go; he doesn't know what he will do; then he turns, knowing what he will do, past hourly hotels and vacant lots where palm trees sprout through cement, and in the distance, billboards and apartment buildings and the Astrodome's huge gray disc, an ancient UFO, looking over his shoulder at the rushing cars; and just as he despairs, he sees an empty place, a bridge, the bayou.

He scrambles down a foot trail, holding the black leather bag against his side, clutching at the tall grass, the veils in his eye taking his balance, until he reaches the bike path. Ahead, the bayou's sloping concrete walls curve into the distance, and above them, the curving grassy slope of the bayou's banks, and within its banks, a vast emptiness and silence, different from when he's ridden along the bayou with his father. In the stillness and silence, his heart churns in his chest like a fist; he starts out, toward Hermann Park, away from Gramma Turner's house and the school, under an abandoned train bridge and the concrete pillars of a bridge that has never been finished, behind the medical center's huge toy buildings, their faces turned from him, the world of Dumpsters and parking garages and an electrical station's humming metal thicket, the world behind the world; and in the silence, white cranes cock their heads, asking him a question, a white egret waits patiently at an enormous storm drain's dark, square mouth, a black heron skims the unmoving water for fish; and he looks over his shoulder, afraid he will see his father on his bicycle, hovering behind him; but no one is behind him.

In the dark trees at the end of Hermann Park, bicyclists zip around him, joggers with terrycloth headbands huff past; through the moss-covered trees, past a statue of a man holding a cane, he sees the red-roofed zoo, the planetarium's white dome, Sam Houston rearing back on his horse, and as if on a tiny, distant stage, himself, his mother and father, Gramma and Grampa Turner at the zoo, hot dogs, blinding sunlight, the leathery smell of his grandfather's car on a forgotten summer day. Near a gray-columned marble shelter, an ancient bus stop or tomb, is a small, slanting bridge. Across the street, the trail curves out of sight beneath a stand of nodding trees; he crosses the street, his eyes downcast, his stomach already aching with hunger; and when the brown-brick building of his mother's hospital peeks out from behind the trees, his heart lifts, then clenches and sickens; downtown seems more distant than before, and for a moment, he thinks that he should turn back.

The bayou curves, and above it in the empty sky, the sunlight presses like a hand on his head; he keeps going, past the Tip Top Grocery Beer Wine and Milk, the Ardmore Apartments $59 Move-In Special, pale brick, greasy-smelling apartments, and on the bayou's other shore, three-story houses set back on spreading lawns, at the end of curving drives; past the Loyal Baptist Church and Bert's Mini Mart, the pink BarBQ Hut, one tiny building that is Floss Fashion and The Fragrance Club and Best Nails, past the end of the bike path, and in the emptiness and silence, someone follows him, not his father or a boy from the field, but a boy who looks like him, but isn't him. The boy whispers to him, and though he whispers from a great distance, invisible to him, always hidden, his voice is close, as though he whispers in his ear; the boy speaks words that are also pictures, so that he can see Gramma Liddy, turning away from him, her mouth a bitter line, and Sam's face, hard and still as an upper-school boy's, and Simon's broken, haunted face, and Mrs. Quine, turning from him behind the dark glass, and Alex, staring at him from inside the cage, and Mr. Torres, looking at him with his dark eyes, as if he can see into his soul; and the boy puts the rough weight of the rock in his hand, and the hollow crack of rock against bone; and the boy tells him that what he's seen in the drawings is true, that everything is only a lie, that he is only a lie; and he mocks his plan to map the vast city, to make a movie so beautiful it will leave his mother speechless, that all of it is only a lie to cover what he will have to do when he reaches his mother's house.

Beneath him, on a bridge, cars rush past above a moaning concrete canyon where the bayou crosses the freeway. Look, the boy says; and he looks down into the echoing chambers, into storm drains as big as houses, clinging to a fence, afraid the rushing cars will sweep him away; and the boy mocks his fear, and tells him how easy it will be to drop into that darkness, smash his head on concrete, slip into the dark water that will carry him out to the Gulf; and the darkness will not be lonely, the boy says, not dark at all, but a world like his grandfather's movies, where everything is light, where he can join his real father in the secret world. Everyone will love him, and everyone will mourn for him, and in the darkness will be the end of the hollow ache, its true and only end. He stands a long time, pressing his forehead against the cool metal links, rough with soot, staring down into the echoing darkness, while the boy whispers: better to erase himself in that greater darkness, better to free his mother and father from their mistake. He raises himself up, bearing his weight with the toes of his shoes in the fence, the rough metal links cutting into his fingers, afraid of dropping into that darkness, and of what he will face at his mother's house; he doesn't know if the boy is lying, if he will go to the secret world, or the cold heat of Hell, or nothing at all; he doesn't know what will happen if he slips over the fence; and he lowers himself carefully and turns from the fence and keeps going.

কৈ ৯ৎ

When he reaches the 7-11 at Telephone Road, near the yellow apartment where the men who buried the boys lived, it is almost dark, and his feet are as tender as if he walks on coals, and he is so tired the cool air passes through him, as if he were a ghost. After he left the bridge, he looked for the horse, in tree branches and clumps of garbage at a bend in the bayou, an ancient shipwreck where herons perched, and downstream, dove into the rushing brown water, their sharp black heads, their long necks curving like whips; and a flock of white gulls overhead; and past the end of the bayou's concrete banks, the enormous slabs abandoned, as if a child tossed them there, the only sound the slap of birds' wings as they dove into the water, and a bird's long, patient call – *tchritt-it-it-it*. He has crept to Alex's house, on the dark side of the street, watching Mr. Torres' truck, white in the dusk, and Alex's window, whose curtain glowed orange; he has knelt beneath his window, imagining Alex hunched over a drawing at his desk, the white gull or a heron or something else he can no longer imagine, and took the camera bag from his shoulder, and unzipped it, and pressed a switch, releasing the cartridge of film, and stuffed the cartridge into his pocket, while the boy chattered in his ear, telling him it would make no difference; he knew it would make no difference, but he tapped a secret signal on Alex's window, to let him know the camera was his.

He crosses Telephone with mincing steps, as if he walks on glass. Above his mother's house, in the huge sky, a gilt-edged armada blooms, borne out to the Gulf, and beneath it, the house looks small and empty, the windows of its first story dark; he hobbles ahead, remembering the gray morning when he thought that both of them died, and he beat the walls, trying to follow them.

He creeps toward the house, his arms and legs and breath sunk in sand, and touches the hood of his father's car, still warm, ticking in the silence, and unlatches the gate. Above the yard, the sun slides like a shutting orange eye across a window in Mr. Knight's house. He touches the film in his pocket, his vision clear and sharp; and in the sharpness of his vision, the small, dark yard is like a stage, still and silent, with the stillness and silence of death.

The back door shudders open, a white shape slides down the steps. His father descends, his face convulsed, his face at the track, and presses him into his sharp scent of sweat; his back shakes, his rough cheek wet against his neck; and Buddy holds himself still, telling himself he smells the sweet, coppery scent of blood, the cool, dusty smell of dirt under the house, where he knew his father has buried his mother, telling himself his father cries a murderer's tears, though he knows that this is only a childish thought.

"Buddy?" his father says. "Are you okay? Are you okay?"

He closes his eyes; and in the darkness, the screen door slaps shut, his mother clasps his shoulder, pulling him from his father, shaking him.

"Are you okay?" she says. "How did you get here? We looked all over for you."

His father wipes his face with the back of his hand, turning from him; his mother stares at him, fierce with love, and Buddy wonders what his father has told her. In the darkness, their faces are like ancient masks, and he thinks of their voices — *for him*, they'd said, *for him*. "What happened?" she says.

He turns from her, wrenching his arm from her grip.

"What are you doing?" she says.

His father catches his shoulder, half-turning him, buckling his legs beneath him. "Buddy?" he says. "What are you doing?"

Buddy doesn't look at him; the yard's dark corner is impossibly distant, as if he sees it through the wrong end of a telescope.

"What are you doing?" his mother says. "Let go of him."

His father lets go of him; he stumbles, his legs folding beneath him, fitted together from spare parts, toward the corner, the darkness there deeper because of the light in Mr. Knight's back yard, and kneels, the dead leaves chattering beneath him, their sharp, curled edges catching on his fingers.

"Buddy?" his father says. "Don't do this."

He scrabbles at the leaves; his father wrenches his hand behind him, a pain like a knife in his shoulder. "Buddy," he says. "Don't do this. She's gone."

His father's face, in the lamplight: each bristle of his beard sharp and distinct; his face in the movies, and only a hollow mask. Buddy turns from him, and reaches, trembling. His father ratchets his arm behind him, catches his other hand, then falls, bracing himself with his arms; and Buddy turns, scrabbling away from him, as his father falls, turning with him, reaching out to catch his hands, as he and his father turn in a dark place that smells of dust.

"Let go of him," his mother says.

His father holds him, pressing him into the sharp, sour odor of his sweat, his heart pounding against the cage of his chest.

"Buddy," he says. "Don't do this."

"Let him go," his mother says.

His father looks down at him, lamplight reflected in his eyes like glass; and he sees that his father is afraid of him.

"I'm sorry, Buddy," he says.

He reaches out, to grasp his father's hand, but his father's hand slips from his, as his mother asks his father where he is going, and what he is doing, and his father answers her with silence; he turns to the dead leaves, as the gate latch clicks, and his father's car door clunks shut, and his father's car roars to life, knowing he is evil, knowing he will go to Hell because he has betrayed his father; but he keeps digging, past onion skins and eggshells and worms that runneled like water over his fingers, not as if he is digging something from the ground, but as if he is digging himself up, as if he has been buried alive; he will show them, not the story in the drawings or the story of the woman or even in the pictures and letter and movies, but the real movie, the movie of his father's barracks at Fort Polk and of the room with the coiled sheets, of the new house and the dirt beneath his mother's house and his father's shy, stunned smile, and his mother talking lightly to the camera, and Gramma Liddy and Grampa Liddy and Gramma Turner in her canary yellow dress, clapping her white-gloved hands; and all of it will be beautiful, because it cannot be true, what he saw at the bayou, what the boy still tells him, that there is only darkness and silence; behind him, his father's car whinnies out of the driveway, the gate latch clicks, his mother's footfalls tap the cement walk; and in the small, dark yard that smells of coffee he can picture her clearly as she weeps, covering her face with her hands; but he keeps digging, not knowing how he will face her, not knowing how he will begin.

Acknowledgments

This book has been composed over a period of fourteen years. I have many people and institutions to thank for their support, primarily, Robert L. Giron at Gival Press for giving *Ghost Horse* a chance; also, the Wallace Stegner Fellowship Program at Stanford University, The National Endowment for the Arts, the Dobie Paisano Fellowship Project, the Helene Wurlitzer Foundation, the MacDowell Colony, the Vermont Studio Center, and the St. Botolph Foundation, for their generous gifts of time and money. Many people have contributed their time and encouragement, reading and re-reading this book as it has slowly developed: Pamela Painter, Kate Wheeler, Stephanie Reents, Daphne Kalotay, Rishi Reddi, Julie Rold, Eric Puchner, Andrew Altschul, Tom Kealey, Stephen Elliott, Otis Haschemeyer, Malena Watrous, Katharine Noel, and Margot Livesey; also, my teachers, who have been so generous with their time: Elizabeth Harris, James Carroll, Tobias Wolff, Elizabeth Tallent, John L'Heureux, and David MacDonald; and thanks, also, to Susan Siroty, Michele Cotton, and Ivan Gold; and above all, to my wife, Cheryl McGrath, and my daughter, Alice McGrath, who have taught me how to love.

About the author

A former Wallace Stegner Fellow, Thomas H. McNeely has also received awards from the National Endowment for the Arts and the J. Frank Dobie Memorial Fellowship Project. His fiction has appeared in *The Atlantic, Ploughshares, The Virginia Quarterly Review*, and various anthologies, including *Best of The South: The Best of the Second Decade of New Stories from the South*. For more information, please visit his website: thomasmcneelywriter.com.

Books from Gival Press—Fiction & Nonfiction

Boys, Lost & Found by Charles Casillo

The Cannibal of Guadalajara by David Winner

A Change of Heart by David Garrett Izzo

The Day Rider and Other Stories by J. E. Robinson

Dead Time / Tiempo muerto by Carlos Rubio

Dreams and Other Ailments / Sueños y otros achaques by Teresa Bevin

The Gay Herman Melville Reader edited by Ken Schellenberg

Ghost Horse by Thomas H. McNeely

Gone by Sundown by Peter Leach

An Interdisciplinary Introduction to Women's Studies edited by Brianne Friel and
    Robert L. Giron

Julia & Rodrigo by Mark Brazaitis

The Last Day of Paradise by Kiki Denis

Literatures of the African Diaspora by Yemi D. Ogunyemi

Lockjaw: Collected Appalachian Stories by Holly Farris

Maximus in Catland by David Garrett Izzo

Middlebrow Annoyances: American Drama in the 21st Century by Myles Weber

The Pleasuring of Men by Clifford H. Browder

Riverton Noir by Perry Glasser

Second Acts by Tim W. Brown

Secret Memories / Recuerdos secretos by Carlos Rubio

Show Up, Look Good by Mark Wisniewski

The Best of Gival Press Short Stories edited by Robert L. Giron

The Smoke Week: Sept. 11-21. 2001 by Ellis Avery

The Spanish Teacher by Barbara de la Cuesta

That Demon Life by Lowell Mick White

Tina Springs into Summer / Tina se lanza al verano by Teresa Bevin

The Tomb on the Periphery by John Domini

Twelve Rivers of the Body by Elizabeth Oness

For a complete list of Gival Press titles, visit: www.givalpress.com.

Books available from Follett, your favorite bookstore, the Internet, or from Gival Press.

Gival Press, LLC
PO Box 3812
Arlington, VA 22203
givalpress@yahoo.com
703.351.0079